WHY US

WHY US

BRIAN CLARK

First Printing, 2025
This story is written in US English.

CONTENTS

Dedication vi

Prologue 1

1 Waking to a New Life 7

2 Learning About the Changes 18

3 Settling In 36

4 Mike Arrives 52

5 Zane and School Bullies 71

6 Enhanced Senses 85

7 Colors and Collars 100

8 Extending Protection 118

9 Zane Falls Apart 136

10 Gardeners Found 153

11 The Attack 172

12 Attack Response 191

13 Zane and the Rabbits 208

14 Zane and the Cows 225

15 Massages 243

16 Mindy's Wishes 260

17 Discussion About Mindy 278

18 Mike and the Sensors 296

19 Decision About Mindy 313

20 New Mates 330

21 The Laugh 347

22 The Contempt 365

23 The Pictures 383

Teaser for Why Us 2 402

About the Author 409

Goodbye to Max, by Adam Webster 411

Dedicated to everyone who has lost someone close to them, especially through sudden events, leaving them to grieve and needing to learn to continue with their life without the loved one, be it a parent, sibling, child, or just a close friend.

As the saying goes, "Friends are the family you can choose."

Friendship is the hardest thing in the world to explain. It's not something you learn in school. But if you haven't learned the meaning of friendship, you really haven't learned anything. – Albert Einstein

Prologue

Zane sat on the edge of his bed as he tied his shoestrings. He'd finished his homework and felt like going for a run. Thankfully it was right near the end of school, and he had one last meet before he finished junior high. The idea of becoming a freshman was scary and exciting. He was in track and field, and they had trained earlier, but he just felt like getting out of the house for a while. There wasn't any reason, other than he simply loved running and some days it felt like he could run forever. He wasn't sure where he came by this, since his father had never played sports and his mother was a former cheerleader. For some reason when they had talked to his father's older brother, he hadn't seemed to be surprised.

Once he was done getting ready, he grabbed his phone from the charger and plugged the earbuds in. As he headed towards the front of the old house his family lived in, he made sure he had everything he needed. He poked his head into the living room and smiled. His sister was sitting behind their father doing something with his hair. His father had a very patient look on his face as she did whatever she was doing, "Hey, I'm going to go for a run. Back by nine or so. Would you like me to deal with the stinker for you?"

His sister stuck her tongue at him, "Go run what little brains you have left out. This is important, for your information. I promised Ava I would do her hair for the dance, and she is going to do mine." She had her phone sitting next to her and would periodically check it as she was working.

His mother was grinning at her husband and youngest child, "Have fun Zane and have a good run. Try not to forget the time again. This time, I might just call the police and report you as missing." She had to tease him since he tended to forget the time when running. Last week he had gone out for a 'short run' and came back two hours later.

Zane had to exaggerate the eyeroll and mock whined for good measure, "Mom!!! It was a Friday night for heaven's sake. Besides, I told you I was trying to get away from all my admirers." Considering he didn't date and was just average looking, his family knew he was joking. He flashed a grin at her and headed out. One thing he liked about where they lived was how quiet it was. They might not be well off, but his parents had managed to find a decent place to live. It was old and showed its age but was in decent shape.

They lived in an old subdivision which was one reason it was so quiet, and the trees were old and massive which he loved as well. With the area they lived in as well there was what was loosely termed a forest which he used to train for cross country. Tonight, he wasn't in the mood for running through the forest as he enjoyed being in the trees, so he was going to run the edge of the forest which normally took him about an hour. After a slow jog to start warming up he started stretching.

Once he was warmed up and stretched, he started running. As he was running, a light cloud cover moved in, and the moon shone down through it, almost creating beams of light. The moonlight was bright enough to read by, so it seemed. The air was cool and crisp which made it even nicer to run in. It didn't take him very long to settle down into the pace he was going to use. As he was listening to his music, he had to roll his eyes since his mother had apparently added a few songs to his list. Right now, Turn Me Loose by Loverboy was playing, and it messed with his pace.

Zane was going to have to mutter at his mother again about doing it. It was a good beat to run to, but it just wasn't what he needed now, "Mothers are such a pain in the ass sometimes. She won't admit it, but I know she thinks she is funny when she does it." Just to be a pest he was going to run a bit longer and then tell her it was her fault due to the songs messing with his pace.

He dipped into the forest on a small path he liked and for some reason even though he'd run this path for ages, it felt creepy tonight. The sudden darkness of moving into the thick foliage and the light cloud cover which blocked the moonlight was probably the cause. Zane still started moving faster than normal since he just wasn't comfortable. Added, it felt like there was something watching him which made the hairs on his neck stand up, "Brr, what the heck? Time to hurry up and get back on the road."

He stretched out his legs and leaned into the run. Zane wasn't going full out, but he had increased his pace. Somewhere behind him, he heard a howl which sent a chill up his spine and urged him to really start running as fast as he could go. As he was running his earbuds fell out and he heard what sounded like paws hitting the ground behind him. It made him panic even more and he started running as fast as he possibly could. He didn't realize just how fast he was going. Even though neither he or his parents knew, he had some werewolf DNA, which gave him an edge and right now it was showing.

Behind him, he could hear the animal speeding up to match his pace and though he knew running was a bad choice, he didn't know what else to do. In the distance he could see the end of the trail which gave him additional energy. When he reached the end of the trail he was panting heavily and stumbled and fell. As he was falling, he felt something hit his back and his head struck the pavement of the road. The last thing he remembered was a sudden burning and tearing pain in his back and shoulder which seemed to spread farther.

*****

The two were coming back from a quiet evening on the town. Neither were spring chickens anymore; they preferred a quiet dinner over any sort of partying. This evening they had met up with several other older couples and after dinner had hit the bingo place. It had been very successful for them since they had won just over two hundred and fifty dollars.

As they were coming around a corner out of the corner of her eye the woman saw something almost jolt into the road. She started screaming to alert her husband but before she could, some monster of a dog hit the back of whatever it was. It was the moment she realized it was a person who had stumbled and fallen in the road.

The old man hit the brakes as hard as he could and was thankful he had good wheels and brakes. It wasn't enough though and they struck both the animal and the person. He did swerve, but it wasn't enough, and he knew he'd hit the person. The woman screamed again since when she looked at the animal its eyes were a glowing red color as it seemed to glare at them. The animal jumped up and with a very loud, ugly snarl ran down the road.

The man sat there for half a moment before scrambling out as fast as his bad hip would let him, "Ma call for help. We hit a boy and he's bleeding badly. He is alive though." From what he could tell in the dark it looked like he had run over one leg but not the rest of him. There was blood though and it looked like he had been bitten, "Relax son, we are calling for help." He said, but not sure if the kid was even awake.

His wife tried dialing for help, but she was shaking too much. Thankfully, they had the OnStar thing and the car spoke into the silence of the night, "This is OnStar emergency services. We detected a possible accident. Do you need help?" The voice could be heard outside the vehicle.

The man called in, "Yes, we do. There was an animal attacking a boy and before I could stop, we hit the boy. I think he is a young teen and is bleeding badly and isn't responding. Send help as soon as possible." His voice was quavering, and he was gasping for breath.

His wife came around the vehicle and pulled out his bottle of Nitro and gave him one, "My husband is having an angina attack. He needs help also." She helped him sit down in the seat and stood there next to him.

"Understood and I have contacted 9-1-1 and assistance will be there shortly. I will remain on the line in case you need further help till they arrive." Almost immediately, in the distance sirens could already be heard.

*****

Zane's parents were notified he had been injured, from an animal attack and then an accident with a vehicle and had been taken by ambulance to the hospital. Once there, they were forced to sit in the waiting room until a doctor or nurse came for them. Though it didn't take very long, it seemed to take forever and when the doctor came out, he looked very serious, "If you'll come with me, I will show you to my office where we can talk."

They stood up and Zane's sister was between the two of them. Both had an arm around her for comfort as they followed the doctor to his office. Once inside they settled down in chairs across from the desk from the doctor, "Tell us straight doc, how bad is it?" His father asked.

The doctor adjusted his glasses before speaking, "Well in that case, there are several key issues. At some point, he hit his head, and a CT scan shows he has some bleeding in his brain. It doesn't appear serious but is bad enough we recommend keeping him in an induced coma until healed. There is accordingly increased intracranial pressure. Where he was run over, his femur was severely damaged and is going to require major reconstructive surgery. The repair can wait for the time being, and currently his leg is in a bulky dressing to keep it immobile. The last issue was his upper back and shoulder was badly mauled by some large animal. There is extensive damage, and he is going to need surgery soon to correct the damaged tissues. Due to blood loss we've had to start a transfusion."

Olivia, Zane's sister, started crying even more than she had been and was pulled close to her father as he tried to comfort her. He looked at the doctor and after forcing his jaw muscles to relax spoke. When he did his voice was rough and hoarse, "Do what you need doctor, what do you need us to sign? What is going to happen now?"

The doctor nodded and leaned forward and rested his elbows on the desktop, "I will send in a nurse and have you sign a few documents. Once that's done, we will get to work. For the pressure in his brain, we will insert a probe which will monitor it. Before we take him to the O.R. we will induce the coma before starting the work on his back. With his leg, we will give him time to recover from the initial surgery before we do anything. This is going to take some time, so I would recommend going home and trying to get some sleep." Most refused but it was a good idea.

Zane's father tensed at the suggestion and then again forced himself to relax, "I don't like the idea, but it is better than sitting around here for hours on end. Have the nurse bring what we need to sign, and we will take care of it and then head home." When Liv tried to say otherwise, he hushed her, "Liv this is the best thing we can do. Even if we don't sleep well, it will be better than not sleeping here."

The doctor stood up and gave them a professional nod, "She will be in momentarily and I'm going to start and get ready for what we have discussed." He left the office and a brief time later the nurse came in. She made sure to get both parents signatures, "We have your numbers and will call as soon as we know anything." Once that was finished, she showed them out of the E.R. and to the waiting room.

CHAPTER 1

Waking to a New Life

*Zane...** a voice called. He was barely there and didn't have the energy to even start to think, he ignored it and didn't think any further.

*Zane!** The voice was more insistent, and he started waking up, but still couldn't think about why he was so out of it.

Zane, you need to wake up! The voice was starting to be annoying. He didn't want to wake up.

Zane, it's time for you to wake up. You need to wake up! Come on, wake up!

Zane slowly woke up at the insistence of a voice he had been hearing for some time. The voice was definitely male but wasn't any voice he had ever heard before. What was odd was the voice almost sounded like it was inside his head. It had been there for some time, and he had been hunting for the source, but it had been keeping just out of reach. Once in a rare blue moon he could almost touch it, but it kept telling him he wasn't ready. Ready for what, the voice couldn't or wouldn't explain.

When he woke there was a quiet beeping next to him and he was lying in a bed which wasn't very comfortable. Zane did his best to drag his eyelids open, so he could see where he was, and it seemed to take all his energy. By the time he had them open he was feeling totally beat. **There my flipping eyes are open. Are you happy? Now can I go back to sleep?** Since the voice was inside his mind, he pretty much figured he had gone nuts, so he might as well talk to the voice.

Before he closed his eyes, he felt a small hand squeeze his, "Zane? Are you actually awake?" It was his sister, and she sounded scared and tired.

He felt a spark of energy at the sound of her voice, and he slowly turned his head towards her and smiled. Looking at her almost broke his heart since she looked so thin and pale. When Zane tried to speak, he couldn't since his voice was so rusty and unused. She held a straw to his lips so he could take a sip and let the water soak into his parched mouth. He repeated the sips until he could talk, "No kiddo, this is a figment of our imagination."

He let his head roll back on the bed and he had to close his eyes for a moment, "What happened sis and how long have I been asleep?" From the feel of it he hadn't moved for a while since he felt stiff and sore. Not to mention exhausted and weak.

When he teased her, she didn't smile, nor did she do anything else he expected. It had been a miserable time for her while he was in the hospital, but now he had awoken, things were somewhat better, "You went running and were attacked by some animal. You were knocked in front of a car and badly injured. You have been in a coma for about three months." As she had started talking, she had pressed the nurse call button.

All he could do was stare at her as he tried to understand what she was saying. He didn't remember much for the moment, he barely remembered going out for a run... and then nothing, other than the voice seeming to call for him to wake up.

Just a few moments later the nurse hurried in and gave him a bright perky smile, "Oh good, I'm so pleased to see you're awake." She moved over to the bed and checked the readouts, "I will be back in a few." She gave him another one of the perky smiles.

When she left, he frowned at his sister, "Why does her smile make me nervous?" Zane looked back at his sister and had to blink before his mouth dropped open. She was struggling to stand and worked her an arm into an aluminum crutch and limped over to another chair, "Liv what happened?" His voice was still very rough, but his shock could be heard.

Liv shook her head, "Later Zane, let the doctor do his thing and then we can talk." Telling him about the car wreck was going to be horrible and their uncle was out of town working. He had not said anything further about what work was taking him out, but she hoped he would be back soon. She settled down in the chair and stretched her leg out. Since she had shorts on, some of the scars on her right leg were obvious as well as the walking boot she was wearing.

He stared at the scars and then her and almost growled, upset when she wouldn't meet his eyes, "Once they are done, I want to know everything that happened Liv." His voice softened, "I need to know sis, from what you said, I'm missing the last few months of my life and I have to know." When she nodded, he settled back and waited.

The wait didn't last very long before several people came in. The one he assumed was the doctor was an older gentleman who had a stern face, "Good evening, Zane and I'm pleased to see you awake. How are you feeling?" He took a glance at the machines as he was talking.

Zane had finally found the remote for the bed and lifted the head up some, "Confused as much as anything. Liv told me some, but I don't know what to think. As far as how I feel my body feels, stiff and sore from not moving. I do have a headache as well." For some reason he had a feeling saying he was hearing a voice wouldn't be good right now.

The doctor had been reviewing his chart as well as Zane was speaking, "The confusion is understandable as well as the muscle stiffness and headache. I'll have the nurse bring you something for the body and headaches. As far as your injuries and what happened, I would prefer to wait for your uncle to returns from his trip." He finally looked at Zane.

Zane didn't look happy with his response, "Knowing my uncle, it could be some time. What happened to me and how is it going to affect my running? It is my body and I want to know." He really wanted to know why their uncle was involved at all. Shouldn't his parents be there instead?

"It would be better to wait for your uncle to—" The doctor started to say.

Zane interrupted him, "Doctor, if you don't tell me, my sister will. I have the right to know."

The doctor didn't appreciate the tone the boy was using. If he wanted, he could ban his sister from the room, but it would only cause problems. He sighed as he conceded, "I'll give you a summary now, but beyond that, you will have to wait for your uncle to come back. While running you were attacked by a wild animal and pushed into the street by the weight of it. You struck your head which caused a small fracture and a subdural hematoma. When you were shoved into the street a vehicle struck both you and the animal. Your left femur was badly damaged, but it has been repaired. As far as the animal, it clawed your back and bit you several times. As far as how much it will affect you, until you are out of bed and seen by both physical therapy and ortho, we can't say."

Zane stared at him and though he felt like crying, he didn't want to. From somewhere in his mind, he received a surge of strength and comfort and was able to keep the tears back, "Thanks for the info, Doc." He leaned his head back and closed his eyes, "Go ahead and do what you need and then I want to be with Liv." He was starting to feel tired and knew he wasn't going to be awake for much longer.

The doctor didn't say anything more and simply gave him instructions on what he needed to do. Finally, they left but the nurse told him she would be back with some Motrin for the aches, "If you can Liv, I could use a good hug." When she carefully stood up and limped over to the bed, he did start crying. Very carefully he moved over on the bed and patted the mattress next to him.

She was already crying as she struggled up and limped over. He had to help her onto the bed and placed one arm behind her head and pulled her close. He couldn't say anything and simply cried with her. Before he realized it, she had fallen asleep curled up next to him and he drifted off as well, as the crying seemed to use up the last of his energy.

*****

The next morning Zane woke up and groaned since his body still ached from not moving much. He had no idea while he'd been in the coma every several hours they'd come in and adjust his position and had used automatic pressure cuffs. It was to avoid bed sores. After lying there for several moments, he realized his sister was still curled up next to him. About the time he woke a nurse walked in and smiled, "I'm glad to see you are awake Zane and though against policy, seeing your sister sleeping soundly is good. Well, the sleeping isn't against policy, but having your sister sleeping in your bed is." The man walked over and gave his sister a pleased smile, "She hasn't been sleeping very much or very well since she was admitted."

Zane glanced at his sister and then the nurse, "What happened to her and why did the doctor ask to wait for our uncle to return? Has something happened to our parents? This is my family, and I should be told if something did happen." He rubbed his face with his free hand, "I know I'm a minor, but something happened to my sister, and she needs me." He was trying to keep his voice quiet, but he was starting to get really scared.

The nurse had started taking his vitals as he was talking, and he did deserve to know what had happened. He finished the vitals before saying anything, "I understand what you are saying Zane and will make a couple of calls for you. You do have a phone you can use though not for long distance." It was a subtle way of suggesting he try calling any relatives who might be nearby.

Before he could respond his sister started to stir and grunted in pain as her leg started aching. She was starting to get used to chronic pain, but it didn't mean it was fun. Liv looked at her brother to make sure he was actually awake and wrapped an arm around him and gave him a good hug, "Morning Zane and I'm so happy you have finally woken up. I suppose I should be heading back to my room to take a shower and all the other fun stuff."

Somehow, he could sense the pain she was feeling and easily helped her sit up, "Morning Liv and I would say it is nice to be awake but not knowing you were asleep sort of shoots it to heck." He took a moment to gently squeeze her shoulders, "I understand and frankly I want a shower as well as food. I'll see you later." Even though his voice was relaxed his eyes were tense looking.

Something inside was feeling more protective of her than he normally would, and he was reluctant to let her go. It could be due to not knowing what was going on not to mention her obvious injuries. Deep down he knew differently since the voice was making itself known. For some reason it almost sounded like a low protective growl which didn't make any sense. Why would a mental voice growl like that?

His eyes followed his sister out of the room before looking at the nurse, "Someone had better contact my uncle or whoever can and will tell me what happened." His voice was firm as he spoke and the muscles in his jaw were twitching. Part of it was a deep-down fear his parents were dead. It was the only thing he could think of which would keep them from coming to his room.

The nurse managed not to wince at the tone of his voice but again he understood since he would feel much the same, "As I said I will make a few calls. Now, as far as a shower I need to talk to the doctor about what you can do. If all else fails, we will get you in a chair in there and shower you. Breakfast will be here shortly. The TV is controlled by the remote which also has the nurse call. If you need anything, please call." He gave him a polite smile and left the room.

When he mentioned getting him into a chair and helping to bathe him, Zane had to shudder at the idea. The idea of someone giving him a bath made his skin crawl since it was something you did to babies and little kids. By the time Zane had finished shuddering the nurse had left the room which made him growl slightly. Before he could really do much else someone came in with a food tray which totally caught his attention. His stomach rumbled as the smell of the food seemed to fill the room, even with the lids on.

"I thought I heard a stomach growling from outside." The guy bringing in the tray said with a grin, even though he could see the boy's attention seemed to be locked on the food itself. He set it down and removed the lids, "Since you haven't eaten for a while, I would say take it easy while eating. Most of it is easy on the stomach items but still be careful."

Zane gave the man a toothy smile as he finally was able to take his eyes off the food, "I will try but I feel like I haven't been fed in ages. Thank you for bringing the food in." There wasn't a great deal on the tray and if needed he would see about getting more ordered since he was starving. As the man left the room Zane started eating the eggs. In the back of his mind, he could almost feel a pouting sensation. Why he wasn't sure why, other than there wasn't much meat on the tray which seemed to be the cause.

"Why am I feeling these things? Hearing a voice, feeling eyes looking out from my mind, and frankly I feel fine." He was muttering to himself as he was eating the food. Even though he was stiff his leg wasn't bothering him, other than the voice, he seemed to be all there. It didn't take very long before he had polished the plate clean. He was still hungry but decided to wait and see how his stomach felt before he asked for anything else.

The sense of someone else being in his brain had gotten stronger. Frankly, it scared him since the last thing he wanted to do was go nuts. He had his sister to think of and the last thing she was going to need was to have to deal with her brother losing his mind.

When he thought about it, he got an almost mental snort in his mind. His wolf decided it was time to really make his presence known. It had been a slow awakening for both, but especially for the wolf since Zane had been so badly hurt, and his mind had been suppressed with the induced coma. It had also taken time since Zane hadn't been completely infected either. The virus had taken longer than normal to alter his DNA not to mention the time it took for his wolf to really connect with him. Now he could, and it would finish the process. **You are not insane or nuts, Zane. We have a great deal to talk about, but you need* _time. I'm your wolf and when you were attacked, you were infected with lycanthropy._*

Zane almost flipped out when he heard the voice in his mind. Not only that, but the feeling of another being in his mind had him slightly freaked out. Since he was freaking out, he hadn't caught much of what the other said, "Huh? What?" He didn't think when he spoke and felt a grumble in the back of his mind.

Zane, you can speak to me simply by thinking your questions at me. As I said you are now a Lycan—a werewolf. You have been infected with lycanthropy. I'm not going to try and prove it right now. I have a feeling having a wolf in your bed might upset everyone. It was said with a definite huff of annoyance.

Zane sat up and his eyes widened when the voice spoke back to him. *_Well excuse me for thinking I'm losing my mind. It isn't every day I have someone talking in my mind._* He returned huff for huff. *_What do you mean lycanthropy? You mean like on the full moon I will turn into some wolf man thing and want to eat people?_* He sounded horrified by the idea since he had no urge to eat people in any way shape or form.

His statement received a stare by the eyes in his mind and then he started getting dizzy as whatever was in the back of his mind started howling and panting, and somehow he knew it was laughing. Zane wasn't sure how he knew he was being laughed at, but he was, and it was making him grouchy. *_Oh, go bite your tail, assuming you are what you say, and I'm not nuts. If I'm nuts, then it will be interesting seeing the voice in my mind trying to bite a non-existent tail._* It was most definitely a snippy and grumpy comment.

The eyes seemed to roll over like a dog was rolling around. *_Oh, you are silly. No, we don't turn into some human hungry monster. Yes, we will change forms, but you won't have the urge to eat people. Now a nice bunny or even a chunk of venison would be tasty._* He became serious after mentioning it. *_There are wolves known as rogues who don't have a problem breaking the rules. They are hunted down and killed to protect the rest of our species._*

Zane's stomach grumbled at the sound of having a bite of rabbit and then lurched. The lurch was because he knew the voice wasn't talking a nice, cooked rabbit but raw and bloody. **Oh great, so I just turn into a rabbit hungry monster. So, being a rogue is a bad thing huh? How do you know this stuff? If you are part of me then shouldn't I know all this stuff?** Well if nothing else this was keeping him occupied until someone came in to tell him what was next.

His wolf laughed at him again when he muttered about being a rabbit eating monster. **Hey, don't knock a yummy bunny until you try it. As far as knowing all this stuff, I don't know it all.** It seemed to shrug as the answer to how it knew anything. **We are pups since we are a brand new Lycan. We need to find a pack to teach and protect us.** He rested his chin on his paws and whimpered. **And your sister, though she isn't a pup like us.** The wolf didn't even try to answer his question about *how* he knew about things, as he wasn't ready for it, and hoped he didn't press for more.

Zane frowned at being called a pup. **I'm not a pup darn it. I'm a teenager. Puppies are little and cute, and I'm not little and cute.** Then again, he wasn't very tall yet though he hoped he would be reasonably tall, but he was not cute and would stand by it. **Why a pack?** Now he wrapped his arms around his knees and rested his head on his knees. **Why won't anyone tell me what happened to my parents? I want my parents and not some group of strangers. Can't we just remain with my uncle?**

The being in his mind sent him a mental nuzzle. **I don't know what happened to them or why nobody will tell you. A pack will protect and take care of us. They will teach us what we need to know. It is how wolves survive and taking care of each other. I don't know your uncle, so I can't really say much more. Do you know if your sister will be back? Much like you, I feel the need to protect her.** His wolf had seen how she moved and was worried much like his human was about her.

He started sobbing and crying since his fear was starting to really show. He wanted his parents and his sister back the way it had been,

"Why the hell did I have to decide I like running at night? Why couldn't I have stayed at home? Damn it, I want someone to tell me about what happened." Zane was wrapped up enough in his fears and concerns he hadn't noticed an older nurse walk in.

She moved over to the bed and settled down on the edge of the bed, "Hey Zane, I would ask how you are doing but I can see you are upset. The nurse's assistant talked to me, and I will answer what questions I can. I can't tell you everything since I don't have all the answers, but I'll do my best."

He twitched when she sat down and spoke to him and jerked up to a seating position and tried to wipe his tears away, "If someone would tell me what is going on, I would be doing much better. What happened to my parents and sister? Tell me please?" There was desperation in his voice and as much as he hated it, he sounded young and scared.

She moved a box of Kleenex over, so it was on his bedside table, "Well you just woke up and we really haven't had a chance to say much to you." She gave him a slightly sad smile when she spoke, and she decided to tell him more, "Now speaking about your parents, I'm sorry, but they are no longer with us. There was a car wreck as they were coming to see you. Your sister was in the car as well and was badly injured. Right now, she is living in the rehabilitation center." When he started crying again, she lightly rubbed his back.

Zane had been expecting it but had hoped not. Having her say it really brought it down to him, his life was going to be totally different now, "Oh god, mom, dad, what am I supposed to do now. How am I supposed to take care of Liv?" He was starting to panic until his wolf stepped forward and gave him some strength and a feeling of love. He was still very close to falling apart but, for the moment, he had a bit of breathing space. It felt like his wolf had curled up around him to hold him steady.

The nurse kept rubbing his back and gave him some time to calm down, "For right now if you don't mind a suggestion, just focus on your sister and getting her spirits back up. She has been very down though she has been trying not to show it." By having him focus on his sister, she was hoping he would be distracted from any other questions.

She comforted him for a bit more before he asked her to leave him alone for a while. He needed to cry now that his fears were true. He rolled on his side and was trying his best not to cry too much but it was enough he hadn't noticed the door open. He was so tied up in his emotions not much else impacted on him.

When the bed shifted as someone sat down, he rolled over and found Liv there. He held his arms out to her and hoped she could give him some comfort, "Oh god Liv, I just found out." The tears started up again even though he tried not to, "What happened to you, sis?"

She crawled into the bed carefully and into his arms. She wrapped her arms around him and held onto him as they both cried, "Later, Zane, please, I don't feel up to talking about it. It is so good to see you awake."

Both cried for a while before eventually drowsing. It wasn't really sleep so much as their bodies deciding they needed to relax. How long they drowsed neither knew until the door opened again.

When it did Zane sat up and looked at the strange male and female. Something about the male set him and his wolf off. Thankfully his sister was on the other side of him. A low growl of warning could be heard from his chest since his wolf recognized another and knew they needed to protect their sister at all costs.

CHAPTER 2

Learning About the Changes

The male couldn't help but glance at his wife and grinned slightly, "Yup, he takes after his uncle, doesn't he?" He turned back to the two children, "I'm Kadrian and this is my mate, Esther. Your uncle works for me and is out of town taking care of some business for me. Do you mind if we come in and sit down for a few?"

Esther lightly smacked Kadrian's shoulder, "Relax Kad, you are probably going to scare the poor pups to death." She moved over and sat on the edge of the bed and rested her hand on his ankle, "Please relax Zane, we aren't a threat. We can talk about it later. Since your uncle is out of town, he asked my mate and I to swing past and check on you. He really wanted to be here when you woke up and is pretty upset he can't be here when you woke up."

Kad sat down in a chair and let his wife do her thing. She was the Luna of the pack and dealing with scared and wounded wolves was part of her job. She was essentially the peacekeeper for the pack. Unless you were a rogue wolf, very rarely would a wolf not be able to respond to her presence. Even some humans would respond to it as well.

Zane did relax slightly but he simply didn't know these people. They were setting the voice in his mind off. It wasn't in a bad way so much as not being sure who they were or why there were here. It was very hard to describe what he was getting from the voice since he just didn't know what the feelings meant. When the female sat down and rested her hand on his ankle for some reason the voice seemed to calm down. He did as well though why he wasn't sure.

He had to try and stay protective of his sister since she was all he had left, "How do I know you are who you say you are? All I know is my parents are dead, my sister was badly hurt, and I have been asleep for several months." Zane's voice was hard yet brittle. He didn't even think when he wrapped his arms around his sister for comfort, "The only people I have left are my sister and my uncle. I don't even know where I am now, so don't tell me to relax. I want my uncle here." He had an aunt, but so rarely saw her that he totally forgot about her in all the issues. She was gone so much for her photoshoots, and therefore difficult to contact.

Liv was holding on to him as well though she wasn't nearly as concerned. She had met them before since they'd been moved here, and they were nice, "Relax Zane, I know them, and Uncle Mike does work for Mr. Kadrian." She made a slight face though, "He won't talk about his work other than it's in security. He says it's all hush hush stuff." Her voice was very quiet and sad as she spoke. He had said they would be told more once they were out of the hospital.

Zane turned towards Liv and met her eyes. His were showing his concern for her, though his face now had a hardness to it, "I don't know them Liv and Unc isn't here, and you are all I have left. I can't trust anyone right now. Not when it comes to you, sis."

Esther looked at her husband and she had a sad expression on her face. There was both sympathy and hints of pride for how he was acting. Even as young as his wolf was, he was showing what was important: pack and family. For him, he didn't yet consider either of them as Pack, so was keeping some distance. What he had to deal with was upsetting since it had been a rogue who had done it to him, one who seemed to have vanished. So far none of the packs involved had been able to track him down and there were many looking. As soon as they heard a pup had been Force-Turned, everyone had wanted to help. Word was even getting out ahead, and other packs were requesting information, thankfully the Council had taken over it and was now sending out the details to all the packs in the area.

"I understand what you are saying Zane. I have a cell phone you can use to call him. Your sister knows his number so call and talk to him. He is busy, so he might not be able to answer immediately but he will call you back." She pulled the phone out and set it on the table.

Kad gave the two children a smile, "I will give him a call as well and try and get him back as soon as possible. You have our sympathy son and especially waking up to learn about everything. As soon as you talk to him, give us a call. He has asked when the two of you are released to have us take you to our place. Mike lives there also. He has had most of your clothing and personal items moved here. The rest of it he will talk to you about."

He stood as did his wife after giving Zane's leg one last squeeze, "I will swing past later with some things for you if you would like. Have your sister show you to the room she has here, if they will let you. She has some games and movies you might want to use or watch." She paused and then grinned, "Then again I have a feeling you might not want to watch some of the movies she has." She let her husband lead her out of the room.

Zane watched them leave before glancing at the cell phone. He growled again and got a weird look from his sister.

"Zane will you please quit growling? It is rather irritating, you know." Her uncle had told her some about changes in Zane from what had happened to him. The growling was just a bit too strange, since it really did sound like a dog... or a wolf.

Zane had to blink when she said it, "Huh? What are you talking about?" Since he hadn't changed yet and didn't really understand what he was, it didn't make sense. He was still staring at the phone and finally picked it up, "What is Uncle Mike's number?"

She rolled her eyes at him, "I can't really tell you why, but you were growling as a wolf would. Uncle Mike said if he was here, he would talk to you and if not, Mr. Kadrian would." She leaned against her brother and sighed, "Mr. Kadrian and Mrs. Esther are nice people and I have met them several times. Uncle Mike trusts them as well. His number is..." She gave it to him and once he started dialing.

Zane wanted to trust them, and something was telling him he could, but he just couldn't. He didn't know the two and with everything that happened the only person other than Liv he trusted was their uncle. If he told him to trust them, then he would but with a grain of salt. They were going to have to prove to him they were trustworthy. When the phone was picked up Zane almost cried in relief at hearing his uncle's voice.

"Hey Zane, I spoke to Kad, and he told me you were awake. I'm so pleased to hear it and damn it, I wish I was there right now." He took a slow breath, *"Zane, you can trust Kadrian and Esther. They won't lead you wrong and since I'm not there, Kadrian is going to have to talk to you. I'm sure by now you have noticed a voice in your mind. He can tell you about it. Go home with them and they will take care of you."* Both he and his wolf had been horribly upset when they heard about what had happened to Zane. The pack where he had been had a doctor who worked at the hospital and knew what the bites meant, as the hospital listed him as having a specialty for animal bites so called him in. Originally, they were going to explain it to his parents and sister and offer their assistance, but when the rest of Zane's family had been killed or injured in the wreck, the two became his uncle's responsibility. The doctor had slumped after a good sniff and had just bluntly told him his nephew had been turned by a rogue, then all the other stuff. It had almost killed Mike when he'd found out. Only thing which was a positive, was they didn't need to explain Weres to him and find a pack near them.

Zane barely managed to gather his emotions enough to reply, "I'm scared Uncle Mike. Our lives have been destroyed while I was in the coma! My parents are dead, and my sister was horribly hurt. I don't know what to do. When will you be home? I really need to see you." He was forced to take a ragged breath, "I will try to trust them but right now it is going to be hard for me. Why did I have to go for the damn run, if I hadn't none of this would have happened." He lost the battle he had fought hard and started to cry.

Mike had to lean against the building he was at now. He could feel and hear the distress in Zane's voice, and it was starting to drive his wolf nuts. It was going to be very hard to keep working when both he and his wolf wanted to be there right now; they had a hurt pup who needed them, *"Zane when Esther comes back let her give you a hug and some comfort. She is really good at it and will take good care of you. If the two of you are released before I get home, she will take care of you. I have to go Zane but call me anytime and if I can't answer I will call back or text as soon as I can."*

"I will try Uncle Mike; I will try but it is going to be hard. Please hurry back. I need my family with me right now." He was glad his uncle had to go since he was close to losing it. It helped that as soon as he had called; Liv had wrapped her arms around him and held on. The phone fell out of his hands as he turned and returned the hug and held on. When Liv leaned against him it helped a great deal.

Mike hung up and leaned his head back against the wall and had to take several slow deep breaths to calm down before he started crying too. Even if he wasn't all that close to his baby brother, he still loved him, and he really missed him and his sister-in-law. He hated how he couldn't be there for their pups, but he was needed elsewhere.

*****

It was later in the day when Zane had finally gotten approval to try to walk around. It had been difficult at first since he had been lying still for so long. Even though they had done physical therapy and muscle stimulation while he was in the coma, he was still stiff. Once he had been helped around the room, it got easier to move , "Man, it feels good to be out of bed for even a few minutes." He was sitting in a chair while they were changing the sheets.

The Nurse Assistant gave him a grin, "I can't imagine how it would feel but I know after being sick once or twice getting out of bed was nice. If you want to sit there for a while it would be fine but before you move, call for one of us. Hospital Policy and all that." The man finished with the bed and with a casual flip folded the blankets and sheet back, "Dinner will be soon, and your sister is planning on joining you. If you need anything, please call." The NA left the room quietly.

Zane leaned back in the chair and wished it was more comfortable, "Thanks for letting me know." As he was sitting there relaxing someone cleared their throat. Even with his eyes closed he knew it was the lady from earlier and didn't think about how he knew. He sat up and opened his eyes and he was right, "Good afternoon, Ma'am. If you would like to come in, it's fine." It wasn't but since his uncle had told him to trust them, he would try. His face was still almost frozen with the same expression from earlier.

"Thank you, Zane, I appreciate it even though I know you aren't comfortable with me coming in." She wasn't going to be in your face about it, but she was going to let him know she was seeing through his politeness, "Mike called earlier and let us know you did call and talk to him. I left my husband at home, since I know sometimes he can be somewhat overwhelming. I did want to bring you a few things, so you have something to do." She had a gym bag with her, and she set it down next to his chair.

For some reason in the back of his mind the little voice he had been hearing was almost whining. Zane wasn't sure exactly why but wherever it was coming from didn't approve of how he was feeling. There was some undefined feeling of they could trust the woman and they should respect her. Why he felt both coming from the voice he didn't know, and it was bothering him. When she did call Zane on his not really being happy with her there, he figured it wasn't hard to tell. He didn't know her or her husband and even his uncle and sister vouching for them didn't help, he just wasn't ready to let anyone else in. Zane contemplated her for several minutes, "Thank you for taking time but you didn't need to Ma'am. Since I've started walking, tomorrow I was going to go to my sister's room."

She almost sighed at him since he wasn't going to make this easy for her. He was going to have to learn his place eventually, but it could wait. Right now, he was a scared pup who had lost almost everything. He basically had a pack of four; the leaders were gone and the other badly injured. "It really isn't a problem Zane, and I would do the same for any of our family or workers. We firmly believe in taking care of those who are important to us. You and Olivia are important to Mike, therefore you are important to us." She kept her voice relaxed as she was talking.

Damn it, the voice was grumbling at him, and it was almost giving him a headache. While he was listening to her, he wasn't thinking when he reached up and rubbed his temples. It didn't really help but it was something to do. **Leave me alone damn it! I need to think.** When he thought it there was an almost wounded whimper and the voice withdrew. It seemed to make his headache even worse which upset him, "Ma'am the only family I have left is my sister and Uncle Mike. Uncle Mike will take care of us even though he isn't here now. You don't need to worry about feeling the need to check on us." He had decided to settle on what he hoped was a distantly polite attitude. He had already said his piece earlier and she didn't need to do anything for him.

She could both smell and see the tension in his body as he was rubbing his temples. For a very brief moment his eyes flickered to a lighter color before they faded back. She didn't know what had happened, but Esther had a feeling he was having issues with his wolf. His wolf's urge would to be to trust her because of who she was as. She narrowed her eyes slightly and her expression firmed up slightly, "You have more family than you know but that is something you need to discuss with your uncle. I can tell you are not in the mood to talk right now. I will leave the room since I do not wish to upset you any further." When Esther spoke, there was a slight chill in her voice. It was directed at his wolf more than him. The bag she left behind.

When she gave him a look, he tried to keep his eyes on hers but couldn't. He ended up settling for looking at her chin. In the back of his mind, he felt the whine again and almost growled at it. When she stood and left, he almost stood but again for some reason ended up lifting his chin slightly. Once she was gone, he glared at the bag before pressing the nurse call button, "I would like to get back to my bed please."

When the NA came back in, he simply stood next to Zane, "I think you can do it without my help. I will just stay close in case you run into problems."

Zane gave him a nod, "Thanks," And after placing both hands on the arm rests carefully stood up. It took more energy than he was used to, but he did it without help. Once he was vertical, he stood there for a moment before slowly walking to the bed and climbed in.

The NA was close enough to catch Zane if needed but when the boy made it to the bed unaided, he gave him a solid grin, "I think in the next day or two you will be cruising the hallways. Would you like me to bring the bag over?" He had seen Mrs. Mac Tire' Dona come into his room with the bag and figured it had some things for him to keep busy with.

"I hope so since I would like to be able to go and visit my sister. As far as the bag just put it off to the side, please. I don't feel like dealing with it now." If he did look in it and accept anything, Zane felt like it would be accepting a bribe. He would earn what was given to him and not just have it handed to him. Once he was in the bed he settled back and ignored the bag.

The NA was somewhat startled by it but guessed Zane was just tired and stressed, "Not a problem and when you decide you want it just call." He resisted the urge to make sure Zane was tucked in, "Dinner will be soon, and I'm sure your sister will be here since her tray is supposed to be delivered here as well."

Zane leaned back in the bed and after a nod closed his eyes and leaned back. He tried to relax but the damn voice was fussing at him again. It was obviously still very put out with what Zane had said earlier which made him roll his eyes. How the hell could he be getting emotions and feelings from the voice in his head? One thing that really bothered him was he honestly wasn't worried about the voice or his being nuts. **Just who are you? Why am I hearing you in my head and I know*

*I'm not bug nuts?** He wanted to know and hoped it would say something back to him.

His wolf was feeling a bit peeved with how he had been talking to the Luna. He didn't understand why he wasn't giving her the respect she deserved. If his uncle was in the pack, then it would make her *their* Luna as well, since they were pups. When his other half sent a thought to him, the young wolf growled at him and turned away. He walked deeper into Zane's mind and curled up with his back to his other half, clearly offended.

When Liv walked in, Zane was lying back in the bed with an arm across his eyes and looked very grumpy. She rolled her eyes at him and poked him with one crutch, "Zane if you keep it up you are going to be a grumpy old man before you even make it out of high school." Since Mrs. Esther had visited Liv to check on her too, she knew there was a bag for him. When she glanced around it was sitting off to one side unopened.

Zane growled at her for the teasing, "Not in the mood for it, Liv so don't, please." Just for good measure he made his expression even grumpier.

She snorted at him as she carefully sat down in a chair near the bag, "So, what did Mrs. Esther bring you? Did you even open the bag yet?" She wasn't going to let him be a total grump and just for good measure she poked him again before jerking the crutch away. He had snatched at it and almost gotten it.

"Nope, didn't open it and no clue sis. I started to get a headache and decided to lay down and ignore the world. For some reason the world doesn't want to ignore me and keeps poking at me." When he said it, he had tried to get the end of the crutch she had poked him with only she was faster than he was.

"It isn't a problem; I can take a look for you." She pulled the bag over with her crutch and started to unzip the bag. When he started to sit up and really growled at her she yelled at him, "Zane don't you growl at me again like that. If you want to be a grouch, then do it but don't take it out on me. She is a nice lady, and she does care. If you can't or won't accept it, you are the only one you are hurting." She finished unzipping the bag and looked inside. There were some games, a game boy, a variety of magazines, and a few movies. There were some new clothes for him as well for when he could wear them.

Zane had to put his hand to his throat as he was growling and looked rather shocked. Yes, she had mentioned something about it earlier, but it was an honest growl. He could feel the vibrations in his throat and finally really heard it. His eyes widened in shock and for a moment, he almost freaked out. When he started to, a calming sense flowed over him which had a definite impact on him. He was sitting up in the bed with his eyes wide open in shock.

As he was sitting there, Esther walked back into the room and gave him a quiet smile, "That was one of the things I had wanted to talk to you about, young man. Do you think you would like to talk now? Some things my husband will have to tell you, but I can answer a great deal." As she walked past Liv, she gave her a light hug with one arm and stroked her hair for a moment. Once she had greeted her, Esther settled on the edge of the bed.

Zane's hand was still on his throat when she walked in and even when she sat down. For the moment he had been shocked enough he didn't even blink when she sat down, "Um, can you tell me why I'm hearing things?" As he was talking, a scent hit his nose and his mouth started watering. Whatever she had in a large bag she had carried in, there was food in there and man it smelled good. He barely managed not to ask what she had. He had no idea how he was smelling it, either.

Since she had his attention, or the attention of his wolf, it should be easier for the moment. It was going to take some time to figure out just what was going on in his mind, "I hope you don't mind but I decided you could use a real meal. Mind you the food they have here is decent, but I'm sure you will find this better." Out of a bag she pulled out two trays. One had a huge burger and pile of fries. The other was a smaller portion which he assumed was for his sister.

As Esther pulled the food out, she could tell Zane was barely able take his eyes off it. It was his wolf as much as anything, since the meat was rare and even she wanted to eat another, as she had eaten one when she had got the takeout for the pups., "Eat Zane, and I will talk. Some things will have to wait for a variety of reasons which you will understand when you are told, but as far as the voice, relax. It is part of you." She glanced over at Olivia who simply shrugged.

Zane moved his tray over in front of him and to be honest his hands were shaking slightly. The food smelled so bloody good he wanted to devour it. He wanted to ask what things and why but before he realized it, he had a mouthful of burger. When the flavor hit his tongue, he could both feel and hear a growl of appreciation from the other. Now he did lift an eyebrow in question at her as he ate.

She smiled a little bit wider at his appreciation of the food, "Not all of this has been explained to your sister, since we wanted to talk to both of you at the same time. I don't want to bring up bad memories but what can you tell me about what you remember of your accident?"

Her question made Zane stop eating and he had to shiver in reaction, as memories of that night came back... for a moment, he was back there as he remembered more than he had before. His breathing was starting to speed up and he could feel his heart starting to race. The pupils of his eyes dilated as well. Before he realized it, Esther had her arms wrapped around him. When she did, for some reason he started to calm down though he was still reacting. He could finally speak, "I don't remember much. I had gone for a run and when I cut through the wild area where we lived, on my normal route, something started chasing me. I never saw more than a large black shadow. It jumped on me and... And... I don't remember anything else until I woke up here."

In his mind his wolf took some control and almost forced his other half to lean into the hug. They were both new wolves and it felt good to be held by their Luna and surrounded in her scent. If he had been in his other form, he would have had his chin resting on her shoulder, even as their ears and tail were tucked.

Esther didn't stroke his back like she would normally since she didn't want to chance chasing him back to where he had been, "I hated having to ask you, but I needed you to think about it before I could answer you. This is going to take all your belief, but I'm sure you have heard stories of the supernatural all your life. Children's stories, TV shows, books, possibly even stories which were told to you by your parents or other relatives. Many of them have some basis in reality, Hun. You were attacked by what we call a rogue wolf. A rogue werewolf, that is." She paused for a moment to see what he might have to say. She was speaking quietly enough that nobody outside the room would be able to hear but was loud enough for the pups to hear.

Zane was frankly glad she didn't push him more than to just hold him. It felt damn good and something about her calmed the voice significantly. For the moment while he was being held, he could somewhat accept what she was saying. Now tomorrow or tonight, in the dark of the night might be a different story, "Something like Dracula by Bram Stoker or Hans Christian Anderson? Is it what you mean and if you tell me I'm a vampire then just stake me right now." So much had been tossed at him he'd forgotten what the voice said earlier.

Olivia had been listening but when her brother mentioned vampires, she almost choked on the food in her mouth. She finally managed to get it down before commenting herself wanting to tease her brother, "Well I have noticed you seem to be getting a bit furrier, but I think you just need a good shave."

Esther turned and looked at her before making a face and rolling her eyes at Olivia, "Well yes and no. No, you aren't a vampire and frankly the only good one is a staked one." She didn't bother to tell him that if he had been attacked and changed by one of those, he wouldn't have woken up. He would have 'died' in the hospital as soon as he arrived. "No, as much as your sister is teasing you, you are almost done with becoming a werewolf." She had to roll her eyes at Olivia to keep her from saying anything silly.

Zane stiffened slightly, “Oh, is that all? So, I only need to worry about wanting to eat things once a month instead of finding a nice juicy neck every couple of days? I suppose I could live with it though a rotten little sister might get bit for teasing me.” He kept his head on her shoulder as he was talking.

For his teasing Esther had to thump him lightly on the back of the head, “Silly pup, after your first change, you can change whenever you want, to an extent. As far as biting your sister you will be nice and no biting, as we do have strict laws about it which you will need to learn. Seriously though: yes, you will have the urge to hunt and eat the kill. Just no bringing a dead rabbit back to your sister.” She figured a gentle bit of teasing was in order for both of them.

In the back of his mind his wolf started doing a ‘Yummm...’ thought and was wondering what a kill would be like. Zane groaned, “Thanks, now the voice in my head is contemplating a rabbit and biting.” He didn’t mention which one it wanted to bite.

His sister made a face at her, “Thanks Mrs. Esther and now I know he will be bringing me something. I wonder if I can teach his wolf how to clean and cook it first.” She shuddered for good measure since she could just see him dropping a dead rabbit in her lap.

Zane let out a rather strangled sounding chortle before he choked it off, “Fine, so I’m a werewolf now. Great and all that stuff but when can we get out of here?” He wasn’t going to cry but he wanted to go home, “I want to go home. I want our house, my room, and my family back.” He knew it would never happen again, but he needed to be elsewhere. Somewhere that wouldn’t keep reminding him of what both he and Liv had lost. He didn’t even know what was wrong with Liv other than either a leg or hip was badly hurt.

She gave him a light hug but again didn’t force anything beyond it, “Well actually as soon as the doctors release you, we will take both you and Olivia to our place until your uncle finishes his work. Olivia has been staying here, in order to be near for when you did wake. She must do therapy every day, but doesn’t have to remain here, as we have those who can help her as well as those here. I will talk to the doctor, about when you can be released. For the moment, we have two rooms at the main house for you and Olivia until your uncle gets back. Once he is back, we will go from there." Esther leaned back and nudged the food towards him. She could feel his agony at never being able to go home again. It was several states away and by now was rented out to someone else. There had been no reason not to have them moved here to be near to his uncle. The pack nearest to their place had packed everything up and shipped it out to them here and had dealt with getting the house cleaned and ready to be released. They had already known about what happened, since one of the pack's healers worked in the hospital, so notified their Alpha when they realized Zane had been attacked by a Rogue and not a wild animal, as the humans thought. When they realized his uncle was a werewolf, and his nearest kin, they arranged for Zane and Olivia be moved to the hospital near where their uncle lived.

He looked down at the food and started eating again. His sister had been eating for some time and was mostly finished. Zane didn't take very long to finish eating, "Thank you, Ma'am, it was very good." He didn't realize it, but his mask started to settle back down over his features. Zane had broken for a moment from his perceived need to be remote. Now that he was full and had some answers, , he was starting to tense up again.

Esther noticed this because of both his scent and his posture changing. She really wanted to hold him and tell him everything was going to be okay. Her experience and her wolf told her this wasn't the right way to handle him. What was right, she wasn't sure but if he didn't open up eventually, he stood a good chance of becoming a lone wolf. It wasn't necessarily a bad thing but for someone so young, it could be very difficult, "You are welcome, Zane. I need to get back home. Assuming the doctor or nurses don't have a problem, I included some shorts and a loose shirt in the bag for you. I don't know about you, but the open back gowns always bothered me."

Olivia had to give out a sort of giggle groan at her, “You are telling me Mrs. Esther. Waking up in nothing but a gown was not nice.” She shuddered at the memory but then again, she had been on so many meds much of the first few weeks were rather vague, “Thanks for the food and it was really good.” She yawned before starting to gather up her trash.

“Thank you as well Ma’am, it was very good. I appreciate it.” Now he was back speaking in the formal yet distant manner he had been earlier.

Both Esther and Olivia winced slightly as Esther stood. “We will see you in the morning and tomorrow my husband will talk to you more about this. Relax and sleep well tonight young wolf.” She collected the trash even as she lightly impressed the urge to go to sleep somewhat early and sleep well. With the information she had given him, he could have a nightmare and call his wolf forth too early, which was never good, especially for those who didn’t know of them. They had no need to have an upset wolf waking up where Zane should be.

*****

When Zane woke the next morning, he contemplated the night before. Once Mrs. Esther had left the room, Olivia had brought the bag over and dumped it on his lap. Well, actually she had called for help since she couldn’t carry it easily. She still wouldn’t tell him what all was wrong with her, which was very upsetting. As he was laying there contemplating the evening before he sighed. Zane did want out of the hospital but in a way, he didn’t. This would never be somewhere he would consider home but once they left, he would lose what little he knew and there would be no returning to his old life.

Before he had a chance to get too worked up, a young man walked in. He appeared to be slightly older than Zane was, maybe sixteen or so. Just looking at him he could tell he was related to the two from the day before, “Morning Zane. Mom and Dad asked me to come and give you a hand getting ready to leave. I don’t expect you to need one but...” He rolled his eyes when he said it. It was almost as if he was saying ‘parents will be parents’.

Zane blinked as the teen walked in. He was tall and broad across the chest with a narrow waist and presumably muscular legs. The expression on his face was open and pleasant without being annoying. What really hit Zane, was his voice. It was a deep mellow baritone, with something in it, which almost demanded his attention, "Ah, well Liv packed the stuff Mrs. Esther brought over other than some shorts and a shirt." It was rather obvious since he was wearing it.

"Excellent and..." He frowned slightly and then laughed, "Sorry but I forgot you have no clue who I am. My name is Damien and Esther and Kadrian are my parents. My little sister is Polly..." He had to roll his eyes at his parents giving her such a name, "It is short for Polly Anne, and she hates it. Call her Anne unless you want a fight." A slow smile crossed his face when he said it.

Zane could only stare at him before turning away to try and keep control of the laugh. He really didn't want to laugh, since it felt wrong. Once he had managed to get his control back, he turned and looked at Damien, "I will keep it in mind and thanks for letting me know." More stilted and rather distant speech.

Since his mother had given him some information, Damien didn't blink but he could see what she meant about keeping people away. The most annoying part was she had told him to do his best to befriend the other boy. The befriending he didn't mind but just from the moment or two of speaking to him, this was going to be difficult. It was like he was a wary wolf from another pack, and didn't know if he was enemies or not, his wolf decided they needed to show they were friendly, "Mom and Dad are working on the papers to spring you from this joint and Olivia and my sis should be here shortly. Do you have any questions or anything for me? I was asked to show you around when we get home as well."

Zane flipped the covers back and after sitting up slid his legs over the side, "I hope the bloody car is at the entrance and the engine is running. If I have to, I will crawl out of here to safety." He flashed a smile though it didn't reach his eyes, "Well only if Liv gets out also. If she didn't, I would have to figure out how to break in and kidnap her..."

Damien snorted at him and grinned. At least the other had a sense of humor, even if he wasn't going to let much in the way of emotions show. To a wolf the eyes were close to the old 'windows of the soul' thing since they could be so expressive. He had seen his father get the truth from someone simply by watching their eyes. Zane was similar, but it was obvious he was doing his best to keep them from showing anything, "If I didn't help to spring both of you, sis would take a two by four to me."

Just about then the two girls came into the room, "Damn straight I would, even if I didn't know what you were guilty of." Anne's hair was a mixture of brunette and red with a pixie like face and a slender body. At a guess she was probably thirteen or so.

Zane glanced at her and minutely froze since he had always had a problem with cute girls and she was very cute, "At the moment he isn't guilty of anything I know of." He barely managed to keep a slight shy smile from his face. He guessed she was maybe a year younger than he was. Thankfully their parents walked into the room, or he might have blushed.

"Ready to leave Zane? Everything is packed and taken care of for Olivia and I'm sure my son can handle the bag I brought over." There was a grin on her face as her son pretended to struggle to lift it and groan.

Olivia snickered at Damien though there was a slight blush as well. She might only be twelve, thirteen shortly, but Damien was really cute, "Should a girl save you from the weight Damien?"

Zane sighed patiently at her, "Olivia, leave him alone and no more teasing for at least five minutes. I want out of here now." He growled at her for good measure even though it was a mock growl, "Sisters can be such a pain can't they Damien?"

For some reason Anne punched Damien in the ribs, "Don't you dare answer or else you will regret it. Now I'm going to escort Olivia out of here and away from both of your senses of humor." She turned and with a look at Olivia slowly stalked out of the room to everyone's amusement.

CHAPTER 3

Settling In

When they arrived at the house Zane was honestly shocked. It was huge, and he could see it appeared to be made of several connected buildings of various ages. There were houses of various sizes scattered around nearby. In a way it made him think of a subdivision, only this one had a massive forest around it, and more trees between the various buildings, some were partly hiding the buildings. For some reason when he saw the forest, he wanted to go for a run. Even though the idea of a run scared him. After what had happened to him, he wasn't comfortable around woods that looked like the ones he had been running in, even if there were more pines in this one. He forced his attention back to the house and had to wonder how many people lived there. His wolf whined in the back of his mind at being scared of the woods. He thought he understood, but it hurt thinking behind each tree was a monster like the one who'd turned them. They weren't monsters, just the rogue was, and it made him upset.

After a few moments of wondering, he forced the thought out of his mind and almost asked to ensure he and his sister had rooms next to each other. If anyone looked, his eyes were rather bleak as he tried not to contemplate what both had lost. What he'd been told the day before, he was of mixed emotions on how much he believed so for the moment he had tabled the thoughts. It wasn't that he didn't believe them so much as he simply didn't have enough emotional room to think about it. Yes, he had a voice in his mind—and he'd decided it was real—but what it was he wasn't ready to deal with.

His wolf was sitting in the back if Zane's mind and trying not to whine. He knew his other half had been really hurt and the loss of pack always hurt but to close himself off this much hurt both. If he opened up to even the Luna it would be so much better, but Zane had almost closed off everything. If it didn't involve his uncle or sister, he was almost cold and dead to it. It really upset his wolf and his wolf wasn't sure how to deal with it. Both were young and needed the contact with an older and more knowledgeable wolf. His wolf had a feeling for the moment it had to be his uncle.

Esther didn't trade looks with Kad, but she did contact him. **I'm not sure how to help him, Kad. It really hurts to say, since I can't remember the last time I had to deal with a wolf so hurt. It isn't just that he is hurt; he is withdrawing into himself and doesn't want to show feelings for anyone but his sister and his uncle. How do I deal with it?** As Luna, she was used to having hurt wolves come to her for comfort, even when they couldn't trust going to anyone else. She tried to remember the last time she felt or dealt with a wolf this withdrawn and she was worried. There wasn't a Mind Healer available within the state, but through their Council, they had requested one. They didn't know if one would be available who was willing to come; there was no way they would be able to send him to another pack for the help; it would break the slight trust they had gained so far. Some travelled, but the two she personally knew were already busy with those needing their help and were not available to come.

Kadrian wasn't sure himself, even though he had dealt with many hurt wolves. This was, in a way, a unique case since he hadn't ever heard of a changed human who was in a coma for so long. Yes, their healers had kept a close eye on him and his sister, but they didn't have an answer for why he had been down so long. Based on how he was reacting to his sister he had to wonder how he would react to young pups. **Maybe have most of the older pups give him room and have the younger pups say* *hello? Beyond that, I'm not sure but for the moment we need to try and give him a bit of room until his uncle comes home.**

Esther sighed quietly and was silent the rest of the ride home. When they pulled up, she stepped out with a cheerful smile on her face, "Well we are here, I hope you like it. For the time being, you will be in the main house. I have assigned two rooms to you and there is a shared bathroom. There are some clothes and toiletries for both of you until your uncle comes back. After that, it will be up to him where you live. Zane, can you offer your sister an arm inside?" She had opened the door to the SUV and stepped out.

He had already planned on it. He slid out of the car and moved around to the other side and helped Liv out of the SUV, "Once inside we can relax in whatever is the living area if you needed." He really hoped they were on the first floor. Several others came out and gathered the luggage. For him it was the one bag but for her there were several. When they grabbed the bags, he and his wolf, stiffened up slightly though they didn't growl or do anything else; his wolf seemed to sense that they were not a threat for some reason. He settled for slowly walking his sister into the massive building.

Liv gave his arm a light squeeze, "I would prefer to go to our rooms first and unpack. It is warm enough I want to change into some lighter shorts and a t-shirt." She was also feeling somewhat overwhelmed since the building was large and impressive. When they walked in, it had a very homey feeling which helped her relax some.

Damien smiled at the two, "Follow me and I will show you the rooms. Both of you are on the first floor for your sister's sake. It will make it easier for her to move around right now." He could see how it pained her to move around. He had to wonder what they could do to help her. They had some of the best doctors he knew of, but she had come to them already partially healed.

Zane gave him a tight smile, "Thank you Damien and it is appreciated." He didn't know the higher up in the building you were the higher the rank you had. Since their uncle was the senior enforcer and a Beta, they should have been in better quarters on the second floor. He kept his eyes on who was around them and as hard as he tried not to, he was rather twitchy. He wasn't sure if it was because he knew, in theory, they were wolves or because they were around his sister. Or if it was for something else entirely. All he knew was it was hard not to growl at them.

Eventually they reached the rooms and after Zane helped Liv into her room he had to stare. They were very well furnished. Even though it was a single room with a joining bathroom, it was huge. Well to him it was huge, and he had to stare around and wonder if everyone had a room like this. It was obviously a girl's room based on the colors and furniture. Inside was Anne. It was bigger than their parent's room.

"Okay you two out. I will help Olivia sort her stuff out and if needed, change into something more comfortable." She looked at Zane as her brother left the room, "Git or else. Your sister is safe with me and if we do need anything I will come and get you. Go to your room and check it out." She stood there with her hands on her hips as she both glowered and yelled at him.

Zane debated and finally decided the safe way was to go and check his room out. Instead of saying anything he turned and walked through the bathroom and to his room. This room was far more masculine based on the colors and décor. He hadn't realized both rooms had been adjusted for the two of them. It was rather generic since there weren't any posters or personal items such as pictures on the walls. He was comfortable, as best possible, in the room. On his bed were several bags which he moved to investigate.

*****

Eventually he was done sorting out what was in the bags, and he had found many of his clothes as well as his old laptop and Kindle, which he put on the desk. Now he was done he stood there feeling somewhat lost. Before he could start tensing up there was a knock on the door, and he moved over and opened it. Outside was a girl about his age, "May I help you?" His voice was quiet and mostly emotionless.

She gave him a shy smile, "The Luna asked me to see if you wanted to be shown around. My name is Melody." The Luna had decided on someone his age and less dominant than Damian to show him around. She'd briefly talked to the Luna about him but hadn't learned much. The boy standing at the door to the room was cute but had a strained look on his face, "I can show you to the game room, outside, if you are hungry, the kitchen, and answer some questions."

Zane had to frown since he didn't recognize the term Luna, "Luna? What do you mean by that? I don't understand." Before he asked to be shown around, he wanted to know what the girl meant. His voice—he had trouble saying wolf—seemed to recognize it but couldn't really explain it to him.

Melody tilted her head for a moment, not understanding his not knowing, "Mrs. Esther is the Luna for the pack. Her mate Mr. Kadrian is the Alpha for the pack." It seemed strange to her he didn't know what she was talking about. Melody didn't know Esther hadn't told Zane much, intentionally, to force him to ask questions. Even if he didn't show many emotions, it would get him involved, and hopefully open up more.

Zane sighed, "I don't have any clue what you mean. All I know is I woke up from my coma to find our parents are dead and my sister badly hurt." Damn it he was struggling not to show anything, but he could feel his jaw muscles twitching, "I don't know what you mean by Luna or Alpha." His wolf started to whine in the back of his mind again, but Zane couldn't snap at the girl.

Her face saddened, "We heard about it, and I feel so bad for your loss. The Alpha is the wolf in charge of a pack and the Luna is his mate." She did look upset at the mention of his losing his parents. She knew it meant his sister had as well, "If you would like we can go to the kitchen and get something to snack on and talk. Would you like that?" She could smell his tension, anger, and sadness which was upsetting her. She wanted to cuddle and help show that she would help him through his loss.

He was forced to look down at the floor when she gave him her sympathy, but he chose not to say anything, "Thank you for telling me what those titles meant." Something from his wolf demanded he accept her offer. He could phrase it how he wanted though, "If you want to get a snack, I can go with you. I would like to see what all is here." It would help him avoid those he didn't want to talk to.

She was starting to feel lost as far as what to do for him or with him. **Luna what do I do? He is barely reacting to anything I say. What do I do?** She sent, "Then come this way and Anne will bring your sister when she is ready." She didn't say if she wanted a snack or not. When she turned from the door, she felt him step out and close the door behind him and start following.

Esther kept up a strong front for the girl. **Melody, he is a badly hurt wolf and for now simply talk to him. Even if he doesn't say much, keep talking and show him around. I would take him outside for now, since I have a feeling the game room wouldn't be right.** She sent a wave of comfort to the girl even as they were talking.

It didn't really help her much, but she trusted her Luna and went with she was told to do, "This way to the kitchen and then we can go for a walk." She tried to keep a cheerful expression on her face as she was talking. Her wolf was whining as well since she could smell the distress coming from him. Since he was a new wolf, she had a feeling he didn't know just how good their senses were. Even though he hid it on his face, his emotions would be out to all the wolves he was near.

Zane walked next to her to the kitchen, "Do you know if my sister has come out? I want to make sure she is doing okay." For a moment some emotions showed on his face which made him look much nicer. As they were talking, they had walked into the kitchen, and something smelled good. His nose was twitching as he sniffed the air.

Melody couldn't help but give him a shy smile back at his expression, "She is with Anne and will be out eventually. I think she might be lying down for a few minutes." All the pups knew about his sister and to take it easy around her. For a moment she almost wanted to give him a hug but didn't know how he would react. When she noticed him sniffing, she had to grin, "We have some really good food here; want to raid the cookie jar?"

For a moment he almost turned to go back to her room and check on her. Zane knew she was fine but right now he was scared to be away from her. It was as if he would lose her if she wasn't there nearby where he could watch over her, "Thank you for letting me know, cookies sound good." As she headed for a cupboard he walked behind and looked around the kitchen. As far as he could tell a sizable number of people either lived in the house or ate here.

The kitchen was massive and filled with what he assumed was industrial grade appliances. To be honest it was almost overwhelming him. The house he had grown up in was a small, well-used, older building which had seen better days. This place might as well be a mansion, even if there were lots of people living there. His thoughts were interrupted when Melody pushed a glass of milk and a plate into his hands. He looked slightly startled, and a slight smile crossed his lips. They were thick chocolate cookies and were obviously homemade.

"Sit down silly, it's what the table is for, you know." Melody had noticed his looking around and had to wonder what sort of place he had grown up in. When he smiled, she was pleased even if it didn't show anywhere else on his face. She flopped in a chair and started munching on one of the cookies.

Zane settled down as well and started eating the cookies as well. They went darn well with the cup of milk she'd poured. Once done she took him for the tour of the grounds. From what she said this was just part of what she called the pack property and much like the house it was huge, "I think I would like to go back to my room. I want to check on Liv and lay down for a while."

Melody nodded at his request and showed him inside. When they walked in, he heard Liv talking to someone and after briefly touching Melody's sleeve, he turned to follow it. He found she was in what he assumed was a living room of some sort. There were a number of kids of all ages, and she was talking to Anne while holding a young boy. Since she was in shorts, his eyes focused on an ugly scar which was tracing up one thigh. He'd seen part of it before and his jaw muscles tensed in anger though he managed not to show it, "Hey Liv, I see you have a lap buddy huh?" The boy was three or maybe four.

Olivia looked over at him and smiled. She could see his expression and the tension in his jaw but chose not to mention it, "Yup and Caleb is a cutie, isn't he? I offered to keep him, but he growled at me for some reason." She grinned at him until she noticed him staring at her leg. She didn't let the smile slip and didn't bother moving. It was ugly, but she wasn't going to hide it, "Come have a seat Zane and relax. I'm having fun getting to know some of the other kids."

Zane gave her a tight smile and tried to give a warmer smile to the little boy, "I'm sure she was teasing you, Caleb." He settled down next to his sister and leaned over and rubbed the boy's back, "Thank you for watching my sister while I was out and about." He was smiling, and it showed. Little kids he might be able to deal with but older kids and adults he couldn't. Maybe eventually he might start trusting them as they proved themselves to him.

Caleb mock growled at him and grinned, "She nice, smell good." He leaned against Liv and relaxed. He looked very comfortable.

Since her lap was taken a somewhat older girl, maybe six-ish, came over and crawled in his lap. She gave him a hug and sniffed at his chest, "Yous smells good as well." She giggled at his expression. Even if they didn't say it, his distress would draw the young pups to cuddle as even they tried to help.

Zane hadn't been expecting it since he was trying to project a lack of care. It was obvious the little girl wasn't buying it as she climbed on his lap. Just for good measure he frowned at her and growled, "I see I have tricked the little girl and now I'm going to kidnap her and keep her." He wrapped his arms around her as she started to squeal.

He got several laughs, though one older boy, Zack assumed he was her brother, grumbled, "Good, then I won't have to deal with the little beast." He flashed Zane a grin even as his little sister growled at him.

Zane gave him a slight smile before wrapping his arms around the little girl, "Well I guess I get to keep you then. Should I get a doggy bed for you for my room?" For some reason his wolf growled at him for the joke.

The girl turned and growled at him, "Not doggy. Need wolfy bed. You sleep in wolfy bed, and I sleep in bed." She started giggling when she said it.

Liv was doing her best not to show how pleased she was Zane was interacting with others even if it was a little girl. He had started withdrawing and it worried her. She was still worried for him since he was so different from the brother she had known.

Melody was paying as much attention to his actions as possible. Since the Luna told her to get to know him, this was a start. The whole thing with the doggy or wolfie bed was cute. It made him seem more like a person than his cold act showed.

He glowered at the girl, "Nope, bed for me wolfy bed for little girl." He gave her brother a slight smile as she was growling at him.

Most of the older pups had been contacted by the Luna about Zane. She hadn't said much, other than give him room but include him in conversations if he was inclined. Kadrian had let the adults and older pups know why the two were there without going into detail a couple days before.

*****

Zane sat with Liv and the others though he didn't say much other than to her or the younger kids. It never occurred to think of them as pups or the fact they could shift if they wanted. If someone directly asked him a question, he would answer but that was about it. Eventually Kad came into the room.

"Zane, would you come with me please? We need to talk, and I need to explain a few things to you." He was aiming for a mellow tone and not demanding.

He looked up at Kadrian and gave him a nod. Because the voice in his mind told him to, he lowered his eyes slightly after looking at him, "No problem, sir." He picked the little girl up off his lap and set her back down after he stood up, "Sorry, gotta go, lap buddy. I'll see about the wolfie bed." He almost smiled when she growled at him again. When Kadrian walked out of the room Zane followed him and eventually they reached Kadrian's office.

"Have a seat, Zane." He waved towards a comfortable overstuffed chair, "Lap buddy and wolfie bed?" He settled down in another chair and gave the boy a slight smile, "Since you are no longer at the hospital, we can talk more about what is going on. I know you were told you were infected with lycanthropy and it's correct. Normally the initial change only takes a couple weeks to process through your body. Following the initial changes, it takes several weeks for your wolf to present himself, and usually they are waiting with happy anticipation for it. From what we can tell, you weren't fully infected when you were attacked. Between that and being in a coma, it delayed or slowed the spread of the infection and thus slowed your turning."

He didn't bother mentioning Zane had some dormant wolf DNA, which would have been activated as well. The other pack had done genetic tests after he had arrived, even as they stabilized him, to try to detect the rogue's DNA in the wound, to detect if they had other reports; there hadn't been any other turns, but there had been other hits. He wasn't going to overload the pup. With him being in a human medical center, it was a good thing, as werewolves sometimes shifted while they slept, especially when injured or stressed, as their wolf felt better able to protect them with their claws and teeth. Sometimes, it was just their wolf wanting out, almost like a stretch, especially if they hadn't had a chance to shift recently, and the wolf felt comfortable there.

Esther came in and had a tray of food and something to drink, "I thought you might like a snack, Zane. Your sister indicated you liked Dr. Pepper, so I brought a bottle for you." She put the tray on the coffee table before settling down next to her mate.

Zane picked up the bottle and took a drink and had to make a face. He glanced at the bottle to make sure it was the real thing, "Ug, that tastes nasty. Can I get some water instead?" He shuddered much to the others amusement, before going back to answer Kad's first question, "I was teasing the little girl about being a lap buddy and I was going to kidnap her and get her wolfie bed for my room for her. For some reason it seemed to offend her."

Esther had to smile in amusement at his face when he drank, "It really depends on the wolf if they like sodas or not. Lemon water? You'll notice your tastes are going to change. Highly processed food or drinks, you will be able to taste the chemicals... For some, they can handle it, and for others, it doesn't taste good." When he nodded, she took a bottle from her mate's fridge and handed it to him. When he explained what he'd meant about being a lap buddy and wolfie bed she had to laugh when Kad sent to her what Zane had said when he'd gone to get him, "That's amusing."

He carefully took a careful sip and nodded, "Thank you, ma'am. That's better." He contemplated the food but held off for the moment, "So what does this mean for me? I won't get furry or something?" To say he was confused was an understatement. Being honest, he wasn't sure how much he really believed what he was being told. He hadn't seen anyone change and there wasn't any dogs or wolves running around.

Kadrian laughed, "You would be a rather odd wolf if you didn't get furry. Besides I have a feeling your wolf would be offended if he didn't have fur. No, it simply means it took much longer for the infection to progress through your body. You are a werewolf now since I can smell the fur scent of a shifter. Based on your actions, your wolf is talking to you, even if what he says doesn't make sense." This was going to be rough on the boy, since the first change after being turned was hard for new turns. If you were born a shifter, you started shifting when a baby and it was relatively painless, since your body was used to it. You grew up with it being normal to shift between two shapes.

The boy was chewing on his lip as he was listing to what Kadrian was saying. When Kadrian mentioned his wolf being offended, his wolf growled since he wasn't amused. Zane couldn't help but smile slightly, "Sir, I think you managed to offend the voice in my mind. He didn't like the joke." His wolf growled again, this time at Zane, since he could feel Zane's amusement at his displeasure, "So what does this mean? How do you change? And do you only do it on the full moon?" He'd forgotten what Mrs. Easter said about changing.

Kadrian grinned at the boy since he could sense the wolf's reaction. He was going to need to bring him into the pack on the full moon, which thankfully his uncle would be there for, "Well, now your wolf is awake, you will change on the next full moon, if you don't change before. You are going to have to think about if you want to change on the moon or not. The change on the moon is demanded by your wolf and between that and it being your first time, it is going to hurt. If you choose to change now, it is still painful the first several times but shouldn't be as bad." He didn't answer the question on how to change since Zane would have to think about this. By the tradition, and what he had been taught, they usually did the first change in private with the Alpha or the Luna. It wasn't something he even considered there were other ways, it was just how they did it.

Zane chewed on his lip some more, "So what you are saying is either way it is going to be painful, just less painful if I did it now. I don't know about you, but pain isn't something I care for, and less pain is usually good. Now how do I go about changing sir?" He was still on the fence about believing what was being said to him.

Kadrian had to agree, "I will touch on it in a minute. Before you change, it is strongly recommended you strip your clothes off. If you don't, they will tear and irritate your wolf till you are free of them. Now to change, what I think of it as, is calling your wolf forward. Others call it as wrapping your fur coat on. It is different for everyone. The first time I will help you change using my powers as the Alpha. You'll later learn how to shift on your own." He managed not to laugh at Zane's expression.

He sat up straight with a horrified expression on his face, "I have to what?" Zane could feel the blood rushing to his face and knew he was probably bright red. He glanced at Esther and blushed even more before looking away, "Oh god, I... Um... I guess it makes sense. Do you have rooms or something to change in?" If not, then he would have to find somewhere to hide to change. It would be behind a tree if nothing else!

Esther gave her mate a wry smile, "I think it might be time for me to go and check on Olivia and dinner." She knew Zane wouldn't do anything while she was in there. She gave Zane a grin as she walked out since he was very obviously not looking at her.

Kadrian started laughing at his reaction, "Yes Zane, you need to strip down and I'm not pulling your leg. You will grow significantly in size when you change even though you are still young. I would guess you will top about two hundred and fifty pounds right now. Most adult male wolves range from three hundred to five hundred pounds. It depends on your dominance as to how big you will become." He didn't bother saying anything about how he would lose the human modesty he clearly had and would just not think about just stripping off all his clothes and shifting.

Zane was most definitely shocked when Kadrian told him the weight, "Good god that's almost a pony in size. So how will you help me change?" He was still red and was very glad Esther had left the room. He wanted to get this over with and see if it was real. Part of him wanted it to be real but the rest of him had to wonder if the entire group of people were nuts.

He was trying not to laugh at Zane's reaction, "Not really, since our muscles and bones are denser, but we are significantly larger than any wolf in existence. How I help you change would be very hard to describe right now. It's part of who I am. Once you change the first time, you will understand much better. There are also some books you are going to need to read and classes to take. Do you want to take care of it now?"

He crossed his arms and leaned back in the chair and stared at his lap for several minutes. His wolf was almost doing summersaults in enthusiasm at the idea, **Oh for heaven's sake, calm down. You're making me dizzy.** About the only thing keeping him from trying was the fact he would have to get nude. The idea didn't bother his wolf at all, but it did bother Zane. If what Kadrian was saying was true, then he would have to, "Fine, let's get this over with. What do you want me to do?" Zane stood up.

Kadrian had a pleased smile on his face, "We can do the change in here and then you can go and wander around for a while. If you want, step behind the chair when you strip. It is something you will eventually get used to and you will see a fair amount of casual nudity as people strip to change. It is normal for us. Oh, and for the change, I don't need to touch you in any way." He figured it would make Zane a bit more comfortable.

Zane blushed again since several of the girls were cute and the idea of seeing them nude bothered him, since he had grown up learning that nudity was not something you did with anyone else around. He stepped behind the chair and quickly stripped down and waited. As he was looking at Kadrian, he had to stare since the man's eyes were starting to glow. As they were glowing, he felt something call to his wolf and it came forward in his mind. Suddenly an almost agonizing pain hit. It started in his joints before spreading up his arms and legs to his chest.

With a muffled groan he leaned over and clutched his stomach before he fell onto all fours. When the pain finally subsided, he tried to stand up and promptly fell over with a yip. He turned and looked at his body and had to yip again since he was a wolf now. His fur was almost a solid white except for some grey on his tail and back. He would find out later, one of his ears was black too. This time when he tried to stand up, he was able to. He could feel his wolf far better than he had before, and he took more control of their body, leaving Zane still in overall control. Later, he would learn that was the most common mode of sharing their body, although there were times a wolf would take full control, and the human mind would have nothing.

Since now he was standing, he checked his body out better. Kadrian wasn't saying anything, so Zane started walking around the room. He found it was pretty easy to get used to walking on his four paws. Chances were, it was because of his wolf. His wolf had kept making them smell things, as they moved around the room. Eventually he was trotting around and felt more comfortable with his new body. He walked over to the office door and looked over his shoulder and barked at Kadrian.

Kadrian was smiling at the young wolf as he was getting used to the new body. Based on the size of Zane's wolf, he was going to end up fairly dominant, but he didn't say anything. He was almost the size of Damian. From the size of his paws, he still had some growth too. When Zane trotted over to the door he stood and walked over, "All the doors have the lever type doorknobs, so you can open doors yourself." He went ahead and opened it for Zane though, "Go say hello to your sister. I'm sure she'd like to see what you look like."

Zane contemplated the door handle and nodded. It made sense to have that type of knobs and he felt silly for not noticing or realizing it. With a woof he trotted out of the office and instantly lowered his nose to the floor. His sense of smell had changed when he had, and Zane was shocked by how many scents there were. It took him some time sniffing before he could start moving again. His wolf kept a running commentary of what the scents were. Werewolf and if they were in wolf or human shape, what they had recently eaten, if they were happy/sad/upset/depressed, gender, if they were young/old. For those who had come in from outside, several had traces of scents from where they had been. Other scents related to the building itself. Once he was done, he headed back to the living area Liv had been in.

When he walked in, her back was to him, and he slowed down and did his best to be silent when he moved over to her. Once he was behind her, he stuck his nose against her neck and sniffed.

Olivia wasn't expecting it, and she jerked away and almost dropped Caleb. When she turned around, she received a wet dog kiss, "Ewww.... That was disgusting. I don't even want to know where your tongue might have been." Suddenly she realized who it probably was, "Zane? Oh wow, you are a beautiful wolf." She moved Caleb off her lap and carefully slipped off the couch, "Come here and let me give you a hug."

He trotted around the couch and moved into her arms. Zane was careful not to step on her legs as he moved close to her and ended up resting his head on her shoulder. When she wrapped her arms around him and gave him a hug, he leaned into it, and it felt good. Those around them smiled as his tail relaxed more and started to wag.

Liv started stroking his back and sides, "Wow, you are huge, and your fur is so soft." She worked her fingers into his fur, and he was really warm as well, "Hmm... For those cold winter nights, you might have a use..."

Zane was surprised how nice the rubs and scratches she was giving felt. He barked at the teasing. Just for good measure he gave her another good lick.

CHAPTER 4

Mike Arrives

They sat there for a while as Liv was stroking Zane's fur. He carefully settled down next to her though he kept his head on her shoulder as he gently leaned into her petting. For the moment all was well for him, even with the loss of his parents. Liv was hurt yes, but she was still there. Now he and his wolf had started merging, he was feeling much calmer. His wolf also started to understand the hurt inside his human, and it made him want to howl for him. He was going to lend his human the strength he needed to start healing. If it meant being standoffish for some time then so be it, he would support his human.

Zane didn't realize his wolf had made his decision to help. For the moment he was just going to enjoy the moment. How long they sat there he wasn't sure but eventually he moved back. He nuzzled her face for a moment before standing and giving his fur a good shake and turned. He was starting to get tired and for some reason he had a feeling taking a nap here would be a good idea. He twitched his ears at her and then with a flick of his tail he trotted off towards his room.

*****

Later in the evening the two of them were sitting in Liv's room relaxing against the headboard of her bed. They were watching some mindless show on TV and simply enjoying being with each other, "Liv I want you to tell me what happened. I both want and need to know. I want to hear it from family and not someone who wasn't there." He knew this was going to be hard for her, but he had to know.

She sighed and shifted her body to take some of the pressure off her hip and leg, "It was just a stupid accident, Zane. We were coming to see you. Mom and dad were going to drop me off for the morning. They had a few things they needed to take care of, and I was going to spend some time reading to you. We were coming through a green light when someone ran it and hit the side of the car. Mom and Dad died upon impact, and I was badly hurt." Her voice was tense as she was speaking since she didn't like talking about it. "I don't remember much of the accident, just some lights then heard the crash. I woke up in the hospital."

Zane sighed and leaned his head back against the wall, "Thank you for telling me Liv. I had to know and not knowing was killing me. How badly were you hurt? Um, what were you going to read to me?" He glanced down at the scar which was showing below the hem of her shorts.

She looked away and sighed, "My upper leg was badly broken, and the hip joint was damaged as well. They pinned the leg bone, but they are going to have to go back and do more on my hip." She hoped by the time they were done, her leg wouldn't hurt her nearly as much, "It is mostly stiff and hard to move when I have been sitting around for a while. There were some other injuries, but they were mostly relatively minor. Most have healed already." She snickered, "Um, a werewolf story." What she didn't say, was it was more from the female's point of view. It was a story she had been reading.

He lightly grasped her hand as she was talking and gave it a light squeeze, "I'm sorry you were hurt sis. Please ask if you need anything." Just for good measure he lightly ruffled her hair, "You are a pretty good sister, for the most part." When she mentioned what she read to him, he growled at her.

She smacked his hand just for good measure, "And you are a pest for a brother. Messing my hair up is just wrong, darn you." She yawned,

"Well I'm going to head towards bed, and I will talk to you in the morning." She glared at the growl, "Remember no growling at me, darn it!"

Zack took the hint and slipped off the bed and stretched, "I'm going to hit the bathroom on the way to my room." He trudged towards his room and after taking care of business went in and changed to some sleep shorts. He crawled in and settled down on his back. Since he had changed earlier, he was feeling the wolf in his mind much easier and clearer. It was so odd but also in a way so right.

Once in his room he flopped on his bed and realized he wasn't tired yet. He was mentally tired but not physically. As he was wondering what to do, he was staring at the ceiling. The room was very nice, and he could see himself staying here for a while, but he didn't know if he could call it home. Home was the house they had lived in with his parents. No, it wasn't anything special and yes it was old and rather used but it had been theirs, though they rented it.

His wolf was listening to his thinking and sent a suggestion to him. **Go for a run? Get out of the house and see what the nearby territory is like? I would like to run.** Now they had changed he wanted to come forward again and go for a run to see what this pack was like. It sounded fun and even if the moon wasn't full, he wanted to say hello to the Ultimate Luna.

Zane started to smile. It was a slow smile and sounded like a great deal of fun. Nobody said he couldn't do it and he figured if he didn't go too far, it wouldn't be a huge deal. The doors had the leaver type knobs, so it would work fine, "Oh my, that does sound nice. I have to admit I did rather enjoy the feel of our body earlier. Not far, scared of cross country running." Zane rolled off the bed and stripped down. Once he was done, he sighed, "I'm going to need help for this." He wasn't sure on how to change, or what to do.

His wolf moved forward and suddenly the shift started; his wolf knew it instinctually. It was still painful but not as bad as earlier. Once he was on paws he stretched and shook his body. The tail felt a bit odd since he most definitely wasn't used to having one. His wolf snorted at the thought and just for good measure wagged it. Zane had to roll his eyes before lifting a rear paw to get an itch behind one ear.

From the bathroom, he heard his sister close the door on her side and he debated on going and saying hello. He finally decided not to and pawed the door open and walked out. He noticed all the doors seemed to have a counterweight which slowly closed it behind. He hadn't really considered it before changing but it was a nice touch.

Once he was out of his room, he headed towards the main room since there was an exit there. He had noticed it earlier in the day. When he approached the door, he did pause for a moment and wondered if it was okay to go out. He cocked his head and then his eyes hardened. Since nobody had told him not to, Zane decided if he didn't go very far, he would be fine. As he slipped out of the exit he had to pause because he could almost feel the moonlight touching his fur.

After closing his eyes, he lifted his muzzle to the moon and simply stood there for several minutes and almost felt its caress. Eventually he lowered his muzzle and headed away from the house. Something was calling him away from the house. It made him somewhat suspicious, but he couldn't feel anything negative to the call, mostly just a direction to run. He slowly followed the call until he came across a perfectly circular clearing near the edge of the forest which surrounded the property. Zane settled down at the edge of the clearing and his eyes traveled around it, as it seemed that a feeling of peace settled into him.

Now that had surprised him, he could see nice and clear in the moonlight; to his human mind, it looked as bright as day. Eventually he moved into the middle of the clearing and lifted his muzzle again. This time it wasn't simply to feel the light on his face but a low howl broke out. This started with his wolf but soon both were singing to the moon. Since this was his first time it was somewhat awkward since they were both trying to figure out how to say what they wanted.

*****

Inside Esther and Kad were relaxing in their room as Zane was slipping out of the house. Both had felt the change and when Kad started to move Esther shook her head, "I will go and keep an eye on him. If I need anything, I will contact you." She slipped out of her clothing and changed forms. Her fur was like his except since she was a Luna her fur was a soft silver and she had sparkling blue eyes. After changing she padded out of the room and silently left the house via the same exit Zane had used.

She could feel the moon since the full moon was in just a few days. This was a call which neither Zane nor his wolf could resist and should be good for them. Since she wanted to give him some time she didn't hurry to the clearing. Once she made it there, she simply stood on the edge and listened. Though Zane was trying not to, the call he was making showed his anger and loss. It didn't mean he would relax around her but at least he was talking to the moon. All wolves were driven to speak with the moon at times, but most did so much more and made regular songs of their life.

When he finally finished howling, she sent a thought to him. **Hello Zane, may I join you?** She didn't want to force her presence on him, but she wanted to talk to him, and this form was more conducive, since his wolf would be much more in control.

He should have expected this, but everything was so new he hadn't. **If you wish ma'am. This is your territory, and I wasn't going to go very far but I needed to get out for a few.** Since he was sitting down already, he simply waited for her to join him.

She shook her head as she padded over to where he was and settled down next to him. **It is the pack's territory, Zane, not mine. Your uncle is pack, so it makes it his territory as well. When you become pack, it will be yours as well. Wolves don't think of territory as belonging to one person. Yes Kad, and I are the Alpha wolves, but we simply protect the pack and pack territory.** Esther was hoping knowing he would have somewhere to call home might help eventually.

Zane was still looking at the moon as she was talking to him. He didn't want to become pack; the thought terrified him. He had lost his parents while he was unconscious, and he had almost lost his sister. Yes, his uncle was still there but they didn't see him very often. **Ma'am I don't wish to sound rude, but I don't even know where I am. My home is gone, and I will never be able to go back. I lost almost everything after some monster attacked me. Now I'm one of those monsters. My life has been torn apart and tossed into a blender. Why would I want to join a pack of things like me?** He really wasn't trying to be insulting or even say even that much. His wolf had forced him to.

Esther had to look at the moon as well. She could understand what he was saying since it was his wolf speaking as much as Zane. She also could feel the wordless feelings he shared unconsciously with what he was saying, which told her more. **Zane, we are not monsters, though some do act monstrously. It is no different than some humans being criminals. If you act like a monster, then you are one. What we are isn't much different from some of the other biological anomalies humans can have. As far as your life, it has been heavily impacted. Nobody can or will deny it. As far as where you are, the pack resides on property which we have owned for many generations.**

She lifted her muzzle and let out a pleased howl to the moon, not really saying anything since she was in a good mood. **You are currently living in Oregon. We are away from any major towns but as you saw, not very far. The pack owns several thousand acres of property. It includes some heavily mountainous sections, forests, and range land. We run cattle, do some farming, even a moderate amount of logging. Mind you we do our best to keep it ecologically balanced.** For the moment she was trying to draw him into simply talking with her.

Zane didn't want to admit it made sense to him, the acting monstrously bit, so he didn't comment on it. **So why would I want to join the pack? What is in it for my sister and me? We have our uncle and can live with him.** He didn't really care at the moment, but she had piqued his curiosity. Zane did notice she hadn't mentioned where in Oregon they lived but at least he had a state even if it was several away from where he had grown up. His wolf wasn't helping since he really wanted to go and explore the territory.

Wolves are communal creatures. Yes, we do have a hierarchy of ranks much like our lupine cousins but most of us are most comfortable being around others of our kind. For most, the need to be with others is as strong as the need for as food and water. For your sister, there is protection and help with her injuries. Now the healers want her to take some time off from surgeries and concentrate on her physical therapy, letting what has been done to finish healing. In a few weeks we will have her seen by several of our specialist medical staff. It also gives you family in a way, though not quite like the one you lost. Pack takes care of pack. At least he was listening even if he was still being stubborn and closed off, and not making any comments. **Also, since you are a werewolf there are only a few options on how you are viewed. If you are in a pack, you are considered controlled, as the pack can hold you accountable for your actions. If you are a lone wolf, you will be allowed on pack territory once you petition the Alpha and they agree, sometimes they will impose restrictions. Some packs don't allow Loners on their territory. Here, while they are respectful, and don't cause issues, they are allowed. The last category is a rogue. It's the type of wolf who attacked you. They are considered the criminals of Lycan society. Most are insane and have a certain stench to them. The longer a Rogue lives, usually the more insane they become.** She didn't overwhelm him with how a werewolf became a rogue; some were loners who had gone insane from loneliness, and others were sane at the beginning and were kicked out of a pack for some sort of major rule breaking deemed too large to keep them in the pack with a punishment. Usually, it was one related to not being trustworthy or unprovoked attacks of others.

There was a great deal of information, and he was going to need to think about it. For his sister he would do almost anything but the idea of joining a pack just because something bit him was discomforting. **I'm going back in ma'am. Thank you for talking with me.** He stood and quietly padded back to the house and headed to his room. Since he didn't feel like changing back now, he curled up on top of the covers and settled into sleep. His last thought was a slight amusement on how comfortable it was to be in a ball.

*****

Liv had been paying close attention to her brother over the last few days, she really needed to talk to her uncle about him. When spoken to, he would respond but even now his answers were polite but short and nothing else. With the younger children he was more open, but you could almost see the barrier he was creating. The only time he was close to who she had remembered was when they were together. Usually, it was at the beginning or end of the day in her room. Thankfully, their uncle was supposed to be there soon. She was in the back of the house, talking with several of the other kids while she waited.

Mike had finally made it back to the pack and was getting ready to head in when Kad contacted him. **Mike before you see your niece and nephew, I would like to talk to you for a few moments. Nobody is in trouble but there are a few things we need to discuss.** This was going to be difficult since it was about Zane.

He sighed as he responded. **Not a problem Alpha, I will come in the side entrance and before you say anything, I have been kept updated.** He had his team keeping him updated on how the pups were doing, with one or two keeping a discrete eye on them. From what he had understood Zane was almost being too polite or maybe distant would work better. Both were good pups or, so they seemed when he had seen them over the years. It didn't sound like Zane was causing problems since he was doing any chores given to him without complaint. He simply was being distant and to polite to most of the pack.

He walked into the office as he was thinking and nodded at the Alpha, "Morning Kadrian, so what do you wish to talk to me about?" He was curious and wanted to know what the issue was.

Kad waved him towards a chair even though he remained behind his desk, "Morning Mike and welcome back. I already have the report you submitted and have reviewed it. It can wait for the moment though. I would like to talk to you about your nephew." Before Mike said anything Kad held his hand up, "He hasn't done anything wrong and is more than willing to help with what he is asked. What has Olivia and the Luna concerned is he is not allowing others to get close to him. He will talk when spoken to but otherwise appears to want to be left alone. When he is dealing with the little pups, he is somewhat open but with anyone near his age or older he is at best remotely formal. Melody has been doing her best to talk to him since the Luna asked her to."

Mike settled down in the chair and carefully listened to what Kad was saying. As far as the report it was something which could wait. He leaned back and sighed in frustration, "I had a feeling it was something like that. My team has been keeping me up to date on what's been going on." From the sounds of it, Zane might be in the process of becoming a lone wolf. He couldn't see him becoming a rogue no matter what happened if for no other reason than Liv was alive. He refused to even think about what would happen if anything happened to her. Mike didn't know what to do now, "So what can I do Kad?"

Kad had to give him a helpless shrug, "I'm not really sure. Esther is close to tears since she has never had a young wolf refuse to allow her to comfort him or her when they were clearly needing the help. Liv doesn't have a problem with it, but Zane isn't willing. I honestly think he has been seriously scared by waking up to find his family is mostly destroyed. Beyond that I just am not sure what to do. I have asked the elders what they think but it might take some time. They are also looking to see if there is a free Mind Healer willing to come see him, but as you know, they are few, and so far, those willing to travel that we know of, currently are dealing with issues already, and are unavailable. I am not willing to send him to the two which accept those coming to them, as I refuse to send Olivia, nor will I separate the two of them."

He rubbed his face with both hands before talking to his Alpha again, "If I find the fucking rogue, I'm going to give Zane or Olivia a wolf skin rug. I might be a wolf and born as such, but I never expected this to happen." Mike stared at the floor for a few moments as his anger and outrage at not only the rogue but also the driver of the other vehicle warred with his sadness at losing his brother far too early, "I don't know if it will help but after I talk to him and get a feel for where he is at emotionally, I will know more. Maybe I can get him into training as an enforcer and it will help him find a place for himself." Mike looked up at Kad and tried to look hopeful, "If you don't mind, I'm going to find them and talk. If nothing else, he must join the pack for the next few years. An adolescent wolf can't be a lone wolf. He would have to be sent out of the pack and it wouldn't work. Liv can't survive that way, and neither can he. I will deal with it for the short-term sir."

Kad nodded and he hadn't considered it. If Mike explained what might happen if Zane didn't join the pack, it might help. Granted they would never kick him or his sister out, but it might help center him. The training might help as well, "That works, though you do know I would never kick him and his sister out. I know I would lose you and it won't happen. Do your best please." He would never consider kicking out a pup. Even if they were horrible, they would be kept basically on lock-down until they finished their human schooling and reached the end of their second decade before they would be kicked out.

Mike nodded at him and left the office. He paused for a moment and sensed Zane and Liv were outside the back of the pack house. Mike headed their way and stopped at the back door and had to smile. Zane was in his wolf form and was playing with some young pups. Liv was sitting on a bench and was stroking some as well and tossing balls for them to go chase and fetch back. For the moment he could smell a type of contentment from Zane as the wind was coming towards him. Olivia was different since she wasn't a Lycan, but under her pain he could smell some enjoyment.

Outside, Zane was still feeling his way into his new body which was interesting. Playing with the young pups gave him a chance to grow used to how to use his body. His wolf was enjoying being allowed out and he was loving playing with the pups.

As far as Zane's wolf, he was saddened by what he was getting from his other half. This should be good for both, but his other half wasn't willing to open himself up to the pack and ask for help. He was scared by the loss of his parents and what had happened to his sister; he kept fearing the loss of anyone else he opened himself up to loving. He would trust his uncle but beyond it every person was going to have to earn his trust and it was going to be hard. Melody had some, but she was still going to have to work hard to go beyond what she had now. He still had a deep-rooted fear of loss.

When Mike came out Zane quickly knew, as the wind swirled off the building, bringing his scent to them and he turned and had to pause for a moment. He could feel his dominance and after lowering his head in respect for a Beta he realized it was his uncle, he ran over and started rubbing his head against Mike's stomach. He was letting out soft whines as he was doing it. His tail was also wagging hard.

Mike rubbed Zane's ears for a moment, "Why don't you go and change, so we can talk. I'm going to sit with Olivia until you come back. We can go over to my place for a bit of privacy ." He heaved a heavy sigh, "I'm so sorry I wasn't there when you woke, Zane. I was called out of town for my work. I should be here for the next few weeks though." He had asked Kad for some time off from traveling, and other than this one which there wasn't anyone else they could have sent, his request had been accepted.

Zane stepped back and looked up and woofed. For a moment he had to wonder what Mike's wolf looked like. Before he went in, he dashed over to Liv and lightly nosed Liv's leg before dashing inside and towards his room. Almost before the door shut, he was changing and started pulling on some shorts and a shirt. As soon as he was dressed, he ran back out and almost ran Melody down. He barely managed to catch her, "Sorry but my uncle is back." Once she was firmly on her feet he ran out of the house and out back. When he saw his uncle sitting with Liv he slowed down and moved over and sat on the other side of Mike, "Hey Unc, it is nice to see you again."

Melody was rather startled since he was showing an excitement he hadn't since arriving. Once he had made sure she was standing again and ran off, she followed behind but at a slower pace. When she made it to the door, she found him almost leaning against his uncle. She knew

Mike and he had always felt solid to her. She hadn't known he had a human brother, nor that brother had pups; as far as she knew none of the pack knew, other than maybe the Alpha and Luna, as Mike had joined the pack as an adult. Since he was an enforcer, there was a definite sense of danger. Because she didn't want to disturb what was going on, she stayed at the door as she watched.

Mike wrapped an arm around Zane and gave him a light hug, "Hey Zane, I'm so sorry I couldn't be here when you woke. Kad had a last-minute urgent job for me. I had to take care of it. I was thinking we could go to my house for a few hours, and we can talk. How does that sound?" As he was talking, he was carefully sensing how Zane was doing. He knew everything which had gone on with Liv medically but with Zane in a coma, it was different. They had test results showing the changes but that was it.

Liv nodded, "I think it would be nice." She had a feeling Zane wasn't going to talk if they sat there with everyone around. To be honest she wasn't used to living with so many people. They were very helpful, but it was far noisier and active than she was used to. Melody and several of the other girls were rather nice but she wanted some alone time. She also wasn't used to the lack of privacy, where everyone knew almost everything about you.

Zane nodded as well, "I would appreciate it Unc. I would like to talk to you as well. I have some questions only you can answer." To be honest he wasn't comfortable talking to either Kad or Esther about what had happened to his parents and Liv.

"Sounds like a deal and I think I'm going to order some food delivered. I don't know about you two, but I have no urge to cook right now. It was a busy week for me." He stood and helped Liv up as Zane was standing, "My car is out front." He offered Liv an arm as Zane was dusting his bottom off.

All three walked around the house and to the SUV. For some reason it seemed like there were a considerable number of SUV's scattered around. There were some sedans and other cars, but trucks and SUVs were by far the most prevalent. Once at the car Zane waited for Liv to be helped in before he climbed in and buckled up. The drive to their uncle's house was quiet and barely took any time at all.

Once they had arrived, Zane helped Liv out and then let her do her own thing. She had finally yelled at him for hovering which had upset him and his wolf at the time. Now he simply kept a close eye on her and only stepped in when it appeared she needed the assistance. His wolf wasn't completely happy about it, but it was better than having her yell at them. He couldn't help but trade a look with his uncle as well as a wry smile.

Liv noticed the wry smile and smacked him in a leg with her crutch, "I saw the look, Zane." She looked at the house and was impressed. It was a decent sized two-story house which was well maintained. One thing she noticed was a ramp looked to have been recently installed. As much as she appreciated it, the need irritated her. Without another word she started towards the ramp since if she didn't, she knew her brother would try to help her. It was something which not just Zane but almost everyone older than her had been doing, keeping a close eye on her. She had finally had a discussion with Mrs. Esther which only made her want to scream.

Mrs. Esther had told her it was mostly a wolf thing. They had the urge to protect those who were weaker, especially the injured, and all pups, which in her case made it even worse as she was in both groups. It was because their wolves knew she was hurt and had trouble moving around. This almost forced them to hover and help. It apparently made their protective instincts go nuts with them the older they were. It was one reason she was enjoying the younger pups. They didn't have the drive yet and when they were in their pup form, they were so darling even if oversized. In Zane, he had both, but also she was his sister making it even worse.

Zane had to exchange another look with his uncle before he schooled his face. He followed his uncle into the house, though he did hold the door for his sister. Once inside he started relaxing since it didn't feel like he was being watched. He knew how he had been acting had upset Mrs. Esther and she was keeping an eye on him. That, as much as anything, was frustrating the crap out of him. Right now, all he wanted was to be left alone so he could try to come to terms with what had happened in his own mind.

Mike waved them towards the living room, "I'm going to grab some snacks and drinks. Back in a minute." He headed towards the kitchen and for several moments all which could be heard was his moving around. When he came into the living room the two pups were seated and simply looking around, "If I remember you prefer lemonade Liv and you prefer Dr. Pepper. I have some jerky and cheese." He gave Zane a slight grin, "If you haven't already noticed, your taste in food is going to change."

"Not any longer Unc. Sodas are nasty now." He growled since he'd liked Dr. Pepper, "Lemon water or just water now, please." He rubbed his face for a moment, "I noticed and... Not sure what to say."

Mike nodded and returned to the kitchen to get the drinks.

Liv made a face, "Uncle Mike, I swear his burger mooed last night when he bit into it." She didn't mind rare meat to an extent but flash fried burger which was almost right off the hoof? No thanks. When he grinned at her she made a face before taking a piece of jerky.

Zane snorted at her as he grabbed a few slices of both jerky and cheese, "Thanks Unc." He took a sip of the water, "Uncle Mike I want, no need, to know what all happened. Liv told me some as did Mr. Kadrian and Mrs. Esther. They told me much of it I would have to talk to you. I also have questions on why I have to join a pack."

Mike settled down in a chair and took a sip of the beer he had grabbed, "I'm going to start with the pack question. Since you aren't an adult by either human or wolf terms, it is in a way like being in a family. Once you are an adult, you can make the choice to leave home and go elsewhere. It's the same for being in a wolf pack. If you do choose not to remain a member of a pack, you would be classified as a lone wolf. There isn't any problem with it other than if you end up in the territory of another pack you must check in with the Alpha and get permission to stay. Not all Alphas approve of having lone wolves in their territory and won't allow you to stay as a loner." He paused as he was thinking.

"Now, as far as joining a pack, most wolves are most comfortable in a pack since we are social creatures, much more than humans, as you are likely noticing. There is a hierarchy of dominance but for pups it isn't nearly as obvious since you aren't adults. There are other advantages as well such as being able to contact other wolves with the pack bonds. It is what you would call telepathy and works over long distance. It also allows you to join the pack for moon nights when we almost must shift." He stopped to see if Zane had any questions.

Zane looked down at his flavored water and his brow was furrowed as he was thinking. The voice, his wolf, seemed to agree with what his uncle was saying. His wolf more than anything wanted to join the pack. He really felt it was needed, which was making it hard for Zane to do anything but agree to it. It was all so strange to him, and he honestly wasn't sure what to do. He heaved a frustrated sigh, "So what does this joining require? Some special wolfy handshake or something?" There was some mild sarcasm.

Mike almost snorted a sip of beer out and had to cover his mouth for a moment, "I'm not sure what a secret wolf handshake might be other than sniffing the others bottom." When Liv made a face, he grinned at her, "No, you are introduced to the pack, given some of the blood of the Alpha, and indicate your willingness to join the pack. This normally takes place on the full moon which is tomorrow night."

"Ewwww!!! That sounds nasty." Her original expression at the mention of sniffing butts changed to utter revulsion. She really hadn't been expecting it and her reaction was completely open and honest.

Zane had to blink since he hadn't really been expecting it either. In his case he wasn't nearly as revolted since his wolf wasn't bothered by it, and seemed to have expected it, "Shush Liv please. You wouldn't have to do it." He looked up at his uncle, "Would she?"

Mike chortled at her reaction and answered Zane, "No she wouldn't unless she became a wolf, or she chose to join the pack. We don't turn people without consent, except in very exceptional circumstances if it will save their life, and without it they will die. The primary reason for changing someone, is if a human is your mate. Since we live significantly longer than humans, they will age and die well before we would. With their informed consent, we can change them though there are some dangers with it as well."

Zane really didn't like the idea, even though his wolf did. When he spoke, he was rather grumpy sounding, "I don't like this idea whatsoever Unc. But for Liv's sake I will." For her he would do almost anything.

"Thank you Zane and I think in the long run you will realize this is for the best. Now as far as your parents, it was just an accident. The other vehicle had a mechanical malfunction with the brakes which caused it to not be able to stop at the red light. It was fully investigated and found the other vehicle needed some work which they were not aware of. Since the other vehicle needed work, they were found to be at fault, but no charges were pressed." From what he had been told, the other driver was clearly devastated that they had caused the deaths and the injury of a child. They had fully cooperated. "The other insurance company has been covering the expenses for your sister as well as damages. The pain and suffering money as well as the money from your parents' life insurance has been placed in some investment accounts for when you two are older. All your belongings which aren't here have been placed in storage." They were in storage on the pack's property, but he didn't say it. There were reasons he'd been told not to mention it for now. If they asked for something, he would get it for them.

Liv stood and carefully limped over to Zane and settled down next to him and started crying. She hadn't wanted to talk about this, since every time it came up, she cried. When he wrapped his arm around her, she leaned into him.

He held his sister close and when she didn't say anything, he kept speaking, "I know we were renting the house." Zane was really missing the house. It was old and used but he had liked the neighborhood, "Do you have a room downstairs for Liv to use and what about if you have to leave again?"

Mike gave Liv a sad smile as she moved over to her brother, "I have talked to Kad and Esther and there are two things we can do, you can live here while I'm here and then at the pack house if I must leave. The other option would be for you to stay there and come here for meals or to get away." He scratched his chin as he contemplated telling him about how normally they would be in rooms on the second floor due to his rank, and decided not to, "If you want to do the first, it can be doable and the two rooms you are using would be assigned to you. As far as here, I do have a room on the first floor. I have been using it as an office, but I had it cleared out and moved to a different room. I have a nice bed, dresser, and other furniture moved in."

Zane looked at Liv and she nodded before speaking, "We haven't really talked about it, but I think we would both prefer to stay with you while you are in town." Her lower lip quivered as she tried not to start crying again, "We want what family we have left together."

Mike leaned over and lightly patted her knee, "That's fine, and I was really hoping you would say it. In that case, tomorrow we will bring some of your things over. I can take you shopping for some additional clothing and things, so you don't need to worry about carrying stuff back and forth. I will talk to the Alpha about having you join the pack as well."

*****

Zane rolled out of bed and stretched. It had been a week since he had joined the pack, and he still wasn't sure about the decision. Most of it was because he could feel the others in his mind though he had to give permission for them to connect to him. What made it even more frustrating was he could now really feel some of the concern from the Luna and oddly enough even Melody. He sighed as he stepped into the bathroom and started getting ready for the morning.

He wasn't looking forward to school since he was going to be a new student. Thankfully, several of the kids who Liv had started hanging with were in junior high as well. Melody had assured him they would keep an eye on her for him. Melody was also going to high school as well. Both were going to be a first-year student since he'd just gotten out of eighth grade. Once he was done getting ready, he stared at his image in the mirror. His hair was just below collar length which was somewhat odd for him. It had grown a fair amount while he was in the coma, and he'd decided not to cut it as he decided he liked the look.

He had on some black boots, black pants, black belt, and just for a hint of color, a dark blue t-shirt. Zane's eyes were tense and much harder than they had been before he had been attacked. His face had a rather neutral expression on it as well. As far as he was concerned, he was going to go to school, study, and hopefully get out of there without being noticed any more than possible. With a slight nod he headed downstairs, "Morning sis, you are looking very nice this morning."

She had on some nice shorts and a long flowing shirt. Her shoes were what he would call cutesy girly shoes. Her hair had been pulled back and neatly braided. Their uncle was on morning patrol currently, so he was already gone. Liv smiled at him and then rolled her eyes, "Zane, I might have to start dressing you. I don't understand your urge to look like a bad boy."

He stuck his tongue at her and went and grabbed some leftovers for breakfast, "I like the look so deal with it, sis." He settled down and started munching down the food. Both were relatively quiet as they were eating. Zane knew Liv was concerned about him, but he simply didn't know what else to do. He was too damn scared to allow anyone else to get close. Once they were done, they made sure everything was turned off and they left the house.

Since the high school and junior high were next to each other, they would be taking the same bus. That he was pleased with. When he picked up her backpack she started to frown, and he sighed, "I'm just holding it, so you can put it on. I know better than to try and carry it. If I did you would try and break your crutch over my head. It would be hard on your crutch, and it would make my wolf pout."

She snorted but didn't say anything. She liked the attention but also hated it. Even with a bad leg, she was going to do her own thing as best she could. She'd already figured out the other kids her age would be keeping an eye on her. It was annoying, but she was slowly coming to understand it.

By the time they reached the school, he was starting to get a headache and was looking somewhat irritated. Liv and her friends had gotten off already. Once at the high school he hurried off and went to find his locker. It was a small school, and he already knew where his classes were, because his uncle had taken him for a tour and to check in the day before. Once he dumped his bag in his locker, he grabbed what he needed and headed to home room. When he walked in the teacher asked him to sit up front for the moment.

Once everyone came in, she waved for him to come to the front, "Good morning class, this is Zane, and he is new here. Do you have anything you would like to say?" She gave him a pleasant smile.

Zane shook his head, "Not really ma'am." He started to sit back down when she asked him if he was sure. Zane sighed, "Ma'am what am I supposed to say? My parents are dead, I was in a coma for three months, my sister was severely injured, and we were moved in with my uncle, and I woke up to discover all this. I don't have anything I want to say."

CHAPTER 5

Zane and School Bullies

For a very long moment the class was silent as Zane sat back down before a low buzz of conversation started. The teacher almost looked like she had been slapped but recovered quickly, "Well class, pull your books out and turn to page..." She managed to recover and decided not to say anything else to the boy. He didn't look happy, and she wasn't going to push it. Right before the class ended, she had someone pass out some papers, "Have the papers filled out, signed, and return them in the morning."

When the bell rang Zane left the room quickly since he really didn't want to talk to anyone. He knew some people would be trying to give him sympathy, others probably just to stare at him, and a few to say something nasty. He wasn't in the mood for any of it now, so he used just a hint of his new wolf speed and hurried out of the room. Since he had one more class before break he headed in that direction.

When he walked in, he hoped he would be one of the first since he didn't want a repeat of the previous class. Thankfully there were only a few kids in the room, and he found a seat in the back. After pulling what he needed out he settled back and stared out the window. It only took a few more minutes before the bell rang and the teacher called attendance. When he came to Zane, he gave him a look and then kept going. Zane was thankful and had to wonder if the first teacher had gotten a message to him. Frankly for the moment, he didn't care but he just didn't want to be pitied or given sympathy by anyone.

When lunch rolled around, he had a headache. **Okay if you are supposed to make me stronger, faster, heal really fast, why am I starting to get a headache?** He thought to his wolf. Zane received a snort back. **Because you are a stubborn human.** For some reason Zane had a feeling his wolf was laughing at him, which was really annoying. **Thanks for nothing, you fur rug.** His wolf almost laughed at him at the reply. He could feel his amusement.

As he walked into the lunchroom, he found Melody waiting for him and he had to resist the urge to groan. She hadn't been acting like she was glued to him, but she had been keeping at the edge of where he was. Since she was a nice girl, he didn't growl at her, "Yo Melody, hope the food is edible. I have to admit the food at the house has started to spoil me." His mother had been a very good cook, but that food was rocking.

She cocked her head at him and gave him a knowing smile. It was almost as if she knew he was feeling irritated by her hanging around and was saying 'deal with it', "It is if for no other reason than a number of students would hold a rally for better food." As in the wolves would go on a rampage. They would likely storm the kitchen and eat the meat raw, leaving nothing to be made badly. Or the few who enjoyed cooking would just take over to make it up to their standards.

Zane blinked and snickered before he realized it and was almost horrified. He hadn't laughed much since he had woken up. He had laughed with Liv and Uncle Mike at the house but nowhere else, "Um, I can see as how it might not be a good thing." He managed to keep a straight face as he walked past her, and she joined him. Once they were done getting food, he had to admit it did look decent and there was plenty of it. **My wolf is not pleased since the burger isn't going to moo when I bite it.** He had found the way Liv had described his new food choices totally funny.

Melody had been taking a drink of chocolate milk when he said it and almost choked on the sip. Once she managed to clear her throat, she gave him an annoyed look. **Zane that was... Actually, fairly accurate, but* *don't try to kill me like that again.** She patted her lips dry before she took a bite of food. Once she had finished the bite, she glanced at him, "So how was this morning?" They didn't have any morning classes together.

Zane tensed up slightly and the skin around his eyes tightened up slightly as well even though he tried not to, "It was okay. All I really care about is making it through school without any more crap happening." His teeth clenched slightly before he started eating again.

She wanted to sigh and lightly leaned against him for a moment before sitting up and continuing to eat. Melody had felt him start to tense up, but she had ignored it. Even though Zane had tensed slightly, she could feel appreciation from his wolf. It was something Zane was going to have to get used to. Wolves were tactile creatures, and he needed the contact. It would help him deal with his loss. After talking to the Luna, she had decided to make it her personal mission to keep close to him and spend time with him.

Zane did tense up when she leaned against him, and he wanted to... He didn't know what he wanted to do. Part of him did want to accept the comfort but another part was still too damn scared to take the chance with anyone getting close, as he couldn't handle any more loss. A third part was somewhat twitchy since she was cute and her paying attention to him was both nice and not sure how to handle it. He'd never had a girlfriend before and though he had liked some girls he had been too nervous to say anything. When she sat up, he finished eating.

"You know one thing which is going to drive me nuts? I can hear everything being said nearby. I really don't want to know what people are talking about, darn it." He grumbled quietly at her. As of yet, he hadn't really been impacted by his increased sense of smell. It was along the lines of trying to figure out which sense he was going to be paying attention to. Right now, he kept hearing snatches of conversations which were interesting.

Melody bumped him with her shoulder, "I wish I could say I understand but I was born this way. I grew up with the expanded senses and learned at an early age to filter out what I didn't need. You will learn, though it might take some time." She was keeping her voice quiet as she was talking.

Zane stuffed some food in his face before replying, "Sooner than later would be nice, you know. I really don't have any urge to listen to who has done what recently. It is enough to make my... I mean make me want to plug my ears." He wasn't going to mention his other half even if many people knew about them.

She was stuffing her face as well. Since they were both eating, she tried to contact him via the pack bonds only to realize he had them almost totally blocked. It made her want to fuss at him, since it was nice to be able to talk without being overheard. She also wouldn't need to stop eating to talk. It helped their wolves stay comfortable as well. Instead, she sighed, "Zane... Oh, never mind for the moment. I'd like to talk to you later please."

He had felt her trying to contact him and he had tensed since he was most definitely not comfortable with that stuff. It wasn't something he had grown up with at all, "Maybe this weekend. I have the extra training this afternoon and then a pile of homework." Zane didn't want to talk about somethings, yet he knew she wanted to. What didn't help was his wolf was trying to urge him to open up. He wasn't ready for it and was still too scared to let them that close. With Liv and Uncle Mike was one thing since they were family but anyone else? It was going to take time before he could even contemplate it.

Melody sighed, and she knew he would hear the frustration in the sigh, "Maybe this weekend then. I hope you have fun with the training. It is going to be difficult at first, but it should help. I go to it twice a week though you will be in the beginner's group." She might end up getting a hug from the Luna when she went home. Her wolf was quietly whining in the back of her mind now as well, wanting to help Zane, and not liking how he was keeping them away.

He heard the sigh and felt bad, but it didn't change how he felt. Melody had been trying to be friendly with him and Zane did appreciate it, but it was also driving him nuts. He quickly finished the food, "Gotta go find my next class. See you later." He hurried away from the table and left the lunchroom.

*****

By the time he made it home after the training, he was feeling seriously used. When he walked into the house Liv looked up at him and both eyebrows shot up, "Goodness Zane, did you fall in a pool?" His hair was soaked with sweat, his shirt was clinging to his chest, and upper arms and his shorts were almost as damp.

Zane glowered at her before a very loving and innocent smile crossed his face, "Let me give you a good hug, sis. I missed seeing you most of the day." He started towards where she was sitting.

She grabbed one of her crutches and held it over her head, "If you even think about it, I will bend this over your skull. I know for a fact it will hurt, even if there isn't anything up there to damage." Just the thought of a nice big sweaty hug was totally gross. Even thinking about it made her want to take a shower and get clean.

He started laughing as their uncle came out from his home office, "I'm going to take a shower. I will give you a quick hug later." He grinned at his uncle as he headed upstairs to his room. He liked not having to share a bathroom. Zane didn't like having to clean the bathroom by himself, but it was his.

Mike covered his eyes and gave Zane a patently false sigh, "Zane, if you do it and she breaks her crutch I will take the cost out of your allowance." When Zane had headed upstairs Mike traded a look with Olivia and both smiled slightly since Zane had actually laughed. It hadn't been a very big one or a very long one, but it meant something.

Zane wandered back down and gratefully took a bottle of water from Mike and collapsed in a chair, "You know before all this crap happened, I used to be in much better shape. Running cross country and from monsters tends to keep you in decent shape." He slugged down a good slurp of water. He didn't want to admit he hated it now. He kept seeing monsters behind trees, or coming up behind him, when it was just another runner.

Mike grinned at him, "That's the spirit Zane and give it some time for your new wolf muscles to really develop and you will feel much better. Whether you are turned or born wolf, as you get to be a teen, your muscles and other abilities will gradually grow. Most people accept this is to keep a young pup from having access to their full strength." This was the most relaxed Zane had been for some time. Just the idea of an infant having full access to wolf abilities was enough to make one shudder. They were bad enough once they started moving but full abilities? Nothing would survive.

Zane groaned at the comment, "Thanks for the info Unc but it is embarrassing to be shown up by a thirteen-year-old girl. I know it's silly, but it still makes me feel weird." When Liv poked him with a crutch, he grumbled at her, "I wasn't trying to be sexist or whatever they call it now. It just feels weird to have a girl out run me. My wolf was even annoyed."

Liv poked him again and laughed, "I know Zane, but it was too good to resist. How was school?" It had been hard for her to get around and she had taken something when she made it home, "It was nice having Anne and the others helping me around. I finally gave up on carrying my bag." She was rather upset about needing the help, and it showed.

Zane stood and moved over next to her and wrapped an arm around her, "I wish I could say I understand, sis. Just don't push yourself too hard. The pain isn't worth trying to do everything. At least you don't have Damien and me hovering over you." He slugged down the last of the water, "So Unc is the cow out back? I'm starving." The joke was just for his sister's sake since she'd poked him several times.

Liv leaned into his hug, "I know but having half the kids hovering over me is really starting to drive me nuts. I know what Mrs. Esther explained to me, but this isn't how I grew up. I don't have some overprotective wolf occupying part of my brain." Yes, she was fussing but she figured she deserved to. When she heard him mention a cow, she elbowed him, "Ick and if you ever try and bring me some rabbit or a flank of whatever, I won't talk to you for a month."

Mike leaned his head back and started laughing at the two, "Zane you shouldn't tease your sister that way, even if flank of cow is darn good. I brought some dinner over from the main house since I had a feeling both of you might be feeling tired. For this evening it is some chicken and beef enchilada's, refried beans, red rice, and bunnies, I mean burritos." He stood and headed towards the kitchen.

Zane stood up and offered his sister a hand and waited to see if she wanted help. When she gratefully took one arm, he knew she was hurting, "Do you want me to see if Melody or Anne would come over and massage your leg?" It was something which the therapists had mentioned would help with some of the pain.

"Maybe after dinner, I didn't take my pills very long ago. Before anyone starts massaging my leg, I want my pills in me tonight." When she sat down Liv leaned against Mike when he came over and gave her a light hug, "Thanks for the food. I would have cooked something but had to sit down."

Mike gave her shoulders a light hug before he moved over to the table, "It really isn't a problem, and I would prefer you don't strain yourself. They are used to either bringing me food or me coming for food." He started passing the food around and made sure she had enough to eat before he and Zane took any, "Oh, I know you don't want anyone else poking and prodding you. We have a healer from another pack coming to look at you after school tomorrow. She is an orthopedic specialist and deals with wolves whose bones haven't healed correctly when broken." She also dealt with those who had injuries where shifting had made them worse as they healed wrong, and the regular healers had not been able to resolve it.

Liv paused what she was dishing out as she made a slight face, "You are right I don't want anyone else poking or prodding my leg. Frankly I'll do almost anything, the pain is constantly there and even if they could get rid of some of it..." She started rubbing her face to keep from crying.

Zane's jaw tensed and when he looked at his uncle it was obvious both he and his wolf were angry. Later he was probably going to have to go for a run to work some frustration off. **Damn it Unc this is... It doesn't help being constantly reminded of what happened. I know some people are worried about me but how can I let someone else in when I know they are either going to die or get hurt?** It was his wolf as much as Zane asking. His wolf wanted and needed help.

Mike leaned over and rested his hand on her shoulder, "She is one of the best and has consulted with a number of packs. Once a bone in a wolf has started healing, it must be rebroken to fix. If it is healed, it might have to be broken and fixed before it can be set correctly. This is her specialty. If anyone can make it better, I know she can." Mike mentally sighed. **Zane, I understand where you are coming from. My wolf and I can feel your fear and anger. The answer I want to give you is one you don't want to hear right now. Until you are ready, simply do your best, let Melody give you some comfort. She is a good pup and does want to get to know you.** The last time he had mentioned trying to go to the Luna, Zane had shut down emotionally for several days. The only person he would open up to was Liv at that point.

Zane took a good pile of food and tried not to growl. He did manage not to, since the last time he had his uncle had forced him to submit. That had been rather shocking, and his wolf had carefully explained why they had been forced to, "Would you like me to come with you until they take you into the room for the exam?" He asked his sister, hoping she wouldn't shut him out. **I will consider it, but she isn't giving me much space to think about it. Every time I turn around, she is somewhere nearby. Never obviously but she is always somewhere nearby.** It was a definite huff.

Liv leaned back in her chair and glared at them, "Stop having conversations in your brains. I don't know what you are talking about and even if it isn't about me, it is as rude as whispering. You can come with me, Zane, only if you stop talking with your mind while I'm around." She wasn't a member of the pack, but she had started to learn the look of wolves using the bond.

Both Mike and Zane glanced at her and looked embarrassed, "Sorry sis, we were discussing some wolf specific issues. I don't want you to feel left out of the loop by us discussing this around you. I will talk to him later and it wasn't about you." His wolf whined when they were yelled at.

Mike changed the subject, "So how was school and training, Zane?" He was keeping his nose out of things for the moment. If anything happened, he would be informed immediately, or the Alpha would inform him. It was the biggest reason he was staying out of it; he didn't want Zane or Liv to feel he was hovering. It was damn hard since he wanted to be there for them, but he didn't want them to feel caged. The other parents also suggested letting them find their footing without him hovering. They were old enough to start learning their own limits.

Zane shrugged, "School was okay, and I have stuff for you to sign. No homework yet, since it just started. Melody and I ate lunch together which was nice." At the thought of the training, he wanted to groan, "As far as the training, I swear one of the pups could take me out."

Mike snorted and snickered at him along with Liv. She reached over and patted his arm, "There, there, I'm sure Melody would protect you." Her eyes were dancing with amusement when she said it. When he did growl at her she grinned at him.

He growled at her, "Not a nice idea, darn you. Melody is nice but the idea of her protecting me makes me and my wolf grumble. Might bite you later." He growled again just for good measure.

*****

Melody went looking for the Luna again. By now it was every couple of days she was going there for a hug and sympathy. She knocked on the door to her office, "Mrs. Esther do you have a moment for a hug?" Both knew why she was there.

"Of course, Melody, come in." She had felt the girl coming her way and had settled on the sofa. She held her arms out and gave her a big hug before settling her next to her, "So how did today go?" Her mate was talking to Damien and Anne about how the two had done.

Melody leaned against Esther and started to cry, "I know he is hurting, and I know his wolf is trying to get him to open up. It's just making me want to smack some sense into him. I'm not saying we have to be bosom buddies, but I want to help him." She hadn't really heard about his first class, so as far as she knew he had an okay day.

Esther pulled her close and settled back in the sofa as she was thinking. She felt bad for Melody but even if she didn't realize it, Melody was having an impact on Zane, "Melody, I know how much you want to help him and how upset you are by his refusal. I can tell you it is helping though. He might still be acting cold and distant but between your obvious concern and his wolf, he is starting to recover. I'm not saying tomorrow or the next day he will just wake up and be perfect, but you really are helping him."

Melody looked up Esther, "Really? He is getting better?" It was obvious she wanted to believe her Luna. She didn't believe her Luna would lie to her, but she was very upset with Zane.

Esther leaned over and pressed a kiss on her forehead, "Really Melody, you have taken on a very large responsibility. I'm very proud of you, young lady, now why don't you go back to your family and get ready for tomorrow."

Melody gave Esther one more good hug, "Thank you Luna." She left the room feeling much better and headed out of the pack house to her home. Before she went to bed, she considered going for a run.

*****

Kad was looking at Damien and Anne, "So how did Olivia do today, hun? Did she have much trouble getting around?" He was going to wait to talk to Damien until after he was done talking to Anne. The conversation about Zane was going to be something Anne didn't need to listen to.

Anne shrugged, "When we walked in, she tried to act like she wasn't having any problem. By lunch time, she was really hurting and finally let some of others help her. She did okay in school and seemed to be happy enough." She was a year younger and didn't share any classes with Olivia, "I did help her into her house though. Her leg and hip were really hurting her." It upset her since as a wolf, she healed really well and hadn't helped anyone with an injury like Olivia's before. She could smell how much pain the other girl was in, even if she tried to hide it.

Kadrian gave her a comforting smile, "She has an appointment to see a specialist tomorrow to see what can be done for her. She is one of the best out there. I'm sure she can help her even though she will be hurting for a while." Kadrian gave her a peck, "Go find mom and make sure you are ready for tomorrow."

Once she left, he turned to Damien, "Okay son how did Zane do and act?" He had several reports on how the day had gone but they were from adults. He wanted a kid's point of view.

Damien scowled, "Well he definitely made an impression in his first class. The teacher asked if he wanted to introduce himself. After she didn't accept his not wanting to say anything, he asked her what he was supposed to say and then mentioned what had happened. Well other than being bitten and turned." He carefully thought about what he wanted to say next, "From the beginning, he alienated a number of people. He also brought himself to the attention of some of the bullies in the school. Then again, his current dark and brooding look did get some attention as well." He was chewing on his cheek as he was still thinking.

Kadrian frowned slightly. He had asked his pack who worked at the school to pass it around to the teachers not to push. This was something he was going to need to look into and see what had actually happened, "Great, it's not what he needs right now. If someone bullies him or tries to, it could get very ugly for the person or persons." His eyes were watching his son's body language, "There is something else you want to say or ask?"

Damien made a face, "Dad, I can tell he will end up being reasonably dominant. It might cause him problems with some of the other wolf pups. I have to admit I'm concerned about his becoming a lone wolf, even if he stays here until he is eighteen."

His father smiled at him even as he shrugged, "It might happen no matter what we do. It is as he, his wolf, and the Goddess decides. Being a lone wolf isn't wrong, if it is right for you. As you know, there are several lone wolves in our territory, and they don't cause problems. For now, simply keep an eye on him and let me know how things are going. Your mother and I are keeping an eye on him while trying to give him room to try and come to terms with what happened. Go and make sure you have what you need as well."

Once his son had left the room, he sighed in frustration. He knew Mike was concerned as well and neither had any idea what to do, "Damn it boy, talk to someone. I don't care if it is one of the pups or Esther but talk to someone." With a sad sigh he stood up and walked over to his mate's office. When she stood up, he stepped over to her and gave her a good hug.

*****

"Hey Unc, I'm going to go for a run in my other form." Zane called out as he walked outside. Thankfully, it was starting to get dark so stripping down didn't make him feel too odd. He still hurried taking his clothing off and changing. Once his wolf was free, they dashed for the forest and lengthened their stride. This was better than the running he had done for cross country, since he could really move. For now, he was staying to the trails due to his fears of monsters behind trees. His wolf's body was more flexible and maneuverable than his human body. For some reason he was called to the clearing again. Once in a blue moon, he felt the need to go to the location and it really did help. He did take a roundabout route to get there since it felt so good to be running. Once he arrived, he walked part way into the clearing and looked around. The moon was only half full and his wolf always wanted to say hello to the moon.

Even though Zane hadn't been a wolf for very long, he could feel the draw as well and lifted his head and joined with his wolf in saying hello. To his wolf, they were greeting their Goddess. To Zane, it made him uncomfortable since he had been raised as a Presbyterian and the Christian idea of there being Only One True God and all others were lies. He settled for simply saying he was greeting the progenitor of the Lycans. The first time or two he had howled out his anger, fear, frustration, and pain. Since he had called the Luna to him, he finally quit including those feelings.

Instead, he simply called out a greeting and let his wolf say what he wanted. Once the howling was done Zane simply sat down and kept his head raised to feel the moonlight on his face and fur. Interestingly, it was rather like feeling the sun on his face as a human.

Back in the main house, Melody had also decided to go for a run and on the porch stripped and changed. She normally went towards a different part of the property when she ran but for some reason Melody headed elsewhere. While she was running, she heard a wolf howl and knew it was Zane. By now she knew the sound of his wolf's voice and it always sounded sad and lonely. Melody wanted to howl out her frustration at how hurt he was and how he wasn't willing to accept any help. It wouldn't help anything if she did, since she knew even if Zane didn't understand, his wolf would. It would eventually lead to Zane knowing.

Instead, she settled for a fast lope in the direction of the howl. By the time she arrived at the clearing he was in the howling was done. She paused at the edge of the clearing and had to admit he was a handsome wolf. With his head lifted and eyes closed, he looked content and relaxed. **Zane, I'm coming over.** She walked over and settled down next to him and lifted her face as well.

Zane, for some reason, was feeling relaxed enough having someone, even Melody, settle down next to him didn't disturb him. He didn't move and kept his face towards the moon. **Hello Melody and it's fine.** For some reason, he was relaxed enough her presence didn't bother him at all. **I would ask what brings you here but since this is where you live...** There was some traces of amusement in his voice.

Melody was close enough to rub against him after she sat down. **You live here as well Zane. You are pack as well, you know.** She lowered her head and looked around and if she had been human would have frowned. It was familiar, but it wasn't, and she couldn't quite place where they were. She didn't remember a perfectly circular clearing existing before, nor how it somehow had a feeling of peace. **You do have a lovely wolf, Zane. If you don't mind talking about it, how did it happen? The Alpha and Luna only said to the pack you were turned by a rogue.**

Zane lowered his head as well. **It still sounds so strange to me. Frankly, it really bothers me.** He contemplated her question and huffed at her. **Since I was in cross country, I went for a run. When I decided to run through a section of forest near our house, something started to chase me. I started running even harder and when I broke out of the forest it jumped at me and bit me. I guess having the car hit it and me saved my life. I was in a coma for several months. When I finally woke up, I discovered my parents had been killed and my sister badly injured in a car wreck.** As he was talking, he could feel his agony, fear, and anger welling up, as well as traces of regret and a feeling of it being his fault.

Melody almost asked why it felt weird, but he started talking about what had happened. She had known some of the details but mostly he had been turned and his parents dying. When he explained what had happened, she leaned against him and resting her head on him, instinctively trying to give him comfort. **I'm so sorry Zane. I can't even begin to imagine what it might be like.** When he didn't resist her leaning against him, Melody stayed where she was. **Can I ask another question: is it why you are resisting the pack, the Luna, and letting anyone in?**

Zane lowered his ears and looked down at the ground. He had to think very hard before replying. **Yes.** His mental voice was almost a whisper, full of pain and fear. He finally stood and left the clearing.

CHAPTER 6

Enhanced Senses

Zane quickly stood and stepped away from Melody. He had given too much away. After giving his fur a good shake, he trotted away, quickly moving to a full out run, heading back towards the house. Why he had so easily given up the information, Zane wasn't sure, but it scared him badly; he had no idea what she would do with it. It was why he ran away so quickly. He was going to have to work to keep it from happening again.

Once back at Mike's house, he quickly changed and dressed before going to his room. Once there he took a moment to ensure he had everything ready for the next day, before getting ready for bed.

He changed to sleep shorts and crashed. He didn't sleep well during the night, but he hadn't expected to; he hadn't slept well since coming out of his coma. By the time he woke, Zane was most definitely feeling grumpy. Even after a good shower, he was still out of sorts.

For the day, he picked out clothing similar to what he had worn the day before. Dark pants, boots, and a dark shirt. Once he was done getting dressed, he grabbed his backpack and headed downstairs. Breakfast was already served, so he settled down and started eating. Right now, he wasn't in the mood to talk to anyone. Once done, Zane stood and carefully watched his sister. It looked like she was still in some pain, "I will carry your pack Liv and no arguments."

She sighed and made a face at her brother before agreeing, "Thanks Zane." Liv wasn't happy about it but frankly she could use the help. Even with the meds and the massage last night, her leg was aching. When the doctor saw her later, she hoped she would have some good news for her. It had been several weeks since the two of them had been released from the hospital and her healing should be progressed enough.

Instead of saying anything, he settled for grabbing her bag and carried it out to the bus stop. Liv slowly walked next to him and thankfully her light meds had kicked in and started working. She hated to say she had started to get used to the pain but to an extent she had. Most of the time Liv was in low grade pain and managed to ignore it for the most part. Once at the stop, she greeted one of her new friends and they stood slightly off to the side talking quietly.

Zane nodded to one or two people he had somewhat come to know but otherwise didn't get involved in a conversation. He had a feeling the Luna had talked to many of them, since they were giving him some space. Zane had watched how many of the other kids acted, and even with the dominance starting to show with the older kids, they tended to be rather touchy feely. It wasn't in a bad way, but they tended to brush against the other pack members, trade hugs, and even lean against each other. Even though he was changed, it still seemed strange to him.

Thankfully, his wolf wasn't trying to force him to do the same, other than with one or two people. Melody was one his wolf was very comfortable with. Damien was another though in his case it was because he was to be the next alpha someday. In a way, Zane almost wished he could relax enough to trade even a shoulder bump. Even before he had been changed, physical contact wasn't something he had been comfortable with. Part of it was because he was growing and trying to figure himself out.

When Melody came over and stood next to him, he politely greeted her. After a great deal of thought, he had decided to pretend last night never happened, "Morning, ready for another fascinating day at school?" His voice indicated he wasn't looking forward to it.

She couldn't help but smirk at him, "Most definitely ready for another *fascinating* day at school, we get to expand our brains, learn new words, and other *fascinating* stuff." Now she was teasing him somewhat. Melody could feel his slight retreat from how he had been last night, but she was going to ignore it, even as she was going to keep what he had said to herself. Come hell or high water she was going to help him open up. Something Melody had considered was getting one or two of her other friends involved over a period of time. She also decided she wasn't going to betray his trust and share what he had told her.

Zane looked at her and wondered if she was teasing him with her reply. Since he was so new to being a wolf, he couldn't tell if she was or not based on her scent. Zane settled for keeping his neutral expression on his face. He didn't think when he lifted one eyebrow above the other, "It is fascinating isn't it?" Thankfully, the bus pulled up and he followed Liv onto the bus and had to smile when a boy helped her on. He could sense her annoyance, but she didn't say anything. It showed Zane just how sore she was, which again had his wolf growling in his mind.

Melody wrapped a hand around his arm and gave it a gentle squeeze. She could feel his reaction to his sister needing to be helped onto the bus. It was something few of the pack had to deal with. It was obvious to her many of the pups Liv's age were keeping an eye out for her. Even more than normal, since she was such an open and nice girl. Liv and Zane were almost opposites in both how they dressed and came across.

Yes, Liv was a girl, but it was beyond Liv liking colors and not having a problem wearing them. She laughed even when she was in pain. Liv played with the pups and chatted with those who were her age and didn't have a problem yelling when she felt she was being too protected. Melody decided a good way to describe Liv was that she wore her emotions on her sleeve. Rarely did she show her fears though she knew from Anne, she had cried a few times.

Zane was... well, Zane. Since he had arrived, he had been wearing darker clothing and didn't want attention. He would talk when talked to but gave very little of what he was thinking away. He did what was asked but other than that he just didn't talk much. What Zane might have been like before he had been bitten Melody really wished she knew. Last night was the most emotional she had seen him since he had arrived. It was also the most he had ever said about what had happened.

Zane managed not to change expression when Melody gave his arm a squeeze though he didn't try and remove her hand. To be honest it felt nice knowing there was someone who cared. Zane didn't want to admit it, but he simply wasn't ready for much more than that. Maybe if it had been further from what had happened but for now, he was too scared to let anyone closer. His wolf accepted the comfort though and very carefully sent subtle traces of comfort to his other half.

*****

Zane had passed the backpack to one of the boys from the pack who was in Liv's grade. He gave him a nod in thanks for helping his sister. For Liv he really was willing to bend slightly from his self-imposed isolation. As much as he cared for his uncle, for Zane Liv was the center of his world now. Having a wolf only reinforced it. She was human and hurt and they had to protect her.

When they walked into the high school, he looked at Melody, "Later, I'm going to assume you are going to drag me to lunch right?" There were traces of amusement in his voice when he said it.

Melody grinned at him, "Most definitely though nothing is going to moo, you know." She turned away and headed towards her locker as Zane headed towards his. Now her plan was going to be set in motion.

Fredrico caught her very subtle nod as Zane walked away. He followed Zane. His locker was next to Zane's and they both reached them at the same time, "Morning Zane, ready for class? I don't know about you, but I hate history." Both had history first thing in the morning.

Zane glanced at him and recognized him from the pack. After flipping a mental coin, he finally replied, "About as ready as possible, just remember he who ignores history is destined to repeat it." He flashed a faint smile before opening his locker. After pulling out the books needed as well as the forms signed, he slammed it shut and spun the dial before heading towards class.

Rico, as he was known, did much the same, "You know if you listen carefully to the tumblers, you don't even need to know your combo to open the locker." It was simply something to say to see if he could get a reaction from Zane. Normally he would have steered clear of Zane and the bad boy look but Melody had asked him to try and get to know him.

Zane wanted to growl but knew better, "I'm trying to ignore all the lovely crap my ears are hearing. It's giving me a headache." Now he was almost whining since his nose had decided to kick in and the scents were starting to hit. His ears weren't quite as obvious now since it seemed as he was learning, it was one sense at a time.

Rico had to grunt in reaction, "Tell me about it. Between my ears, nose, and eyes high school can be a pain in our butts." He grumbled quietly, **I might have been born a wolf but once everyone started growing... I don't want to know who is doing who, who is at that time of the... Yah, just ick.** He did understand what Zane was saying.

That made him want to gag. **Thanks dude, not what I wanted to think about or consider.** Even his wolf lowered his ears and whined in the back of his mind, "Maybe a bit of Vick's Vape-o-rub might help. At least the menthol might kill the scents." He hadn't run into an issue with his eyes and was rather curious. About then they walked into class and Zane headed towards the back. Thankfully Rico settled down in the middle since Zane had talked more than he had wanted to.

*****

Lunch was interesting to say the least. Melody had ambushed him as he was getting some food and hauled him over to a table. Several of her friends were sitting at it and working on some large trays of food. Rico was there as well, and he gave Zane a nod as he was eating. Melody urged him to sit down, "Zane this is Rico, Simone, and Paul." **They are pack members, some of whom you have met.**

Zane glanced at them and again settled for a nod of his head as he started to dig into the food. **Melody don't try and force me to be friends.*

*I know we talked last night but I'm not...** He wasn't sure what to say. **Don't push me.** He relented slightly, "Rico and I talked a bit this morning." He admitted between bites.

Melody didn't reply to his sending and settled for some general conversation. Most of it was related to school and stuff like that. She had been paying close attention to what the pups in her classes had been saying and as of now, not all of them had heard about what Zane had said yesterday. They had noticed him since he was new and most of the pups had been going to school together for ages. For some of the girls there was the somewhat mysterious bad boy vibe as well as the emotionally hurt aspect. For some of the boys, there was a sense of he might be easy to pick on. Other boys felt a negative feeling which gave them the urge to stay away from him.

It was going to be interesting to see how he ended up fitting into both school and the pack. Melody had to admit she wasn't totally immune to the bad boy vibe, but it included knowing how hurt he was. It was half the reason she was doing her best to befriend him.

Zane wasn't sure what to think when Melody didn't reply to him. As the others were talking, he settled for eating and once done he stood, "I need to get my books for the next class. Later." He picked up his tray and left the room. Once he was away from the table, he wanted to say he relaxed some, but it wasn't totally true. He did relax but also almost missed the feel of being with the others. It was enough to make him grumpy, which showed. For the rest of the day his expression kept anyone else from coming close.

Right as the school day ended, he was contacted by his uncle. **Zane, I'm outside with Olivia. Come out to the pickup section and we will go to the pack medical section. The healer is waiting for us to show up.**

Once he was contacted, he hurried out of the building and after jumping down the stairs he ran to the car, "Hey Uncle Mike, afternoon Liv." He climbed in and settled down. Olivia was in the front which didn't bother him too much. It gave her more room to stretch out besides which the vehicle was large enough he didn't feel squished.

Liv gave him a tired smile. Since she was more active than she had been, even with the physiotherapy, Liv was feeling the pain more than normal. It was also a case of the chairs weren't very comfortable in class which didn't help. She might need to start bringing a small pillow along with her.

Zane's wolf took a deep sniff, and their eyes changed since they could smell her pain. As much as he tried to keep the low growl of anger inside, it didn't work, "Sorry Olivia, we can smell your pain, and it has my wolf worked up." He leaned back and tried to relax.

Being honest, Olivia did feel protected as her brother growled. Being her mother's daughter, she wanted to yell. Her mother had been a strong woman even if she had mostly remained at home. Their mother did have a job, but it was part time just for some extra income, "Shush both of you, Zane. Life happens, and I'm dealing with it." There, she had stood up for herself, "Thanks for caring though." It was said very quietly, but he heard her clearly.

What she said helped his wolf calm down though they were still feeling upset. For the rest of the drive to the Pack House everyone remained quiet. Mike was hoping Zane wouldn't be to upset since he had asked to have someone check on his nephew as well. On the surface it was to ensure there wasn't any remaining issues about the odd change. Beneath that it was to check on how he was doing mentally, even if it wasn't going to be as deep as what a Mind Healer could do.

Soon they pulled up in front of the medical section for the pack and Zane hopped out and opened Liv's door, "Please let me help, sis. My wolf is feeling rather worked up right now." His voice was quiet though there was some distress showing.

Liv let him help her out and gave him a hug, "I know I've been somewhat grumpy about the attention Zane, but it does mean a great deal to me. Now back off and let me get my crutches." She grumbled at him as she turned to pull what she needed out.

Mike managed to turn his laugh into a cough though he was sure they knew better, "Inside you two, Zane once Liv has been seen I have someone to check to make sure your change is progressing properly. I had meant to mention it, but it slipped my mind." He tossed it off as a simple oops.

Zane managed not to growl at his uncle thanks to his wolf. Mike was more dominant than Zane, he and his wolf knew it, "Gee, thanks for the notice, Uncle." It wasn't something he wanted to deal with since after getting out of the hospital, he found he disliked doctors.

Mike chose not to say anything, since the boy had submitted, even if Zane might not feel that way or see it as such; he was still learning the way of werewolves. The three of them walked into the clinic and were quickly escorted to a room. The female nurse turned to the two males, "Out. Olivia needs to get a gown on, so out." She chased them out before going back in.

"Here is a gown for you Olivia. Just take your shorts off and pull this on. I have a sheet to cover your legs with as well." She turned and pulled out a sheet and handed it over, "The healer will be in shortly. If you want, I can ask your uncle and brother to come in, once you are changed." She waited to see what Olivia might have to say.

Liv was still standing and slid her shorts off and pulled the gown on over her shirt. Once she was ready, she had settled on the exam table with some help. The sheet she tossed over her legs after looking at the scar. Zane hadn't seen all the scars. Due to the accident, she had several on the leg which had been hurt. There were a number on her hip which her shorts or skirt normally covered. The surgical scars went up the side of her leg to her hip. She didn't like looking at it since she felt it made her look ugly, "Please, it's fine."

Since the nurse was a wolf, she could sense the discomfort from the girl but since Olivia hadn't said anything, she couldn't do much. Instead, she made sure the sheet covered Olivia's legs and up to her waist, "I will get them but if you want, when the healer comes in let me know and I'll have them leave." She gave the girl a smile as she turned to leave the room, "Okay, you two come in but keep it quiet."

Zane and Mike walked in, and Zane took the chair next to his sister. He carefully grasped her hand and gave it a gentle squeeze, "Hey sis..." He didn't know what else to say and settled for looking at their uncle.

Mike settled down in a chair across the room and stretched out, "The healer will be here momentarily. We will leave the room when she starts the exam. No reason for us to be here unless you want. If you want, the Luna will come in and answer your questions."

Liv looked at her uncle and then her brother, "It really depends on what they need. I would prefer if you two were here, but Ms. Ester would be fine as well." She was starting to get scared and wanted her family there. Unless she had to get further undressed, she wanted them there.

Before anyone could say anything else the healer walked in. She was an older- woman who had a jovial face and a pleasant disposition, "Hello Olivia, Mike, Zane, I'm Doctor McMicmallan and I'm here to see if we can help you." She gave Olivia an open smile, "I have reviewed your records and examined your scans and x-rays with my colleagues. I need to examine you, but we do think we can help you."

Zane had to speak, "Hello doctor Please do what you can to help my sister." He glanced at his uncle before he spoke again, "We don't have much money but what we have we will give you to take care of her."

Sasha came over and stroked Zane's hair to give comfort to the pup she could clearly smell was stressed out, thinking it was just about his sister, "Don't worry about it, son. We will do what we can to help her. The pack will take care of what payment is needed. As I'm sure you know, Pack takes care of Pack. Now let me get started." She hated how the US medical system was designed so the rich owners or shareholders could get richer, instead of all the resources going to helping the patients the best they could and was why she liked when she could work with packs, since they would do what was needed, with some even supporting her efforts when she helped someone who couldn't pay. She didn't comment to the two pups, as they wouldn't really understand. She turned to Olivia and gave her another smile, "This is not an exam like you have dealt with before. All Pack doctors are healers. We have special abilities humans don't. All I need to do is to feel your wounds and allow my senses to check on the damages. I'm going to need to move the sheet, so I can touch your leg but that's it."

Zane had to clench one hand since he was still not comfortable with taking support from the Pack. He didn't say anything, but he was sure everyone in the room, other than Olivia, could sense his reaction. Zane looked at Olivia, "If you want me to leave the room, I understand." It wasn't, since his wolf was growling, as they didn't know the other wolf. He had to say it for her though.

Olivia grasped Zane's hand harder, "Zane you might as well see the rest of the scars. There are more you haven't seen, since I didn't want you to be even more upset." She released his hand and carefully tucked the sheet out of the way, so her leg was exposed from her hip down.

Zane looked and had to look away, due to the scars he could see. How many were from the accident and from the surgeries he didn't know and couldn't ask. They ran from her hip down the side of her leg almost to her knee. In his mind, he saw her, injured, in the car crash. Then he saw her laying in the hospital bed, alone... He surged up from the chair and stomped from the room, not able to take it anymore. When he reached the hall, he had to struggle with his wolf and finally lost control. Zane didn't get the chance to strip before he changed. His clothes ripped and the rags scattered in his wake as he ran.

He was so angry and upset he didn't know what to do. As he ran, he tried to keep the emotions and feelings to himself, but he wasn't successful. Too many emotions were hitting, and he ran and ran and ran. When he burst out of the clinic, he was moving at a speed he didn't realize. Again, he was heading towards the clearing which helped him calm down. Even now he didn't know why he was so drawn there but it really did help him. He also had no idea how or why he always knew exactly the way to it and could feel almost a pull from there. Nor did he understand how it could be so calming.

In the clinic Mike almost followed before he was contacted by the Luna. **Don't follow him. He needs to run and doesn't need an adult to get more involved.** She contacted Damien since she felt he was the right one to deal with this. Melody wasn't the right one for the moment either. She would look at it from a female point of view. **Damien, follow Zane and talk to him.**

Mike was forced to grind his teeth for a moment, "Olivia we are taking care of your brother. His wolf took over and they aren't happy. I should have asked him to stay outside." He took a deep breath before responding, **Yes, Luna I will remain with my niece.** He wasn't happy at the moment and moved over to Olivia and took her hand. This was going to change the appointment with the other healer for Zane.

Olivia was looking really upset when her brother left the room. She knew Zane had been upset with the scar but hadn't expected this at all. The healer settled down next to her, "Relax Olivia, this is very normal for male relatives and especially older brothers. With Zane, since he is such a new wolf, he is learning how to deal with his new feelings." She lightly touched Liv's shoulder, "Now let me do my exam and it is painless and doesn't take very long." The healer placed one hand high on the girl's hip and the other just above her knee.

When the healer did whatever she was doing, Olivia felt a slow warmth flowing out of the woman's hands. It almost forced her to relax, and she leaned back. Before she realized it, the healer leaned back and removed her hands.

"Well, I can say we can help you, though it is going to require some more surgery. It is hard to explain but I know what needs doing and once we're done a number of the injuries will be resolved." She pulled the sheet back over the leg and looked at Mike, "I would like to speak to you in an office for a moment." The two of them left as the nurse helped Olivia back into her shorts.

*****

Damien had already figured his mother was going to ask him to go after Zane and had already changed. **Yes mother, I'm already heading in* *his direction.** He wasn't going to run all out since he wasn't sure where Zane was heading. It was going to take some time, but he wasn't going to hurry. Better let Zane wear himself out before Damien approached him.

It did take some time but when Damien approached him it was in a clearing Damien hadn't been to before as it was oddly perfectly circular. He would later think it was odd he didn't feel curious about the clearing and felt comfortable. When he reached the edge of it, he stopped and looked out into the opening in the forest. Zane was there, and he was looking very tense and distressed.

Zane reached the clearing and again wondered why he had been drawn there. It only lasted a few moments before a low demanding snarl broke out from his muzzle. Both Zane and his wolf were so very angry, yet they knew there wasn't anything they could do. Zane's wolf didn't quite understand a 'mechanical issue,' but Zane did. They did know sometimes shit happened, but it didn't help. All they could do for the moment was to stalk around the clearing and snarling and growling in frustration, feeling it was safe to let it all out here.

They paced back and forth trying to work their anger and frustration out, but it wasn't helping a great deal. They finally settled down and lifted their head and let out an angry and frustrated howl. Both knew it was stupid to be so damn angry, but they couldn't help it. Both were feeling a great deal of anger over what had happened. Eventually the howl died down and they dropped down, so they were lying down with their head on their paws, mentally feeling exhausted from all the emotions.

Now Damien and his wolf started pacing over to Zane. **Zane, it's Damien. I was asked to come and talk to you. I hate to say it, but it isn't a request but an order.** He settled down next to the other wolf and carefully sensed his dominance and was rather intrigued. Zane was going to be a more dominant wolf than many; even though he was younger, and still in his Turn, he already had the feeling of a dominant wolf.

Zane let out a slight growl. **I guess it doesn't matter what I want. I'm so angry and pissed it isn't funny, Damien. My life has been destroyed beyond imagining, not to mention what my sister must deal with. I want to fucking bite someone and I don't know why. I want to protect her, but she doesn't want me hovering over her, so what the hell am I supposed to do?** There was definite anger in his voice as he spoke.

Damien almost growled at the other wolf. His growl was almost borderline disrespectful, but Damien had to take a slow breath. **Zane, I don't want to come across as an ass but don't growl at me that way again. I'm more dominant than you and it was almost disrespectful.** He yawned before saying anything else. **It does matter what you think. Zane, if you remain in the pack, you will eventually become a fairly dominant wolf. It's what is causing you to react the way you are. Your wolf is trying to deal with the situation he came to when he joined you. He, much like you, is a young wolf. It is going to take some time to learn who and what you are.** He paused to let the other wolf say his piece.

Damn it but it was all Zane could do not to growl at the other wolf. It wasn't due to dominance but because Zane was so confused. **Sorry Damien but I...** What the hell should he say? He was still learning to be a wolf, working thru all loss, dealing with Melody being so damn attentive, and his sister's problems. Zane started whining though he didn't realize it. **What am I supposed to do Damien? I feel so lost, my sister was hurt while I was unconscious, my family destroyed, I hurt so much that I can't think, only react. Adding in that, my wolf is demanding that I watch out for my sister.** They recognized Damien as being more dominant and lowered their ears as they were talking.

Damien shifted position and leaned against the younger wolf. **That's a tough question to answer Zane. Since you are a new wolf, it is going to take some time to figure out how things work. The best I can say is talk to us. Talk to me, talk to my father, and talk to my mother. We can help but only if you come to us.** Damien knew this was a test for him from his parents. It would be decades, or even centuries, before he became the alpha, but they were training him now. **As far as losing your* *family, I wish I could help you more, there are wolves who have lost mates and pups. It is never easy for those still here. Just, maybe, talk to someone. Melody wants to help. Mom wants to help. She is honestly rather upset you won't talk to her and let her help. She hasn't dealt with a pup who can't or won't talk to her.** He wasn't trying to make Zane feel bad, just stating the truth.

Zane stood up. He looked across the clearing before deciding he couldn't handle any more openness. **I will think about it, Damien. I need to leave.** He turned and started running again since he wanted to get back to his sister. Zane was feeling bad about leaving but it had all been too much for the moment.

When he reached the medical clinic one of the staff looked at the wolf and waved for the young wolf to follow him, "I have some shorts for you and the healer is waiting for you." He led the wolf into a room and tossed some shorts and a shirt on the exam table, "Change and he will be in momentarily." The man left the room.

Zane lowered his head and followed the man into the room. Once he left the room, Zane changed forms and jerked on the shorts and shirt. He settled on the exam table and ended up staring at the floor. He was feeling really bad for having left Olivia the way he did. When the door opened, he glanced up at the man before looking back down, "Afternoon doc." He was looking rather subdued.

The healer walked in and quickly evaluated the dominance and body posture of the boy, as he did with everyone when he entered, to know how to act, and especially when to keep his distance. "Afternoon Zane and I'm just doing a quick exam to ensure your change is going well, since it was not a normal one. Just relax and I will be done in a few minutes. All I need to do is place my hands on your head and do my thing." He moved over and settled his hands on the boy's head and started doing his job.

Zane didn't bother responding since he was still feeling rather depressed since he had wanted to be with his sister. Even though he didn't realize it, his shoulders were slumped as the healer did his thing. When they had finished doing whatever he was doing and stepped back. Zane didn't even bother asking what they might have sensed, "Can I go to my sister and uncle?"

The man wanted to sigh at the young man, but it wouldn't do any good, "That's fine, she is in the next room. Go and see how she is doing." He was going to need to talk to both the Alpha and the boy's guardian. He was a very upset young wolf, and he needed help, even if he didn't want to admit it. If they had a Mind Healer, he would have notified them about the urgent issue, if they weren't already involved. He knew the Alpha and Luna were trying to track one down who was willing and able to come to them, but they were extremely rare, and often dealt with pack-level issues, like when a leader or elder passed suddenly. They didn't often come to deal with a single wolf, even if they were a pup. The pack itself usually was enough to help them.

Zane slipped off the couch, "Thanks Sir." He left the room and after knocking on the other door walked in, "Sorry Olivia, I... It... Just sorry." It was all he could say. What else was he to say? He'd lost it and he knew it.

CHAPTER 7

Colors and Collars

Liv lightly squeezed Zane's hand when he sat back down next to her. She still didn't really understand why he was so overprotective, even though it had been explained to her. Yes, the old Zane had been protective but now since he'd changed, he was far more protective as well as more irritable and had more abrupt mood changes, "Zane please try and relax. I know you are really upset by what happened. I know it was hard to wake up and find out about everything, but I need my older brother and not an overprotective brother." She gave his hand another squeeze.

Zane was still feeling fairly bad for reacting the way he did, "I will try Liv, I really will but it isn't just me. My wolf is also reacting to your pain and the scent of your pain." He returned the light squeeze before rubbing his face with his other hand, "Damien tried to explain it to me. He said something about me probably becoming a dominant wolf. That and something about being a dominant wolf makes my protective urges even worse." Zane had to shrug since it still didn't make a great deal of sense to him.

Olivia had to shake her head, "Zane listening to you talk makes it sound like you have an extra voice in your mind." She was trying to make a joke when she said it, "All the wolf stuff just doesn't mean a massive amount to me. I'm not a wolf, so I don't have some weird set of rules I have to live by or make sense of."

He snorted at her, "Should I let my other voice talk to you? I'm sure he'd be happy to growl something at you." He was trying to make a joke of it and got poked for the teasing.

Olivia snorted, "He already growls, and I don't understand wolf. You'll have to interpret for me." She laughed when he didn't get the end of her crutch though she realized he hadn't really tried hard.

*****

Mike followed Dr. Macmillan out of the room and into an office nearby. He sat down in a chair across on the other side of the desk, "So what can you tell me Healer?" He was really hoping they could resolve most of Liv's issues. Since she wasn't a wolf, they couldn't completely heal Olivia, but they could do more than a human doctor could.

She settled down in the chair by the desk and started typing on a keyboard, "I'm sure you have seen these, but I want to show them to you before I say anything else. First off, the femur was broken..." She pointed out where the damages were, "As far as her hip, there was some damage as well which is..." Dr. Macmillan finished discussing the damages, "The human doctors did a damn excellent job with what they had to work with. We can resolve many of the issues but even if we had been there in the beginning, we couldn't have fixed it all. If she had been a wolf, we could have resolved it. Since she isn't there is only so much we can do, with the limitations on how well humans heal."

Mike listened to what she had to say and nodded at all the right spots. He had heard most of this but for a fair part of the time he had been away working. The recap was appreciated since it gave Mike everything in a nutshell, "Okay, I understood most of it. What can you do and when can we see about the surgery?"

Dr. Macmillan rattled her nails on the desk as she ran through some ideas, "What we will need to do is re-break some of the bones, adjust them to the proper position and then heal them. It will reduce the time needed for healing, but she will still be down for a while. As far as when we can do it, I will need to get my surgical team together, review the notes as well as what my abilities showed me. Once I have done that, we can schedule it, I would say I need at least two weeks since we will have to reserve a surgical room to do the job." Both knew the price didn't matter; for any pup the pack would just pay it and consider it an investment into the future of the pack, even if she technically wasn't a member, she had her brother and uncle as members and she lived at the pack, so they would consider her under their protection.

He ran his fingers through his hair as he considered what she had to say, "Go ahead and talk to your team and start getting things setup. I'm going to need to talk to Olivia and Zane before we schedule it. Zane is having trouble dealing with his anger and fears over what happened to both of them and their family. If we just randomly schedule it, it will stress Zane and his wolf out even more. He doesn't need it right now."

She shrugged, "I understand what you are saying and it's fine. She is mostly healed now, so putting it off for a while longer isn't a real issue. We are going to have to re-break the bones no matter when we do it. I would recommend sooner than later, since the longer we wait some of the scar tissue will heal even more. It will delay her recovery for a while though not a great amount."

Mike stood up, "Thanks Healer and I will be in touch with you in a few days. I will talk to them this evening. Once they have decided what they want I will contact you." He left the room and was met by the other healer, "Are you done with Zane?"

Healer Markov gave Mike a slight nod, "I am and let's go to my office." He turned and walked into a different office and settled down behind his desk and waved Mike to a chair, "As far as his physical change is concerned, it is complete. I didn't sense any potential issues due to the odd change. I have a feeling it is because he was in a coma and his wolf couldn't talk to him until he woke up. Before then, his wolf simply couldn't connect with Zane which would keep any changes from happening."

Markov leaned over and pulled a bottle of water out of his bag and took a sip, "As far as his mental status, I briefly talked to his wolf and much of it is fear. All he knows is he went for a run, was attacked by some animal, only to wake up and find his family destroyed. Add to that his sister had been badly hurt in the accident which killed their parents, toss in a new reasonably dominant wolf pup and it is understandable. Frankly, he is terrified of getting close to anyone other than you and Olivia. He is scared if he does, he will lose them as well, so he is creating walls to keep people away. Other than that, I didn't notice any issue and believe the separation between he and his wolf is due to the fear of loss."

Mike had to lean his head back as he sighed and frowned, "So what am I supposed to do, Healer? I'm single, haven't found my mate, and know very little about being a stand-in parent. I don't have the faintest idea of how to help him deal with this." If only Zane would go to the Luna, she could help him start to come to terms with this. No, it wasn't going to go away overnight, but she could help him start dealing with his feelings and fears.

Markov looked at the back wall while he was trying to come up with something to say. It was hard since this really wasn't his specialty and when something like this happened to a wolf, there were only a few options. Sometimes the wolf would *will* him or herself to death. If they lost it, went rogue, and went on a rampage, they were killed to keep them from hurting others. In some cases, having the Luna step in helped but that was about it. If a wolf had a mental illness, though it was rare , in many cases they either died or had to be killed. With their strength and abilities, and the fact restraining one would only make it worse, they were very limited in their options, "I'm honestly not sure. Since this happened before he was a wolf and woke to the news as a brand-new wolf, it is outside my experience. I can say at the moment I don't expect him to do anything stupid, though he might end up being a lone wolf, if he can't let anyone in. I wish I could say something different but as you know wolves and mental issues only have a few options." How he wished they had access to a mind healer, but none of the ones they knew of were available. Sending him to another pack where one was would not help and might even cause more issues.

Mike sighed, since it was pretty much what he had expected. He did know the various options, though in Zane's case, he didn't think it was going to be an issue. Zane had someone to care for and to remain for in the pack. Zane was almost rabidly protective of his sister and Mike knew he wouldn't leave while she was around and needed him, "Thanks Healer, and it's pretty much what I had guessed. I needed the official exam to confirm what I was thinking. I'm going to go and get the pups and take them home."

He left the office and walked back across the hall to the room Liv was in and he knew Zane was in there as well. Mike knocked and walked into the room without waiting for an answer, "I talked to the healers about both of you. I will tell you what they said when we get home. I don't know about you, but I would prefer to have a cold drink before we discuss this."

Zane looked up at Mike when he walked in, "If you don't mind Uncle Mike, I need some time to think. Damien came and had a talk with me when I shifted. I will be home for dinner, okay?" He really did need to talk to someone but who he wasn't sure. Zane didn't want to talk to his uncle now since he felt he needed someone outside his family.

Mike strongly considered telling Zane to come with him but managed not to. Since he didn't have any idea what Damien might have said it might be the wrong thing to do, "Be home by dinner and it's fine. I will expect you to do your homework after dinner though." He stood and waited for Olivia to get her crutches before they slowly walking out of the pack house.

*****

Zane walked to the main house and out back. He leaned against one of the trees in the yard. As he was leaning against it, he was doing his best to really think about what Damien had said and wanted to huff. He didn't want to talk to anyone or have anyone try and pick his feelings apart. What he wanted was to be left alone so he could do his own thing. Yes, Zane was starting to figure out what pack meant but it was going to take time. He was getting some training on the weekends about the pack and pack law, but it just wasn't what he had grown up with.

He finally moved away from the tree and walked into the house. Even if he didn't want to go to the Luna, he did need to talk to her. Zane needed to try and explain to her where he was coming from. This was something he had to deal with. Mrs. Esther was a nice person but she both drew him and scared him. There was something about her which made him want to curl up and cry on her shoulder, and that scared him, since it reminded him of his mother, which led to too much pain. Zane simply wasn't ready to ask for help or let more than one or two people into his life.

Zane's wolf was trying to project comfort... and blast it, *he* did want the comfort of the Luna since *he* needed it. It wasn't quite what Zane would get but he was a new wolf and didn't know how to manage the fears and concerns his human had. Even if Zane wasn't willing to lean on her, he wanted to, and man, it was hard trying to give support, while needing comfort too.

Zane finally walked into the house and headed towards Mrs. Esther's office. It only took a few minutes even though Zane wanted to drag his feet and go somewhere else. Once he had reached it, he knocked on the door jam, "Mrs. Esther do you have a few minutes?" He really didn't want to do this, but Zane was almost feeling forced to.

Esther looked up and managed not to smile since Zane had come to her. To an extent it didn't matter what he had to say, he had come to her, "Please come in Zane and have a seat." She stood and walked around her desk and settled down in a chair and waved him to another one. Even if she was busy, she would make time for him... not that she would tell him that she would reschedule almost anything to help him. She would do that for any of the pups, regardless of whether they were members of the pack, or not. The fact he was also hurt, and rogue-turned, just made it even more important she help. Pups were the future, for werewolves, it meant they were the most important, and he didn't know that each and every adult would help however they could.

Zane came in and settled in the chair, though he didn't lean back. Once he was as comfortable as he was willing to be, he started speaking, "Mrs. Esther, Damien spoke to me earlier; I assume at you or your husband's request. He indicated you are upset because I can't or won't talk to you. I'm not sure why he said it, but this is something I must deal with. I lost everything in a matter of a few short minutes." in his mind, the time he was in the coma didn't really count. "My family was destroyed, I lost my parents, my sister was badly hurt, and all because of some damn rogue." His hands were clenched though they were resting on his knees, "I'm sorry if I'm upsetting you, but I have to deal with this. I... I... I'm not willing to get close to someone right now." It was better than saying he was scared to let anyone close to him other than Mike and his sister.

Esther didn't move or say anything as he was talking since if she did move, it might chase him away. As he was talking her heart went out to him since she could feel his tension, "Zane, I know you are being taught what being a Lycan includes but there is a great deal of information. It will take time for you to really learn and to understand and it includes your wolf. I have been keeping an eye on what your studies for the pack, but they haven't yet hit on just what the Alpha and Luna are. The Alpha is the protector of the pack. He protects and controls the pack. He deals with the enforcers of the pack, normal punishment and discipline for pack members who mess up."

She now shifted slightly so she was more comfortable, "The Luna is in a way the mother of the pack. Yes, she helps the Alpha protect the pack, but she is also the comforter of the pack. When pack members are having issues, have had a bad day or week or losses such as you had, they come to her. They come to get comfort and a hug and shoulder to cry on. Sometimes I can only listen as they talk and explain what is going on. Other times I can help them look for solutions to what happened and how to deal with it. This is especially true with pups, or as you would have said kids. You and your sister went through a very traumatic experience. In ways, it was far worse for you, since you woke up to find your sister badly hurt and your parents killed. It doesn't even include suddenly having a new voice in your head and getting furry once a month."

Zane's hands were still clenched on his knees, "Thank you for explaining it Mrs. Esther. It is still something I need to deal with. My wolf is trying to force me to feel things I'm not comfortable with right now. I know he is trying to give me room, but I'm still being impacted by what he feels which is not something I have grown up with. It feels like it would be going to the principal and crying on his or her shoulder over something which didn't matter." He was feeling tense now since this was almost as open as he had been with Melody last night without the comfort of the clearing.

Esther was listening to both Zane and his wolf. From Zane she was getting one set of feelings and from his wolf she was getting something different. The wolf wanted her comfort, but Zane was just too new to the Lycan life, "I will have a talk with your wolf later and no I don't need you here. I think I understand what you are saying. It is so very rare to have someone your age changed and even worse by a rogue. If you aren't comfortable talking to me or Kad, talk to Melody and Damien. Both are good pups and can answer your questions in ways I can't, since they are close to your age. Is there anything else you want to ask or talk about?"

Zane was glowering at the floor even as hard as he was trying not to, "Thank you Mrs. Esther. I just wish I could get my wolf to relax around Liv. Every time we smell her start hurting, even if she doesn't say anything, he gets worked up. It makes it hard for me since she tends to yell at us. When she does it hurts me and my wolf, since it makes us feel like we are... bothering her." It was the best description he could come up with, even if it didn't really fit.

Esther couldn't help but smile slightly at him when he said it, "Zane I would say give her some room, but it won't work. It is something you, your wolf, and Olivia will need to work out, together. She just doesn't really understand why you have suddenly become so protective. I'm sure if you had woken up as a human, you would be protective, but wolves have an extra dose of it. As Damien said you are going to be a reasonably dominant wolf eventually, so you are feeling a sort of extra protectiveness. This is especially true because of what happened to your family. Talk to Mike, Kad, and even Damien about it. It is something you are going to have to work out with Olivia."

He kept his hands clenched since it allowed him to focus on them and not the pain he was feeling inside, "Thank you Mrs. Esther, I will think about what you had to say. If you don't mind, I need to start back towards Uncle Mike's house." He stood and after submitting slightly he left the room. He quietly stalked out of the house and ended up out back again. Zane almost gave his wolf control to go for a run but he, Zane, needed to think as much like a human as possible. **Melody, do you have a few minutes? I would like to talk to you before I head home.**

Melody was doing some homework when Zane contacted her, and she quickly sat up and closed the books. **Are you still at the pack house? If so give me a few minutes and I can be there.** She almost asked what he wanted to talk about but chose not to. The fact he was asking to talk to her was almost startling.

Her house was close to the pack house, since her father was close to Zane's Uncle Mike in rank. It only took her a few minutes to locate him. Once she had found him, she slowly walked up, "Hey Zane, how is it going?" She was trying to come across as just being friendly.

Zane rolled his eyes at her. **Considering I asked to talk to you why are you trying to come across as if you just wandered past? If it won't get you in trouble, can we talk as we walk? Uncle Mike wants me home soon and I need to head in that direction.** He did keep his eyes on her as he was sending to her.

Melody returned the eye roll and bumped him with her shoulder, "Fine and I do have some time to talk. If you are going to be all growly, I'm going to be growly back at you." Just for good measure she gave him an amused growl.

Zane ignored her teasing. **I'm being serious Melody. I talked to the Luna for a few, but I need to talk to you as well. Don't try and force your friends or anyone else on me. I'm not ready for more than one or maybe* _two close friends. I just can't do it and if you try and force it, I will retreat. I don't want to hurt you, but I just can't at the moment._* He had started walking towards the house and thankfully it wasn't very far away.

She bumped his shoulder again as they were walking, "Fine Zane. I'm not going to let you hide though. I'm going to drag you to lunch, introduce you to some of my friends and encourage you to do stuff. Go to movies with us, go to the mall, and other things like that. I won't ram them down your throat, but they will be with me when we do things. Maybe even a good run in the forest." Just for good measure she wrapped a hand around his arm and leaned against him.

He wanted to growl at her for the teasing but could tell she really did mean it. *_I'm not hiding, I'm just trying to deal with what happened to my family and my sister. Just please don't push it. I will try not to be a total dick but please give me some room._* He looked down at the ground as they were walking. Zane could feel her hand on his arm, and it was rather comforting. *_I can't even begin to explain how..._* He just couldn't say scared, *_How worried I am about Olivia and what is going to happen with her._* Thankfully they were approaching Mike's house.

Melody gave his arm a light squeeze, "Zane I won't push but I won't let you hide either. I don't know how you are feeling since I haven't had anyone I cared for die. I do know we, the pack, want to help you and your family. I will be here for you to talk to, as will Damien. Just don't close us out." By now they were at his uncle's house. She gave his arm one last squeeze before letting him go and turned and headed back towards her parent's house.

Zane walked into the house and found his sister at the table working on some homework. He picked up his backpack from near the door and walked over to the table and settled down across from her. Zane wasn't in the mood for homework , but he needed to do it. He pulled out his math and actually growled at the assignment, "I hate math, darn it. The teacher is cruel and mean as well, giving us this much this soon."

Olivia looked up at him and then leaned over and bonked him with her pencil, "Zane no growling at the table. Be a good wolf and do your homework or I will make sure your meat is well cooked." She was grinning when she said it before turning back to her homework.

Zane frowned at her when she bonked him and threatened him. He growled one more time just to annoy her before he turned back to the homework. By the time their uncle walked in both were mostly done with their homework and Zane was working on something to eat, "Uncle Mike, food will be done soon." It wasn't anything special or complex, but he knew how to cook good solid food.

Mike walked into the kitchen and looked at the food, "Just make sure Olivia's meat doesn't moo. I don't want to listen to another argument about how rare or well done the meat should be." After grabbing a drink from the fridge, he flopped down in the living room. Thankfully, dinner was going to be soon since he was starving.

Olivia gave Mike a knowing smirk, "We already discussed it, and he knows what will happen if I poke the meat and it bleeds." She was putting her books into her backpack. When she started to get up to put it by the door she frowned when Zane took it from her, "Zane..."

Zane looked at her, "Liv... Let my wolf help you. Not everything obviously but let him help. It really makes him feel bad when he can't, or you don't let him. Having a pouty wolf in the back of my mind makes me grumpy and you don't want me to be grumpy, do you?" He leaned over and gave her a quick hug before taking care of the bag.

She had to frown some more, "I might have to have a discussion with your wolf. I can do some things by myself you know. As far as you being grumpy, would we notice the difference? All you do is the grumpy bad boy look." Olivia had to grin at him though, "I know of at least three girls who are feeling drawn to your grumpy looks. Would you like me to introduce them to you?"

He froze and turned and glowered at his sister, "I can be grumpy if I want to. As far as the bad boy look is up to whoever looks at me. As for as the girls, I have the feeling they are in your grade so no thank you." What made it worse was Zane's wolf was amused by what Liv had said. When he walked back to the kitchen he was still glowering at his sister.

Once he was in the kitchen, he relaxed the expression and managed not to laugh.

Mike managed not to choke on his drink as the two were talking and called out, "Are you sure Zane? I have seen a few older girls appreciating your bad boy look. I can introduce them to you instead." He was grinning as he spoke.

"Uncle Mike!!!" It was most definitely a whine when he said it, "I already have Melody interested in being my friend. I don't need a gaggle of either younger or older girls following me around." His wolf had his ears pricked forward in interest. When Zane noticed it, he mentally grumbled at him, "Thanks both of you, now I have my wolf staring at the two of you and he is looking curious."

Olivia and Mike decided to stop teasing Zane, since he was cooking. It was possible Olivia's food would be rare and Mike's well done. Eventually they did eat and after clearing the table Mike settled down at the head of it, "I talked to the healers who looked at both of you. Olivia, the healer said she believes she can take care of many your problems. It is going to require more surgery, and you will be down for a while again. I don't know how long you will be down since it partially depends on how your body heals. It won't be anything like what it was since they will be healing you as they are working. It is going to be at least two weeks before they can schedule the surgery. If you want, I can talk to her and have it scheduled for a Friday, two weeks from now."

He turned and looked at Zane, "I know you are going to want to be there at the hospital while they are working on your sister. I will excuse you for the day of the surgery if it is on a Friday. If they have to schedule it for the middle week I will excuse, you for the day of the surgery and the day after. It should give your wolf some comfort. After that you will need to go to school, though you can take her homework to her."

Zane was sitting next to his sister as their uncle spoke. He could hear her heartbeat speeding up and smell her anxiety. He wrapped an arm around her without thinking. He had a feeling as much as she might want to be able to get around without pain the idea of being in the hospital scared her. **Thank you Uncle and I'm going let you and Olivia talk about this. I do have one question? When I changed, why didn't the rod they put in my leg stick out of something?* He'd seen the x-rays and there had been a metal rod and things in his leg.*

Olivia leaned against Zane and chewed on her lower lip as she was thinking about it. She didn't want to have to keep dealing with the pain, but she also hated the idea of going back to the hospital. She only had bad memories of it between seeing Zane in the coma and then when she was hurt. Olivia finally looked up at Zane, "What do you think?"

He looked down at his sister and gave her another gentle squeeze, "I hate the idea of going back to the horrible place, but I can see and smell how much pain you are in even on a good day. I think you should get it done and the sooner the better. I want my little sister back. You've said I've changed but so have you." Zane gave her a teasing smile, "Just think if you get it fixed as best possible you won't have me and my wolf hovering over you all the time."

She poked him for his teasing and made a face at him, "Well for that alone would be a good reason to get fixed. Then maybe you won't be as growly and grumpy and might actually smile once in a rare blue moon." If he was going to tease her Olivia was going to return the favor.

Mike snorted at them, "Then I will see about having it scheduled as soon as possible. Once I know when it is going to be scheduled I will tell both of you. It was made of a metal which would change as you do. Also, over time it will dissolve, as your body replaces it with normal bone." He stood and stretched, "Oh, Zane, the healer said your change is complete and though rather delayed, appears to be a normal change." He was going to keep an eye on Zane while keeping what the healer said in mind. Nobody realized though about how Zane was still considering his wolf as a totally separate mind, or what it could mean.

Zane didn't really know what to say or think, "Thanks for letting me know. I'm going to go to my room and relax before bedtime. The idea of metal moving inside is disturbing." He stood and stretched before slouching off towards his room. The afternoon had been very hard for him to deal with, and he needed some time alone.

*****

The next morning Zane rose and after considering the selection of clothing in his closet, he went with all black. It was mostly to tease his sister about her comments about the bad boy look he had going. Just to make it even better he made sure he had the bed head look going as well, "Now if I actually had to shave, I could add the scruffy look as well. Oh well, eventually I suppose." His wolf snorted a laugh about being scruffy but didn't say anything further. After one last look in the mirror, he left the room and clomped down the stairs.

Olivia was already downstairs and rolled her eyes, "Hark, I think I hear an elephant on the stairs." When she looked at him, she rolled her eyes at him again, "I was hoping you might at least put on a more colorful shirt. You know, maybe a pastel color. They you could do the pretty bad boy thing and you need to comb your hair as well."

Zane settled for smirking at her as he collected his breakfast. After he sat down, he simply grinned at her before starting to eat, "I don't think you could catch me or my wolf in a pastel shirt. Chances are good he would bite someone who tried it." Mike was already gone on a patrol of the property. This afternoon Zane would be doing the training again which he was looking forward to. Zane could feel he was starting to get stronger though he was still weaker than a regular Lycan currently. He had no comparison to a human to know he was getting into elite athlete range.

She had to cover her mouth when he mentioned his wolf and pastel colors, "How about we get him a really nice collar with rhinestones? I'm sure he would look really cute with one." Olivia was most definitely teasing him when she said it.

Zane's normally blue eyes turned almost ice white and he growled at her, "If you even mention it again, you might wake up one morning with teeth marks on one of your crutches. My wolf is not amused." He growled a very displeased growl.

Olivia snickered as she stood to take her dishes to the kitchen. By the time she made it back Zane had her bag and was opening the door for her. One thing he had to get used to was nobody locking their doors. There were there but they didn't use them. It felt just so weird to walk out of the house and not lock the door. As he expected, he found Melody there at the bus stop.

He gave her and Rico a nod and said a brief hello as they climbed on the bus. Zane settled down in his usual seat and knew Melody was going to sit down as well. **So, are you telling me my grumpy bad boy look is drawing you also?** He figured he could tease her a bit.

Melody snorted and had to cover her mouth to keep from laughing too hard, "That was horrible Zane and I'm not going to answer the question." She turned, and her eyes were twinkling in amusement, "I do know of a couple of girls who tend to like the look though." She gave him an amused grin, **There is even a boy or two, if...**

Zane almost choked on the sending, **Not funny Melody! Girls are my thing, or will be, if I ever decide to date anyone.** He glared at her but decided not to say much, "I think I will bypass on your offer." He lightly thumped her leg with a finger for her teasing, "The doctor Liv saw last night feels she can repair most of Liv's problems. I really hope so since it hurts seeing her in pain." Zane leaned lightly against Melody as he was talking.

She returned the thump for good measure and leaned against him as well, "I'm so very glad to hear it. Maybe once she is doing better you won't be acting like a wolf with a sore tooth as much." Melody was pleased he was being somewhat more open.

Being the mature young teen Zane was he settled for sticking his tongue at her. Just for added benefit he crossed his eyes. **At least you didn't offer to get my wolf a dog collar with rhinestones... Liv did it and my wolf offered to chew up one of her crutches.**

Melody and Rico were still laughing at his comment as they walked off the bus. He had sent it to Rico as well, since Zane figured he would get a laugh out of it. Zane was even smiling slightly though as with so many things it really didn't reach his eyes. He felt safer not showing any real emotions or someone might try and comfort him, "Later Melody and see you at lunch." He headed towards his locker and then walked with Rico to class.

While they were in class Zane had to resist the urge to growl. One or two kids were whispering in the back of the room and his name kept coming up. Chances were good they were talking about his comment the first day of school. If they made a big deal out of it, they would find it almost useless to get a rise out of him.

When lunch rolled around, he had noticed two boys were whispering and talking about him. It was starting to irritate his wolf not to mention what Zane was feeling. Frankly, he didn't care. The only people, currently, whose opinion mattered to him was Liv, Uncle Mike, and Melody. If you weren't one of those three, then he really didn't care. What bothered him was the whispering since it kept distracting him from what the teacher was saying, when they mentioned his name. Since they were human, he wasn't worried about them trying to pick a fight with him.

It was one of the first things he had been taught both at training and in the classes he had to do on the weekend. If a human picked a fight, be very careful not to hurt them. With the increased speed and strength, it was very easy to badly injure one and even kill a human. It was not something Zane was very worried about since he had mostly managed to avoid fighting. Now he stood out because of the damn teacher. If she hadn't pushed, he wouldn't have snapped at her.

Once they sat down at the table they normally used, Zane shook his head. The two boys and what he assumed were several of their friends sat down at the table next to them. **If they keep whispering about me, I'm going to have a talk with them. I'm not amused, and neither is my wolf.** Zane sent it to everyone at the table even as he was starting to eat.

Rico rolled his eyes. **Go for it. They are some real pains in the ass. David's parents are well off and they think he can do no wrong. Leon's parents work for David's, and they feel the same. It is hard for us since we* *can't really break them in half like they deserve.** Many of the pups in school had dealt with them and it was so frigging annoying since virtually any wolf could beat the shit out of them without breaking a sweat, not that they knew it.

Melody had to lift a corner of her mouth in annoyance as well. **They are such a pain and spoiled brats. The only reason people hang around them is because they have money, and they are willing to use it. They will bully anyone they can.**

Zane really wanted to growl. He didn't like bullies and had dealt with some during his school life. **God that makes me want to beat them up just because. My parents had decent jobs and we lived well enough, but they taught Liv and I what deserved is.** As he was talking his eyes were wandering around the room. He noticed a boy and girl walk past with trays and he knew they were wolves due to their scent. When they walked past the table the boys were at David and Leon started calling them names. Both flinched slightly. **Who are the wolves?**

Melody glanced over and sighed. **They are twins, and their parents are two of the most junior wolves in the pack. They work for Beta Mike.** She was starting to stand when Zane did.

He didn't try to hide what he was doing when he walked over to the other table and rested his hands on the top. He met David's eyes and stared at him, "Listen dickhead. I don't give a fuck what you have to say about me or what happened. You have been following me around for most of the day trying to get on my nerves. It won't happen since I don't give a shit what you say since you mean nothing to me. If you think I'm lying, look deeply in my eyes and see if there is any sign of give a shit." He kept his eyes on David's and made them as empty and emotionless as possible.

David looked up and a sneer started to cross his face as Zane spoke until he did look into Zane's eyes. When he did, he had to shudder since they were so blank. He had never seen anyone with such bleak and empty eyes before and for the first time in a long time he flinched and looked away. David could tell that Zane honestly didn't give a shit and was almost begging him to try something. For some reason he had to lower his eyes to avoid looking at the teen.

When David did, Zane stood and turned away as if nobody at the table was worth any of his attention. Instead, he walked over to the twins, "Hey, why don't you come and have a seat at the table I'm at."

Both wolves looked at him and lowered their eyes since they could tell Zane was more dominant, "Yes Zane, that would be nice." The girl said and followed him over.

He settled back down, "I'm sure you know Melody and Rico. As far as the rest of the menagerie I'm sure you know them as well. Sit and relax." His wolf was rather worked up and wanted to go and smack David down but not here, not now.

Damien had watched the entire incident and smiled slightly. Zane might have his issues, but his wolf knew what was important. If Zane hadn't gone over, he would have asked one of the other wolves to go and gather the two up. With being so low in the pack, they simply didn't fight. It wasn't part of their nature which made them easy targets for bullying. With Zane involved, he could only hope it would help bring him out of his shell.

CHAPTER 8

Extending Protection

By the end of school Zane was still worked up. Those two dickheads had seriously annoyed him. It wasn't what they said about him since they didn't matter to him. It was what they had been saying about the twins. Both had been quiet at lunch and were somewhat more petite than the others. They were also rather quiet, which his wolf had indicated was normal for such junior wolves when confronted with more dominant wolves. It still sounded strange to him but pulling them away from the two had felt right. Even now, he wanted to break David's face in half for what he had been saying to the two.

Before they left the lunchroom, he had their locker numbers and had told them to find him once school was out. For some reason, it helped calm his wolf for the moment. When he reached his locker at the end of the day the two arrived shortly after he closed it, "Afternoon." He made a face, "I'm sorry, but I meant to get your names earlier and forgot." Now Zane felt stupid.

Both looked up at him and then looked somewhat down. In this case the boy spoke, "I'm Oscar, and this is my sister Tessa. Thank you for earlier." Most of the more dominant wolf pups tended to keep an eye on them but some didn't care. Zane seemed to care more than others to personally take care of them, and to want them close.

"Nice to meet you and I think I introduced myself but I'm Zane and you might have seen my sister Olivia." Zane slung the pack over his shoulder as they were talking. About then Melody walked up, and he gave her a bare smile, "Thank goodness school is over. I'm so ready to get to training and work some energy off."

Melody snorted at him, "Try not to break anything Zane. I would hate to have you annoy your uncle." She gave him a knowing look. Him protecting the two was a good sign that he wasn't totally blocked off from either his wolf or what his wolf felt.

Zane settled for simply walking away from the locker and loftily ignored her, "I will resist the urge to imagine David's face on some of the training dummies." Since David was nearby, he felt it only right to say that. As of now, David was his enemy, and he was going to be keeping a very close eye on him.

Melody snorted at him and rolled her eyes for good measure, "Zane... Sheesh, boys will be boys, I guess." Just for good measure she deliberately bumped him with her shoulder, "It will be good for you to get back into training. Helps to keep the urge to tromp on things under control." Part of the reason most wolves went through the training was to teach them control. It wasn't just about fighting and protecting the pack, though that was a good portion of it. It also included discipline and knowing when to fight.

Zane smirked at her, "Yup and proud of it!" When she bumped him, he bumped back and grinned when she grumbled at him. The twins were being relatively quiet though Rico was talking to them. Once they settled on the bus he turned and looked at the two, "Let me give you my number. This way if you need anything, you can call me." He gave them his number though he had to lift an eyebrow at the phones. They were some of the most basic available. Yes, they were smart phones—he wasn't sure you could you get a phone which wasn't—but appeared to be older. He also made sure to get their numbers as well.

Both looked down slightly before getting the number from him, "Thank you Zane." They could feel his dominance and it felt good to know a dominant wolf was taking personal interest in taking care of them. Tessa seemed to do most of the talking.

"Don't worry about it. Ass-wipes like them make my knuckles ache. I have been there and won't stand to see it happen to others." Now that they were away from the school, he was calming down and was starting to wonder why he had done it. It confused him. It wasn't anything against the two, but his reaction was odd for him. He was going to probably need to talk to Mike about it later. Now he was just feeling somewhat confused. Zane was still pissed off but not nearly as much.

Melody settled for leaning against him slightly. If he wanted to talk, he would and if not, she wasn't going to force it. Eventually they made it to the pack house, and everyone split off to what they needed to do. Zane headed towards the training after giving everyone a nod, "Zane you did good today. Later." She hurried off towards her house.

He wondered what she meant but the training distracted him since it was hard, but he'd started to enjoy it. For some reason the short sticks, he thought they were called half staffs, called to him. There was the sword and knives and hand to hand. He wasn't good yet, but he was working to do his best.

He didn't realize Malcom, his trainer, was sending reports to Mike about how he was doing. If he kept going the way he was, he was going to be an Enforcer nobody would want to encounter as their opponent, and likely be looked to by those on his side for leadership and protection. His training also included using rifles and pistols and he was becoming a dead shot with them as well.

*****

Once home, Damien immediately headed towards his father's office and knocked, "Do you have a few minutes, dad? I wanted to let you know about something that happened at school today." He was grinning as he was talking since it did amuse him.

Kad looked up and waved his son into the room, "Close the door if you need to." Since he hadn't heard anything from the school it couldn't have been too bad. If it had, Damien would have sent to him immediately, "So what happened and for some reason your smile has me curious and concerned."

Damien smiled even more, “Can we just say Zane drew a line in the sand as far as David and Leon are concerned. They were whispering crap about losing his parents and how all he wanted was sympathy and pity. At lunch, it came to a head when David and Leon started to pick on Tessa and Oscar. Zane went over and had a very short discussion with David before ordering the twins to join him at his table.” Now he was looking more serious since what Zane had done was protecting the pack. It was a very important step for him.

Kad listened to what his son was saying even as Damien was sending his memories of the incident to him. Kad had to raise his eyebrows and contemplate his son; he figured Damien didn’t quite get what else Zane had done. Even if Zane didn’t realize it, he had taken not just the twins under his wing but some of Melody’s group of friends, not all but some, “I hope David and Leon don’t push Zane’s buttons or it will get messy for them. I will have to have a talk with Mike and then Zane. Do you realize what else Zane did?” Just because they were a single pack didn’t mean more senior wolves didn’t have their favorites.

With Damien, even now, he was starting to build his personal connections. His best friend would be his beta, several of the others he kept an eye on would become his staff. It was an instinctive action for a wolf who was senior enough. It helped to ensure continuity of command if something happened. For the most part it only happened with the Alphas, Betas, and Deltas. The junior wolves didn’t need to have such a structure in place.

Damien lifted a hand and started rubbing his nose as he tended to do when he was really thinking. He carefully thought back to everything he had seen at lunch, but he didn’t quite catch what his father meant, “Well it shows he is starting to feel something towards the pack. Protect those more junior than he is. Zane is very comfortable with Melody even if he isn’t admitting it. As far as her friends, he is still distant with them, but chances are good he will probably end up being friends with them.”

Kadrian nodded at each point his son was making. Once he finished speaking, it was obvious to him, Damien hadn’t quite made the connections, "Son he is doing the same thing you are with your friends. You are already selecting those who will become part of your team once you are old enough. You have a future beta, a delta, and others who will support you. He is doing much the same. For now, I would guess he might end up being a lower beta though until he is older, I can't really say. Melody will probably become his assistant, maybe a delta, her friends, those who he claims, will be his staff. As far as the twins, they will probably end up being part of his support staff. Cooking, cleaning, things like that." He had to smile since it really did show good things about Zane. Zane might not ever be a warm or friendly person again, but his heart and mind were in the right spot.

Damien stared at his father before he started laughing, "I have a feeling we shouldn't mention it to him or he will close up, but it's too good. It is exactly what he needs to start fitting in." After he wiped the tears from laughing from his eyes he sobered up as well, "Sorry dad but it really hit my funny bone. He is trying to push us away but instinctively pulls towards us. What do you want me to do about it?"

Kad had to quirk an eyebrow as his son started laughing. Once he was done, he leaned forward and started tapping a pen against his desk, "For now just keep an eye on him and don't tell him or anyone about what is happening. Some will notice but I will have a talk with the adults. Try to avoid his ending up thumping on David and Leon, if possible. I know they are less than sterling examples of humanity, but we don't need the exposure." He tapped the pen a few more times, "I think that's all for now. I will take care of the adult side, and you take care of the pup's side." He hoped it wouldn't come back to bite them.

Damien stood and walked out shaking his head. If nothing else, it was keeping things interesting. Hopefully in a good way though since he wanted a nice quiet school year himself.

*****

When Kadrian had mind linked with Mike, he was honestly caught flat footed. It wasn't something he would have expected yet. Maybe down the road in a year or two, once Zane settled down, but this soon after being changed? Even if he hadn't been so withdrawn, he wouldn't have expected it. As far as the incident with David and Leon, he would talk to Zane about it and remind him he had to be careful. Not careful as in not to step on the human's toes but to keep from hurting them too badly if there did end up being a fight. Sometimes fights happened in school and honestly it was rather expected. What did matter was Zane didn't hurt him too badly in the fight, **Thanks for letting me know Alpha. Tomorrow is going to be interesting.**

Asking Zane to toss the fight would be pointless since his wolf would reject it. If they were beat fair and square, it was one thing. To toss a fight without a very good reason simply wouldn't happen. It would indicate the wolf wasn't worth his or her level. As far as Melody and the other friends she hung around with, they were close enough to Zane's dominance it wouldn't show. With the twins it was a different matter. They were going to feel drawn to his protection since his wolf had essentially claimed them. It was going to be interesting to see what developed. Tomorrow morning would be enough time to talk to Zane though.

Mike turned back to his work and waited for Zane to get home. So far, he had gotten complimentary reviews for the training. He was going to need to talk to them since he was going to be gone the upcoming weekend for work. He needed to report to a nearby town where there had been some rogue sightings. They needed to verify they were rogues or lone wolves before they did anything. It was usually his job, as he had the seniority in the pack, and the Alpha trusted him to make the decision on his own, and he was good at being able to tell quickly.

*****

When Zane rolled out of bed the next morning he grumbled at the clock. It looked like he had hit the snooze one time too many, so he had to hurry. Once he was done in the bathroom just to tease Liv, he pulled on a white V neck t-shirt with the dark pants and boots. After grabbing his bag and clattering downstairs, he had to stop since Mike and Liv were at the table and the twins were serving them. It smelled like waffles, bacon, eggs, and toast. Zane was frowning when he walked in and received an amused look from Mike.

Mike had a feeling Zane was going to be confused by the twins being there, so he had waited to go to work, “Morning Zane, did something happen yesterday?” There were traces of amusement in his voice as he was talking.

Zane glanced at the twins and Tessa gave him a small smile, “Morning Zane, we were waiting outside for you when Beta Mike invited us in.” Their bags were sitting next to the front door.

He was very confused by their presence, “You didn’t have to make breakfast, you know.” He sat down as Oscar placed a plate on the table for him. Zane glanced at his uncle, “Nothing major happened, just a bully picking on them. I had a brief discussion with him about it and invited them to the table Melody and I were sitting at.” Zane’s wolf was feeling relaxed and content in the back of his mind.

It was pretty much what the Alpha had explained. Mike took a sip of coffee, “Well Zane, by doing what you did and inviting them over to your table, *you*, in a way, took responsibility for them. You protected them, made sure they were safe, and even if you didn’t realize it, extended your *personal* protection around them.” The Alpha had asked Mike not to tell him too much but left it to Mike’s discretion.

Liv almost coughed out the bite of food she was eating. Zane looked like he had been smacked by a board and it was all she could do to keep from laughing. Instead, she managed to swallow the bite she had before speaking, “That was very nice of you Zane.” She turned to Oscar, “Thank you and the food was really good.” They had already informed her and Mike they had eaten.

Zane glared at Oliva before glancing at the twins. Both looked rather pleased by what Mike had said, or Zane assumed that was why, “Ah, can you repeat it in a way I can understand? I just did what anyone should have done.” He wanted to glare at Mike since Zane knew he was laughing at him.

Mike looked at the two, "Have a seat and relax." He turned back to Zane. His arms were crossed and resting on the table. His fingers were tapping on one arm, "Yes and no, Zane. Yes, one of the more dominant pack members would have come over and taken care of them. Once they had gotten them away from those two, they would have continued to where they normally sit to eat. The more dominant wolf would have gone back to where they had been. This would have taken care of the pack and nothing else needed. By inviting them over to your table and inviting them to eat with you showed the other pack members you took responsibility for them and would see that they were protected. In this case, it is a wolf thing and not a human thing."

Zane had started eating as his uncle tried to explain. As Mike was talking, he was glancing at the other two wolves, and they really did look pleased. He finished a mouthful of food, "Okay, but what does it mean to me or for them?" His wolf wasn't being helpful currently but seemed to feel what they had done was right and was content having them to protect.

Mike kept tapping his fingers on his bicep as he tried to not overload Zane with too much information, "This is going to be hard to explain and maybe later the twins can do a better job from their point of view. As you are learning in the pack, there are several different ranks. Alpha, Beta, Delta, and Gamma are the most senior. Below Gamma technically the wolves are just 'junior' wolves. The junior wolves have their ranks as well. It isn't defined such as the top four, but they are still there. At the very bottom of the pack are the Omegas who are those being punished. Above them are the most junior wolves." He took a sip of coffee since Zane was going to choke on the next part, "As I'm sure you have been told, you are a fairly dominant wolf. You are just learning what rank you might end up, but I'm leaning towards a Gamma in the beginning and if you work hard maybe a Beta when older. Anyone of the top four ranks start to gather a... mmm... I don't want to say following so much as a team. It starts once they hit puberty, since it's when you really start discovering your dominance level." He looked at Zane to see if he followed.

Zane took a sip of the coffee, and it was darn good, “Good coffee and thanks.” He told the two since Zane assumed they had made it. Now Zane was frowning but it was trying to understand and not because Liv was laughing still, “Ooookay, I guess it makes sense, but it still doesn’t really say why they are here and making breakfast for us.” It was good food, but they didn’t need to since he had just used them as a reason to confront David. Well fudge and he did want to protect them.

Mike shrugged, “This team, for the most part, will end up working with you as your support staff. I would guess Melody would become your assistant, Rico and his friends will be somewhat like office staff. For Oscar and Tessa, they will end up taking care of you. It means preparing food, doing laundry, cleaning, things like that. Most of the senior rank wolves have a similar relation with the most junior wolves. It allows us to focus on the pack and not have to worry about sundry details.”

He did get a reaction and Zane ended up coughing as a drink went down the wrong way, “What?” He had to cough a few more times before he could really speak, “You don’t have any staff like them.” Zane had never seen anyone doing that sort of stuff for Mike so far.

Mike gave Zane a grin, “I do but they don’t normally start working until after you are at school. Who do you think cleans the house and keeps the laundry done?” For now, it was all he was going to say about it. There were a few other things which Zane was going to choke on later, but it could be dealt with down the road. Maybe when Olivia went in for surgery.

Zane could only stare at his uncle before his eyes flickered across the other two, “And you two don’t have a problem with this?” He was sounding slightly strangled as he was talking. It almost sounded like he had just acquired indentured servants or something.

Oscar spoke this time, “We don’t Zane, since it is how the pack works. We keep you comfortable and you protect us. Our parents have been working for Beta Mike since they were in high school. We were really pleased when you offered to take responsibility for us. Our parents were so very happy as well." Both twins looked up at him and their eyes showed just how much it meant to them.

Liv hadn't realized what the two showing up meant and she was looking rather gob smacked as well. She didn't say anything since she didn't know what to say. To her it also sounded like they were almost property of his, but Olivia knew better, or so she hoped.

Mike looked at the twins, "Tell your parents they are invited over for dinner this evening. I was trying to keep the information Zane is learning to a minimum. Since this is in the open now, I need to introduce them. Now all of you off to school and we will talk about this later." He stood and after finishing his coffee, left the house.

Zane sighed before turning back to the food. He needed to eat, and they needed to get going. Once he was done, he looked at the two, "That was a lot of information, and I need to think on it before I can ask anything else. Thank you for breakfast, it was really good." Before he could pick his plate up Tessa collected it which made Zane sigh again.

Even as Tessa was clearing the table Oscar was packing up the leftovers for later. Zane watched them do the work and frankly he was at a loss what to think about what he had been told. He was going to need to really think about it. Instead, he turned to Liv and smirked at her, "See, I do understand the concept of not dark colors. See, a white t-shirt."

Olivia wrinkled her nose at him and poked him in the leg with a crutch, "I'm so going to sneak a tie-dyed shirt into your drawers and hide all the others." She stood and started towards the door. When Oscar picked her pack up, she didn't even bother sighing, "Thank you Oscar." The four of them walked out of the house and down to the bus stop.

Melody glanced at Zane and managed not to laugh at his expression. Something had happened which managed to penetrate the wall he had. **So, Zane, how was your morning? I see the twins came over to say hello.** She had for some reason expected them to, though she didn't know why.

Zane managed to keep his expression neutral when she sent to him. **If you so much as say anything or poke any fun at me, I will bite your tail* *or an ear or something. I just discovered by my actions yesterday I have taken responsibility for the twins, and they are now... Um, report to me I guess?** He just couldn't say belong to him.

Melody's face went blank as well before she responded. **Huh?** Yes, she was a wolf, but it didn't mean she knew everything about the pack. Even though her parents were Gammas there was a fair amount of the pack structure she didn't know about yet.

He decided to poke fun at her. **Well according to Mike, I'm starting to assemble my team, or so he said. I guess it means you get to be my assistant and the others my flunkies... Oscar and Tessa will start taking care of me and the rest of us as the other very junior wolves do for the seniors.** He was waiting for her response to his joke.

Her reaction was even more stumped, "What?" All Melody could do was stare at him and then the twins, even if her wolf sort of gave a confirmation it was true and was content with it. She was going to have to discuss this with her parents and maybe the Luna. When she noticed the slight twitching of Zane's face, she growled at him, "Not flunkies." With a huff she turned away from him.

Zane kept his face mostly still and settled for standing next to her. The twins were somewhat behind him and were glancing between the two. They exchanged looks and shrugged. They knew what their jobs was and let the more senior wolves worry about everything else.

*****

School had most definitely been interesting since Zane could almost feel a shift in the structure of the wolves. Several of various senior dominances came over and quietly congratulated him on taking care of the two. It also included a murmur of appreciation on how he had dealt with David and Leon. Others, Zane had no idea why they were talking to him, which was annoying since he didn't want to talk. Eventually after some half grunting responses many of them went away.

One who was annoying him was a she-wolf who seemed to be intent on getting close to him. Again, he wasn't sure why, but she was trying. Melody, another girl in their group, and even Tessa seemed to be growling at her. Frankly by the end of the day he was ready to go and scream. What helped was every time he came across David, he made sure he met the other boy's eyes. When he did, he made sure his eyes were empty and almost begged for a fight.

Leon and the others, Zane simply ignored. He did look at Leon once with a scathing look. After the look he said, "Not even worth a fight." He walked off with a slight smirk since Leon had bristled at being dismissed so easily. Zane knew they would try and get back at him but for now they were keeping their distance.

That evening Zane and Olivia had met Oscar and Tessa's parents, and they seemed like nice people. Much like their children they were quiet and reserved. It was obvious they were extremely happy for their children. It was still driving Zane nuts, since it just felt so wrong from the human way of looking at it. His wolf was still feeling content and pleased with what had happened which wasn't helping.

The rest of the week had gone smoothly for the most part. Zane was still feeling rather grumpy since every morning when he got up, the twins had breakfast ready. In the evenings they followed him home from school and sat down and did their homework with him. What was also frustrating was Melody and her friends were doing much the same after the second day. Once homework was done the twins and one of Melody's friends would work on dinner. Once dinner was over the twins would head home.

Since he hadn't really had a chance to talk to them, Zane was about ready to pull his hair out. The one thing that kept him from screaming was they had adopted Olivia. Tessa would help her with her physical therapy exercises, massage her leg and hip when it became sore and stiffened. For that alone he could deal with the sudden intrusion into his privacy. It didn't stop the urge to scream though.

Friday evening, Uncle Mike almost did have to deal with a seriously pissed off Zane. Mike had informed him Oscar and Tessa would be spending the weekend since he wasn't going to be there. There was one last small room which had been converted into a room for the two.

Zane was glad the two had left already since he didn't want to hurt their feelings, "Uncle Mike, why do they have to stay here? I appreciate all the help they have been giving Olivia, but it is starting to drive me nuts." He was keeping his eyes down and trying to control the tone of his voice. It was hard and coming out between gritted teeth though.

Mike contemplated Zane, "Zane, grow up. This is the life you are going to be growing into. Unless you cast them free and chose to become a lone wolf, get used to it. Just warning you, if you do cast them free without a damn good reason, you will be telling everyone they weren't good enough for you. It will also impact on those you are calling to you as well, and your trustworthiness in the future. I'm sorry you have to deal with this now, but it is part of being a wolf." His voice was stern but not hard or denigrating. It was a simple statement of fact.

Mike's comment hit Zane almost as if he had been slapped. His wolf was giving agreement and sharing a possessive feeling towards the others; he wasn't willing to cast them out for any reason. His body jerked, and he had to lift his head and stare at Mike, "What? Damn it, Uncle Mike how am I supposed to know this crap? You are starting to make me scared to even talk to anyone now. How the hell do I know what will mean what? I just don't really understand." Zane was almost ready to cry again, "I just want to... I just wish this had never happened. I didn't grow up this way, I don't know what anything means anymore. I want my parents back."

Mike moved over to Zane and pulled him into a hug, "I know Zane and I wish it hadn't happened to you or your family either. It was a horrible thing to happen and believe me, it hurt me as well. I miss my brother and sister-in-law as well. I hate watching Olivia hurting as she moves through the day. I know the surgery is scheduled but even after the surgery, she is going to have some problems. I want the damn rogue in our cells, so I know he won't do anything again. I know this is so damn scary, Zane, I'm also so proud of you and I know your parents would be as well." He gave him one more squeeze before stepping back,

"Why don't you shake your fur out and go for a run. It might help since it will bring your wolf forward."

Zane held onto his uncle and let him comfort him. It was almost the first time he had asked anyone for comfort other than Olivia. He had to take a number of deep breaths before finally stepping back, "Yes Uncle, it's a good idea. At least I can ask them to keep an eye on Olivia, since I make her want to smack me with a crutch." He turned and walked out of the house. After stripping down, he lifted his nose, and his wolf enjoyed the cool night air and the clean scent of the forest. As they were sniffing, they were identifying nearby wolves based on their scents. It was almost as if each one had their own 'flavor' or 'color' and left a trail of where they had been, which slowly faded. When Zane thought of it, it seemed strange how much more nose-oriented his wolf was.

Since he wasn't angry as he had been with some of the other runs, he settled for a reasonable lope. Zane was frustrated, it was true, but he wasn't angry as he had been with many of his runs since changing. Before he realized it, Melody was there next to him and pacing along with him. A few minutes later Rico, or he assumed it was Rico, and several others joined. Zane finally stopped and looked at Melody. Before she realized what he was doing, he lunged at her and took her out. **Gonna get an ear or some other part, like a tail.**

She yipped in surprise and then returned the attack. As they were playing two other wolves came over and settled down nearby. They would have liked to have joined but they were smaller than the others and didn't want to get hurt.

Zane instantly knew who they were and jumped out of the play fighting. **Calm down, the twins are here.** He trotted over to them and was shocked at how small they were compared to even his wolf. They were far larger than any normal wolf, but he was easily a head and shoulders above them in height. Once he was facing them, he leaned forward, or his wolf did, and gave both a good sniff before giving their muzzles a swipe of his tongue. **If you want to join in, we will be careful. I have a feeling we would all feel bad if we accidently hurt you.**

Melody came over and greeted them as well. **Come and play. Zane will know if we start getting too rough and let us know.** With it she lightly bumped Oscar before attacking his shoulder.

Oscar had lowered his head in greetings, and he also had to yip in surprise when Melody took him out. He should have been expecting it, but he and his sister only played with the other wolves of their ranks. It wasn't nearly as rough and was almost like pups playing.

Tessa moved over to Zane and rubbed her head against his shoulder. **Sounds like fun, Zane and we will follow you back. Mike informed us he was leaving and for us to take care of you and Olivia.** She didn't know about the argument Zane and his uncle had. It wasn't any of their business.

Zane sat down and rested his head on her back and huffed. **We do need to talk but it can wait. I'm still trying to figure out how I should feel now. It is not how I grew up and even if my wolf is content, I'm confused. Tomorrow will be fine.** He relaxed for a moment before using his body to knock her on her side and then jumped away. **Now come and get me, Tessa.** His wolf was in charge for the moment and Zane allowed him to take charge.

Tessa rolled over and came to her feet. **That wasn't nice Zane.** She jumped at him, and the play was on. They played for a while before Zane ended up feeling somewhat better. He finally rolled away from the play and stretched and yawned. **Guys, I'm tired. I'm heading back home. I know some of us were given a group assignment for history, so I guess I will see all of you at Uncle Mike's house tomorrow?**

There was a general agreement with what he said, and they separated to head back to their houses. Melody followed Zane and the twins, instinctively protecting the two weaker, smaller wolves between them. Once there he gave another good stretch before shifting and pulling on his clothing, ignoring the fact others could see him nude, "I know you had some clothes brought over so go in and shift. I'm going to bed and will see you in the morning." Zane leaned over and gave Melody a good hug and pet before he turned and let the other two inside.

*****

The weekend had turned out fairly well even though Zane was still not comfortable with having the twins taking care of him. They had talked a reasonable amount about what it meant to the two of them. It had made Zane feel bad, since they were so pleased to have been picked to help take care of a more senior wolf. Not many were, and it became a mark of seniority and prestige. It still really bothered him, and he was going to have to talk to someone but right now with Olivia's surg looming he was focused on her.

At one point during the week before the surgery, Zane was sitting out back with a bottled water and Tessa came out. She had simply settled next to him and leaned against him. It had helped, since she had been taking care of Olivia and he'd made sure to tell Tessa how much he appreciated it.

Tessa simply relaxed against the more dominant wolf, "Thank you for allowing us to help take care of you. I know this isn't comfortable for you but Oscar and I—we feel so wonderful being accepted by you and Olivia. If there is anything we can do to help, just ask." She really was growing to like Zane, and he was keeping a very close eye on her and her brother. Even if he wasn't happy about what was going on, it showed what sort of person he was.

Zane wrapped an arm around her and took a sip of the lemon water, sodas just tasted nasty now, and he wanted to sigh, "Tessa, it does bother me since to my human side it is almost like I have acquired servants. It bothers me because you are people and some of the terms used almost make it sound like you belong to me. It is as if you and your brother are possessions. I know it isn't true, but it is how it feels or sounds to me."

Tessa almost preened when he wrapped his arm around her shoulders. As he was speaking, she tried to understand and she thought she somewhat did, "Well in a way, servants are right but not as if we aren't people. Think of us as hired help. People who clean and cook and take care of you. Even if you don't realize it, we are now getting paid for this.

It comes from the pack funds and for now, most of the money is going into a savings account for us."

Zane had to blink at what she said, and he glanced down at Tessa and wondered where the funds were coming from. It was something he was going to have to talk to Uncle Mike about. He also wanted to know what money they had from the death of their parents and any settlement from the accident. It had been mentioned that some of the money was going to Olivia's treatment which was good. He wanted to know so they knew what they might have for college. He had yet to learn how the packs generally paid for the education of all members, as long as they passed. Even older wolves could easily go back to training programs, or even back to school for a whole different education.

"That does help and thank you Tessa. It is just hard since I grew up in a small house, my parents were middle class and we had some money, but Olivia and I did a fair portion of what you and Oscar are doing now. It just isn't something I'm used to. I will try and talk to you or Oscar when I'm confused." He finished the water and after one more hug he stood, "Well time for you two to head home I guess." Somehow Zane knew they were eventually going to end up moving in but for now he didn't want to think about that.

Tessa stood up and stretched. Zane made her feel so protected and the bullying from some of the humans had dropped drastically. She hadn't mentioned it, but she could tell Zane wasn't a happy wolf, even before he had extended his protection to the two of them. She did know about the accident and what had happened, as everyone knew the basics. Beta Mike had explained it in detail to the two of them. Even now he was just so hurt and trying to keep people away from him and to a lesser extent from his sister. She turned and gave him a good hug, "See you in the morning."

Oscar came out about then and gave Zane a nice smile, "Olivia has headed towards bed and has taken her meds to sleep. We will see the two of you in the morning Zane." He didn't think when he gave Zane a good hug before the two of them hopped down the stairs and headed home.

*****

The following Friday, Mike took Zane, Olivia, the twins, and Melody to the hospital. It was very early in the morning and most of them were looking barely half alive and on the grumpy side. He had noticed Zane was being almost too protective of Olivia since she was going into surgery. Mike had taken time the evening before to let Olivia know Zane was going to be that way and not to fight him. It was a case of the protective older brother and a protective wolf hovering in the back of Zane's mind, with both being extra protective because of the operation. On top of that, Zane's issues with the loss of their parents, and the need to keep her close and protected.

Olivia dealt with it as gracefully as possible but had almost demanded Oscar help her to the car. She liked the older boy even if he was a very shy person. They had talked a fair amount and had discovered they had many similar interests. He was always helpful and polite.

Eventually they were at the hospital and just before they took her to pre-op Zane gave her a good hug. He didn't want to cry before she went in, so he asked his wolf for help, "We will be waiting Olivia. I'll see you in a few hours." After one last hug she was taken away on a gurney to get ready for the surgery. One thing she hadn't been informed of was that Zane and others had been asked to donate some blood for her. Since he was a Lycan, it would help her heal. Mike had been asked as well.

Once she was gone, they had gone to the blood bank. Mike, Zane, Oscar, and even Melody had donated. If they didn't need the blood for Olivia, one nurse knew how to deal with the blood to help those who might need it. It wouldn't turn them, but it would help with the healing of whatever injuries they might have. They might get slightly enhanced senses or a reduction of allergies as a side effect, but it would be temporary.

Now came the fun part, Zane and everyone else sat in the waiting room. Melody was on one side and Tess was on the other to give him comfort. How long this was going to take Zane didn't know but until Olivia was out of surgery, he was going to be going nuts.

CHAPTER 9

Zane Falls Apart

Once they were in the waiting room, Zane was finding it almost impossible to sit still. Last night he hadn't slept very well, which combined with nerves was putting him on edge. He kept having to stand up and stalk around before trying to sit down and relax again. He knew it was probably getting on his uncle's nerves, but he just couldn't help it. Zane's wolf was almost pacing around in the back of Zane's mind as well, which wasn't helping. Both wanted to be in the room to protect Olivia, but they knew they couldn't.

Finally, Zane settled down between Melody and Tessa again and closed his eyes after exhausting his nervous energy. Eventually he fell asleep and started snoring. Since the Luna had come to the hospital as well, she stood and moved over to where he was, "Tessa, move to the other end of the couch. We will lay Zane down and he can use your lap as a pillow." Once Tessa moved, the Luna helped lay him down, "He should sleep for a while which will be good for him." Sleeping was one way a wolf dealt with stress, but needed to be with those they trusted fully, and it was a good thing Zane was starting to trust, even a little.

Once Zane's head was settled in her lap, Tessa started stroking his hair and face. Even though he was acting distant and remote she knew better. She could feel the torment he was feeling and could smell his distress, and it helped her feel better being able to help him. His feet were resting in Melody's lap. Tessa glanced up at her brother and he was sitting next to Beta Mike, who was relaxing with an arm around Oscar.

The Luna settled down in a chair next to Tessa and gave the girl a light pat on the shoulder, "I'm pleased for you and Oscar. I think this will be good for the three of you. By taking care of Olivia, you are also helping to take care of Zane." She told the three pups, before sending silently, **He will accept your helping with Olivia in ways he will have a tough time accepting for himself. Remember, if any of you need a good hug or to talk, come to me.**

Tessa and Oscar couldn't help but look pleased again. It meant a so deal to them having the Luna feel they were the right ones to help Zane. **Thank you Luna and we had come to that conclusion too. We figure once Olivia is released from the hospital, we will move into Beta Mike's house to help her. It will give Zane time to get used to us being around.** Oscar sent since his sister was focused on comforting Zane at the moment.

*****

Zane eventually woke up and stretched before he realized where he was. When he noticed Tessa smiling down at him, he stared at her for a moment before he sat up. Now he was blushing slightly since he had been using her lap as a pillow, "How long was I asleep? Is Liv out of surgery yet?" He took the large sandwich Melody handed him; his stomach rumbled since it smelled really good.

Mike grinned at Zane's reaction as he replied, "You have been down for close to three hours. A nurse came past and let us know she had about two more hours of surgery. Once she is done, there will be an hour to an hour and a half of recovery before she is moved to her room." He was probably as concerned as Zane was right now, "The nurse did say she was handling the procedure well."

He glanced at his uncle even as he was eating the sandwich and sides he was handed. After swallowing a bite, "Well at least I slept through half the procedure. For the balance, I'm likely to scream if it takes longer than what you said." He continued eating the sandwich since he was starving. It also gave him something to focus on as well.

Melody reached over and gave his arm a squeeze, "Relax as much as you can Zane. I'm sure she is going to be fine. Just think, once she heals, she won't be able to threaten you with her crutches anymore." She figured Zane would get a laugh out of it.

Oscar almost giggled at Melody's comment. It was a standing joke around the house, "I'm sure she will keep one just in case it's needed Melody." He moved over and settled down next to Melody and leaned against her for a moment before pulling an electronic game thing out and started a game, "Beta Mike had us pack a bag of things to distract you with."

Zane snorted at Melody and frowned at Oscar, "You are not to help her hide one or else..." He relaxed and finished the food before sucking down a good portion of water. Zane wrapped an arm around Tessa and rested his head back against the wall, "I know I have said it but thanks to both of you for helping Olivia so much. I don't know why but she will accept the help from you she won't from me." That was an annoyed grumble.

Oscar tensed for a moment before he realized Zane was teasing him. Both he and Tessa were learning Zane's moods and actions. The longer they were with him the better they would know him. It would help them know what the boundaries were when it came to taking care of him. One thing they were learning was Zane really wasn't comfortable with their helping him. Mike had explained it to them, but it still sounded odd. Then again Zane was—or had been—a human until just recently. One memory of their learning came back as he was thinking.

It had been last weekend while Zane and Melody had gone for a run. Oscar and Tessa had gone into Zane's room to tidy it up. They hadn't even considered it might bother him when they did it. Tessa was putting some clean laundry away while Oscar had picked the room up and cleaned it. He hadn't moved anything on the desk or bed side stand. It was mostly things on the floor and collected dirty laundry.

When Zane had come back, he'd not been happy. Oscar wasn't quite sure why. Zane had told them the only reason they were to go into his room was either to put laundry away or collect dirty laundry. Beyond that they were to ask, or Zane would tell them. Both had felt really bad for the rest of the day for having upset Zane. They knew it was part of the learning process, but it had still upset them.

Tessa gave Zane a quick hug, "Because you are her overprotective older brother." She leaned slightly against him, and relaxed, **We are just junior wolves who are taking care of you, so we don't have the same urge to protect her as you do. That and she gets along with Oscar pretty well. That helps alot.** She then pulled out a book to read.

Melody was enjoying the byplay between the three. Even if Zane didn't realize it, he was reacting to the two which was helping him to come somewhat more out of his shell. Just to tease him she settled down on the couch with her head in his lap, "Since you had a nap earlier..."

Zane frowned as he looked down at her before asking Oscar what was in the bag. He settled down with an electronic game . Just for good measure he lightly thunked her forehead with it before starting one of the games.

She snickered but quickly fell asleep as they were waiting. His lap was warm, and she felt content relaxing in his protection.

The rest of the time passed even if it seemed like it was glacially slow. They were finally told Olivia was in her room. When they were told Zane almost jumped off the couch. The only reason he didn't was because Melody was asleep still and it appeared even Tessa was snoozing as she leaned against him, "Okay, time to wake up. Olivia's in her room."

Mike stood and stretched as well. The Luna had gone back to the pack once they knew the surgery was going smoothly and Zane was asleep, not thinking she might have still been needed, "After we see her for a few moments, I'm going to take you home. Right now, as much as you want to be here, she needs the rest. Part of her healing is going to be sleeping a great deal." He warned, **She is also going to be eating a great deal, thanks to the Lycan blood she was given. The demands it is going to place on her body is a big reason why she is going to be sleeping so much.**

Before they left the waiting room, they grabbed the bags packed for her. How much she would feel like reading or watching movies they didn't know. Zane had decided the best idea was to give her plenty of options just in case. She also had her phone, so she could call if she needed anything.

When they walked into her room, Zane had to grab the door frame. She was so pale and looked so tiny in the bed, since it was sized for an adult werewolf. Her leg was in some massive bulky dressing which only made her look worse. There was an IV, some cables coming from under her gown and some other stuff attached. His eyes started to tear up and all he could think was this was probably how she had looked after the accident. He started shaking and his breath was coming in gasps. This was something he missed and should have been there for.

Melody pulled him into the room and wrapped her arms around him. Tessa and Oscar did as well and once the door was shut, they held him for all they were worth. Mike came over and wrapped his arms around Zane as well. He could feel what Zane was feeling and it had never even occurred to him Zane might have some sort of flashback. **Oh hell, I'm so sorry Zane, it didn't even occur to me you would react this way. Olivia is fine, she really is though she will probably be asleep for a while. I'm going to take you home and bring you back later.**

It felt like Zane was holding onto Tessa and Melody for dear life. Having Oscar and his uncle holding him helped as well but he had to get out! He was having horrible visions of wrecks, his parents staring at him with dead eyes as they were mangled in the car. Visions of waking up and finding Olivia had died. Frankly he was starting to fall apart. **Please Uncle Mike, I can't stay!** He felt horrible for saying that. If he stayed any longer, he was going to break down and scream.

Tessa, Melody, Oscar, bring him to the entrance. I'm going to go and get the car. He made sure they had a good hold on him before he hurried away. **Luna, can you please come to my house? Zane lost it when he saw Olivia. It is almost like he is having flashbacks to when she was hurt,* *and his parents killed. I never even considered it.** By the Goddess he felt like crap at the moment.

Esther sighed since she should have thought about it too and remained. **I'm on my way, and Mike don't beat yourself up. I should have considered it as well.** She poked her head into Kad's office, "Zane had a bad reaction to seeing Olivia post-op. Mike is bringing him home and I'm going to go and wait for them to arrive. I will contact you when I can." Esther hurried away and headed to Mike's house. Once she was inside, she started coffee brewing for those who would want it.

Back at the hospital, Melody was holding on to Zane as they walked towards the elevators. When people looked, she shook her head at them to keep them away. She knew Zane didn't need the attention and it would only make it worse. Oscar was almost running interference for them since he could tell Zane wouldn't handle the attention. The three of them could feel Zane's wolf very close to the surface as he was mentally growling.

Eventually they made it to the entrance and Mike was there with his SUV. Melody and Tessa helped Zane into the back seat and sat down on either side of him. Once everyone was inside Mike pulled away and hurried home. It was hard not to speed and get Zane to the Luna, but he had to be careful. The last thing they needed was to be pulled over for a ticket. Eventually they made it to the house and as soon as Mike had parked, Melody was helping Zane out and taking him inside.

As they walked in Zane felt the Luna and this time, he didn't resist the pull. He staggered over to her and wrapped his arms around her before finally falling apart. Esther helped him over to the couch and settled down next to him and pulled him into a good hug. For the moment, his walls were down, and all his fears and concerns were flowing out. His thoughts were so jagged and scattered she couldn't really get a sense of what was going on for the moment. As badly as he was reacting, she was forced to start applying her powers to calm him down. Zane was going to need to cry before he could even begin to talk about what he was thinking.

Mike was in a chair across from them with his head resting in his hands. His elbows were on his knees, as he was forced to keep his wolf from raging. Zane was a pup and his responsibility, and he felt horrible about Zane was experiencing right now. Mike finally stood up, "I'm going to talk to the Alpha." He stalked out of the house and towards the main pack house.

The Luna met Mike's eyes before going back to comforting Zane. Melody and Tessa were helping as well. **Kad, Mike is coming over to talk to you. He is really upset because he never thought that Zane would react so badly. I can't get much of a sense of what is really going through Zane's mind. What I am seeing are images of his parents being dead and Olivia dying as well. He is terrified he is going to lose her.** Once she let her mate go, she turned back to Zane.

*****

Before Mike made it to the office Kadrian had gone to his wet bar and poured two stiff drinks. just as Mike reached the door Kadrian called him in, "Come in Mike and close the door. Have a seat and a drink. Esther let me know what was going on. I wouldn't have considered it either, so try not to take it out on yourself. If all else fails, we can go for a good hunt and enjoy a deer." Hunting was controlled since if they randomly hunted without some sort of limit there wouldn't be anything living nearby.

Mike dropped heavily into a seat and tossed the Scotch back without even thinking. It hit the back of his throat and burned on the way down, "Damn it, Kadrian, I feel like warmed over shit right now. I just never even considered it. This isn't something I have ever dealt with before; hell, I haven't even had a mate or pups. I'm doing my best but what do I know about raising pups, much less emotionally damaged pups? I feel so out of my depth." Damn it he was whining but he didn't know what else to say for the moment.

Kadrian poured some more Scotch into Mike's glass before taking a sip from his own glass, "Mike, you are doing an admirable job of taking care of the pups. Yes, it is a learning process and harder for you since they came to you hurt and injured. What happened today we should have expected but as you know it isn't something we normally deal with." Or not from a human point of view. If pups lost their parents, the pack would take care of them. They would have grown up knowing about the Luna and how she could help. Even if they didn't have additional blood-family, the pack was an extended family and they knew they would take care of them and protect them, "It's good that Zane is finally opening up to Esther however unwillingly it was. She can begin to help him heal. How long will it take? I don't know but it is a start."

He looked at the glass and after doubling the amount in it tossed it back again, "I still feel like shit for not even considering it. I have been keeping an eye on them and both are having trouble dealing with what happened. At least Olivia has been talking to Esther and going to her for comfort. Now it is Zane's turn, I guess." Mike could feel the large shots of Scotch hitting since he had taken them so close together, and it had been a while since he ate. He knew it wouldn't last long.

Kadrian took another sip, "She will help him and having both Tessa and Oscar there will help as well. I would suggest having them move in now. It will force his wolf to take care of them." Having Melody spending time with him would help a great deal as well. The rest of his small group would help although not as much as Tessa and Oscar could.

Mike slouched down in the chair and nodded at the suggestion. Now he just looked tired and worn. What had happened to his brother and sister-in-law had hurt him badly as well. "Thanks for listening Kadrian, it really helped. I think I'm going to go for a run and see about finding the keeper of the rabbits and eat a few." The fresh blood would help his wolf.

Kadrian stood and waited for Mike to stand as well and gave him a good hug, "Go and tell them I said you could have several extra rabbits. I will be here if you need me. It might sound bad but maybe find a she-wolf to dally with. It will help work some of your feelings out." Besides, he knew Mike hadn't dallied since the pups had come to the pack. It didn't mean it was wrong not to dally, just when unmated, wolves liked to play.

*****

Zane had finally cried enough; he had worn himself out. When he realized where he was, Zane had to wonder when he had come home. He knew the Luna was holding him and Tessa was curled up next to him. Melody was nearby as well based on her scent. He slowly sat up and when the Luna tried to hold him, he spoke, "I need a Kleenex." He sounded really stuffed up and Zane couldn't breathe through his nose. After he blew his nose and wiped his face, he leaned against Ester again. He didn't have the energy to fight it anymore. Even if he had, his wolf would have forced him to accept her help.

Esther let him move before gathering him close again, "Do you want to talk about it, Zane?" She didn't bother telling him his wolf had tried to tell her what was wrong but couldn't. It would only upset Zane more, which he didn't need now.

He had to shiver before he could say anything. When he did start talking his voice was very hurt sounding, "When I saw Liv, all I could see was her after mom and dad were killed and her hurt. I wasn't there for her, and they wouldn't be dead, if it wasn't for me. I didn't have to go running that night. If I hadn't gone running, I wouldn't have been attacked or run down by the car. If I hadn't been hurt, they wouldn't have been coming to the hospital to see me." He started sobbing again since he knew it was his fault his family had been destroyed.

Tessa rested her face against his shoulder and started quietly crying as well. It was both because of what he had said and how shattered he sounded, as well as the pain she wanted to take care of him. Her wolf was crying for him and what he had gone through.

Melody rested her head against Tessa's head and comforted her even as Tessa was trying to comfort Zane. All three of them were feeling really bad. Oscar had left not too long ago though Melody wasn't sure why. To be honest she hadn't noticed him leaving until after he was gone, and his scent started to fade. It made her feel somewhat bad, but she had been focused on Zane.

Esther kept applying her powers to comfort him, "Zane, I can see why you might feel this way, but you had no idea what would happen. You did nothing wrong and from the sounds of it, you tended to run fairly frequently. You were simply doing what you normally did. The rogue is the one who is responsible. He attacked you, Zane. I know it might take you a long time to come to terms with this, but he is the one who caused this. We have added his DNA to our rogue database and put out a reward for finding and turning him in." She figured he needed to know it.

It didn't matter since he felt how he felt. True, the rogue had attacked him, but he had decided to go for the run. Zane didn't know what to do now. He had run from Olivia again and it hurt as well. Even if she didn't know he had, Zane knew and it was probably going to haunt him, "I don't know what to do anymore. I just don't know." He just didn't know how to handle all the changes in his life. He was lost and floundering as he tried to deal with everything.

Now that he was talking, she could help him, "Zane, what you are feeling is normal. It horrible when you lose someone special to you. It is also normal when someone close to you is badly hurt. In your case it is even worse since you were in the hospital yourself when it happened. You woke up to find out the unimaginable happened to you. Add to it discovering you are no longer completely human, and you have a second voice. It isn't even mentioning struggling to learn about the pack and being a werewolf. I know this is going to be hard for you but don't close yourself off. Melody wants to help you. Tessa and Oscar want to help you. The pack wants to help you. It is one of the nice parts of being in a pack. You do have a family even if it isn't by blood."

About then Oscar came back in. **Luna, Tessa, I brought our things from our house over. The bags are in our room. We can unpack it later. I'm going to start on dinner. You keep helping Zane.** He quietly walked into the kitchen and after some serious thinking decided on a comfort food meal. It was simple but very good. Once he had decided what he was going to cook he started pulling out what he needed. Earlier in the week he and Tessa had come up with a shopping list of what they wanted and needed to have here. With Mike being single, he mostly just came to the pack house for meals, or had someone collect it and bring it over, often their parents, and he and usually some of his team would have a meal together. They had submitted the order to the head of the house and collected the food the next day.

Zane had finally stopped crying, “I have never lost anyone before like this, Luna. I don’t even know where to start. When I saw Liv, I just couldn’t handle it.” He had said it, but he just couldn’t get past what seeing her had made him think about, “She looked so little and hurt in the bed. I know this is to help her but all I could see was her after the accident, with nobody there for her.”

Esther started stroking his hair, “I can’t even imagine what it might have been like. I have lost people I have cared for, and it always hurts. For now, let your friends help you and comfort you. Let Tessa and Oscar take care of you and support you. Melody and some of her friends are here for you and I will be here anytime you need me. If it gets too bad send to me and I will come and help you. If needed, there are a few people who I can ask to talk to you and help you deal with your feelings. Just don’t hide from us Zane. We can’t help if you don’t allow us to.”

He finally sat up again because he had to blow his nose again. Once he was done, he turned to Tessa and gave her a good hug before reaching across her and giving Melody’s arm a good squeeze, “I will try but I can’t even describe how much it scares me since I don’t think I could handle losing anyone else.”

Esther felt better since he had admitted one of his deepest fears, they could start to deal with them. She settled down to keep talking to him and comforting him. It was going to take him a lot of time to deal the fears because he had bottled it up for so long.

*****

When bedtime rolled around, Zane didn't even bother saying anything after realizing the twins were moving in. He simply didn't have the energy to raise a fuss, especially because his wolf wanted them close. When he went to bed, he curled up in an exhausted ball and was quickly asleep. As he had expected it wasn't a good sleep, until at some point something soothed and comforted him.

When he woke up the next morning, he found a small wolf curled up on his bed on top of the covers, pressed against his leg. Based on the scent he knew it was Tessa, not realizing he had just used only his nose to identify her. "Great, I don't even get my bed to myself. I might have to grumble later." He yawned and stretched before sitting up and giving Tessa's wolf a good pet, "Thanks but I'm going to grumble later just so you know." He rolled out of bed and stumbled to the bathroom.

Eventually he came out and Tessa was gone from his room. After pulling on some clothes, he headed downstairs and was pleased when he found a cup of coffee on the table for him. He flopped in the chair and yawned again, "Thanks." He took a sip of the coffee and tossed in another yawn for good measure as his uncle walked into the room.

Mike flopped in a chair as well and took his cup of coffee from Oscar and took a sip as well, "Morning Zane and I know the feeling. Esther said she would drive you to the hospital and sit with you and Olivia for a while." Nobody wanted a repeat of yesterday afternoon, since it had been messy and extremely hard on both Zane and Mike, "I will come by later when Ester needs to come back. Tessa and Oscar have a few things to keep you occupied including your homework..."

Oscar had just slid a plate in front of Zane, and he had been about ready to eat when Mike tossed in the bit about homework. Zane turned and glowered at him, "Uncle Mike you should know better than to swear like that this early in the day." He did end up snickering though and turned back to the food and started munching it down. He had eaten some last night and this morning he was starving.

Eating didn't take very long and about the time they were done Esther showed up. Zane made a point of walking over to her and leaning against her and giving her a hug, "Thank you Luna." He just couldn't quite say what he was thanking her for, but Zane figured she would understand.

She returned the hug before urging him away, "Shall we go? The doctor called, and Liv is doing fairly well for the moment. She does have some pain, but the medications are helping to control it. She isn't all there due to the meds, but it's expected." Esther urged them to the vehicle and waited for them to climb in before she pulled away.

When they arrived at the hospital Zane had to stop and take deep breaths before he could go inside. When he finally walked in, it was obvious to Esther he was only entering because he had to. She was sure his wolf was helping as well but she had a feeling he would never be comfortable in a hospital again. The trauma was too deep, and it wasn't something she felt he would want to 'fix', "Come Zane, I'm here and lean on me. Allow me to do my job. let Tessa and Melody to help you too. ."

They slowly walked in, and it was so damn hard for Zane since he had to keep stopping to take slow deep breaths. Having the Luna there was helping more than he wanted to admit. Tessa was a warm presence next to him. There was just something about her and Oscar that made him want to take care of them. Even with Tessa next to him he knew Oscar was behind them and he was carrying a bag of things to do. Much to Zane's annoyance, it did include his homework. Mike hadn't been joking when he mentioned it.

When they finally walked into the room, Liv had her head elevated some and she was awake. Looking at her Zane figured she really wasn't all there because her eyes were somewhat glassy. He let go of the Luna and moved over next to her and sat down on a stool, which was next to her. Zane gently grasped her hand and held it, "Hey Liv how are you doing? I hope the pain isn't too bad sis."

Olivia turned her head and looked at him. She gave him a wan smile before yawning, "Hey Zane, doing okay." She yawned again and blinked sleepily at him. It was good to see him. As he was holding her hand it made her feel safe and protected, "Falls sweep soon." Her eyes drifted closed, and there was a smile on her face.

Zane settled for sitting there and holding her hand. If it helped, he could sit there the entire day while holding her hand. The homework could go to hell. He moved slightly so he was lying next to her and wrapped an arm around her. He closed his eyes and did his best to relax with her next to him.

*****

The rest of the weekend had been much the same. Sunday morning, Zane found Oscar curled up in wolf form on his covers and rolled his eyes, "Dude I'm going to have to set a few ground rules." He had slept well last night, and he did appreciate the affection they were showing him. Sunday night he hoped he would sleep decently since it felt so weird waking up with someone, even in wolf form, in his bed. They had never had pets, not that they were, so he had never gotten used to waking up with a dog or cat next to him.

Finally, Monday morning rolled around and when Zane walked into his bathroom, he looked in the mirror. Frankly, he looked like crap and wanted to go back to bed for a few more hours. He had looked like this for a while after waking up from the coma. Now it was back, and he really didn't like the look. With a disgusted grunt he left the bathroom and got dressed.

Breakfast was good, but he just wasn't feeling civil and settled for just a few words. When they climbed on the bus, Zane figured Melody had talked to the others since other than a greeting, they didn't bother him much. They gave him comfort, but it was about it. Once at the school, Zane did his best to pull on his emotionless face. It would help keep some at bay though the one annoying she-wolf tried to get him to talk to her again.

When she did, he turned and stared at her before furrowing his brows at her, "Just what do you want? I don't want some hanger on trying to make me her boyfriend. I'm not interested in having anything to do with that. I thought I had made it obvious the first few times. Unless you have a valid reason to want to hang around, just don't. I'm not in the mood for it and won't play the game." Zane turned and walked away before she could say anything. He knew she was a wolf, but he didn't know who she was and honestly didn't care.

Melody was very pleased he had slapped her down. She was okay but tended to try and hang with the current 'in' crowd. What made it rather pathetic, her parents were reasonably senior, so she really didn't need to do it. With a glare at the girl, Melody turned and walked away with Zane. If she had to, she would slap the girl down during training.

Zane normally would have kept half an eye on David and Leon but this morning he just didn't care. Because of this, he didn't notice one of their flunkies watching the entire thing. During first period Zane didn't even try to act interested. He settled for just taking notes and ignored most everyone in the room including the teacher. He was tired, still worried for Liv, and frankly his wolf was as grumpy as Zane was.

When lunch finally rolled around, Zane settled at what was now his table. He glared at the food since he, and his wolf, now wanted something which was mooing as he ate it. He might have to talk to Mike later about getting one of the rabbits they raised for the wolves to chase and hunt. He still wasn't very skilled at it, but it would still help. One thing Zane did notice was David and his posse were whispering and they kept glancing in his direction.

By Wednesday he was so sick of it, Melody had been forced to grab his arm as he was getting ready to confront the prick. When she did, he glared at her. **Don't stop me. He is pissing me off and I'm sick of it.**

Melody gave him a smirk. **I never said you shouldn't deal with him but there are other ways... We know where he lives, and his mother has a prized flower bed... She doesn't do the work, but she routinely enters the flowers in gardening competitions and takes the successes...** She wondered if he would get the hint.

Zane was forced to stop and look at her as she sent to him. As pissed as he was, it took some time to realize what she had said. When he did his eyes went round in appreciation of the depths of the horribleness she was suggesting, **Oh hell... Oh... Oh god that's so wrong... Um...** His eyes were starting to dance as ideas went through his mind. His wolf had sat up in the back of his mind and he let out a low appreciative growl.

Rico glanced at Zane and sniggered at him. **Oh yes, Melody has a mean streak when annoyed. It is a good thing you slapped down Mindy earlier or Melody might have done something.** He was grinning like it was going out of style. **So when and where?**

Melody was looking rather angelic for the moment. It wasn't working because anyone who looked would probably see the horns holding up her halo. **At Zane's house about 10pm? It will take about a half hour to get there and then we can have some fun.**

Zane pretended to lift a non-existent hat to her in respect. **Sounds like a deal. Shall we all turn and smile at David and Leon? We can deal with Leon later...** Almost as he mentioned it, they all turned and gave David huge smiles before turning back to their food.

That evening Mike was thankfully on patrol and when Zane checked, he was on a completely different part of the property. He met everyone out back and quickly shifted after stripping down. He was still uncomfortable with casual nudity and turned his back to the girls when he stripped. Melody, Tessa, and Simone were all rather cute, which made it worse. Once he had shifted, he turned back to them. **Lead the way, Melody.**

They all streamed away from the house and tore across the property. It didn't take very long to find David's house and Zane had to admit it was pretty nice. It wasn't anything like the pack house, but it was better than many houses. When they arrived, they all dropped to their chests and looked over the back yard. It was very nicely done and well groomed. To be honest to Zane it was almost too pretty and nice. **My wolf came up with an idea. Before we tear up the lawn, those of us who need to... can go and make some deposits on the lawn and porch. Anything worth chewing on, go for it. If we don't get to her prize flowers tonight, we can do it later. The light is going to be a pain though.**

Rico had to cover his muzzle with his paws to keep from making any noise at the suggestion of dropping a pile of do-do on the porch. **I can take care of the light.** He quickly shifted and skinned a rock at the porch light, which went out. Once he was done, he shifted back. To make sure he wasn't seen, he had moved back into the forest and stepped behind a tree.

Zane looked at Tessa and Oscar. **I do not want you to be involved with this. If we get punished, so be it but you two would do this simply because I asked you to, and it would be wrong. We will be back later. Keep an eye out and send if you see or sense anything.** He turned and led the group into the yard after easily jumping the fence. The damage only took a few minutes and he had decided to wait on the flowers. Several slippers were chewed to death, a load of crap was dropped in front of the door and the rest scattered around. Once done they jumped the fence and vanished into the darkness.

CHAPTER 10

Gardeners Found

The following morning, David was just getting ready to get out of bed when his mother screeched. It was a sound he was somewhat used to, but this shriek was not quite normal. Because of that, he rolled out of bed and hurried downstairs. Chances were good his father was already gone and at work. As he followed the sounds from his mother, he finally reached the back door and froze. His mother was standing there with a horrified expression on her face. She was clutching onto the door frame with her long scrawny fingers and one foot was in the air.

When he glanced down, he could only stare at the missive pile of crap on the porch. It was obvious she had stepped in it since there was some on the bottom of her foot. David knew if he laughed, he would regret it later, so he forced the guffaw back and tried to speak normally, "Mom? What..." He didn't know what to say since they didn't have any pets and had a tall fence around their property.

She screeched again and shook her foot. It didn't work well since it scattered the crap around, "Get me a wet towel David and hurry!" She screamed again in disgust. This was why she had never wanted a pet or allowed an animal in their house. They were disgusting nasty things who crapped and pissed wherever they wanted.

David hurried to take care of it. When he came back and quickly wiped the shit off her foot, he glanced at the yard and almost stopped moving. There were several piles of crap, anything chewable had been shredded, and, well, it was a mess. Damn it and if he didn't get out of there shortly, he might have to clean the mess up. If he could hurry out of there the hired help would take care of it, "Let me help you inside mom."

*****

The next morning Zane woke up and sighed. Tessa was again in her wolf form curled up next to him. He wanted to glower at her, but he didn't have the energy. Last night he had nightmares again and he figured she had sensed them. Since he had a feeling grumbling at her would just make her feel bad, he decided not to. Instead, he rolled on his side after a good stretch, "Morning Tessa and thank you." He curled an arm around her wolf and gave her a good hug. He did appreciate their concern even if he still wanted to push people away.

With a groan he rolled on his back and stretched again before rolling off the bed. He stumbled over to his dresser and pulled out some clothing before heading towards the bathroom. At some point he was going to need to talk to Tessa and Oscar about just what he needed and or wanted. Their actions still confused him, since it was so foreign to his human side. After brushing his teeth, he stepped into the shower and smiled at the warmth of the water. It did help but he couldn't stay in too long. They needed to get to school and then afterwards go and spend time with Olivia. Anne had taken to coming with them, since she was bringing Olivia's homework to her.

Most of it was done by Anne but they were doing their best to keep Olivia in the loop, so she knew what was going on. By now he was out of the shower and glanced in the mirror and was pleased to see he didn't look quite so much like crap as he had . Most of it was related to his not sleeping well and the nightmares he was having. Zane didn't want to admit it but having either Tessa or Oscar curled up next to him was helping. He could feel their concern for both him and Olivia as well as the others in their small group.

Zane finally made it downstairs and gave Oscar a smile as he placed a cup of coffee in front of him at the table. Just to be silly, Zane started chanting 'coffee, coffee, coffee', much to their amusement, "I so don't have any urge to go to school, darn it. I really don't but if I didn't Unc would growl, and Liv would hit me with a crutch." He sighed and started eating. What he really wanted to do was sit at Olivia's bedside and be there with her.

Melody and Rico had taken to coming to the house in the morning and Melody gave him a hug, "We know and so does Liv, even if she is still recovering. At least she is doing better than expected, thanks to the wolf blood."

Zane couldn't help but lean against Oscar when he also gave Zane a hug. It bothered Zane as he didn't even think when getting a hug from anyone in the group, including the guys. It just wasn't something he was used to or ever considered other than maybe a 'bro' hug, "I know, but I'm still feeling bad seeing her in the bed. It scared the crap out of me and it... It makes me want to hide even more." He sat back up and started eating again and forced his fears away. Olivia was doing well. . He was just feeling stressed and upset about waking up with her hurt and his family destroyed.

Rico leaned over and lightly punched Zane's shoulder, "Zane, we are here for you." He rolled his eyes and grumbled, "Several of us had a talking to by the Luna and explained what has been going on. We know you are scared but at least talk to us. If you don't, Melody and I are going to deal with you on the next run." What the Luna had said had shocked him since he had never dealt with the higher dominance wolves. He had never needed to interact personally with the Luna before. The draw to Zane was also something he was surprised about, especially with how everyone expected him to be ranked more senior.

Normally Zane would have glowered at Rico or made some sort of bad threat but now he wasn't feeling like it, "It is hard, Rico. It still terrifies me to let anyone close." He glanced up and looked at Tessa and Oscar before looking back down at the cup of coffee, "With Tessa and Oscar my wolf and I agree we will protect them. They just call to something inside us. Not saying you and the others don't, but you will fight, and they won't unless they have no choice." His hands made a tight fist before he stood up, "Time for school, I guess." He needed to move.

Melody flashed a look at the others, and they slightly nodded at her. This was more than Zane had said to anyone as far as Rico knew. The breakdown with the Luna hadn't been mentioned by anyone in the room at the time. It wasn't what they needed to hear. If Zane wanted to discuss it, that was his choice, **Zane, we are here for you and Olivia.** She stood as well and stretched, "Definitely time for school and then to the hospital. From what I understand, Abby is going to take us."

*****

When Zane's group reached the school, he was feeling somewhat better. **Remember, avoid looking at David or Leon with anything other than irritation.** They all got off the bus and walked inside. After splitting up for their various lockers they headed towards class. When Zane and Rico walked into the classroom, it was all they could do not to smirk. David was looking seriously pissed off about something. Presumably, it was related to what they'd done to the back yard the night before.

With a casual flop Zane settled in his chair and glanced at Rico as he was pulling his books and stuff out. **Someone looks somewhat irritated, doesn't he? Gee I wonder why?** Both knew why or assumed why. Chances were pretty good David had seen the mess they had made of the backyard.

Rico flopped in his chair as well and stretched and yawned, "Thank goodness tomorrow is Friday. I could use a weekend off." Rico knew everyone would be listening to see what had happened, **He even looks grumpier than normal. Something must have happened. I will keep my ears open.** They just got the first shot since David was in their class.

Behind them David was glaring at the two. Somehow, he knew Zane was at fault. How he knew it, he didn't care; he just knew it and he was going to pay for it. Even after helping his mother into the house David had been forced to go and clean the pile of crap off the back porch. The rest of the yard would be taken care of by their workers, but it had been nasty. Even though he had used doubled up store bags, he felt the crap squish as he was trying to pick it up. The way it felt made him want to barf alone, which didn't even mention the smell! It had ruined his appetite and now he was starting to get hungry.

Instead of saying anything, he settled for glaring at Zane's back most of the class. He didn't even give a crap about the homework now, since he was so angry. What David was doing was thinking up ways to get back at Zane. Even if he didn't have anything to do with what had happened, he had still shown him up in front of his group. He would find out some way to return the favor big time.

Eventually lunch rolled around, and everyone settled down at their table, "Well school was an absolute blast as usual. I think the math teacher is in cahoots with the English teacher. Not only do I have a pile of math, but I also have some essay due next Monday and it isn't short." Zane muttered. Rico and Simone groaned as well since they had the same teachers.

Even as they were talking everyone was listening to David at his table. Leon looked at David, "What has you so worked up man? All you have been doing today is swearing at everything." David hadn't said anything, and Leon was curious. He wondered if David had another run in with the jerk squad.

David snarled something before answering, "Some wild animals decided to have a party in the back yard. They left crap everywhere, chewed up anything not nailed down, and as a final note left a pile of shit on the back porch. Mom stepped in it this morning and I ended up having to clean the porch up." His face was red with fury and his expression was pretty bad.

Zane ended up coughing into a hand to cover a laugh. It was even better than he had expected. **I almost feel sorry for him. Almost but not quite. Hopefully now he will leave us alone.** No, there wouldn't be any connection between them and the wild animals, but he hoped it would distract David. Frankly in the mood he was in, it would be the best for David to leave him alone. Zane knew it wasn't going to take much to set him off until Olivia was back home and healing.

Maybe for his mother... No, she is still an upscale bitch. Simone didn't like the woman at all. She, like many of them, had encountered her. She always came across as better than thou and was especially if you weren't white. Simone's parent's ancestry was from India, and it showed; she had the black hair, dark eyes, brown skin. At least she didn't have a caste mark. Even though David's mother frequented the pastry shop her parents owned, the witch came across as better than everyone else.

David glared at Zane when he coughed into his hand. Even if the jerk didn't have anything to do with it, he was still laughing at him. For laughing at him, Zane was going to pay. His eyes wandered the other table, and a slight smirk crossed his face. He knew who he was going after though he was going to have to be careful.

Now David had made his decision he was going to have to talk to Leon and make plans. Feeling much happier with the world he turned back to his food and started eating. He didn't say anything right now since he didn't want anyone to overhear what he had to say.

*****

When Zane and the others arrived home the twin's mother was waiting there for them. Abby smiled as Zane, Melody, and the twins climbed in, "Good afternoon and I already picked up the homework for Olivia in case she is awake enough to do some of it." Once everyone was seated and belted in, she pulled away from the house.

Zane hopped in and yawned, "Thanks for the ride, Abby, and Anne for getting her homework. I'm not sure how much she will appreciate it though." He grinned as she pulled away, "I hope they have an idea when she might be able to come home ." Zane knew the doctors were going to be doing some x-rays and tests today.

Abby glanced at Zane before looking back at the road, "I have a feeling anything to distract her will be appreciated." She focused on the drive while the pups relaxed. Having finally met Zane, she knew her pups had been accepted by someone who cared. He might look and act cold but from what her twins had said as well as what Beta Mike had said, she knew better. Even she, maybe more than most, could feel the pain he was feeling. Mike had spent some time talking to her and her mate once the boy had been hurt and even more when his brother and sister-in-law were killed. It had hit him hard, since their family wasn't very large. Both her and her mate had spent time cuddling Mike, helping him with his loss.

Once they reached the hospital she pulled up to the entrance, "Go in and I'll come to Olivia's room once I park." After they had piled out, she pulled away and went looking for a parking spot.

The four of them trooped into the hospital and headed towards Olivia's room. When they reached it, and walked in they found Mike inside, "Hey Unc, hey Liv, I hadn't expected to see you here." He gave his uncle a quick hug before moving over to Olivia. She looked more awake today. Zane gave her a quick hug before settling down, "Hey sis, you look better. How are you doing?" His expression softened as he was talking.

Olivia returned the hug and then grasped his hand, "I'm doing okay and feeling more awake." She glowered at him, "Next time you donate blood, I might just whack you with a crutch. I was told about it earlier." After one extra glower she squeezed his hand again, "Honestly, I'm feeling far better than I expected. How was school?"

Zane took her hand when Liv held hers out to him, "We were told not to tell you to keep you from feeling scared about it. I did talk to Uncle Mike about it though. As far as school?" He rolled his eyes at her, "I have some more homework for you to work on as you can. Has anyone said when you might be able to come home? I have been missing you and even though I know you are doing fine. It really scares me knowing you are here."

Tessa came up and settled behind Zane and wrapped her arms around him and leaned against his back. She settled for simply relaxing against him and not saying anything. Even though he had been somewhat grumpy about it, she and her brother had been alternating nights curled up with him. They could tell it was helping so they were ignoring his grumping at them. In a way his grumping about it, because he never asked them to stop let them know he did appreciate their attention and help.

Mike cleared his throat after meeting Abby's eyes, "Actually, I do have some information on your sister. Assuming she keeps improving as she has, she will be moved to the pack medical section either Sunday evening or sometime Monday. The doctors are very pleased with her recovery and her healing. She still has a way to go but Olivia is doing much better." He glanced at Abby again as Tessa tried to comfort Zane. At one point he and Abby did have a relationship, though both knew it was only until one or the other had found their mate, as she had. **I can't wait until she comes home since it will help Zane to be able to step back and recover even more.** He could feel Zane's fear of walking into the hospital.

Abby met Mike's eyes briefly before looking at Tessa as she comforted Zane. She had an arm around Oscar and another around Melody, "I know I'm pleased to hear it. It will be good for all of you to have her back on pack territory." **I understand Mike and so does my mate. We know how hard it had been on you to hear about what happened. He is working on some food right now for when everyone goes home.**

Zane couldn't help but rest one hand on one of Tessa's as she wrapped an arm around him. **Can everyone give me some room to talk to Olivia?** He sent a different message to Tessa. **Not you since this is going to be hard enough.* He needed her comfort,* "I want to talk to you for a few minutes Olivia. Nothing horrible but I do want to." Well maybe moderately horrible depending on how she might look at it.

Everyone traded looks before Mike chased them out of the room. Once they had left Olivia looked at Zane and was almost worried by what he might have to say, "What do you need to talk about Zane?" Somehow, she had a feeling it was going to be hard for him to talk about. She also noticed how Tessa was relaxing against Zane's back.

Zane had to look down at their hands, "When I saw you right after surgery, I lost it Liv. I freaked, and they had to take me home. I ended up crying my heart out as the Luna held me. All I could see was how you might have looked coming from the first surgeries and being all alone. I kept seeing you dying as well. It almost destroyed me and if the Luna hadn't been there, I don't know what might have happened." Zane was feeling like he had failed her twice now. First at the doctor's appointment and then when she came out of surgery.

Olivia used a hand grip to sit as upright as possible and pulled him close, "Good for you, Zane. I'm glad you were finally able to go to the Luna. I'm sorry you were so scared but good for you." She had to wince as her movements hurt some, but it honestly it wasn't very bad, "I have been so scared for you. You changed and weren't the brother I knew anymore unless nobody was around. I didn't want to lose you either." She didn't cry but it was obvious she was considering it.

Zane helped her sit up and wrapped his arms around her and he did cry, "I'm still so scared Liv. It is terrifying to even consider letting someone else close though there are some who are trying to force it." He wasn't going to cry even more so he resorted to some humor, "I don't know why but certain people are refusing to fall for my grumpy bad boy attitude."

Tessa ended up nipping him on the side of his neck lightly for the joke. She still didn't say anything since she was just there to help support him. If she hadn't been around, it would have been Oscar. This was more than he had said to anyone even after breaking down with the Luna.

Liv held on to him and relaxed in his arms, "Zane, I think it is too late for you to try and hide. Melody is most definitely your friend, Rico, Simone, and Paul are in your corner. Tessa and Oscar are now living with us, well us when I come back home. Let them help you." She leaned back and carefully shifted position in the bed, "Now bring me the darn homework. I don't want to do it and don't have the urge, but I need to start doing it again." She didn't care but it would change the subject. Just for good measure she grumbled as she said it.

Tessa gave Zane one more light hug before moving away and found Olivia's pack and started pulling the stuff out, "There is a fair amount since you have been mostly asleep or not all there this week. Oscar and I can help you with it while we are here." This was to give Zane some room as well.

*****

The next morning rolled around, and Zane stretched and gave Oscar a good pet since he was curled up next to him. The twins hadn't even bothered waiting for him to fall asleep before hopping into bed. At least they weren't stripping and shifting in his room before hopping into bed, "Morning Oscar and I will see you in a few." He rolled out of bed and grabbed some clothes from his drawers and headed towards the bathroom.

When he came out, he was grumbling since at some point it appeared Olivia had slipped a ringer in on him. His shirt was a dark purple with traces of red and orange. When he had checked his drawers most of his shirts had been replaced with similar colors. Right now, he felt like a really bad sunrise or sunset. When he stomped downstairs, he glowered at everyone in the kitchen and just for good measure growled, "I know Olivia had something to do with this. I will deal with her, and nobody will interfere." He was thinking about trading all her clothes out for something goth looking. Maybe something with lots of red and black for good measure.

Melody stared at him and had to turn away even as she started laughing at him, "It looks good on you Zane... It really does."

Even as she was dying laughing, Oscar and Tessa lowered their heads, "We didn't do it Zane. Even if Olivia asked us to, we couldn't have gone against your wishes." It did leave several people who could.

Zane glowered even more just for good measure, "I will find out who is responsible for this and either glower, bite, or kick them." Just for good measure he turned to Melody, "So not getting invited to the dance next weekend."

Melody returned the glower before turning to her food, "Thank you Oscar for the food, it is really good. Might you like to go to the dance next Friday? It appears I'm not interested in inviting anyone else." She silently added, **I'm teasing Zane but to be honest we are probably all going and yes it includes both of you.**

Oscar blushed deeply and settled for picking up the table with his sister. Both had traded looks and had finally decided Zane and Melody were just messing with each other. It still wasn't for them to get involved in the disagreement. It was their job to keep the team running smoothly even with ruffled fur.

*****

David had invited Leon over the night before and they were sitting out back. David's mother had been so horrified by stepping in the animal crap she had ended up deciding to remain late at a spa after she had finished work. Since his father tended to be gone many evenings, because David knew he had a mistress, it left David to his own desires. In this case both he and Leon had a beer as they were sitting on the porch, "I know the fucker was laughing at me at lunch. He is going to pay damn it. I'm going to get even with him."

Leon took a slug of the beer before saying anything, "David, you know I agree he went too far but I saw his expression. Do you really think he gives a shit about anything?" Frankly the expression Leon had seen from Zane had chilled him to the bone. It was almost as if Zane had been begging them to take a shot at him. Leon honestly didn't think Zane cared one bit about anything. Why, he didn't know and didn't care. Zane had scared him though he wasn't going to say it. There was just something chilling about him.

David tossed back a good drink as well, "But he does Leon, he might not show it but look at the way he protected those two losers. The moment we started to put them in their place he jumped up and came over. God knows why he should care since both are probably fucking gay." He snarled it out before spitting on the lawn. At least most of the damage had been cleaned up. David was sure he could still smell the stink of the shit which had been scattered around.

Leon sipped on the beer before tossing the bottle in a trashcan. Once he had finished it, he had pulled another one out and opened it, "It might have been simply an excuse he used to glare and snarl at us. Ya know, to try and provoke you into doing something stupid. I saw the look he gave you. Something happened, and he don't care." As far as the twins, Leon didn't give a damn. They were skinny little pansies and were fun to push around or had been.

He finished his beer as well and grabbed another one as he considered what Leon had said. After David flipped several mental coins, he grudgingly had to agree, "Yah, might be true but yah know they might still be a way to get to him. He put his foot out and made a stand. Even if he doesn't care, if he doesn't keep watching them and something happens..." David gave Leon a malicious grin, "He will lose a fair amount of the rep he gained."

Now that was something Leon hadn't considered, and he returned the malicious grin with one of his own, "Now that is a good point. So are you thinking about..." He gave his long-time friend a look. When he met David's eyes he started laughing and to many the sound would be chilling.

David smirked at him, "Damn straight and what I'm thinking is..." They started discussing it as they sucked down a few more beers before going back inside. It was common for Leon to spend the night at David's house.

*****

Friday at school seemed to go well and for the moment David and Leon seemed to be ignoring Zane. It was appreciated but it also made Zane rather suspicious of what was going on. In his experience, until a bully was faced down and sometimes even smacked down, they didn't back off. They were cowards but as long as they thought they had power, they wouldn't go away. Zane was going to make a point of watching them to make sure they didn't do something stupid enough to get his wolf involved.

When they reached the house after going to the hospital he was feeling rather beat. He had been doing the training as well as going to the hospital, doing his homework, and watching those two. Zane needed the weekend to recover. It also hadn't helped having Olivia almost order him to take tomorrow afternoon off. Melody had run with it and decided they were going to catch a movie and relax.

It had made him growl and grump at both Olivia and Melody though he had a feeling they were amused by it. It had made him want to grump at them even more, but he had finally settled for glowering at them until it was time to head home. When they had arrived, dinner had been fixed and it had been darn good. Since Zane now knew about the twin's parents, they were making their presence more known in the house, he figured they'd helped. It still bothered him to be, what felt like, waited on hand and foot. It wasn't all that comfortable since he had grown up where you did everything for yourself and were self-reliant.

Eventually the twin's parents had left, and Mike had gone to the pack house for some reason. Once everyone was gone, he flopped in a chair. Zane had been wanting to talk to the twins, but it seemed like there was someone always there. He hadn't wanted anyone around when he talked to them since he didn't want to embarrass them in front of their friends. Now it was one thing he was sure of; they were all becoming friends.

Almost before he realized it Oscar had brought him a bottle of cold water before settling down next to his sister on the couch. Zane took a sip of the water and sighed, "I'm glad everyone is gone since I wanted to talk to both of you. I do appreciate what you have been doing for both Olivia and me. I know I haven't been the happiest about this. It isn't because you are doing anything wrong but because I just don't feel really comfortable with it." He took another sip of the water and waited for them to say something.

Oscar traded looks with Tessa before he spoke. When he did his voice was quiet yet still happy, "We can tell Zane, you appreciate what we have been doing. This is something we grew up knowing would happen though. It isn't something *trained* into us, it is who we are. Our wolves feel this as well. Our parents have been taking care of your uncle for long time. Our mother even before she found her mate. They love and care for Mike and he feels the same. They take care of him, and he protects them. It is a wolf thing and just part of pack life." He stopped talking but Tessa took over.

"We like you Zane and not just because you protected us. Most of the more senior wolves have protected us but you invited us to your table and introduced us to your friends. We can feel your wolf watching over us and wanting to protect us. The other night when you ordered us to remain behind and told us why it felt so special. It showed you cared as well." She gave him a very pleased smile as she was talking, "Even as hurt and scared as you are, you protected us. It's why we want to help take care of you." Just to tease him she had to add, "Even if you are sometimes grumpy and growly."

Zane did his best to try and understand but it was still so foreign to him. His wolf tried to explain it but, in this case, it was the wolf vs human aspect. Zane hadn't grown up with this and his wolf simply couldn't understand why Zane felt this way. It was rather frustrating to both, which did cause both to be grumpy at times. He took a moment to try and come up with something to say after listening to both before what Tessa said hit. Zane sat up and glowered at her, "You deserved to be both frowned and growled at for that Tessa."

He sighed before continuing, "Oscar, I honestly used what was happening as a way to confront David and Leon. I was sick of his whispering and needling me behind my back. When he started to bully the two of you it gave me a reason to go and face him down. Call it what you want but that started it. I wanted a reason to confront him and almost force him into a fight. Yes, I'm glad I kept him from bullying you more than he did, but that was the main reason I did what I did." He honestly felt bad for admitting it. Zane was growing to appreciate them, but it was still hard for him. He did not want to stop, as they deserved his protection, and it was something his wolf was firm on.

"I'm sorry but as hard as I try and as hard as my wolf tries to explain this to me, I just don't understand." Zane took another drink from the water bottle as he struggled to understand and even try to accept what they said, "I do appreciate everything you have done for Liv though. Especially you Oscar, since she will let you help her." Zane had to yawn and then sat up, "I'm going to head to bed and try and work this out in my mind."

Both had come to understand the first day had been due to David. It did hurt some knowing he had used them to get to him, but he had protected them then invited them to his table. Both stood and came over and gave him a good hug, "We will try not to get too obvious as we help you, Zane. You do care and that's what matters." Both held him for a few minutes before stepping back.

Zane grumbled at them, but it was half-hearted at best, "I'm going to bed. Sleep well both of you and see you in the morning." He knew one or the other would curl up with him as they had been doing. Maybe once Liv came back, he could convince them to do it for her instead. Zane headed upstairs and after changing to his shorts crawled into bed and crashed.

*****

The next morning after going to the hospital and visiting Olivia for a while, Zane stood, "Before you yell at me or something I'm going to head out. We are catching a bus to the mall and see what is playing. Is there anything you might want?" Today he hadn't bothered bringing his bag with him since he had done most of his homework. Tomorrow, he would finish it after coming back from the hospital. Zane gave Olivia a good long hug before leaving.

Liv grinned at him, "Good, I was about to break out a crutch and wave it at you." She returned the hug and waved at the others as they left. She was feeling much better and though Olivia was still on pain meds it was nothing like the first few days.

That comment received a snort and laughter from all in the room, "Just for that I'm going to expect you to have all of your homework done tomorrow before I leave." Zane stood and headed towards the door, "Later sis, we will let you know how the movie goes." It took a moment or two for everyone to leave the room since everyone stopped to give Olivia a hug.

The bus ride to the mall was not something Zane enjoyed. School was one thing, but this was enough to drive his wolf up the wall. He was used to the scents and people on the school bus. For public transportation, it was a whole different category of misery. Unwashed bodies, the stench of bad food, alcohol, drugs, and others he didn't want to identify. By the time they made it to the mall and climbed off the bus he was almost ready to ralph, "God, how did I used to do it? It was bad enough as a human but now?" He shuddered as he was speaking. Zane did make sure nobody else was around when he said it.

Rico had to blink and then gave Zane a friendly pat on the shoulder, "It will get better Zane, you are getting used to the sounds, scents, and things at school. This you will get used to as well." He had to agree it would never be his preferred way of getting around.

With a shake of his head, Zane headed into the mall. This was really the first time he had left the property other than school. From what he understood most of it was due to him being a new wolf. Now he was starting to form a team, the idea still bothered him, he was being given more freedom. They were talking as they walked in, and Zane caught a whiff of food, "Let's check the time for the movies and then get something to eat." He was hungry though chances were good it wasn't going to be as good as at home.

Everyone agreed with him and headed to the theater. The girls were trying talk the guys into going to some romance movie which they shot down. After a great deal of discussion, they ended up going with the newest hunger games movie. After purchasing the tickets, they headed to the food court. **Damn it, my nose keeps getting distracted. Even my wolf is starting to get a nose overload.** A sneeze caught him unaware and it almost felt like his hair stood up he sneezed so hard.

When he sneezed, everyone jumped and started laughing at him before ribbing him a bit just for good measure. He had to sneeze one more time before he felt somewhat better, "Well crap, it did help somewhat. Now for some food." As they were teasing them, he returned the favor. To be honest he was starting to enjoy the afternoon. Chances are he wouldn't admit it, but he was beginning to feel relaxed.

Tessa couldn't resist and patted him on the shoulder, "There, there, I'm sure you will feel better after some food and a nap..." When Zane turned and looked horrified at her comment, she had to giggle at him. **You feel more relaxed Zane and it's nice to see.**

Once they reached the food court, they looked around and settled on pizza. There was a place that had deep dish by the slice and after placing an order moved off to the side while waiting for it. Eventually it was done and all of them were starting to drool. It didn't take very long before the trays and plates were almost licked clean. Simone burped and sighed, "Food at home is good but sometimes a nice greasy slice of pizza just hits the spot."

They were all agreeing when Tessa stood, "Back in a moment." She headed towards the nearest bathroom as the others were starting to pick up the mess and toss it out. By the time she was entering the bathroom the others were headed in the same direction.

As she was walking in, she didn't notice Leon start to walk out of the men's room and jerk back in. Leon turned to David, "Hey, the stupid girl just walked into the bathroom. Wanna wait for her to come out and screw with her?"

David didn't even think twice before a malicious smile crossed his face, "Damn straight." The idea the others in her group might be there never even crossed his mind, "Push her around a bit and make a few threats before shoving her back into the bathroom and leaving. Sounds like fun."

They gave her a moment to get inside before coming out and loitering near the girl's room. This set of bathrooms weren't used much which was why they were there in the first place. The lack of people gave them a chance for the occasional bit of random vandalism. When Tessa came out, David grabbed her and shoved her against Leon.

Leon leered at her, "Oh what is this? Some skanky girl? Bet you are putting out for the bad boy, right?" He shoved her back to David.

Tessa didn't even think before screaming, even as they were shoving her back and forth between them. What they were saying was horrible and vile. How could they even think such things?

Zane and his group were almost at the entrance to the hall which led to the bathrooms when they heard the scream. All of them instantly knew who it was but almost before they could react, Zane had vanished. Based on the feelings from his wolf they were going for blood. By now they could also scent David and Leon. **Oh, damn this isn't going to be good.** Melody shot down the hallway as fast as she could. To be honest she was shocked at how fast Zane had moved since he was still growing into his wolf. Maybe if it had been mentioned he had been born with inactive wolf DNA, it would have been understandable, but it hadn't, so it had caught the others almost flat footed.

When Zane came around the corner, the only reason he didn't take David out was because Tessa was between them. He had to alter his path some but as he approached, his hands were reaching out. He hit David from an off angle which was about the only thing which saved the boy. By the time Zane recovered enough to do anything the others were there in the hall as well.

Rico and Simone were restraining Leon while Oscar had his arms around Tessa and was holding her for all he was worth. Melody had made the decision to 'run into' Zane to keep him from killing David. She knocked him enough off balance it gave her a moment. **Zane don't! Don't kill him or hurt him too much. Not good for pack. Remember Pack comes first. Tessa needs you.** Thankfully her wolf was thinking at his wolf as well.

Zane staggered but recovered even as Melody was sending to him. It was just enough to keep him from killing David. He jerked the larger boy towards him even as he whirled around and slammed him against the wall, and it wasn't a gentle slam. It was hard enough to knock the wind out of David. Even as one hand was curled up in the others shirt, Zane's other hand went for his groin and grasped, "If you ever come near Tessa, Melody, Simone, or any other female I will rip your pencil dick off as well as your balls. Remember I don't care what happens to me. I will not kill you but that's all I will promise." His face was inches away from David's and the sound of grinding teeth was clearly heard even as Zane was talking. His eyes were even more empty than they had been the other day, "Remember this, you yellow chicken shit bastard. I don't fucking care." After one more good squeeze of David's nuts he dropped him.

He looked at Leon, "The same goes for you. I won't kill you but start to imagine what can be done which is worse than death." His eyes were almost pitch black as he was talking, "Rico knock the breath out of him and then we are leaving." He walked over to Tessa and Oscar, "They will not hurt either of you again. This I promise." All thoughts about the movie were completely gone from their minds. **We are leaving.**

CHAPTER 11

The Attack

Zane heard an ooph from Leon as Rico slugged him in the gut. He didn't give a damn since he had his arms around Tessa as he was urging her and Oscar away from the bathrooms. **Does anyone know if there might be a wolf nearby we can get a ride from? We need to get to the pack house and talk to the Alpha.** He had to do it before anything else, since it was about the only thing keeping him from going back and killing David.

Oscar looked up at Zane. **Mom is here since Beta Mike had asked her to pick up a few things for Olivia. Some nice sheets, something to put up in the hospital room at the pack, stuff like that. It was to keep the room from looking boring and white.** They knew Olivia would probably be in the clinic section for at least another week and maybe two. Now that much of the initial healing was taken care of, she would heal slower. It would still be faster than a normal human until the wolf blood was out of her system.

Zane nodded, **Thanks Oscar, Abby it is Zane. We had a confrontation with a bully from school and need to go to the pack house and talk to the Alpha.** Even now he was having to struggle not to do something stupid which was half the reason he was holding Tessa. She needed him now more than he needed to kill the bastard. **I'm very close to shifting and need to get out of here. I will explain later.**

Abby could sense just how on edge Zane was and turned to her mate, "Something happened, and Zane needs me to take him to the Alpha. I will have someone come and pick you and the stuff up." **Where are you? I can meet you at the nearest entrance to your section. Get outside and wait for me.** She was also sensing shock and fear from Tessa, so it had to involve her in some way.

Since all were included in the sending Zane nodded at Melody since he had no idea where they were. Instead, he contacted his uncle, **Uncle Mike I need to talk to the you and the Alpha and the Luna. David and Leon caught Tessa alone and were pushing her around and making some very nasty comments. He is alive and mostly in one piece but if this isn't dealt with, I will kill him if he ever comes near them again.** At this point his wolf was impacting heavily on Zane. **Abby is going to bring us to the pack house.**

Abby had already contacted Mike, and he was already heading towards the pack house. **Have her bring you straight to his office. We will be waiting for you. Tell me briefly what happened. Keep Tessa in your arms to keep your wolf from clawing his way out. She needs you right now more than anything else.** He was most definitely not happy even though he didn't know what had happened.

As Zane was dealing with Abby and his uncle the others were surrounding the two and Oscar. Simone was comforting Oscar since he was reacting to what his sister had experienced. With the bond between twins, it was in some ways as close as a mating bond, though not quite the same. Almost the second Tessa had screamed he had been hit by her panic and it had felt like his heart had stopped.

Zane sent his uncle what little he had heard and seen before his wolf had taken over. Once he had sent it, he turned back to focusing on Tessa. **Tessa, I'm here, and I'm going to take care of you. The Luna is going to be waiting as well and she will comfort you.** Frankly, he was about ready to ask if they could call the cops and have charges pressed.

They walked out of the mall about then and Abby was at the curb and waiting. Thankfully, Mike had her bring his large SUV, so there was plenty of room. Mike had told her a bit of what had happened, and she was most definitely an angry mama wolf. Her pups had other run-ins with those two and even though the pack had mostly taken care of them she was done. Abby wanted this dealt with and now. She might not normally be a fighter, but these were her pups and she wanted them taken care of with, "Get in pups and then we will leave."

Shortly after the pups had headed towards the exit, several people including security headed into the hallway to the bathroom, checking out reports of screams. They found the two boys struggling to get back up. Frankly Zane had scared David so badly he had damn near pissed his pants. If he hadn't just used the bathroom, he probably would have. Leon was trying to catch his breath, and he was just pissed off as of now.

Since Zane had been focusing on David much of what he had said hadn't carried over. Leon had still felt some but when Rico had slugged him, he had been shocked. Rico was a rather scrawny kid and didn't look very strong. When he had slugged him, it had driven the air out of his lungs and took him several minutes to catch his breath. By the time the security guards had arrived he had finally caught his breath. Leon didn't even bother to look at David to see what he might want. He just opened his mouth, "We were beat up by some kids from school. They beat us up just because."

The security guard placed a call over his radio to have a police cruiser sent out, "Contact your parents and have them come down here. We will take it from there." He had dealt with these two before, but he had to follow procedure.

*****

When they finally arrived at the pack house Zane was still worked up and barely hanging on. As soon as they stepped out of the car Mike came over and grasped Zane's shoulder, "Look at me, Zane. Do not shift. Do not allow your emotions to take over right now. This is an order from your uncle and a more dominant wolf. Later we can deal with what you are feeling but for now we need to focus on Tessa and Oscar.

He needs your support as well." Mike urged him towards Oscar since Tessa was being held by their mother.

The Luna had come out with as well and came over. She took a moment to comfort Tessa even as Zane was being ordered not to shift by his uncle. Esther took several minutes to comfort and calm the others even as Zane wrapped an arm around Oscar. She wanted to smile but it wasn't the right thing, "The Alpha is in his office. Follow me and keep calm. We need to know everything which happened."

Everyone followed the Luna into the house and to the Alpha's office. For this he was seated at the head of his conference table, "Come in and sit down please. Mike, you and Zane need to be..." He told everyone where to sit to both show dominance level as well as for support for each other, "What happened Zane. Tell me everything you know."

Zane settled down with his uncle on one side and Oscar on the other. He had to take several slow deep breaths as he was being taught in the wolf class. It was to calm down you and your wolf and to try and step back from what had angered you. Zane wasn't very good at it yet, but it sort of felt like it might be helping. Both of his hands were clenched on the top of the table. **I do not think I can speak and be understandable. What I saw today was...** Zane detailed hearing the scream, smelling the two, then coming around the corner and seeing David and Leon shoving Tessa around. He didn't realize it, but he was also showing the memory of what he had seen.

What he had seen had included one shoving from the back and the other shoving their hands against her chest. **I don't really know what they might have been saying Alpha. All I saw was them attacking Tessa and then red. If Melody hadn't stopped me, I would have...** He didn't know what he would have done and that scared him badly.

Kadrian didn't bother getting worked up at the moment. **Damien, I need you in my office, now.** He needed to get to the bottom of this. **Thank you, Zane, now look at me.** His sending had power in it. When Zane looked up and met his eyes Kadrian spoke again. *_Zane, calm_ *down. I need you to calm down to discuss this.** He didn't bother saying it was an order.

Zane forced his head up and met the Alpha's eyes and it was like they looked into his soul. When he spoke, Zane and his wolf had to respond. Both lifted their chin and lowered their eyes in total submission. **Yes Alpha.** He felt a surge of calmness hit and he instantly started to relax. Somehow, he knew it was to give him a time to be able to talk reasonably.

Kadrian looked at Esther before looking at Tessa. When he spoke, his voice was far quieter and gentle, "Tessa, I need to know what happened. I know this is hard, but the Luna is here to help and the same for your mother. Zane is here as well as your friends. Please tell me but if it is to hard tell Esther and she can relay it to me."

Tessa had ended up moving over to the Luna's lap while her mother took the seat Tessa had been in. She tucked her face into the Luna's neck as Zane was talking. Once he was done and started talking to her, she started shivering even more. After trying to send to the Alpha she ended up simply opening her mind to the Luna, so she could get what she wanted.

Esther very gently took the memories from Tessa. Even though it didn't show in the way she dealt with Tessa her eyes were starting to change colors. Once she was done, she turned and looked at both Kadrian and Mike. **Those two people were making very nasty innuendo's including suggesting she was putting out for Zane and the others. This has gone too far. We have had other complaints about these two and I'm sick of it.** She had to swallow her growl, "Abby, your mate is going to be here very shortly. Take Tessa to the clinic and have her checked to make sure she is okay. Simone and Melody, go with them. Rico, you will remain here."

Zane could feel his wolf wanting to get worked up again, but the Alpha's command was forcing them not to. He finally settled for pressing his palms against the granite tabletop and staring at the fine grain of the stone. When a bottle of water was sat down between his hands he glanced up at Oscar, “Thank you Oscar.” He was most definitely going to have to do something very nice for the two. Zane would talk to Mike and their parents later about it.

Even as Mike and Kadrian were discussing this over the pack bonds, Oscar settled down next to Zane and Rico on the other side of Oscar. Zane stared at the water bottle and wondered if it was safe to pick up. Not because Zane wondered if Oscar did anything to it but as worked up as he was, he could see squeezing too hard if he touched it. It would be rather messy and get the water all over the place.

Zane finally sat up and rubbed his face for a moment before stretching. **I'm sorry I wasn't there sooner for Tessa, Oscar. I just never expected anything like that.**

Even as they were talking Damien walked in and had Mindy with him, “Dad, Mindy has some information for us, she also was at the mall but was too late to do anything about what happened. She did see mall security respond and a short time later, police showed up. Mindy listened and heard David and Leon giving a report Zane and the others beat them up for no reason.”

Kadrian had glanced up and then snarled, “Thank you Damien and thank you Mindy. Sit down and wait to see if we need more from you.” He pulled his phone open and dialed 911, “This is Kadrian Mac Tire' Dona and I need to report a sexual assault. It happened at the Twin Pine Mall about a half hour to forty-five minutes ago. The assault was done by a David Walpert and a Leon Baker. Please have an officer come to One Varg Drive and at the gate have them ask for Mr. Kadrian Mac Tire' Dona. Thank you.”

Kadrian and Mike were less than pleased by what they had learned, and they were done. Even though they hated making waves in the human world, there were some things which wouldn't be allowed. Most of the wolves were capable of taking care of themselves when it came to bullying by humans. The junior most wolves couldn't for the most part. It just wasn't in their make up since they were more inclined to run than fight. It wasn't to protect unlike the more senior wolves, this included the more senior of the middle rank wolves as well.

Oscar leaned lightly against Zane and shook slightly. **Not your fault Zane and you did protect her. Why can't they just leave us alone? All we want to do is go to school and then take care of those who protect us.**

Zane looked at Kadrian before glancing away, "With your permission sir, we are going to go and wait for Tessa to be done. We won't leave the house until you say we can." The meal tonight was going to be flash fried to the point it was barely brown on the outside.

Kadrian looked at the three, "Go and I will send someone for you when the police arrive." He had sent instructions for Damien and Mindy to remain in the office.

As they were walking out Zane stopped and looked at Mindy, "Thank you for your support." He kept going after saying it though. When they reached the medical waiting room, they found the twin's father waiting. He sat down next to him. Zane couldn't think of anything to say and settled for relaxing with Oscar between him and his father.

*****

It wasn't much later when two police cars pulled up. Once was a patrol car and the other an unmarked vehicle. The officers were escorted into the Alpha's office. He looked up and waved them to the seats across from his desk, "Pleased have a seat. Since there are two groups of you, I'm going to assume one is about the alleged assault and the other the alleged sexual assault, correct?" Currently, Mike was in the office since Zane was upstairs.

The two dressed in suits nodded, "I'm Detective Luis, and this is Detective Sanchez. We need to take statements from those reporting the sexual assault. These two officers are here to talk to the parents of the ones reported as having assaulted two people at the mall."

Kadrian nodded to Mike, "This is Mike Donovan who is the uncle of Zane Donovan. Zane's parents were killed in an accident several months ago and he is Zane's guardian. Right now, Tessa and the others are in our small clinic waiting while Tessa gets checked out. I will have someone escort you to the clinic and then bring the others back. Once you are done talking with Tessa you will be escorted back, and you can talk to the others. I assume they will be mostly done by the time you get back." As he was talking one of his wolves stepped into the room, "Take the detectives to the clinic and bring the others back."

The detectives gave Mr. Mac Tire' Dona an odd look as he gave instructions. They knew of him and his odd family, but they also knew he treated all his workers well. His companies were good for the local economy, and they donated and supported several charities. Later they might ask but for now they wanted to talk to the victim, and they were getting what they needed without delay. Later they could ask as to why he was taking care of this, "Thank you Mr. Mac Tire' Dona." Both stood up and walked out of the room.

*****

Once the doctor was done examining Tessa, she opened the door, "Mr. Fletcher, Oscar, Zane, you can come in. Everyone else needs to wait." She stepped off to the side and allowed the three in as the two other girls left the room. Once they had left the room the doctor closed the door, "She is physically fine though she does have a few bruises." They would be gone soon enough but since they were so junior, they weren't as strong or healed quite as fast as the more dominant wolves.

Zane hurried over but stopped at the edge of the bed. **Do you want a hug or a shoulder to lean on?** He had no idea what to do or how to act now. This was not something he had ever dealt with before and was feeling lost.

Tessa held her arms out to Zane and gave him a stricken look. **I can't even begin to believe anyone would say that.** When Zane settled down, she wrapped her arms around him and clung on. When Oscar settled down on the other side of the bed and leaned against her, she sent him thanks.

Zane took the hint and gathered her close and held her as she started to cry. **Because they are cowards and have to tear down others, just so they feel big. I know better, Oscar knows better, and so does everyone else.*

*I might still have issues with being waited on by you and Oscar, but I like you and Oscar and both of you are really nice.** He was doing his best not to squeeze the stuffing out of her as his emotions were surging back and forth. He and his wolf did like the twins and they did feel protective of them. Zane was also feeling the urge to keep others away from him. For the moment he was going to lean on his wolf to give him the strength to comfort both Tessa and Oscar.

As he was holding Tessa, he wrapped an arm around Oscar as well. **Abby, Brandon, I'm sorry I wasn't close enough to protect Tessa. My wolf and I are seriously pissed off about what happened.** Zane felt odd using their first names, but it was expected. He felt really bad about not being able to protect the two which again was causing an emotional surge.

Esther moved forward and stroked Zane's hair. **Zane, you couldn't have expected this or known it was going to happen. When it did happen, you took care of them. On top of that, you listened to Melody and avoided hurting them too badly. The police are here and going to want to talk to both you and Tessa. I know you are going to want to be in the room when they talk to her, but you can't. I will take care of her for you. I'm also going to ensure your wolf doesn't take over. This is a great deal of stress for both of you and we don't need a stress-based change.**

Zane moved away from Tessa slightly and took several slow deep breaths, "Tessa I'm going to have to leave shortly. Lean on the Luna and your parents. I will be here for you and tomorrow we will talk about what the two of you can do for Liv, assuming she is transferred here." He leaned forward and gave her and Oscar a good hug before standing up.

Moments later there was a knock on the door followed by it being opened. The wolf at the door gave everyone a polite nod, "I have some detectives who wish to talk to Tessa about what happened. Doctor, they will probably want to talk to you as well. Zane, Oscar you need to come with me. There are officers downstairs who need to talk to you." He waited for the two in the room to follow him. The other pups followed behind. The wolf knew Abby would remain behind, though Brandon came out with the others.

Zane was back to his almost expressionless face and empty eyes. He couldn't help it, since it was a defensive reaction. He silently walked out of the room and followed the wolf along with the others. Even with the Luna's help, he could feel both he and his wolf starting to tense up again. This was not going to be fun, and he was going to probably go for a run later. He needed to howl his brains out now.

When they walked into the room, he found the other parents there as well as his uncle and the officers. Since everyone was seated at the table Zane moved over and sat down next to his uncle. Frankly, he didn't want to talk to anyone, for any reason right now, other than his family and friends. When Oscar and his father sat down as well, Zane glanced up and gave Oscar a tight smile.

One of the officer's stated, "We had a report of an assault at the Twin Pine mall. It was filed by David Walpert and Leon Baker against Zane Donovan and..." The officer listed the names and then what they had been told. Once done he looked up at Zane and his uncle, "It was indicated Zane was the first and Fredrico Phillips assaulted Leon Baker at Zane Donovan's request."

Zane glanced at his uncle and received a nod from him. **Zane, mention the other things David has done to you. Don't mention what you have heard about David's history. Let it be drawn out.** "Go ahead and tell them what you know Zane. Tell them the truth and don't hide anything."

Zane pressed his hands against the top of the table and did his best to keep from losing it. As he was speaking his voice was tense and rough, "Today at the mall we had been intending to go to a movie but had time to eat. Once we were done eating, Tessa left to go to the bathroom. We stayed to pick up the table and headed that way ourselves. We were almost there and..." Zane talked about hearing the scream and dashing down the hallway. He admitted to shoving David away from Tessa and slamming him against the wall. He did his best to be as factual as he could, but it was obvious he was extremely pissed off.

The second officer had been making notes, "Do you have any sort of history with David which might explain this? I mean what you say happened to Tessa and why he might have done this?" This officer didn't take anything at face value and until proven he didn't take sides.

Zane wanted to growl but it was blocked as well. He had to take a ragged breath before he could speak again, "There is. I lost my parents a while back. On the first day of school..." He went on to describe the first morning and then when David and Leon tried to pick on him and bully him. Zane explained how he had finally faced the two down and made sure to explain he had also done it for Tessa and Oscar. He did not mention why he had done it as it had offended him.

After a some more questions they started questioning the other kids involved. When it came to Oscar, Zane linked to him and sent him as much comfort as he could. Zane knew Oscar was still feeling the impact of his sister's emotions on him and he needed it. As Zane was helping it, he felt the others in his group starting to pull together and support the boy. It both scared Zane and felt good since Zane knew this was drawing the junior wolves closer to him. He might have to talk to the Luna again and then Uncle Mike at some point.

Eventually they were done with the questioning shortly before the detectives came back. The four officers stepped out of the room to discuss the two sides and eventually came to a conclusion. For now, they decided the children were going to be released to the parents, pending charges. When they came back in the senior detective spoke, "The reports will need to go to the DA's office for further review. For the moment, we are releasing the children to their parents. Remain at home and no going to the mall or anywhere else without supervision. Monday, I would suggest you keep them at home as well. This is going to be sent to the school administrators, and we don't want any involvement with those charged." After getting some documents signed the four officers left the house.

When they walked out Zane looked down at the top of the table and frankly, he was having some significant issues. His feelings were at war and even Zane knew he needed someone to talk to, "If the Luna is available would it be possible to talk to her?" He could feel his hands wanting to curl into fists and his wolf wanting to break free of the compulsions.

Mike was less than happy, as were the other adults. This spoke to their wolves and their wolves' reactions, "I'm going to take Oscar, Tessa, and their parents' home. The Luna will be able to talk to you and the others. Don't be gone too long if you can Zane, Tessa and Oscar will need you as well." He stood and gave Brandon a nod. The twins didn't need to see Zane losing it again . **We will talk at my house and go from there.**

Most of the adults stayed with their pups to be there when the Luna came in. It was only a few minutes longer before she walked in with Abby and soon they were out of the room. Once they were Zane kept looking at the tabletop even as an angry and frustrated growl broke loose. **Ma'am, I need your help. I... I...** He finally lifted his hands to his face and covered his eyes. Zane was so angry and frustrated!

The Luna came over and pulled him up and into her arms. **Come Zane, you and the others need to shift.** She gave the more dominant pups a nod, "I will bring them back shortly. They need this to calm down and relax some." Esther led them out of the Alpha's room, "Strip and shift. The keeper of the bunnies is going to release a number for you to hunt. Let your wolves take care of the need for blood and then you will feel better." She quickly shifted and stood there waiting.

Zane was a bit slower to strip since he was still uncomfortable . Eventually though he had changed and after giving a good stretch he bumped shoulders with Rico and Melody. He even bumped Simone's shoulder before one more good stretch. **I have a feeling I'm going to need help catching a rabbit.** It was almost a mortifying comment but both he and his wolf knew they still had a great deal to learn.

Esther hid a smile. This was actually a good thing since it should distract him from what had happened for a short time. **Then that's what* *we will do. Some hunting training will be perfect now. Shall we?** She deliberately bumped Zane off his paws before dashing away. As she was leaving, she sent a message to the keeper of the rabbits to release several in one of the hunting compounds. They were large and had plenty of space to allow the rabbits to run and hide.

Zane had to yip when the Luna bumped him off his paws and huffed at her. **Not nice Mrs. Esther, darn it.** He rolled to his feet and dashed after her. Even if it only ended up being a nip somewhere, he was going to get her if he could. **Mrs. Esther would it be allowable for Oscar and Tessa to shift and come over? I want to bring them a rabbit to help their wolves.** Damn it this was confusing the crap out of him. He was feeling the need to protect both of them; it included Olivia from before the crap happened, but this was a totally different level.

That is a good idea. I will take care of it. Esther and her wolf mentally smiled at Zane's request even as she ignored his huffing at her. **Mike, bring your helpers and their twins to hunt pen three. You need to help Zane learn to hunt. His wolf wants to give Oscar and Tessa a rabbit to help them.** She was so pleased with Zane's request, and it was obvious when she sent to Mike.

Mike couldn't help but smile when Esther contacted him. **Good and we will be there shortly.** "Zane is wanting some hunt training and wants to give a rabbit to the twins. The Luna contacted me about this, so we are going to change and go for a run." It would be good for the twins as well. Moments later they headed outside and shifted.

With Mike in the lead, they flashed across the property to the hunting area. It was barely a challenge for Mike to jump the fence. When he landed, he was panting in enjoyment. He could smell at least a dozen rabbits scurrying around or frozen as his scent reached them. **Zane, come and I will continue teaching you to hunt.** He lowered his nose as he was talking and caught a scent.

Zane started towards his uncle before pausing and going to Tessa and Oscar. He gently bumped Tessa and rested his head on her shoulder. Even now, he kept being shocked at how much smaller she was than he. *Tessa, relax and I will bring a rabbit or two back for you and your brother.* He nuzzled her a bit longer before turning to his uncle. Zane didn't bother apologizing for not coming directly to Mike. He knew his uncle would understand. *Thank you, Uncle, and shall we?*

They hunted for some time, since even now Zane was still getting used to the idea of killing a rabbit. His wolf wanted one and badly, but Zane was still weirded out by wanting warm blood and fresh meat. It didn't matter he teased his sister about enjoying a cow which was mooing, it was just not something he was used to yet. The first rabbit he did catch, he carried over to Tessa and dropped it in front of her. *I will be back with one for you Oscar. If you want to share this one, then share the next with Tessa, he grinned.* He nosed both before heading back into the fray.

Eventually he had caught three rabbits though it had taken him a while. The last one he devoured much to the enjoyment of his wolf and Zane felt much better. He still wanted to rip David's head off, but Zane was feeling much calmer. *Can we go home now please? I need a shower to relax before we eat.* His friends came over and bumped and gave him some comfort before they headed out of the hunting pen.

*****

It was late in the evening when Zane finally decided it was time for bed. Currently he was sitting outside with his uncle. *Mike, I need to talk to you. Not about today but something else.* Zane had been feeling rather confused by his reactions to both Oscar and Tessa. There wasn't anything sexual to it, but he felt odd crawling into bed with either or joining him even if they were in their wolf form.

Mike had fired up one of his rare bowls of pipe tobacco. Being a wolf, he didn't need to worry about cancer, and it wasn't possible to become addicted to tobacco, it did work to calm him down, although the smell did offend many werewolves, so he would shower, and his clothes would be washed. It was a pipe he had for many years and was a beautiful meerschaum pipe. The carvings on it had wolves running and playing. *Zane, you can talk to me about anything. I have been a wolf for a very long time.*

*I know your father was my brother, but I'm a fair amount older than he is. He had some wolf DNA which is probably why you are as dominant as you are. What do you want to ask?** He had fired the pipe up a short time ago and tamped the coals and tobacco down a bit more for an even burn.

Zane looked into the woods and tried to organize his thoughts. He was so worked up the scent of the smoldering tobacco didn't even affect him. **Uncle I'm confused by my feelings for the twins. There isn't anything... Um, it's just feels so odd to wake with a wolf who I know is also a person in my bed. I didn't grow up with pets and having pets in my bed. Tessa and Oscar aren't pets but... I'm not sure what to feel.** God It was embarrassing to say not to mention if you did read between the lines there could be an interest shown. It wasn't there currently, and Zane didn't want to come across that way.

Mike stared out at the woods and smiled very slightly. **Zane, it is so hard to explain, since you didn't grow up this way. You protect them and they, in their own way, protect you. They do this by comforting you, taking care of many of your needs such as food, laundry, and more. How your relationship with them develops is something the three of you will have to work out.** He wasn't going to mention it might end up in a somewhat sexual relationship with Tessa for a while, since he could smell the slight attraction. It was something Zane was going to have to figure out and decide on when he was older. Every team had to work out how they were interconnected themselves.

Zane had a feeling there was some parts his uncle wasn't telling him, but he didn't know how to ask. He had to sigh since it wasn't an answer he wanted. **Damn it, Uncle, this is really hard for me. I'm so scared, yet they and the others are calling to me and my wolf. I don't want to let anyone close to me other than you and Olivia. They are forcing me to accept them, and it scares the crap out of me.** Yes, he was repeating what he had already said but it was life. He had to work through this in a way he could understand.

Mike kept looking out at the dark forest and contemplated what to say. **Zane, I can't really give you advice on this. I wish I could, but you and the others need to figure this out. I know you have talked to the twins, and they do understand. So do the others in your team. Just do me a favor and don't force them away from you. It might sound strange but as much as I say they belong to you; you belong to them. As the leader of the team, you will tell them what to do and provide them protection. On the flip side, they will help you control your urges to be overprotective as they take care of you. It will take you time to really understand since any young wolf of sufficient rank will be dealing with this. Now why don't you go in and head towards bed. Olivia is going to be in the clinic tomorrow.**

Zane stood and slowly walked inside the house. He found Tessa and Oscar resting on the couch. Tessa was asleep, but he could tell it wasn't a good sleep. She was twitching, and slight sounds of unhappiness could be heard. Zane walked over and very carefully picked her up, "Go and shift Oscar. Tonight, she needs both of us." He started towards the stairs.

When he reached his room, Oscar was there, though he was in human form. **I'm just pulling the covers back, so you can tuck her in.** The anguish in his mental feel could be heard. Once Tessa was tucked in, he left the room.

Zane could feel his wolf starting to get worked up again. **Don't please. I can't handle it right now. Tessa and Oscar are under our protection and here. We will take care of them.** He chided his wolf before going into the bathroom and stripping down before shifting. Once he did, he trotted out and found Oscar was already curled up on the other side of Tessa. Zane hopped up on the bed and curled up, so Tessa was between them.

*****

The next morning Zane sat up and stretched before hopping down and heading to the bathroom. He changed forms and started brushing his teeth. Even as he did it, he was trying to hope against hope Liv would come home today. He wanted and needed her to be back on the property but if he hoped too much and she didn't, he was going to end up being in a bad mood. Once he was done, he stepped into the shower and relaxed under the flow of the hot water. Eventually he was feeling more relaxed and after toweling off, he peeked into his room. Thankfully both were gone, and he walked out and pulled some clothes out. Once he was done getting dressed, he almost growled since he had on some shorts and one of those damn shirts.

One thing Zane had noticed was after changing, the scars from his being hit had started to fade slightly. As of now he had some pale stripes but that was it. The scars from his being bitten were still livid red, and he had been told they would only fade a bit once all the lingering effects of the Turn were finished, and even then, the marks would be with him after that. As they started going away it made what had happened somewhat more remote to him. Once he was done, he slouched downstairs and gave his group a yawn and a nod, "Morning and, oh, coffee, coffee, coffee..." He gave them a slight grin before flopping down in a seat at the table.

Melody snorted at him and started laughing at him, "Morning to you as well Zane. I'm not sure I have seen another wolf as driven to have coffee the moment you stagger to the kitchen." Even as she was talking Oscar settled a cup in front of Zane. Right now, Tessa was relaxing in Rico's arms and trying not to think about what had happened the day before.

Tessa didn't have to have comfort from only Zane, any of the more dominant wolves in their team would work. In this case she had a feeling Zane needed a bit of space and Rico hadn't minded her asking for comfort, "Morning Zane and thank you." With both Zane and her brother curled up next to her she had slept adequately.

Zane ignored Melody as he took the cup and after checking started sipping from it, "You are welcome, Tessa. I so hope Liv comes home today. Even if she is at the pack house, I will be far more relaxed." He hated being restricted to the property since it meant he couldn't leave to be with her. Zane was going to have to wait for her to show up if she did. When a plate of food appeared in front of him, he started digging in.

The others did as well though Zane had to smile slightly when Simone ended up helping with the food. It was obvious Tessa needed the comforting and when they were done eating Zane started to help clearing the table. When Tessa stood up Zane turned and looked at her, "Relax Tessa, you need it, and I don't mind helping. Let Rico help you." He turned back to the table and continued clearing it.

*****

Eventually Zane couldn't help it and had to go for a run. Mike had contacted him and let him know Olivia was going to be there shortly. His wolf was so happy it wasn't funny, and they needed to work out their nervous energy. When he finally had to go for a run the rest of his group did as well. They had all wanted to be with Olivia when she was released but none of them could. It really upset Zane, and this was how he was going to deal with it.

When his uncle informed him Olivia was on the property Zane couldn't help but stop and lift his muzzle in a very pleased howl. Yes, there was still an under-laying sense of grief but there was pleasure that his group sensed and started howling as well. Once they were done Zane set out towards the medical section.

As they approached the house something burst from the undergrowth, what was left, since it was starting to get into autumn. Zane and his wolf didn't even think before they lunged at the small furry object and were more than shocked when they found they had a small kitten in their jaws. They hadn't bit down and simply caught it. **Um, what am I supposed to do with a kitten? Can anyone sense more of them?** He didn't tighten his mouth down since if his sister found out about it, she would beat him with a crutch or whatever was handy.

Melody snorted and came over and sniffed the kitten before trotting away. **I will check and see but go and maybe give it to Olivia? Maybe she would like a little kitty?** Frankly she was somewhat startled since cats tended to stay away from wolves due to their predatorial scent.

Zane whined before he started towards the house again. When he entered through the doggy door, several wolves glanced at him before they had to blink in confusion. Why the hell was he carrying a kitten in his mouth? Zane ignored them and kept going as he followed the scent of his sister to the room she was in. When he arrived, he scratched at the door until someone opened it.

As soon as they did, he trotted over to Olivia and dropped the somewhat damp and goober covered kitten in her lap. Once he did, he almost danced in place even as his ears twitched, and his tail wagged in happiness.

At first Olivia started to reach for a crutch until the kitten started to meow at her. When it did, she grabbed a small hand towel on her bed stand and wrapped it around the little kitty, "Oh Zane, thank you." She lifted the kitten to her cheek with one hand even as the other reached for his head. At first, she had thought it was a bunny since he was in wolf form. Even as she held the kitten the other wolves in the room were giving her odd looks.

CHAPTER 12

Attack Response

David and Leon were doing their best not to act smug when the mall cop called for the police. It was hard, but they were used to pulling the innocent kid thing. It had worked in the past and expected it to work this time. Neither even considered the others might make counter charges since they were pansies. They hung around with those two losers and protected them as if it made them look big and tough.

As the security officer was providing more information to his superior the two boys called their parents. When they called, they did their best to sound scared and pathetic though normally it didn't matter. Their parents were almost oblivious to what their boys did. They were the perfect children and obeyed when told to do something. None of their parents could believe their precious sons could be bullies. Those calls took a short time before they were told by their parents they would be there soon.

David caught Leon's eyes, and both knew this was going to be fun. They were going to get back at the others and make sure nobody fucked with them again. This would get around the school and very few would even consider getting in their way. Granted there were some people neither boy would screw with simply because they were stronger or meaner. That still left most of the little fry they could push around and not have to worry about.

When their parents arrived, David hurried over to his mom and threw his arms around her and sniffed into her shirt, “I was so scared mom, I thought they were really going to hurt me.” Leon could do his own sniveling to his mother. David’s father was furious, and he was ranting about wanting those horrible, rotten kids arrested for this. The police had arrived just before the adults.

After the officers took the statements, they talked to the crowd to see if anyone had witnessed anything. By this time David and Leon’s parents had taken them home to comfort them. As they were leaving, they were demanding justice and satisfaction for this brutal attack on their innocent children. As they were leaving Mindy made her way home since she had heard the police calling for a patrol car to go to the pack house to get their side of the story.

*****

Both sets of parents decided to go to David’s house and wait for the police to inform them the others were arrested. They simply couldn’t believe that it wouldn’t happen. While they were waiting, David and Leon slipped upstairs to David’s room. David flopped on the bed while Leon did the same in a chair, “It was so perfect. I had simply wanted to fuck with the stupid cunt. Now we get to have them arrested. Even if nothing happens, we have paid them back.”

Leon gave a crude laugh and sighed since he would love to have a beer right now. It wouldn’t be a good idea, since chances were they would be called down when the cops came back. At least now the pigs would actually earn their pay, “Her reaction and scream were great. Good thing nobody else heard it or we might be in trouble. Who would believe those losers even if they try and say something happened?” Their parents were well respected throughout the community and were always invited to the various balls and parties. The others? Who cared, they lived in some sub-division outside of town. It was probably some run-down place which was dirty and nasty.

Eventually David’s mother knocked on the door, “Come downstairs, the police are here.” She turned and walked back down and settled down next to her husband. The Detectives had asked for their boys come down before they said anything. Having a detective or two deal with this was only right. They gave enough to the police and fireman's fund to be given the best treatment.

The two boys clattered down the stairs and settled down in some chairs and were doing their best to look upset. The Detectives glanced at the two boys before looking at their parents, "We went and interviewed the others involved in this issue. We have a few more questions for these two if it's okay." They had to ask the parents since the boys were minors.

Both fathers glanced at their wives before agreeing. Whatever questions the police had were probably just routine stuff, so it was fine, "That's fine Detective. We want this taken care of as soon as possible." He was sounding rather gruff and angry.

The Detective glanced at his notepad before looking at the two boys, "When this assault happened was there anyone else in the hallway before the assault happened? Anyone who can be talked to as an independent witness?" His voice was calm and relaxed as if this was a regular question.

David and Leon traded looks before turning back to the Detectives, "Someone had just left the hallway before we were attacked." It was a lie, but he didn't want to say nobody had been there. This put the cunt there but not involved.

The Detective made a few notes and stood, "There have been counter charges stating that you were sexually assaulting Tessa Fletcher. For the moment, while we are doing further investigation, we are going to turn you over to your parents. Do not send them to school on Monday or until we contact you."

David and Leon were shocked at what the detective had to say, and it showed. All four parents stood up and started yelling. David's father finally got the upper hand, "I do not believe this. Those brats who assaulted my son had better be arrested for the assault and false report. My son would never do something like that. He is a good boy and that is that. If they aren't arrested, you will be hearing from my lawyer."

The detective stared the man down, "Sir, this needs to go to the prosecutor. If you insist I arrest the others involved, then I will in turn have to arrest your son and his friend. What would you like to do?" It was obvious the boy was the darling of his parent's eyes.

*****

Mike looked at the kitten Olivia was holding and then looked at Zane's wolf. It was obvious the silly thing was tickled pink over finding the kitten and giving it to her. He glanced at the Luna who was in the room and her expression was a duplicate of his. Where the hell did Zane find a kitten and when had he found it. Mike didn't know much about cats, but it couldn't be more than two months old. **Zane what the hell is it and where did it come from?**

Zane had stopped his dancing in place as Olivia started petting his head. Frankly, the kitten looked rather worse for the wear, since it was dirty and rather scrawny as well, not to mention having been drooled a bit on. He could tell Olivia was really touched by his giving the kitten to her. When his uncle contacted him, he looked up and almost fell over at Mike's expression. **Are you saying you don't know what a kitten is, Uncle Mike? I was running over here, and the silly thing dashed out of a bush. I snapped it up without thinking. When I realized it was a kitten, I figured Olivia would brain me if I didn't do something to take care of it.** His tail was still wagging in happiness. **I thought she might like its company.**

The Luna contacted Mike. **Don't make a big deal over it Mike. Look at Zane, he is looking both pleased and happy. This is about the first time I have seen him this happy since he arrived.** She still had an odd expression on her face, "Zane, you and your sister are going to get some really strange looks having a cat in the pack. Mike, you are going to need to take it to a vet to make sure it is healthy and doesn't have fleas." When both Zane and Olivia shuddered at the idea of fleas, she started laughing as did the others in the room.

Melody walked into the room and heard the last bit. She had to turn away to keep from laughing her head off at Zane's revolted expression. When she finally was able to catch her breath, Melody turned back around, "Zane, fleas don't like us. We haven't really bothered to figure out why, but some think it is our blood and others the shift kills them. Now your sister is a different matter..." **I'm not sure where the kitten came from since the trail just faded out after a while.**

The healer sighed and shook her head, "The cat is not going to stay in medical. You are going to have to take it home, Zane and clean it up as well. Be glad you heal fast, since cats have very sharp claws and teeth." She was giving Zane and the kitten an odd look as well. Chances were good he would be getting *that* look for some time from all the wolves.

Melody handed Zane a pair of shorts, so he could change, "We will take the kitten back and make sure it is clean and fed something. I asked Abby to run to the store and get some kitten food since I don't know what else to feed it." To be honest she was looking at the tiny thing with a perplexed expression on her face.

Zane took the shorts in his mouth and trotted to the bathroom. He might be starting to get used to needing to strip to change but if he had some privacy, he would use it. Zane walked back out and settled on the bed next to Olivia, "I'm so glad you are here, sis. I'm going to ask Tessa to remain here with you and help you as you need. I would ask Oscar, but I'm feeling the need of his support currently." He looked down at the kitten and reached over and gently touched it with one finger. Thankfully, it didn't hiss at him, or he would have been offended.

Tessa came over and settled down on the other side of Olivia, "I would be more than pleased to help you, Olivia." Frankly, she could use some contact with Olivia since she wasn't part of the 'group'. All of them were still so worked up and pissed over what had happened the day before. It felt good knowing it, but she didn't want to think about it now, "I will get a bag of some things for you to do as well as clothes you can wear soon. I think my mom picked up some shorts which are designed to wear with a cast, they have Velcro on the legs to make them easier to get off and on." Very carefully she shifted onto the large hospital bed and curled up next to Olivia.

Olivia reached over and stroked Tessa's arm and gave her a tired smile, "I have a feeling much of what you might be doing is watching me sleep. I'm eating like a pig and fall asleep constantly." The pain meds were far less than they had been last time. When Tessa curled up next to her, Olivia could feel a tension which hadn't been there before. When she glanced at Zane his eyes were hard and he subtly shook his head. She furrowed her eyebrows at him, "I will talk to you later, Zane. I'm feeling like a nap right now. It feels good to be closer to home and it is making me relax."

Zane stood and gave her a good hug after Melody, relieved her of the kitten, "I will talk to you later Liv and if you need anything, I do mean anything, have Tessa contact me." He stood and gave his sister a mostly happy smile, "Talk to you later sis." He turned and left the room. Everyone else, other than Tessa, left. Zane stopped at the door, "I will have Oscar pack something up for you and have it brought over." He finally left the room and took a slow thankful breath. His sister was back home. He could visit her anytime he wanted.

Mike bumped Zane's shoulder once the door was closed, "I know the feeling, Zane. I think I was almost as stressed and worried as you were." He looked down at the boy and mock frowned at him, "A cat? Really? You are going to be getting some strange looks for the next week." There was a slight chuckle in his voice as he was talking.

Zane returned the bump and leaned against his uncle for a moment, "It is Uncle Mike. It really is. If it wasn't for two certain non-pushy individuals curling up next to me, I'm not sure how I would have done." The twins had helped a very great deal, and he really was thankful for them, "Don't ask me Uncle, the silly thing jumped out of a bush and almost got eaten. It was blind luck I didn't bite down and if I had, Liv would have broken a crutch over my skull. Thank goodness it wasn't a bunny or Liv might have ended up with a less nice present in her lap."

Oscar was leaning against Simone since Melody was on Zane's other side and Rico had to head back home. He was going to meet them later but for the moment his parents were keeping him close. Zane had some serious restrictions, since he was the senior pup in the group. He didn't care since both he and his wolf did understand. Zane also didn't give a damn, because he knew he'd put the fear of pain into David. When Zane teased him about being non-pushy, he couldn't help but quietly snicker. Oscar knew Zane had appreciated it but his saying it meant the world to him. He would tell Tessa later.

Melody bumped Zane for his comment about the rabbit, "Zane if you did, I might bring a few back up crutches for your sister. No bloody rabbits in her lap or else. Once the bag is packed, I will take it over for you. I think it would be good for you and the others to relax." She figured Tessa would appreciate having her there as well.

Once they finally reached the house, Zane settled down in a chair as Melody and Oscar went to get some stuff for Liv. Once everyone was seated, Zane looked up at his uncle, "So how much trouble are we in? I know I was defending both a pack member and a very junior pack member who I extended my protection to. What are we looking at? As far as Rico, he followed my orders. Melody kept me from hurting David badly. Simone wasn't directly involved and most definitely not Tessa or Oscar." For the moment his wolf came forward and impressed on Zane they were in charge. No matter what, he was responsible for the wolves under his protection.

When Zane started speaking Mike met his eyes and wanted to cry. There were actual emotions in his eyes. Even though he was still somewhat distant with the rest of the pack, he was starting to heal. Mike knew much of it was a combination of the twins, and finally turning to the Luna for help. He probably had a ways to go but he was doing much better. To keep from it showing in his voice he leaned on his wolf for support, "As far as the pack, the Alpha will talk to you about what happened. This doesn't necessarily mean you are in trouble, but he will need to talk to you. You protected not just pack but also those who you swore to protect. Rico did what you ordered as would be expected. Melody also did what a good second would do by keeping you from doing something which could hurt you and the pack. When you reacted to protect Tessa, you did what a good pack member should do."

After a moment, Mike shrugged, "What will happen with the legal system, I can't really say. Since I know you, and can feel over the bonds what you said is true, I want to say you will be exonerated. It would be a case of you protecting a friend from physical or sexual assault. The best option would be for them to be prosecuted and at the very least removed from the school. This isn't because they might come after you again but many of the senior pups will start gunning for them, when this comes out." Not only because they had attacked a junior member of the pack, but they might come after other junior members as a warning to the other bullies; attack any member, and the whole pack would respond. "It is for their safety I'm saying this. For the moment, follow the Alpha's instructions on where you go and simply let us deal with it. You focus on Oscar and Tessa since they need it." Even if they didn't respond first, the senior pups would have their wolves on a hair trigger to respond for any issues with those under their protection, and likely would overreact.

All of them listened carefully, though Zane was sending what Mike had to say to Rico, so he knew what was going on as well. He had already gotten so used to the benefits of the mental bonds he didn't see any issues with using them. Once Mike had finished, Zane started to relax, "I'm trying to care about what might happen to David and Leon, but it is hard. As far as my wolf is concerned, they threatened what is ours..." He groaned and let his head flop back, "That didn't come out the way I wanted blast it. It makes Tessa and Oscar sound like property and I'm having enough problems with this. My wolf doesn't care if they end up broken and bleeding behind the gym. I do though, since it isn't something I grew up with. I just want them to go away and not bother us again." He might need to go and talk to the Alpha, even before he called for him to talk about it.

Melody came down, "I'd forgotten I was going to give the kitten a bath. Simone, would you mind running this over?" She had a reasonable sized bag packed. Melody could also tell Oscar needed some comfort, "I am going to have Oscar help to keep the blood shed to a minimum."

Oscar stood next to her and slightly behind. Zane projected one type of protection, but Melody was providing another. Zane was security and even though the more dominant wolves had it, Melody and Simone also presented comfort. Even when Melody made the joke, he didn't bother smiling. Both he and his sister were still terrified and horrified by what had been said and done. For him it was worse because of the twin bond.

Zane stood and after a glance at Mike, as he decided he needed to talk to the Alpha sooner than later, he walked over and took the bag, "I need to go to the pack house myself, so I will walk Simone over. Go help clean the kitten Oscar and once you are done why don't you and Melody look up the proper care for the kitten." He gave Oscar a slight grin, "It might save you from additional blood shed down the road."

Oscar met Zane's eyes and nodded, "I will take care of it, Zane. Mom is going to be back soon, so we should have some food for the kitten also." They had left the kitten in a box in Olivia's room, but he didn't want to leave it alone for very long.

Zane reached over and gave Oscar's shoulder a slight squeeze, "Thank you and I will talk to you later." Silently, he asked Melody, and also letting his uncle hear too, **Melody if you think it might help, maybe see if you can spend the night to help comfort Oscar. I'd appreciate it.**

The two of them left the house and walked towards the pack house. When they arrived, he handed the bag over, "Simone, give Tessa as much comfort as you can. I have a feeling she might need a female to comfort her right now." He was starting to get worked up again and he had to turn away from Simone and hurried towards the Alpha's office. When he arrived, Zane was thankful the Alpha was in. He knocked on the door frame, "Alpha do you have a few minutes? I need to talk to you and to try and understand something."

Kadrian had been contacted by Mike since Zane had chosen to come to the pack house. On the off chance he had been looking for Esther she was in her office as well. Kadrian looked up from his desk, "Come in Zane and close the door if you need. Help yourself to a drink if you want." He closed the folder he had been looking at, "How can I help you?"

Zane simply walked over and sat down and after briefly meeting Kadrian's eyes before he looked down, "I need help trying to figure out what I'm feeling. My wolf says one thing, but my human side says something else. They are completely different reactions to what happened yesterday and what we are feeling now." Frankly, his wolf's demand for blood scared him. Protect he could understand but the other was more than he could handle.

Kadrian met Zane's eyes and noticed the subtle changes in emotions as well. He was rather pleased even if the cause was not something he was pleased with, "Before I actually say something, tell me what the conflict is, Zane. It will make it easier for me to understand and offer help." Kadrian was pleased Zane had come to him as well.

Zane had to stand, and he started a somewhat jerky fast pace back and forth in front of the desk. He started to talk several times before he could articulate what he was feeling. When he spoke, his emotions were obvious. There were hints of contentment for having protected those who he had taken charge of. There was more revulsion though than pleasure, "Alpha, my wolf wants David gone. He views him as an enemy; it would be best if he couldn't threaten anyone anymore. I sort of understand but not really. I want them punished but not the way he does. I just want him and Leon to leave us alone and go away. I don't need this right now since it's taking us away from my sister and Uncle. How do I deal with this?"

Kadrian sat in his chair for a few minutes and tried to figure out the best way to address it. To be honest, there really wasn't since it was something most werewolves had to deal with. Yes, they grew up with a slightly different point of view, but they still had the conflict at times between the human half and wolf half. For Zane it was far more obvious since he was such a new wolf. He was also being exposed to more ideas and stress than most pups his age. He finally stood and walked over to one of the large windows in his office and looked outside. Interestingly enough, as dark and intense as the topic was the day was a bright autumn day. The trees were starting to turn even though many of the leaves were still green.

As he was looking out the window, he had to smile since there were many the pack relaxing and playing, "Zane, come here please. I want to explain this somewhat differently than you might expect." His voice was calm and relaxed as he was speaking.

Zane slowly came over and looked out the window. All he saw was just people outside doing whatever they wanted. He wasn't sure what the Alpha was going to say to him, "What are you seeing Alpha?" He did hope what Kadrian had to say would make sense to his human half.

Kadrian smiled and it showed in his voice, "What do I see? I see our pack members playing and relaxing. Mothers with their little pups, older pups playing games, and mates being able to relax with each other. They are relaxing, and they are feeling safe since they know two things. First, pack takes care of pack, and the senior wolves will take steps to protect them. This gives them safety to raise their pups, for new mates to relax and get to know each other better. For older mates, they can relax with their adult pups and their grand pups. This is what the pack is. No, we aren't all related by blood, but does it really matter? We are family, in ways humans can't define or explain. What you did, was to protect pack. Even a normal human can feel the urge to protect those they would consider weaker or junior to them. It isn't the same, but it is there." He stopped talking to see what Zane might see.

Zane had to chew on it for a while before he spoke. He looked out the window and tried to see what the Alpha was talking about. Yes, there were many of the pack out there and they were relaxing. For a moment he closed his eyes and called to his wolf. **I don't understand what he is saying. Protection is one thing but what you want I don't understand. Talk to me please. Help me understand.** It was a cry to his wolf for understanding.

Kadrian simply stood there as he felt Zane call on his wolf. He didn't try to pry into what they might be talking about, even though he had the right. This was something Zane was going to have to talk to his wolf about. Zane needed to really start understanding what both his wolf meant and what pack meant. He was struggling with what he was learning as he was struggling with his feelings about what happened to his family. Zane was also struggling with what his wolf was making him feel about the junior pack members. For the most part, it was different than what those who were adult when they were turned, where a pup saw more absolutes. I was different enough he didn't think there was anything they needed to do.

Zane lowered his head and closed his eyes as they flickered between the color of Zane's eyes and his wolf's. His wolf came forward and pulled Zane into his mind. Both were struggling to understand each other even though they were two parts of a whole. How long the conversation went on Zane wasn't sure but eventually he opened his eyes and looked out. When he spoke Zane almost sounded normal, "Alpha, do you have any idea how hard it is for me to let anyone in? I lost almost everything due to that damn rogue. My family, almost my little sister, I don't live where I used to, and everything we owned is in storage right now. I don't have any pictures of my parents or of us growing up." He had to stop speaking for the moment. This was different from talking to Mrs. Esther. This was man to man and not a boy needing comfort from a mother figure.

Kadrian kept looking out the window, "Zane, I can't say I know directly since I haven't had such a loss. I have known what you would call husbands who lost wives or wives who lost husbands. I have known pups who lost one or both parents. I feel each and every loss my pack has had over the many years I have run it. One thing I do know is the pack is a family. We do bicker and fight. There are people who at times intensely dislike others and even occasionally hate each other. Just because we are were-wolves doesn't mean we don't have our issues. One thing is we are still family with many of the human aspects."

He looked down at the floor for a few minutes as he considered what Kadrian had to say. Eventually Zane spoke though it was a whisper, "I'm so scared to let anyone inside. It makes it even worse when I do think of *family*. It scares the crap out of me. I can maybe understand saying Tessa and Oscar need me in some wolfy way but for Melody, Rico, and Simone it's harder. It scares me because I don't want to let them in only to possibly lose them. It scares me also that they are looking to me as the leader of our group and as the protector."

Esther had been listening in since Kadrian had opened the mating bond with her when Zane had arrived. She mentally leaned against her mate. **Don't ask for much more. Maybe nudge him towards his sister and Tessa for some comfort. He is admitting his fears to both of us but if either of us push he might start to close up again.**

Kadrian listened to both what Zane and Esther had to say and after thinking about it he figured she was right, "Zane this isn't something you can deal with instantly. It is not something one single conversation will resolve. You are going from one world to another, and it takes time. This is especially true when it is from a human world to a supernatural world. Why don't you go and relax with Olivia? Maybe change forms so you don't have to answer questions?"

If he was honest it sounded like a really good idea, "Thank you for talking Alpha, I could have talked to Uncle Mike, but he is worried enough. I needed to talk to someone not family." Being Alpha, he should have more of an idea how to answer his questions. Zane stepped away and pulled his clothes off and rolled them up before changing. Once he did, he picked the roll up in his mouth and slowly left the room.

Moments after Zane left, Esther walked into the office and came over to her mate. She wrapped her arms around him and settled for just holding him. **I think he is finally starting to come around. He still has fears about losing people but finding some people he can care for is helping.** She rested her head against her Mates back and enjoyed the surge of feelings holding him caused. They had mellowed over the years but even when they were old and gray they would be there. That was many years down the road, but she knew he would always be there for her.

*****

Zane slowly walked to Olivia's room and stopped outside the door. **Simone, if it is okay, I would like to come in please. I need the comfort of my sister as well as you and Tessa.** He wanted to be next to his sister and to relax and be able to know his family was relatively safe. No longer would he be able to say he wouldn't worry about anyone dying but he could enjoy knowing they were there.

Moments later the door opened, and Simone took the bundle of clothing from Zane and stood to the side. Zane walked over to the bed and carefully hopped up and settled towards the foot of it and curled up before tucking his nose under his tail and closing his eyes.

Olivia watched him walk in and he looked tired. When he hopped up and curled up, she wished he had curled up where she could have petted at least his head. Tessa was on one side curled up and relaxing against Olivia and even though Tessa wouldn't talk she knew something had gone on, "Zane would you please curl up where I can pet you? I know you have been scared for me and really worried. I'm here for you."

Zane slowly uncurled and stood. He moved around her and settled down. He was on the side of her bad leg since Tessa was on the other side. He rested his head across her stomach and did his best to ensure he wasn't hurting her. Once he lay down again, he closed his eyes. When she started stroking his ears and head, he had to whine slightly before settling down. Eventually he fell into a light doze.

*****

The next morning everyone except Tessa gathered at Mikes house. Technically Melody, Simone, and the twins could go to school, but it was decided they were going to stay home. The kitten had been somewhat of a pain with its meowing and not being house broken, but Oscar had taken care of it for the most part. Mike was going to take it to a vet soon, though he wasn't going to be gone too long hopefully. As far as what had happened this weekend, he honestly didn't expect much to happen until later today or maybe tomorrow. Chances were good he and the other parents would be called in to the school today though. It was almost guaranteed since both Leon and David's father were very well known in the community. Mike would end up being called in as well.

For the moment all the pups were at the pack house doing some chores. Their homework had been done and to keep them from having free time to start getting angrier, or to get into trouble, they were working. They were cycling through Olivia's room as well, to give all of them time with her. Zane's group had finally decided they had adopted her as someone somewhat like the twins. Yes, she was more outgoing and even active, but she was human and from her relationship with Zane, it demanded they give her protection. They would never tell her that, since chance was she would take a crutch to Zane, even if he didn't deserve it.

It was later in the morning when Olivia finally glared at Zane, "Why are you home? It is a school day. If you don't tell me, I will ask the doctor not to allow you in here again." It was a bad threat, but she wanted to know as badly as he had wanted to know what had happened to their family.

Zane sat up at the foot of her bed and looked at her though his eyes didn't show nearly the defensiveness as they had. He looked around the room once he was seated, "Tessa come here please and everyone else leave." When Tessa came over, he settled her on his lap and wrapped his arms around her and pulled her close to his chest.

"Olivia, I haven't said much about the person who decided to try to pick on me. It didn't work and my not responding pissed him off more. Saturday, he, and his lackey, happened upon Tessa while she was alone. They started pushing her around and saying some very nasty things. If Melody hadn't intervened, there would be two dead fuckers." His eyes flashed the color of his wolf as he was speaking, "They pressed charges of a random physical assault, and we returned the favor of pressing charges of sexual assault." His eyes flared with anger and hatred.

Tessa curled even more into his arms as he was talking, and he pressed his head against hers, "Oscar and Tessa are mine to protect. Melody and the others followed my lead to help protect both them and the pack. It's why we are home." His wolf had come forward and Zane's voice had heavy hints of his anger but also his acceptance of what the others meant to him.

Olivia's eyes opened, and she looked horribly shocked by what he had to say. When she finally spoke, it was obvious she was very pissed as well, "I will help Tessa and Oscar as best as I can. Do what is needed Zane and I will help." She wasn't a wolf, but if she had been, she might have been moderately dominant as well.

Zane struggled to control his wolf, "Olivia, we will deal with this. I have already asked Tessa to stay with you since you need the help. Oscar is helping me as well." It was rather obvious he was indicating it would help the two, "I'm coming to learn what it means to be a more dominant wolf pup. I protect them, and they take care of me. I protect family and pack, and pack and family are safe and I'm content." He lowered his head and pressed a kiss against Tessa's hair. She was his to protect and take care of. Eventually she would find her mate much as Oscar would and he would extend his protection to their mates and pups.

Olivia felt tears slowly trickle down her cheeks. This wasn't quite the Zane she had known but it was closer than she had seen since he had been in the coma. When he had come out of the coma, he had been so hard to get close to, even for her. For a moment she started to understand what pack meant. It was going to be a hard concept for her to keep understanding but the edges were there. If nothing else, it gave her an understanding this was giving Zane a feeling for family he had been so scared to accept. She was only twelve, so it was somewhat of a basic understanding, but it was a start. Olivia could see he did care, and it felt so good, "It is bad what happened, but I'm glad you are taking care of them Zane. Go beat the crap out of them. They deserve it." She had to lean back and close her eyes.

Silence fell over the room after the talk and before Zane realized it Tessa was sleeping quietly in his lap. He knew she was still dealing what had happened but knowing she was safe in his arms helped, "I'm here for you Tessa. I will take care of you." He murmured.

*****

Eventually the adults were called into the school. When it had been requested the children come with them, Mike and the other pack adults put their paws down and refused. It wasn't that they didn't want the pups there so much as they didn't want David or Leon torn to shreds and it would probably have happened. If either had started acting up, it would have been a blood bath and not much would have stopped it. Instead, they used the excuse they didn't want Tessa or Oscar exposed to the two.

Unfortunately, the other two sets of parents had brought their sons with them. When they walked into the offices, it had almost gotten ugly until the Luna had pressed her powers on all of them. She hadn't been subtle when she had done it; it was almost as if she had put a strong restraining hand on their shoulders and pressed them down into their seats. Everyone in the room calmed down. As far as Esther was concerned, she didn't give a shit about the others, but she didn't want a blood bath. **Calm down all of you damn it or deal with the Goddess. I will not have snarling and growling no matter how you feel.** Her mental voice was hard and firm.

CHAPTER 13

Zane and the Rabbits

Thankfully, there was the school safety officer in the room as well. The simple fact there was law enforcement there would also keep the urge to rip people apart under control. Moments after everyone had walked in, the secretary showed them into a conference room with a large table and plenty of chairs around it. The principal was already at the head of the table, "Please have a seat. I have talked with the student counselors. Before I get into what they recommended, I want to talk to you and get both sides. It's why I wished you would have brought your children as well." She looked at Mike and the others on their side of the table.

Abby looked back at the principal, and she was not looking either amused or happy, "I discussed this with our doctor, and she strongly recommended keeping her away from the ones who assaulted her. After the threats made and the suggestions of rape, I will not have either of my children in the same room with them." When she used the term 'them' it sounded like she had spit it out.

David's father yelled back, "I have talked to David, and I believe him when he says your brats attacked him and Leon. He said the Zane boy deliberately tried to pick a fight with him in the lunchroom. He started this and not my son." He was getting ready to stand when the principal spoke.

She wasn't a large woman, actually she was rather small and gray, but she had authority behind her, "That is enough from all of you. If you refuse to try and talk like reasonable people, I will have you leave and kick everyone involved out until this is resolved. Is that understood?" Her voice snapped out like the cracking of a whip.

Even Kadrian and Esther were impressed by the authority in her voice. Every wolf in the room automatically turned and looked at her, showing respect in their body language. Mike gave her a rather harsh smile, "Sorry ma'am, we will do our best." He was shocked, **Thank the goddess, she isn't a wolf, or we might be in trouble...** He sent to the others.

Esther mentally laughed. **I would be worried about my job! She would make one hell of an elder though.** She gave the woman more respect than she had expected to since the principal did come across as dominant, almost at the equal of an Alpha or Luna, if she had been a wolf. There hadn't been an issue in the several years she had been the principal where they had to be involved, and she shared a thought with her mate, about how if she used her power to impress on the pups or any parents making a scene, how it would quickly be de-escalated. At most, they had a civil discussion with her, where all shared the bare facts. She felt like she would be honest and fair in her decisions.

David's father glared at Mike, "If you can keep them from slandering my son's good name, I will do my best." David's mother had an arm around David as if to comfort him. It was rather obvious to some in the room, it was mostly for show. They all knew her and her opinions on things, so they knew she couldn't believe anything bad about her son.

Mike started to glare at David's father before the principal spoke again, "I will say this one more time. All of you keep a civil tongue in your mouths or else. I have the school records for all involved with me and if needed, I will break them out and start explaining the facts of life to all of you." David and Leon were pains in her ass though she couldn't treat them differently until something formal was written down.

The officer cleared her throat, “If needed, Mrs. Smith I can call for one of the detectives to come and sit in as well if you wish?” Hopefully if they came, it would keep the room down to a low simmer. The charges and counter charges were enough to make everyone pissed off and upset.

Mrs. Smith contemplated the Officer for a moment, “I don’t think it will be needed, but thank you for the offer. This meeting is only for the school side. I do not wish to have this getting involved with the legal issue.” She turned back, “I’m going to ask questions. I expect honest answers from everyone.” Again Mrs. Smith looked around the room to see what the reactions might be. From David and Leon’s parents was blatant disbelief their children could do anything wrong. On the others faces, it was honestly far scarier. Almost across the board she was getting some very chilling vibes from them. The only two who weren’t as scary were the twin’s parents, but there was a determination to protect their children. She knew Tessa and Oscar and they were very good children.

Kadrian cleared his throat, “Mrs. Smith, here is a verbatim transcript of everything the children told us yesterday. It includes what Tessa told us about what happened. There are pictures of the bruises she was left with as well.” He slid the folder down the table to her, “If you need, we will bring the children in later and you can talk to them. Oh, there are recordings of what was said as well.”

Mrs. Smith quirked an eyebrow at the folder, but she did pull it towards her. She had been dealing with Mr. Mac Tire’ Dona for many years and though a bit odd he was a very good person. If anything happened with his extended family, he was quick to step in and take care of business. If one of the teens did wrong, he dealt with it, often with a punishment which occasionally shocked her. The punishments for those found to have lied, or something which at the root was deceptive, seemed very excessive. If one of his teens was an innocent victim, he also dealt with it and supported them fully often by simply sharing all the facts he could find, “Thank you and I will let you know.”

She turned back to the other set of parents and wanted to laugh at their staring at Kadrian, "David, tell me your version of what happened."

Before David could speak, his mother spoke this time, "It is not fair for you to question him in front of them since their children aren't here. If you are going to question my son, I don't want them in the room, or they have their children brought here." She glared at the others and tried to look elegant as she looked down her nose at them.

Mike ended up staring at her as he tried to figure out if she honestly cared about her son or not. Granted she didn't know what they were, but the fact Zane had damn near throttled her son should mean something. He leaned back in the seat he was in and all he could do was stare at her. **Kad, it would resolve one issue, though how we explained the bodies would be somewhat difficult.** He was almost temped to do it.

Abby snarled at David's mother, "Why the hell would I want my children in the same room with the brats who sexually assaulted her? Give me one good reason? The only reason I'm here is to hopefully keep my daughter from having to see the ones who assaulted her." Damn it, even with the Luna's presence her momma-wolf was struggling not to kill the bitch who clearly just supported her son ignoring what he had done, "On top of it, your precious little baby has pushed my children around before. He is a bully and a chicken. If he thinks he is stronger than someone else, he will push them around. You and your husband are no different. I refuse to be in the same room with cowards like any of you." She stood and slammed the door to the room open and walked out with her mate next to her.

Simone's parents stood up as well. Her mother spoke, "You are no longer welcome in our shop. Goodbye and good riddance you self-centered bitch." They stormed out of the room as well. They were no longer going to deal with either family.

The Luna had forced Abby and Brandon to leave or one or the other would have attacked. They were very junior but for their pups they would have. When Simone's parents stood and stormed out, she hadn't been expecting it. **Kadrian, I told them to go back to the pack house.** She was giving David and Leon's mother's a very cool stare, it was almost as if she was saying they weren't worth the hassle. That would get them going.

The others on their side couldn't help but be impressed. As the scents of the others filled the room, it was enough to make their wolves want to cover their muzzles with their paws and even sneeze to clear the stench out.

Mrs. Smith traded looks with the Officer before looking around the room, "In this case, I see no alternative to removing all the children involved from school. From what I understand based on what I have been told, Simone and the twins did not assault the others. Those three will be expected to come back to school tomorrow. This is unless a valid reason is given for them not to come back now. I will have their various teachers provide assignments to ensure the others do not fall behind. They can get notes from their friends. Mr. and Mrs. Walpert take your son and leave please. Mr. and Mrs. Baker take your son and leave as well. This is to keep your groups from encountering each other. Officer, please escort them from the building."

She turned back to the others, "Wait five minutes and then you can leave. I would have liked to have resolved the school portion differently but as of now, I do not see it happening." She stood and walked out of the room with all the folders she had including the one she had been given. When she did look at it, she almost laughed since she found a thumb drive which appeared to have the entire conversation with the police and the others on it. For that Mrs. Smith had to shake her head. They were some odd people, but they did take family very seriously.

*****

When Mike came out of the school with the others, he found Abby and Brandon waiting in his vehicle. They had keys to it, since they used it when they were doing things for him. He climbed in and rolled his neck, "I need to take the darn kitten to the vet. I have a feeling right now is not a good time to talk to our pups. If you want to take the rest of the day off and try and relax, do so. If you need go for a run and hunt, talk to the keeper of rabbits. If you want to wait, we can go together. Maybe even some of the rest of my team as well." Now that was a good idea since it would be good for all of them.

Abby leaned forward; she was in the back seat with her mate and pressed her hands onto Mike's shoulders. She took a moment to give his shoulders and part of his neck a light massage since she knew it would help, "I think it would really help Mike, a hunt and we can see about ordering some additional rabbits. Between Zane and his team this weekend and what we might eat today they are going to take a good hit." They normally kept plenty of rabbits but when wolves got worked up, they tended to go through a number.

Mike dropped his head forward and let her work on his shoulders since he needed it, "Don't worry about the rabbits, I will take care of it, and I might even see about going and finding a cow." They kept some of those for hunting but most of the time if you wanted to hunt a cow you had to pay for it. Rabbits didn't cost much to raise and keep but cows and such cost much more. They had goats and a few other prey animals as well.

He finally leaned back and headed towards the pack property. Taking the silly kitten to the vet was going to be interesting. He had tried to get close to the kitten the night before and the damn thing hissed and spit at him. Mike hadn't been pleased and could only hope eventually the cat would eventually accept him. He didn't care if it came to him and preferred if it didn't, but as long as it settled for simply glaring at him when it was older would be fine.

The other two had to admit a cow sounded rather good and they didn't have a problem helping to cover the cost, "It would be rather nice, to be honest, Mike. I have to admit right now I don't think a rabbit would really work. A cow would be very enjoyable." Brandon could almost imagine bringing a leg of the cow to his mate. His wolf was looking really excited about doing it.

Mike waited until they pulled up to his house, “I will see about setting it up for this evening.” Even as he was letting them out, Melody came out of the house with a small box and after greeting the other two hopped into the vehicle, “I have the kitten and Zane suggested I help you take it to the vet.” She flashed him a cheeky grin when she said it.

Mike glowered at her as she climbed in and settled down. Once she was belted in, he pulled away from the house and headed towards town. Before heading to school, he had found a vet who was highly rated online and made and had made an appointment. The kitten might not appreciate it, but he had decided to schedule a flea bath as well at a local pet store. He was not going to deal with fleas or ticks even for a brief time.

Melody simply settled back in the chair. As they were driving, she was petting the kitten in the box. As Zane had asked Oscar, the two of them had looked up taking care of a kitten and worked up a list of items needed. They would need to talk to the Vet to make sure it had what was needed. Wolves simply didn’t deal with cats like this, making this kitten a surprising exception.

*****

Zane had finally ended up picking Tessa up and tucked her in next to his sister, “Give her the comfort you can, Liv. I have some chores that I have been assigned to do.” He stroked Tessa’s hair for a moment before briefly touching Liv’s shoulder and did his best to silently leave the room. Once he was out of the room, he let loose with a frustrated snarl. Both Zane and his wolf wanted David and Leon dead. Yes, they knew it wouldn’t be good for the pack but damn it, they wanted them dealt with, so they wouldn’t be a problem again. He had been assigned to help the keeper of the rabbits, so he headed to the rabbit pens.

Eventually lunch rolled around for which he was glad for. Zane honestly wanted a shower after dealing with those bloody things. He was sure he stank of rabbits and their poop and pee. Even his wolf was almost whining in the back of their mind at the messes they made. How the hell the keeper could do it, they didn’t know and didn’t want to. He was a junior wolf and many of the workers were both junior wolves and pups home from school.

Zane had to admit he had learned about what the work involved in the rabbits' care. There were quite a few rabbits and trying to deal with them required a great deal of work. It wasn't just feeding them but breeding them, cleaning up after them, making sure they were healthy and deciding how many were available for hunting. Zane had a feeling he was going to be given an intensive overview of how the junior pack worked. From what he understood, not all of the wolves worked directly for the pack, otherwise how could there be income. Most wolves had some chores for the pack outside of work. It appeared to include the more dominant wolves as well.

Once he was done, he decided to go home and get clean. The idea of smelling like bunny crap for the rest of the day just didn't appeal. **Simone, I'm going to my house to get clean. I will just fix myself something to eat.** He should have known better than to tell anyone, but he was still getting used to the whole pack thing.

Once he was done with showering and dressed, he headed downstairs and almost growled since everyone, other than Tessa, was there. There was a pile of sandwiches on a tray as well as some cold drinks and other food. He sighed, "Guys, I could have made some food for myself. I didn't need all of you to come over and cook or make sandwiches or whatever." He flopped down in a chair, though he didn't pout. Zane had a feeling if he had Simone would have flicked his lip and teased him.

This time it was Simone who spoke, "Zane, how can we not come and support you? You had to tell Olivia what happened. Right now, she is taking care of Tessa, and we know Oscar is also struggling. It impacts you even more than it does us since you are the leader of our little group." She stood and walked over and wrapped her arms around Zane, "We know you care but we also know how scared you are. Don't push us away please."

His wolf forced him to relax into her arms when Simone hugged him. Zane's arms slowly came up and wrapped around her and held on.

He sat there for several minutes before finally letting her go and leaning back, "I'm starving and thanks for the food." He knew Oscar had been involved but who else he had no idea. As hungry as he was Zane didn't care for the moment. All he wanted to do was to eat and maybe go and relax before his uncle came home. Zane knew Melody was with his uncle at the Vet's.

Eventually lunch was over, and Zane was feeling the need of some time alone. He did know Oscar would remain even if he went to the room he shared with his sister, "Guys, I need some time to myself. Thank you for being here and eating with me." He frowned at Oscar when he tried to take Zane's plate, "Relax and I'm going to help occasionally. I might even decide to cook once in a blue moon as well." There were a few things his mother had taught him to make, and he was thinking he would like to make them.

Once everyone left, Zane settled down in what he had come to think of as *his* chair and let his body relax. If Oscar needed him, he would tell him. **Uncle Mike, I ended up having to tell Liv about what had happened. She wanted to know why I was home on a Monday and threatened me with not letting me into her room.** It had both scared him and upset both he and his wolf. **She is not happy with what happened and right now Tessa is curled up with her. Tessa is still very upset.**

Mike was at the vet's since they were waiting to get the silly cat seen. They had eaten before going to the vet because they were hungry. Once they ate, they fed the kitten and headed to the vet. It was shortly after they walked in when Zane had contacted him. **Zane, the meeting this morning didn't go well. As of now, until the legal aspect is resolved, you, Melody, and Rico are suspended. Homework will be brought home, and you should be able to get the notes from your team. The principal said Tessa, Oscar, and Simone will report to school tomorrow. We are looking into it, but they might have to go.** Mike wasn't happy with the idea and knew Zane would be far less happy.

Zane did tense up and a frustrated sound came from his mouth. **Just frigging wonderful Uncle. Take care of the kitten and I need to think. I* *don't want them out of my sight but if it was ordered then they are going to have to go.** He broke the connection. **Oscar, I'm going for a run. I will be back. I need to think and talk to someone.**

Zane stood and walked to the porch. He stripped his clothes off and shifted and started running. He wasn't gone very long or far since the Alpha had ordered them to stay relatively close to the property. After Zane worked off some of his irritation, he headed to the pack house and into medical. He needed to think about how to handle this though he did have an idea. To really figure it, he needed time to just talk with his wolf. Since he was in this shape, he could curl up with his sister and not be bothered.

Once he was allowed entrance, he carefully hopped up on the side of the bed Tessa wasn't on. She was curled up with Olivia and they were quietly talking. **Tessa can you please tell Olivia I need to think? I came here since I know I won't be bothered unless Olivia needs something.** He settled down and rested his head next to his sister's side and closed his eyes and let his ears relax. Once he was relaxed, he moved closer to his wolf, and they started talking. Zane was sure Tessa would notice he was busy and let Olivia know.

Tessa reached over and stroked his head and let him start talking to his wolf before she spoke, "Olivia, Zane is talking to his wolf. He knows he won't be disturbed here in your room unless it is urgent. Please just let him be." She had no idea what Zane was discussing with his wolf and wasn't going to ask.

Liv rested her hand on part of Zane's head and tried to relax, "Thanks for letting me know. Can we keep talking or should we be quiet?" Tessa had been answering some questions for Oliva about the pack and other issues. It helped, since it allowed her to see everything from a more normal view. Well to her a normal view since the junior wolves were more relaxed than the dominant wolves.

Tessa blushed since they had been talking about Zane. He was really cute, and she liked him and not just for protecting her and Oscar. Even with the wall he had tried to build to keep others away he had still shown he cared, "Well some things we can but others not right now." Her voice was quiet when she spoke.

Olivia had already figured out Tessa had a small crush on her brother, and it amused her. Then again, she had a crush or two as well. They had been talking about some of the boys they had found interesting. Olivia had been carefully picking Tessa's mind about the wolf pack and what some of what went on there meant. Even with having been helped by both Oscar and Tessa they hadn't talked about just what pack meant. Now she that she was stuck in the hospital , she was starting to ask questions. Later she could talk to Mrs. Esther but for the moment Tessa would do, "That is fine, now about..." They started talking some more until Olivia needed to sleep.

*****

By now the detectives had received the video footage from the mall. It didn't show the hallway unfortunately, but it did show who was both entering and leaving the hallway. They knew the approximate time of the attack, so they started a half hour before the assault and started making notes. As they were watching they noted general descriptions of who had entered and left the hallway. Close to the time of the reported assault they found the two boys entering the hallway. Two or so minutes later the young teen had entered the hallway. It was maybe three or four minutes later when the others involved approached the hallway.

There wasn't any sound, but they figured when the group suddenly vanished down the hallway was when everything happened. One detective let out a low whistle, "Damn but they moved fast. I almost didn't see the boy react." He had perked up and then shot down the hallway. Based on the angle of the camera they could see his face and he honestly looked like he was out for blood. The oldest girl had a sort of 'oh crap' expression on her face as she shot down the hallway as well.

It was maybe two or so minutes before the group came out. The oldest boy had his arms around the younger girl, and he looked like he wanted blood, "Damn he looked about ready to go back and deal with those two. The twin looks ready to cry as well," The first detective commented, and they rewound the video and started making more notes. Both really wished they could see down the hallway. They did have the images the doctor had taken of the girl's chest, and she had bruises forming. Since she was very pale the bruising showed up quickly.

Once they were done with the video, they made notes on who had indicated they had either seen or heard something. Now was the fun and excitement of the interviews. They broke up and started going to each of the witnesses to interview them. Chances were good they wouldn't have much information, but they had to work all the angles. It was going to take some time for them to get all the information and submit it to the prosecutor for review.

*****

Eventually Zane woke up and silently hopped down from the bed. Somehow, he knew Mike and Melody were back from the Vet, and Damien was home from school, and he needed to talk to him. **Damin, I need to talk to you, please?** He waited on the back porch for a response.

Damien had arrived home from school and had just finished a snack before doing his homework. When Zane contacted him, he could tell Zane was serious and needed talk. **Give me a couple of minutes and we can go for a short run first.** He stripped, shifted, and headed downstairs. When he joined Zane, who looked somewhat tense. **Just a run and no hunting. The rabbits have taken a hit the last few days and we have to wait for an order of new ones.**

Zane settled for twitching his ears before standing on all fours. **I'm not in the mood for a hunt and if I need something raw, I will raid the fridge at home.** He jumped down from the porch to the ground and settled into a lope. He didn't run for long before he slowed down and sat in a small clearing. It wasn't the one he had been drawn to several times and was just a somewhat remote spot.

Damien gave Zane a light bump at the mention of raiding the fridge before he set out with him. They ran in a companionable silence until they found a clearing they could relax in and talk. **How can I help you,*

*Zane?** Zane was feeling both more relaxed and comfortable in his fur, and tense.

Zane lifted his face to get the best warmth from the sun. **Those of us directly involved have been suspended from school. Simone, Tessa, and Oscar have been ordered back by the principal. I'm not sure what to ask or how, so I'm going to simply state it. Damien, will you please take them under your protection until I'm back at school? This is with their permission of course.**

Damien had lifted his head to the sun as well. Even as a wolf they enjoyed the warmth of the sun and the sunny spots on the forest floor were valued locations. When Zane asked him to take care of and protect Zane's team members for the moment Damien was actually honored. He stood and moved closer to Zane until their shoulders were barely touching. **Zane, I would be honored to protect and take care of them for you. With their consent, of course.**

Zane leaned against Damien for a short time. **Simone, Tessa, Oscar, I need you to come and find Damien and me. I need to talk to you please?** Until they showed up, he couldn't, or so he felt, discuss this any further. **Thank you for listening. Talking to your mother and father has helped a great deal. It is still so hard for me because of dealing with what happened.** If Damien hadn't slapped him down, it would have been harder to go to the Luna or have her come to him as it was.

Damien yawned and settled down on the ground. **Zane this is what it means to be pack. If it helps, until you chose to protect Tessa and Oscar, I didn't realize what it really meant. After dad explained it, I have to admit I was rather startled since I have been doing something similar. If it helps, I have also found my junior wolves and started integrating them into my team.**

They finally lapsed into silence until the three showed up. When they did, Zane stood up, he nuzzled all three as well as running his tongue across their muzzles. **I don't know if anyone has told you, but you three are supposed to start school again tomorrow. I have asked Damien to take care of and protect all three of you in my place. This is until I can* *come back to school and take care of you. Once you are out of school I will take back over. Will you accept Damien's protection while I'm not able to take care of you?** He had moved so he was between the twins, and they were leaning against him as he was talking.

Tessa was forced to whine slightly as she leaned against the larger wolf. **I want you there, but I understand. I will accept Damien's protection while you are not around.** It was obvious she didn't want to be away from Zane for very long.

Oscar looked at Damien and met his eyes before looking down. **I want Tessa protected. Simone can watch me while Damien is taking care of Tessa.** Both had been badly hurt by what had happened. Tessa was still recovering from the bruises.

Damien stood and came over and rested his head on Oscar's shoulders. **My team and others will take care of you since Zane asked it of me. You are pack, and pack takes care of pack. All of you will be at my table during lunch.** He lifted his head and howled for a moment. **I need to go back; dad is calling me. I take responsibility for the three of you at school. You can sit with Jason and Margarethe as well. I have recently expanded my protection to them as well.**

Tessa and Oscar jerked their heads up and their joy was obvious. **Oh, thank you Damien. Thank you so much. They will take very good care of you and your team.** Both almost ran the short distance to Damien and rubbed against him in pleasure. The two were friends of theirs as well and it made them happy to know they had found their team as well.

After the quick rub, Damien turned and dashed away. Zane gave his body a good shake. **Time to head home and do whatever homework might have been brought over. I hope someone took good notes and will share them.** He lightly bumped Simone before setting off towards home. He had missed training which frustrated him, and he was going to see if he could get some extra in since he had to be home currently.

*****

When Kadrian called for Damien, he hurried back to the house. After he reached his father's office, he closed the door and hurried to his dad and gave him a huge hug. *Zane asked me to watch over and protect Simone and the twins.** It was obvious he was rather touched by the request.

Kadrian returned the hug, "I'm very pleased to hear it. I'm pleased he feels you can and will take care of them for him. I'm also pleased he trusts you enough to ask you to take care of them. I had been planning to ask you to keep an eye on them, but this takes care of it." He gave Damien another good hug even as he told his mate what Zane had done. It pleased them both he was involved enough to realize it, and to ask for it before others could deal with it.

They stood there for a while longer before Kadrian let his son go. When he stepped back, he looked down at his son and realized he wasn't much shorter than Kadrian was any longer, "Son when it is time, you will make an outstanding Alpha. Now time for you to go and do your homework." He gave Damien a wry grin when he said it.

Damien almost glowed even though he also had to glower. His father did give praise and it wasn't the sparse or grudging. When he said something, the Alpha meant it, "Thanks dad and it does mean so much to me." After one last good hug he left the office to go and do his homework.

*****

When they reached the house, they found Mindy sitting on the stairs. Before anyone could growl, grumble, shift, or snarl she held up her backpack, "I was asked to get your homework. I have copies of the notes from the classes you are in as well. Mrs. Esther asked me to collect them. Some you might need someone who excels in chicken scratching to understand." She had been really upset with what Zane had said to her. Mindy had honestly wanted to talk and get to know him, and the rejection had hurt.

Zane scratched an ear and with malicious aforethought sent to all there. **Oh crap!!! That damn kitten did have fleas!!!** When everyone flinched, he yipped in amusement. **Mindy, we will talk later. Thanks for your help.**

Zane received several growls at his joking from all three. Just for good measure Simone nipped at his tail and growled again. **Not funny Zane. Not funny at all.** She had noticed both Oscar and Tessa reacting before they realized what he had really said.

He pushed the door open and headed to his room to pull on some clothes. Once he was done, he headed downstairs and found the others already there.

"Great, the fun and excitement of remote learning. If I fail a class, I'm going to blame those nut-less idiots." He flopped in a chair and started pulling books from his backpack and glared at the math, "Crap, that damn history thing is due tomorrow!!!"

The others grumbled as well and started getting to work. Eventually Mike came home and found them working hard. When Melody picked up a set of what he assumed was notes and glared at them he almost lost it, "Melody, if you destroy the notes, it will not help. I decided to have Abby and Brandon bring some food over from the main house. All of you need the break and I'm hungry now." He gave Zane a good hug which did get him a grumble.

Zane, I'm so proud of you. Kad contacted me and let me know you talked to Damien. Damien was very pleased you came to him and so am I. To keep all of you somewhat occupied, I have scheduled all of you, other than Tessa and Oscar, to workout at the training center while not doing homework. I think it will be good for you. He turned and sniffed when Abby and Brandon walked in with some baskets heavy with food, "Darn, that smells good! Okay pups, put the homework away, so we can set the table." Mike might need to request permission to move to a larger place at this rate.

*****

While the pups were doing their homework, Abby and Brandon brought in the stuff for the kitten. For the moment the little furball was curled up in a small carrier they had for it and was asleep. Abby gently put the carrier down and opened it, so the kitten could come out when it woke. They set up a small place for the food and water as well as the litter box. Eventually they would be able to get it trained to use outside and not need the box.

After everyone was gone Zane yawned, "Time for bed and both of you can join me. I know you slept better last night Tessa and I understand why." He headed towards his room, pulled on some shorts, and flopped in bed without thinking about it. His wolf was starting to make a difference in him more every day and he wanted to keep their two juniors close. When Tessa settled into the bed, he curled around her and was quickly sleep. Oscar was in his wolf form on the other side and quickly followed the other two into sleep.

CHAPTER 14

Zane and the Cows

Even as Zane was getting ready for bed, Mike was joining his team for a hunt. He had already purchased a steer and had it released earlier. It couldn't roam far, so they didn't have to go off the territory to get to it. Before they started , Mike called his team together. He had more people because he was in a position of authority. Zane had the five following him, and Mike he had ten, total.

When he stopped at the edge of the hunting reserve he paused and called his team around him. Abby and Brandon were on either side of Mike. **This hunt is for Abby and Brandon. With what happened to Tessa and as a side effect to Oscar she is feeling somewhat riled up.** He gently bumped her shoulder before doing the same with Brandon.

I thought I was going to have to drag her from the school conference room bodily today. Her momma-wolf is still pretty riled up, so you might not want to annoy her. She might not bite you, but I have a feeling your laundry might not be done for a while. There was both amusement and pride in his voice when he said it.

Mike's lead enforcer, Malcom, glanced at Abby and his ears lowered in respect. **Seriously? Good for you Abby and Brandon. We were all very upset by what happened.** Most of Mike's enforcers had wanted to personally go and express their discontent with what had happened. It wouldn't happen since they were well trained, but it didn't mean they didn't want to. Malcom moved over and lightly nuzzled Abby and then moved and gave Brandon a good bump.

One of the others sent to everyone. **Anything else we need to know? I might even let her have the tenderloin.** It was one of the prime choices for any wolf senior enough to claim it.

Abby dropped her ears and looked down. **Thank you but a flank or haunch would be fine. I was just taking care of our pups.** She was not used to this much attention. All the wolves who worked for Mike ensured both knew how much they appreciated the two taking care of them.

Mike decided it was time to move. **We will talk more after the hunt. I have a few chores for several of you to keep the pups from doing anything stupid.** He gave a short howl and lead them on the hunt.

*****

Once they were done with the hunt, they were sitting off to one side of the clearing they had caught the cow in. Abby was working a leg bone over as she finished working her anger out. Brandon was lying next to her and after cracking open the leg bone he had, he pushed it over to Abby, so she could have the marrow. She had been very upset when Tessa had been assaulted and he was doing his best to comfort her.

At the moment, as the two were comforting each other the other wolves were somewhat circled around them. **So, what are you thinking about to keep the pups busy and why?** Malcom was rather curious as to what had prompted Mike to say it.

Mike was gnawing on a bone as well. **Well, it seems some pups made an unauthorized excursion outside the property recently. Though nothing has really been said, the pups made a visit to a certain property. They chewed up anything not nailed down, left several wolf loads of crap in the yard and on the back porch. A report was made to the animal control. I would like to ensure said pups are too tired to repeat such an incident.** To be honest when he had heard about it, Mike had damn near died laughing. **Oh, and said pups tore the lawn up some but left the flower garden untouched.**

All the wolves, except for Abby and Brandon, sat up and stared at Mike before they started laughing. Kandy flopped on her side as she died laughing. **Oh man that's so perfect, though if it came to my attention, I would have to yell at the wolf. So, what are you thinking?**

Brandon had to toss his two cents in. **Tessa and Oscar did follow along, but Zane ordered them to remain hidden. He didn't want any trouble to come to them if they were caught.** It was obvious he was very pleased with Zane's concern for their pups.

Malcom sneezed in pleasure. **Good for him, he is hurting but Zane can still feel the drive to protect. So, boss what do you want us to do?** He was very interested since he had a feeling Zane was going to be following in his uncle's pawprints.

Mike returned the sneeze with a snort. **I'm going to have the three remaining at home starting active Enforcer training part of the day. In the morning, I plan on running them through the muck and the mud of helping the pack. Helping with the rabbits, the cattle, cleaning, you know the stuff. In the afternoon before school is out, I want your personal attention on wearing them out. Check their records, find out what they need, talk to the trainers currently working with them. Work out a course to train them and wear them out. Mind you, I don't want it messing with their schoolwork, but I want them too tired to think of more fun.**

He finally stood and stretched. **The only other thing is, I have applied to move to a larger house. I'm running out of room. The Alpha is looking into it, but I'm hoping to have the new place before Olivia is out of medical.** He turned and started trotting away.

Everyone followed him back towards the houses. Tomorrow was going to be an interesting day for the pups. From the sounds of it, Mike definitely had plans for them.

*****

At some point during the night Tessa jerked up sobbing as memories of what happened turned to a nightmare. She pulled her knees to her chest and wrapped her arms around them as she rested her head on them and cried.

Zane was startled awake and thanks to his wolf he rolled off the bed in a crouch. It was only a basic fighting stance, but it was obvious his wolf was looking for danger. After Zane's eyes traveled around the room, he slowly stood. He found Oscar sitting next to his sister with his wolf's head resting on her shoulder. Zane settled down on the bed and stroked Oscar's head.

Once he'd looked around Zane picked Tessa up and settled her on his lap. He wrapped his arms around her and held her close to his chest. Instead of saying anything he simply settled for humming a quiet song his mother used to sing to him when he was little and scared. It might be silly, but he had always loved 'Hush Little Baby'. For the moment, he was going to simply hold her and let her calm down. What he was going to do, he wasn't sure but there had to be something Zane could do for her. Tomorrow, he might have to talk to the Luna and see what she might say.

Eventually Tessa fell asleep in his arms, and he leaned his head back against the wall. Tomorrow was going to be a miserable day, but Zane wasn't going to move unless he had to. Next to him he could feel Oscar pressing against the two of them. Eventually Zane fell asleep though it wasn't very comfortable .

He was woken up the next morning when Mike quietly cleared his throat, "Wake up Zane." Once he was sure Zane's wolf wasn't going to react violently, as it was best to not startle a sleeping wolf, especially when they were in protection mode, he settled down on the bed. Mike lifted one hand and gently stroked Tessa's hair before waking her and Oscar. *Luna, Tessa had a very bad nightmare last night and honestly all three, Zane, Tessa, and Oscar are looking rough. I'm going to drag the twins over to the Healer and have him take a look. I'm not going to force her to go to school.**

The Luna was in her office and had Abby and Brandon with her when Mike contacted her. *Do it. I have their parents in my office. Both felt Tessa's nightmare last night and had almost come over. I will contact the school and excuse them for the day. Tomorrow we will revisit this.**

Mike gave the three of them a sad smile, "Tessa and Oscar, I'm going to take you to the Healer. He is going to talk to you and make a decision on how we are going to deal with your fears." He looked at Zane, "While I'm taking care of them, you will report to the services office. They are going to have some chores for you and the other two. Simone is already on her way to school."

Zane felt the impact of Mike's orders and wanted to resist but he didn't, "Yes Uncle Mike. I will get something to eat at the main house." He gave Tessa a hug before wrapping an arm around Oscar's wolf, "Both of you go and get ready to go with Uncle Mike." He urged the two off his bed and watched them silently leave the room. Instead of saying anything he settled for pulling some clothes out and walking into his bathroom. He was sure Mike would understand his current mood and Zane didn't need to say anything.

The two silently left the room and headed downstairs to their room. It only took them a few minutes to get ready to go. Neither were hungry currently; they could eat at the main house later. By the time they left the house with Beta Mike, Zane was already gone. He had briefly sent to them he would talk to them later and had ordered them to take it easy. Zane had included going to talk to the Luna if Tessa was feeling up to it.

*****

When Zane reported to the services office, he found Rico and Melody there as well. Melody and Rico traded looks when they saw how rough Zane was looking. Before they said anything the she-wolf in charge spoke, "This morning Rico, you are going to be helping with the rabbits, Zane you are working with the cattle, and Melody the housekeeper. Once lunch is over you will be reporting to the enforcer training area. Go get to work."

Even Zane's wolf looked more than revolted at the idea of dealing with cattle unless they were eating them. Zane didn't even bother sighing and after trading wry grins with the other two they left to get to work. Frankly for Zane by the time lunch rolled around, he was not a happy wolf. He had the fun and excitement of mucking out one of the barns. It was nasty and smelly work. From what little he figured out, this was for the cows and baby cows, or whatever you called them. He not only mucked it out, but he also helped move hay around, and hosed remnants of crap and piss into a collection tank. Apparently, it made very good compost. Learning how to use the skid steer was interesting but not worth the smells. Even if he could close the door and limit the smell inside it.

He met the other two outside Mike's house. There was no way in hell Zane was going to be going inside smelling the way he did. He might just have to strip down in back and hose off before anything else. When Tessa and Oscar came out with a pile of food, he made a face, "I'm so not sure if I'm going to be able to stomach anything right now." His wolf was as far back in his mind as possible and whining.

Rico was looking revolted as well but not as bad as Zane was. He had been dealing with the rabbits and though they didn't stink as bad, they still stank. His wolf was less than pleased as well and was glaring from where he was curled up.

Melody looked somewhat ragged and tired as well. She groaned even as the food came out, "They had me helping to clean the attic out. I know they do it routinely, but I'm not sure I'm going to feel clean for a while." She had washed her hands thankfully, so she felt clean enough to eat. She had to agree the other two reeked. She was sitting upwind of them just to keep the stink away, or as much as possible.

Both Tessa and Oscar had to wrinkle their noses at the three and made sure to not be downwind of them. Oscar was looking as revolted as the others were, "I'm not going to ask you what they had you doing. I think I can figure it out. Would you two like to hose off in back? Tessa can get you some clothing to wear until you finish eating."

Zane sighed as he stood, "Anything to help, even if I have to flush my sinuses out." He stomped off towards the back of the house and stripped his clothing off. He was already hosing his body down when Rico came back as well, "Goddess, this sucks. Just another reason for me to do something to David."

Oscar came out with some washcloths and soap. He handed the washcloths and soap over before dumping the clothing and towels on the porch along with a laundry bag, so they didn't have to bring the clothes inside. Once done Oscar headed back out front to wait. Melody was already eating, and he traded another look with Tessa. They knew most wolves went through this stuff, but they were getting dumped in the deep end of the smelliest, most difficult tasks.

Melody had to roll her eyes at the two. It was rather obvious what was going through their minds at the moment. Since her mouth was full and she was starving, Melody didn't bother saying anything. Instead, she focused on eating. By the time she was mostly done the other two had come back.

They still smelled but not nearly as bad. They were both grumbling even as they were stuffing food down. It had been a rather hard morning for all of them and they were hungry and tired. Zane groaned, "Oh, crap, don't forget we are supposed to report to Enforcer training once we finish eating. I have a really bad feeling I might need to crawl back by the time they are done with us." He glanced at Tessa and Oscar, "I hate to ask but I think I'm going to want to soak when we get done. Can you bring some clean clothes to the training center when I send for you?"

Tessa wrinkled her nose at Zane, "Only if I don't have to come near you for a while. Sorry but you still stink, Zane. They do have some hot tubs for soaking after training." She collected the leftover food and plates to take them inside.

Zane didn't blame her for saying it and he really hoped he was stench free before bedtime. Since they were done eating, he stood with a few more mutters, "Well shall we? Time for training."

*****

While Zane and the others were working, Kadrian was sitting in his office talking with the pack lawyer. He was not looking very happy currently since his wolf was feeling pugnacious. He had been in contact with Esther when Mike had contacted her. No, she hadn't discussed her meeting with the twin's parents as well as the meeting with the twins.

He knew she would tell him if it would affect the pack. If it was part of her being the Luna, then in many cases she wouldn't. It gave the pack a sense of privacy and security that what was discussed would be kept protected, "I know you have reviewed the information provided. Before we have access to the evidence both for and against both parties what might we be looking at?"

She took a sip of her flavored water as she took a moment to review her notes. Once she did, she looked back up, "First before anything, we will have to wait until the Prosecutors office decides to file charges and see what they are. Once that happens it depends on what the charges are as to what happens next. If the two in question are charged with something like simple assault it could be passed to a pretrial or settlement hearing. This would be to see if the charges could be resolved without further legal charges or punishments. If the charges are more serious such as sexual harassment or assault, then it could be passed to the Jurisdiction hearing. If one part, the other, or both are found innocent then all charges are dropped. If one, the other, or both are considered guilty then it will go to the Disposition hearing. In the Disposition hearing the judge will decide the charges and punishments. In rare cases it could be passed to the Department of Corrections to be dealt with as an adult." She stopped to see if he had any questions.

Kadrian was tapping a pen on the desk as he listened to what she had to say, "Okay, start with the possible outcomes least to worst. As I'm sure you expect I want a detailed document as soon as possible on what we are discussing." Both knew it was being recorded and saved in a secured computer storage.

The Lawyer gave him a wry smile, "I will skip what happens if the two are let off scot-free. I really don't want to imagine what the outcome might be." Wolves were not believers in letting the guilty go free. Considering how long a wolf could live, if you didn't tromp on them from the beginning it could lead to many decades or even centuries of crime. When wolves turned to crime, they often became rogues and made many of the worst of the human criminals look fairly normal.

"Starting with the two boys, presuming they do end up going to the Disposition hearing, the punishment could range from at home supervision for up to half a year. Next, would be formal supervision via a parole officer for up to half a year as well. If they are put on parole they could be sent to another relative, foster home, group home, or a probation camp." She checked her notes again just to ensure she wasn't missing anything, "If they are transferred to the Division of Juvenile Justice, they would be sent to juvie. If they are tried as adults, it completely changes everything."

After another sip of water, she spoke one more time, "As far as the pretrial or settlement conference, the court will try and resolve this. If the parents can come to an agreement on how to handle it, then the courts will consider it resolved without a record having been made. Before any of the above happens, they have to wait for the DA to press charges. Once charges are pressed the first hearing will be at least ten days after the charges are pressed. I wouldn't expect this to go very fast, it really depends on the charges, and all I mentioned above." The lawyer made a face and sighed, "For juvenile cases, they do tend to try to get through them faster simply due to the impact on the child and schooling. Discovery will start taking place at the first hearing. It's when things will really start taking off."

Kadrian grunted at her first comment, "It might get somewhat ugly and especially if all of the pups ended up back at the same school. Neither boy would survive very long unless we pulled all the pups out. Even if we took Zane and his group out, it would be a win for the others. Damien would try and keep the pups under control but all it would take would be David or Leon being their usual stupid selves. None would allow them to do anything without a major response." He kept tapping the pen as he considered what she was saying. They had never dealt with something like this with the pups before, "Keep me updated and I guess we are going to have to see about getting them started on some sort of home schooling for the time being." He dismissed her.

*****

When Zane and the others were done with their training the three of them slowly staggered to the pack house. Zane was going to visit Olivia and spend time with her or else. When he finally made it to her room, he flopped in a chair and groaned, "I think Uncle Mike hates me. I haven't been this sore for ages."

Olivia looked at him and wasn't sure whether to be sympathetic with or snicker at her brother, "What makes you say that, Zane? You do look somewhat tired but at least you aren't soaking with sweat today." Tessa was back in her room and was helping Olivia do her homework.

Oscar had already contacted her about what they had looked like at the training center. Now he was back at the house, keeping an eye on the kitten. It was old enough not to need bottle feeding but was young enough it needed fairly constant attention, "I will give you a back massage later if you would like Zane. I'm sure Oscar and I can take care of Melody and Rico as well if they need."

Zane ignored her attempt not to make fun of him, "Probably because the three of us are having the fun of learning the pack from the bull crap up. After lunch, we had Enforcer training for two hours. If you try and make fun of me, I will come and visit you after cleaning up the cow patties." He wouldn't but he had to say something, "How are you doing Liv?"

She made an icky face at Zane when he suggested it, "Ick and thank goodness I'm just a human. I will let you have the fun of working with them." Olivia shifted in bed and shrugged, "I'm not hurting as much, and I don't need nearly as much pain meds, but I'm really starting to get tired of being in bed. Tomorrow they are going to do another series of x-rays to see if they can reduce or remove the cast." They had changed the bulky dressing for a two-part cast which was lighter.

Melody had settled down on the other side of Oliva and patted her hand, "Just be glad we did donate blood for you, or your healing would be much slower. Be glad you are here as well, with real food and a much better TV package." She gave Olivia's hand a squeeze, "You also have your brother here, as well as the help of Tessa."

Olivia returned the squeeze even as she made another face, "Don't remind me about the blood stuff. I really wasn't happy when I found out about it." She had to look at her leg, "It has really helped though which I'm very thankful for. Last time, I was hurting far worse this soon after the accident."

Zane tensed slightly before sighing and looking away for a moment, "I really can't wait for you to be home though. This helps but it still bothers both me and my wolf." They talked for a while longer before he finally stood, "We have homework to do so see you later." The three walked out leaving Tessa with Oliva and headed back to Mike's house.

When they walked back in, they found Mindy waiting at the table with their homework. Oscar had already pulled his out and was working on it. Zane and the others flopped in chairs and pulled theirs over. Zane growled at the homework, "I wonder if I can use the excuse my wolf ate it?"

Mindy turned and stared at him for the bad joke. After staring at him for a moment, she looked at the others, "Why does it just sound bad?" Even her wolf was staring at him, "Even my wolf is, I don't know, um, not sure what to say."

Rico started to laugh before several muscles decided they didn't like the laughter, "Ouch! Darn it Zane, don't make me laugh. I pulled a muscle in my shoulder earlier and it is calling you names." His wolf had enjoyed the joke and was howling in amusement. He was howling so hard Rico's eyes had slightly changed.

Melody simply glared at Zane, "I will bite you and your wolf for the horrible joke next time we run." She turned to Mindy, "Just warning you if you do start hanging around you will have to deal with his humor." She thumped a book on the table in Zane's direction and then ignored him for a while.

Zane thumped the table with a book for good measure and started working on the homework. It was somewhat harder since he wasn't in class learning. If this went on too long, he was going to need to talk to Mike about it. The last thing he wanted was any of them to fall behind or have whatever grades they currently had drop. For Zane, it was mostly B's and C's, but he could accept them. It wasn't because he wasn't smart but as of now, he had no idea what he wanted from life.

Right before Zane stood to follow Oscar into the kitchen, his uncle walked into the room, "Hello Mindy, hello everyone else. Mindy, I need to talk to Zane and the others. Thank you for bringing the homework back and we will see you tomorrow." He went to the kitchen and grabbed a glass of juice and came back out.

When he settled down, he noticed everyone looking tense and he shook his head, "Relax, this has nothing to do with those idiots. It has something to do with you, Zane, starting to form your own team. It's simply when I moved into this house, it was when I discovered you had been hurt and lost your parents. I knew I was going to need the room for the two of you. Now you have both Tessa and Oscar, not to mention the foundation of your team, we need more room. I talked to the Alpha about this, and he is getting a house prepared for us. Mind you, only Tessa and Oscar will be living with us, but it will have a small section for you and your friends. We are looking to have this done before Olivia is out of the medical section."

Zane had started tensing up when Mike had chased Mindy out since he figured it had to do with the almost fight. When he started talking Zane did start to relax and then tensed again, "Sorry for the hassle Uncle Mike." He hadn't meant to be such a pain in the ass for everyone, including what felt like most of the pack.

Mike leaned over and grasped Zane's shoulder and gave it a good shake, "Don't even start Zane. You have been making me proud of how you have taken up your responsibilities. It was rough the first month or so, but I don't blame you. You woke up to your entire life not just destroyed but destroyed beyond imagination. You stood up for pack members, you faced down those aiming to hurt the pack. You are trying to do your best for your sister and dealing with your loss. I know your parents would be proud of you as well."

The others remained where they were. This was between Zane and his uncle since it dealt with family. Oscar and the other two quietly stood and moved to the kitchen to let them talk. It was almost time for dinner, so they decided to start cooking.

Zane honestly didn't know what to say. To an extent it didn't matter what anyone said about what happened. He did feel responsible deep down. What the Luna had said was true, he wasn't really at fault, but he felt he was. He had made the choice to go for a run and he had been hurt. If he hadn't been in the hospital, they wouldn't have been at the intersection and killed. It didn't occur to him they could have been killed at any intersection.

Thinking about the pack and his friends, it was far easier to deal with and accept it as being something wolf related. It was so out of his experience Zane didn't connect it directly with being turned. There was something about the twins that almost forced him to protect them. Some of their actions did bother him and probably would for a while. Their cleaning, doing the laundry, and even the cooking he was coming to terms with. Curling up in bed with Tessa and or Oscar still felt really weird. In Tessa's case, she was rather pretty in a quiet way.

It also felt really strange having a *girl* in his bed, even if it was either their comforting him or his trying to protect them. He had managed to avoid thinking about it as much as possible. Oscar was different since he had always been in his wolf form. Tessa had been as well, except the last two nights. Zane had given Oscar a number of hugs and received a number as well which felt really strange as well. He knew there wasn't anything to it except a general affection, but it was weird. To his wolf, it was completely to be expected to help form and strengthen pack bonds. His wolf had no reason to feel differently now about any of them curling up and napping together.

To Zane, it was so very strange and for this he had to lean on his wolf for help on how to act. There had been many times his two halves felt like they were staring across some fixed border trying to figure the other out. If Zane had been older, he might have made a comparison about

Russia and NATO staring across the Berlin wall. It was almost a demarcation indicating there be dragons along with proceed at your own risk. There was also a third wall, demarcation, joined section which both had common ground on. In this case it was the twins. Both Zane and his wolf agreed the twins were pacifists at heart and wouldn't fight.

Even as confused and hurting as Zane was, he knew deep down in his soul they were his to protect. They were also his friends. In a way it gave Zane and his friends a rallying point to center on and base who and what they were to become. Zane had seen how his uncle acted around Abby and to a lesser extent Brandon. There was a great deal of affection and caring there. It was nothing more than that since Abby and Brandon were mates, but it was there. Zane was almost feeling the same way about the twins as well.

As Zane was thinking, Mike sat there with his juice and sipped on it. So many things were being tossed at Zane, but he was holding up reasonably well. Zane might not have noticed but Mike had been talking a great deal with the Luna and the doctors. It was to have an idea where Zane might be heading and how he and the others could help. Before Zane had broken down on the Luna's shoulder and cried his fears out, Mike had been very concerned. Being a lone wolf wasn't a bad thing, if it was right for the wolf. It was more Mike knew his brother would want him to take care of the two. "Zane, think about it and come talk to me or even Damien or his parents. Now why don't we set the table."

Right about the time they had the table set and the food done Tessa walked in and set her pack next to the others. She had finished her homework while helping Olivia. She settled down next to her brother's and leaned against Rico for a moment. She could sense Zane was really thinking about something, so she leaned against Rico for comfort.

*****

The detectives assigned to the case had spent several hours the day before calling and interviewing several witnesses. It had taken some time since there had been several of them who'd been briefly interviewed by the police at the mall. They did take the witness accounts with a large grain of salt. People's memories always had a bit of a bias in them, sometimes very much different than what happened; it was why cameras were much more preferred. One thing most of the witnesses agreed on was there had been a scream just before whatever had happened occurred. Nobody else had been in the hallway, and without any cameras there either, it wasn't much more they could say other than hearing the scream and then some saw the kids take off into the hall before returning with the other shortly.

Once they had compiled all the statements as well as their notes from the interviews on Sunday, they sat down to discuss their findings. Normally there would have been one lead detective and a junior detective but in this case, it was decided to have two seniors. Both were seasoned detectives and had a fair amount of experience with juveniles. The first spoke, "Well on the video, we saw the two boys go into the hallway first followed by the female. Shortly after the others vanished down the hallway only to exit shortly after. Based on some of the witness statements there was a scream, presumably from a young female, about the time everything happened."

His partner ran through his notes and what he had to say pretty much matched up. Even though they had their opinions on what happened they did try to keep it as factual as possible. After comparing the notes and discussing it a while longer they finalized everything and forwarded it to the DA's office. It was probably going to take a few days for the DA's office to review it before anything happened. They turned to the next case on the books.

*****

Zane and the others had finished their homework after dinner and Zane was beat. Between taking care of those damn walking burgers and then training, he was tired. All he could hope was tomorrow he wouldn't be too sore, or he wasn't sure he would be moving much. All the crap about wolf strength and healing didn't seem to apply right now. Even Melody and Rico were looking tired as they slowly headed out for the evening. Zane didn't realize that his workload was geared to a wolf's strength, and if he had to attempted it before being turned, he would have passed out before lunch.

Simone had come by and given them as much help with the homework as possible. She did have training with the other junior wolves still. Once she had finished it and eaten dinner at home, she hurried over to help. It helped since she attended several of the classes all of them did.

When he slowly dragged his body up the stairs, he wanted to scowl at Mike but figured he would get growled at. Sometimes the whole dominance thing was such a pain in the ass. After a short hot shower Zane collapsed in bed and was asleep when the twins crawled in.

*****

The following morning at school, the principal was in her office with the counselors involved. They were discussing what was being done with the five children. The subject of Tessa and Oscar had come up as well. The day before they had received a note from a doctor indicating Tessa had been too upset to come to school. She had slept horribly and woke from nightmares. It was the doctor's opinion forcing Tessa back to school wasn't good.

Added to her headache, was a complaint from several parents about some of the kids who normally hung around with David and Leon. There were a number of complaints about ongoing bullying by several students and a demand to have this dealt with. This was not something the school needed to deal with, especially with a case involving at the least sexual harassment.

In the front office as the three were discussing what they were going to do the secretary looked up when the door opened. When it did her eyes hardened since the four parents and their two children walked in, "May I help you?" Her eyes were on the boys who were not supposed to be on the school property.

Mrs. Walpert glared at the secretary. She was just one of the peons who were below her notice, "We will speak to the principal now. We have discussed it with our lawyer and having our children suspended is ridiculous. Tell her we will not appreciate having to wait to talk to her."

Both she and her husband were looking down their noses at the woman. David was looking smug, as was Leon.

The secretary took a moment to weigh the options before ringing the principal's phone, "Mrs. Smith I have the Walpert's, the Baker's, and their sons wishing to speak to you. They are very insistent." She listened for a moment before looking at the group, "The principal will be with you momentarily."

A moment later Mrs. Smith came out and she had a displeased expression on her face, "Come into my office." She had already asked her secretary to contact the school safety officer. She was one of the local police officers and normally was only at the school part of the day. Currently it had been decided to have her there for the full school day until the end of the week.

As soon as the door closed the Secretary called for the officer and informed her of what was going on, "Please report to the offices in case you are needed, please." Once she hung up, she placed another call, "Mr. Mac Tire' Dona, just to inform you, the other party chose to come to school with their children. You will be updated later."

Inside the office Mrs. Smith sat down at her desk, "Before you say anything, why are your children here? They have been suspended and until the suspension is lifted or the court issue is resolved, they are not to be on school property. Now what do you want?" Her voice was calm and cool as she was talking.

This time it was Mr. Walpert who spoke, "Now see here, this is not right. They were attacked, and the accusations are totally false. We are planning on suing the ones who slandered our good name. We want our children returned to school since they are innocent of whatever the others said."

Mrs. Smith gave him a cool look, "Mr. Walpert, you do not dictate to me how I handle issues such as these. The charges both against your child and the others are very serious. Until this issue is resolved, I will not have or take any chance this will further impact my school. As I said, your child is not authorized to be on school property. Take him and leave, or I will be forced to have the police called to remove you and your child." She looked at the other family, "The same applies to you. If either of you have issues with my decision, take it to the school board. Until they override me , my decision remains." Now her voice was downright chilly.

Mr. Baker glared at her, "Fine, we will go to the school board and be warned we will take legal actions against you and your school district to correct the wrongs our children are facing. We still demand until such a ruling comes down from the school board, our children will return to school." He despised small-minded people.

Right about then there was a knock on the office door before it opened. The school Officer walked in, "Is there a problem Mrs. Smith?" She glanced at the others in the room and her eyes rested on the boys.

Mrs. Smith looked at the six, "Please escort them off the school property. If they resist, I would like to press trespassing charges." This was going to go down like a load of bricks.

CHAPTER 15

Massages

Tessa and Oscar walked into Zane's room; both could tell he was exhausted. Thankfully, Tessa had managed to catch a nap during the day. Olivia had been snoozing and before Tessa had realized it, she had fallen asleep as well. Both had been down for a couple of hours and Tessa had woken feeling much better, "I think I'm going to still give Zane a good massage. It should help him sleep better." To be honest Tessa wanted the physical contact.

Oscar glanced at his sister and gave her a slight smile. **I will give you some time to give him a massage before I come back. He will protect us and help take care of us any way he can. Take care of him sis.** He silently left the room. Oscar knew nothing like *that* would take place, but he didn't have a problem with his sister being attracted to Zane. He was a good wolf and even hurting, he had taken care of them and protected them.

Tessa gave her brother a shy smile since she knew what he was thinking. **Thank you, Oscar. When she is old enough, she will do the same for you.** She turned towards Zane and from a small bag she had pulled out some massage oil. It was something wolves used when they were pushed to their limits in training and would help him relax. In the morning, he would feel better as well.

Since Zane was already lying on his stomach she carefully climbed on the bed and settled down next to him. Once she was sure he was still asleep she rested one hand on his back and waited for him to relax again.

Tessa was sure Zane's wolf knew she was there and knew she wasn't a threat, but she wanted Zane's wolf to relax as well. Once she felt a slight relaxation of his muscles, she removed the hand and poured some of the oil in her hand. After working it to warm it up some, she lightly worked it into his back. She repeated it until Zane's entire back was coated before she started working on the massage.

She finished the massage about twenty minutes later and had to smile when Oscar walked into the room in his wolf form. He hopped up on the other side and settled down next to Zane. Once he was settled, he rested his head on Zane's back and blinked his eyes sleepily at Tessa.

Tessa smiled at Oscar and leaned over and stroked his ears briefly before settling down next to Zane. She was ready for bed and wrapped an arm around his lower back and settled down. Tessa couldn't help but be pleased by having Zane as their protector. He was nice, even if he tried to sound growly and grumpy. She knew he was hurting still and would be for some time. Knowing it only made his choosing them as part of his team even more special.

It was one of the things that was drawing her to him. He felt very comfortable to her and Oscar. Even as he was struggling to get used to having them in his life, he hadn't grumbled very much. There had been a few times he had been put out, such as when they had cleaned his room. Even then, he hadn't been mean or accusatory when he had told him rather bluntly to ask first. She moved a bit closer to him and eventually fell asleep.

It had taken some time for her to fall asleep even curled up close to Zane. Even though Tessa and Oscar had talked to the Luna with her parents in the room, the fear was still there. The nightmare from last night was still on her mind when she fell asleep as was the hope she would sleep deeply. Thankfully all three of them slept adequately thought the night.

*****

When Zane woke the next morning, he felt somewhat better physically. Thanks to his change, he could smell the oil used on his back though he had no idea what it was. It was both astringent and somewhat sweet smelling. As he had been expecting, Oscar was on one side and his head was resting on the pillow next to Zane's head. Tessa was curled up on his other side and one arm was draped across his waist.

He wanted to sigh, since this was not something he was comfortable with, yet. In the classes he was taking on the weekends, it had been made clear to him, this was normal. Family and friends often curled up together; sleeping alone was not common among werewolves. Even if he hadn't seen his uncle with others curled up in his bed, chances were it had happened, "Wake up both of you. I need to get dressed and all that good stuff. I will see you downstairs."

Oscar hopped down off the bed and had a really good stretch before he trotted out of the room. Tessa took a bit longer to wake up. When she did, Tessa rolled on her back and stretched. After a few moments she sat up and stretched again, "Morning Zane. See you downstairs." She slipped off the bed and left his room.

When she had rolled over and stretched Zane had glanced over before looking away and blushing. Tessa was a pretty girl. When she stretched, her night shirt had tightened over her chest and showed more than he was used to. Thankfully, she hadn't noticed his blush as she sat up and left the room. Once his door was closed, he muttered quietly to himself, "So not used to this, damn it. They might be used to casual nudity and everything, but this is almost too much. There isn't any way I can ask her to come to my bed only in wolf form without her asking why. That isn't a conversation I want to have." What didn't help was his wolf snorted at him from the back of his mind, as he quite liked having his juniors beside him, so he knew they were safe and protected.

With those thoughts, he rolled out of bed and quickly took care of getting ready for the day. Zane had slept okay but there had been a few almost nightmares and he wanted to talk to someone. Since they were both his and his wolf's, he was going to see if he could talk to the Luna at some point today. Once he was dressed, he headed downstairs.

After walking downstairs Zane found his uncle there. Zane flopped down in a chair at the table and picked up the cup of coffee already there, “Morning Unc.” He commented after taking a sip, **I need to talk to the Luna at some point today. I’m going to talk to her when I find out what lovely work they have in store for us today.** As usual Oscar had food almost ready, and it only took a moment for a plate to be carried over.

“Morning Zane and I’m going to be talking to both the Luna and Alpha about what we are going to do with your schooling. The other parents are going to be there as well. Since you have been suspended from school until this is resolved, it might be easier if we home school you for a while.” **That’s fine, and I’m sure they have some very lovely work for you to do. I will talk to you later.** In this case each set of parents was going to be called into the meeting.

A brief flash of anger crossed Zane’s face, before he controlled his expression, “I’m sorry it came to this, but I’m not sorry for protecting Tessa and Oscar against them. My wolf feels much the same.” Zane wasn’t going to mention his wolf wanted to make David and Leon go away permanently. He turned back to the food and started to eat.

*****

The Walperts and the Bakers complained loudly as the officer was escorting them from the building and to their cars. Once there, she gave both families’ a neutral look, “Do not bring your children back, unless requested, until told otherwise. Next time I will be forced to arrest them for trespassing. I wouldn’t care to do it, but it will not stop me.” She watched the six climbed into their vehicles and pull away.

The entire time they were ranting and raving about what a crock this was. There were threats to sue the school, the police department, the principal, and more. They swore and cursed about the brats who had started the fight. To be honest, if she hadn’t been an officer, she would have been impressed at the vocabulary they were using.

Once she walked back inside, she reported to the main office. The secretary gave the officer an expressionless look which was returned, “The principal will talk to you later. She needs to finish the meeting before she talks to you. Unless you had to arrest anyone, in which case she would speak to you immediately." There was a knowing tone to her voice when she spoke.

The officer grunted, "Unfortunately the worst I could have done would be giving them a ticket for bad parking and offensive language. I'm going to file a report and start my rounds. Let me know when she is available." She turned and headed to the small office the campus officer had been given.

*****

Zane found he was going to be working in the laundry for the morning, thank goodness. Laundry wasn't something he liked doing but it was better than the damn walking burgers. He did have to admit having Tessa and Oscar saved him from that hassle. As far as the cleaning, he was more on the fence about. It still bothered him knowing they would clean, just because of who he was to them, "Ma'am I need to speak to the Luna briefly and then I will get to work." Once she approved of his request, he left the office.

When he reached the Luna's office Zane had to admit he still wasn't comfortable talking to her. Mrs. Esther had helped him when he had fallen apart seeing Olivia at the hospital, but it still scared him. As he was starting to feel slightly stressed again his wolf came forward slightly to support him. Zane finally knocked on the door frame, "Mrs. Esther do you have a moment?"

Esther was sitting at her desk when she sensed him approaching. Instead of simply calling for him to enter, she waited for him to speak. When Zane did, she looked up and smiled, "Please come in Zane and how may I help you?" She wasn't sure what might have brought him past but was pleased he had.

Zane stepped into her office and met her eyes before lowering them slightly, "Thank you Ma'am, I was hoping you might have time to talk at some point today. Last night I started having some nightmares. They involved both Tessa and Olivia. I also wanted to talk to you about things I can do for both Oscar and Tessa 'cause of Sunday."

She had taken a sip of her tea when he spoke and was feeling very pleased now. Zane might not realize it, but he was taking a huge step by coming to her. He was starting to heal thanks to his friends, and he was moving more towards the pack and being a pack member. Just about then Kadrian contacted her about what was going on at the school. Mentally she fumed but it couldn't be helped, "Right now I have something I have to deal with, but I should have time about 11am. I will contact your supervisor for the morning and let them know to release you just before then."

Zane wished they could have talked now but he understood her being busy, "Thank you Mrs. Esther. I will be here at 11am." He left the room and headed towards the laundry area. Melody was working with the rabbits and Rico the cattle. He felt bad for both and hoped it wasn't too awful.

*****

When Kadrian had received the call, he leaned back in his chair and clasped his fingers behind his head. He looked up at the ceiling and contemplated how to handle this. No, he shouldn't know they were there, so he couldn't call and complain. What he needed to do was to nip this in the bud and keep the pups and certain others from boiling over. Frankly though he didn't have any idea what to do at this point which was rather annoying.

After thinking about it for a few minutes Kadrian contacted Esther. **Can you come to my office? The brats and their parents were at the school. I'm going to have Mike come as well. We need to discuss this before we have the meeting with the parents of those involved.** He sent to Mike as well. The meeting wasn't for close to an hour, so they had some time to deal with this issue. Just for good measure he called for two of the elders who dealt with the training for the pups.

It was only a short time later when those called for came into the room. Esther settled in a chair next to her mate at the conference table. As she was sitting down one of their team made sure to have drinks set on the table and everything neat before they left the room. Mike settled down in his normal chair and grabbed a cup of coffee as they waited for the elders to come in.

Once everyone had come in and settled down, Kadrian glanced at everyone he had called, "I had a call this morning that the other two families had gone to the school with their children. Since the school hasn't contacted , I'm going to assume they left on their own. I will get more information once the pups are back from school. I will talk with Damien to see what he might have heard about this. I assume the secretary will come and talk to me once she is off work as well. I talked to our lawyer yesterday as well. Here is a copy of what she said are the probable outcomes." He passed them out and allowed them several minutes to review the information.

Eventually he spoke again, "I'm leaning towards this taking some time to be resolved unless something happens, such as the charges being dropped. I do not see that happening, but time will tell. Because of this I'm going to be talking to the other parents about homeschooling the pups involved until this is taken care of. Based on what the lawyer said, this could take up to a month or longer. I'm going to try and keep it as short as possible but as we know the courts move in their own time."

One of the Elders set the packet back down after flipping through it, "I will look into what is needed for the home schooling. It can be done here at the pack house in one of the small conference rooms. It will take me a day or two to do the research and get it set up. We can discuss this further when I'm done. There might be a few other options as well which can be looked at."

Mike had started tapping his fingers on the table, to be honest he was pretty damn worked up still. None of this was Zane's or the others' fault but they were being punished simply because they were involved. Zane protected Tessa from something even worse possibly happening. Even if they had been humans, he would have been defending those in danger, "What do you want me to do Alpha?"

Kadrian knew Mike was upset but there honestly wasn't much more to be done, "I want you to talk to your enforcers to ensure everyone knows any actions against the families will be harshly dealt with. I will brook no punitive retaliation against the Walpert's, Baker's, their properties, or businesses. If any wolf chooses not to purchase anything from their businesses that's one thing, vandalism or damaging property is another. I'm going to have a pack meeting scheduled to discuss this as well." With this issue, Kadrian needed to come down hard and firm to ensure the pack obeyed. They didn't need a pack of wolves going nuts and drawing attention to themselves, and the pack .

Mike mentally scrapped his idea of going and ripping up her flower garden or chewing the tires off their vehicles, "I will take care of it once we are done this morning." He was going to have to call several meetings since he wasn't going to pull anyone off patrol unless really needed. Nor was it something he could post a notice about and hope they read it.

Kadrian looked at him and after meeting Mike's eyes turned back to the table, "Esther and I will be discussing this later as well. If needed, we will update you on what we decide. Any questions?" When nobody spoke, he dismissed them and once they had left, he ran his fingers through his hair, "Goddess, Esther I'm probably as worked up as most of the parents are. I might need to go on a walk and calm down for a while."

Esther stood and moved over to her mate and settled in his lap. It was one of the best ways for one mate to help the other relax. She pressed a kiss on his neck before resting her head on his shoulder. **I completely understand and as a mother wolf I have a feeling it is even harder for me. I had to deal with Tessa and Oscar yesterday. Between calming their parents and dealing with the twins I wanted to go and deal with them as well.** She tucked her head against his chest. Both needed to try and calm down.

*****

Zane did his best while working in the laundry, but it was hard. Zane was struggling to deal with everything that was happening . As hard as it was to admit, he was starting to move past the loss of his parents. It still hurt and still made him want to push people away, in an attempt to prevent more pain. Even with Melody and the other more dominant wolves, he was still having some issues. Tessa and Oscar were the only two wolves who Zane didn't want to try to push away. Olivia was the only other one.

This was causing him a great deal of discontent and stress. Thankfully, as he was working, for the most part, he could do what was asked without talking much. It gave him some time to try and focus on what he wanted and needed to talk to Esther about. As he was working and thinking, the other wolves noticed he was not being very vocal, so they left him alone. Zane didn't notice because he was really focused on his concerns.

As he was working, Zane did his best to try and think of one thing or issue at a time. He started with Olivia, and it was both easy and hard. Losing his parents had been beyond horrible and waking up to discover they were dead had really hit his heart badly. Added to it was discovering he had almost lost his little sister. That was almost worse than losing his parents. They were dead, and nothing could be done about it. With Olivia, it was because he had almost lost her only to find out she had been critically injured and disabled.

Finding out he was now the same as the monster who had Turned him, hit hard. Before Olivia had been taken back to the hospital for treatment, had been horrible. Just before then, he had found he had seemed to acquire two very junior wolves as his personal attendants. That was so strange to his human half. It had taken some time to come to terms with it.

When he had lost it, and the Luna had helped to pick him up and help put him back together was almost as stressful. The final problem were those two fuckers who had attacked his wolves. When the two had attacked Tessa in the mall, Zane had finally accepted they were his to protect. His wolf knew this from the beginning, but the human half had to come to accept it. Between the stress of his sister being in the hospital again and then the attack on Tessa, Zane was off center again. The center which his family and team had been drawing him to had been damaged.

Before he could think any more about this, the supervisor caught his attention, “Zane you have the meeting with the Luna in a few minutes. Go and take care of it.” He turned and started giving a few more instructions to the wolves working for him.

Zane tossed in the last of the laundry he had been taking care of before leaving the area. He was still fairly deep in thought as he left and headed towards the Luna’s office. Before he realized it, he was at her door and had to jerk when he realized where he was. He knocked on the door jam, “Mrs. Esther I’m here for the meeting.” He sounded somewhat distracted.

Esther had been waiting for him and called him in once he had knocked, “Come in Zane and close the door behind you.” She stood and walked around her desk to settle down in a chair, “Please have a seat after you get a drink.” She had to tease him slightly, “No beer though.”

Zane twitched and scowled at her, “I don’t drink beer, Mrs. Esther.” After the glower he slowly settled down in a chair, “Thank you for seeing me.” His demeanor changed after he had settled down, “Please Mrs. Esther, no joking. I need some help, and I don’t know who else to go to. Uncle Mike isn’t right since he is an Enforcer and has always been a wolf.” Zane knew he had been a wolf since he had been born from his comments about it.

“Sorry Zane, I was just trying to lighten the mood slightly. What do you need? I can make some guesses but why don’t we start with you telling me and we go from there?” She was still trying to figure out what made Zane, Zane and how he thought. Even with the other day when he finally cried on her shoulder, he hadn’t really said a much. Most of it was his fears about how having lost his parents causing his reaction to seeing Olivia in the hospital. She had read the reports from his trainers, supervisors, and even talked with her son. It said a great deal about him but not who he was.

Zane looked down and took a breath before replying, "Even that's a hard question to answer Mrs. Esther. I'm still dealing with losing my parents, finding out about Olivia, and then her surgery. I think I have accepted the furry presence in the back of my mind, odd looks and all. I'm having trouble dealing with having somehow acquired a team of wolves who look to me. I can feel my wolf is content with them, but it is still so bloody strange. I'm not even going to bother mentioning Tessa and or Oscar curling up next to me at night." He was going to assume she figured he meant in their wolf forms since Zane wasn't going there with Tessa, "Feeling my other half wanting to rip those two into little bloody shreds is not a comfortable thought. Feeling and smelling Tessa's unmitigated terror when she was attacked had me seeing red. If Melody hadn't knocked me away from David, he would be dead right now. I'm scared of these feelings and why I'm feeling them."

Since Zane hadn't gotten anything to drink, she went over and fixed a cup of coffee with some coco in it. Esther listened very carefully as he was talking even as she was fixing the drink for him. She set it down on the coffee table in front of him before settling back in the chair she had been sitting in. Once Zane was done talking, she slowly stirred her drink as she parsed what he had said, "That's pretty much what I thought." She took a sip of her tea and returned to stirring it, "Starting with what you are feeling towards your team and especially Tessa and Oscar for a wolf, it is normal. I have talked with Tessa and Oscar, as you know. While we were talking, they did ask me how to help you become more comfortable with their taking care of you."

As Esther was talking, she was evaluating Zane's body language and what her nose and ears were saying, "One thing I need to hit on before we continue, is wolves look at privacy differently than humans. Even so, it does not mean what is told to me gets spread around. I keep all information given to me private. It is something you need to know; I don't break confidences."

Zane hadn't realized Tessa and Oscar had talked to the Luna about him specifically. He looked down at his cup as he tried to figure out if it bothered him. His wolf simply remained towards the front of his mind, since they were both relaxing in their Luna's presence. Zane's wolf didn't seem to be bothered by what the Luna said, so he left it alone for a moment. He finally looked back up at her, "Thank you for explaining it to me, Ma'am. I'm somewhat accepting of them doing some of the housework and cleaning. What I'm having some trouble with, is how protective I'm feeling and having them curling up with me. I know in the beginning it was to help me deal with what was going on with Olivia but now? Frankly, it is hard to let either out of my sight, even on the property." He finally took a sip of the drink.

Esther completely understood what he was saying, "As a wolf, it makes complete sense, your reaction to not wanting them out of your sight now. You and your wolf took responsibility for them and while they were under your protection, Tessa was attacked. It is making your wolf even more protective of the twins than normal. It is going to take time for your wolf to calm down. Until David and Leon are dealt with, he is going to be extra alert . Right now, they are safe on the property. Believe me, nobody in those two families can come anywhere near this house or your house." She contemplated how much information she should give him.

Eventually she decided to give him a slight bit, "The property close to the pack house and surrounding houses are heavily covered by a variety of sensors. If they don't belong to the pack, they will be noticed, and a team will be dispatched to collect the person. Neither of those two would have a chance to get even vaguely close let alone within sight. You and your wolf will still be tense and twitchy for the time being. What I recommend, is you keep as close to them as you can. You are going to be working both on learning the pack and as a trainee Enforcer. Focus on that, to give you some space from what is going on."

Zane lifted an eyebrow and before he realized it, he spoke, "If you tell me big brother or big sister is watching, I will scream!" As soon as it was out his lips twitched until he forced them to stop. It was so wrong, especially since he despised 1984 by George Orwell. The whole big brother thing made his skin crawl. Zane wasn't stupid since he knew to be careful with what he shared on the internet, but he avoided thinking about it. "Ah, I mean thanks for letting me know. I might have to talk to my wolf later, but it does help. As far as learning the pack I figured it out, though dealing with the burgers on the hoof is not fun. My wolf was horribly offended by having to deal with them. The training is interesting though feeling like I need to crawl home isn't something to look forward to." He took a drink before saying anything else, " Do you have anything to suggest about dealing with Tessa and Oscar?" He felt his heartbeat pick up slightly though he didn't blush.

She gave him a good laugh, knowing the dystopian story, "Something like it, though we don't monitor inside the houses, monitor internet traffic, or monitor phone calls. There are certain areas of the pack house which are monitored but it's expected since many of the senior wolves live here, but even then, private rooms are not monitored. As far as Tessa and Oscar... It's something you are going to need to work out between yourselves. The relationship between a senior wolf and his or her assistants is different for each team, and something you have to figure out." She looked at him and gave him a level look, "I'm going to tell you this since you need to know. It is something we, the more senior wolves, grow up with. At some point you and Tessa might be drawn to each other. Not as mates but simply affectionately. Ask Mike about it, so he can explain it in more detail. I'm not saying anything will happen, but it might. Right now, what both Tessa and Oscar need is the comfort of having a more dominant wolf around. In this case, the wolf who chose them to become part of his team."

Zane couldn't help but look intent as he started to try and consider where those monitored spaces were. Blast it, now he was going to be walking around looking for cameras, heat sensors, and likely things he couldn't think of, "Great, now I'm going to be looking for the darn things. Thanks Mrs. Esther." He had been listening to Mrs. Esther as she was talking, but it had taken him a moment to catch the last bit and thankfully he hadn't taken a sip from the cup he had just lifted to his lips. He was forced to cough several times and damn it, he had turned tomato red, "Um, good to know." Zane's voice was almost a stutter when he replied. There was no way in hell he could talk to his uncle about this.

Esther simply smiled at him, "Relax Zane, I'm just giving you some information you might not have gotten from the classes. What you get in the classes are reasonably in depth and will give you the foundation of how a pack operates. It won't teach you some of the more complex realities we face. It simply isn't possible to cover all aspects. I'm going to make a few changes to what you are learning in the pack classes. What they need is your attention right now. Give it to them." She dimpled at him, "You're welcome."

He avoided thinking about part of what she said, "Thank you for taking a look at my training and adjusting it." Now all he needed to do was to escape from the office, so he could go and try to forget what she had said. Tessa was nice, but it wasn't what he needed to think about right now, "I have answers to some of my questions Mrs. Esther. If you don't mind, I'm going to go and see Liv before lunch." He stood and waited to be dismissed.

Esther had achieved some of what she had wanted. It might have been considered somewhat wrong of her to mention what Zane and Tessa might have but it did what she wanted. It distracted him from some of the other problems for the moment. Hopefully this would keep Zane distracted enough to stop him from doing something stupid. She also knew about the night visit to David's house though she wasn't going to say anything. While his uncle hadn't been around, he had been detected by the sensors and a patrol had been dispatched and had followed them out and then back. As they hadn't done anything which they had orders about, they hadn't intervened, just monitored. "Go and I will have some lunch brought up. Relax with your sister and maybe even talk to her about some of your concerns." When Zane almost ran from her office, she couldn't help but give his receding back a sly smile. **Mike, you might want to find a time to talk to Zane about your relation-*

*ship with Abby and eventually her mate. I briefly mentioned it to distract him from his urges to commit homicide by going and chewing David to death.**

She received a mental groan from Mike, who knew he was going to need to talk to Zane about it soon anyways. No, it didn't mean anything would happen in the near future, but at some point, it probably would. Mike was basing this on Tessa's actions and reactions to his nephew. He was pretty sure Zane didn't see it since he was still struggling to allow anyone very close to him. It was a struggle for Zane and would be for a while. Once Olivia was home and doing better, then Zane would probably relax enough to continue his healing, **Yes, Esther, thanks for dumping this on me.**

*****

When Zane had gone to visit with Olivia, he found Tessa there as well, "Hey Liv, and Tessa. Mrs. Esther said she was sending lunch up." He settled down on the bed and next to his sister. When he spoke his voice was low and quiet, "Hey Liv, how are you doing? Did the doctors have anything have to say?" He wanted her home and sooner than later.

Olivia smiled at Zane when he came in since for some reason, he very faintly blushed when he looked at Tessa. Based on what Tessa and she had been talking about she had a feeling both found each other interesting. As far as she was concerned it was a good thing since it would give Zane something happy to think about, "Hey Zane, they did, and they are going to remove the cast today, but I'm going to have some sort of stiff boot or leg thing for a week or maybe two. Where they broke the bones to fix them is healing well and has good..." She had to frown, "Um, calcium, calci... it looks to be healing well and as long as I use crutches, I will be okay." The terms hadn't meant much to her. All Olivia cared about was she was going home soon. It was what mattered as far as she was concerned.

Zane had to grin as she was trying to explain what the doctors had to say. All he wanted was to have her home yesterday, "Good, I'm so glad to hear it sis. I really need you home and yes, it's my wolf as well as me saying it. It is one less thing I need to be worried about." About then the food had come in and he rolled off the bed and turned to Tessa, "No, I will take care of bringing the food over. You relax and let me do this." His voice wasn't hard, but it was firm. He and his wolf wanted to take care of Tessa and Oscar, even if it was just serving the food for once.

*****

Zane had jumped into the rest of the week to keep from dealing with certain topics the Luna had brought up. Even when Mike had tried to talk to him, Zane managed to dodge his attempts by mentioning homework, needing to comfort Tessa or Oscar, needing a run, and other things. It was obvious, but Zane just couldn't look at that aspect right now. One thing which helped, was the Alpha had found a larger house they could use.

It was another two-story house which had two sections. One could be used for Mike and his needs. The other was something Zane and his team could use. Only Zane and the twins would live there but there was room for the others to relax and bond. The move took place over two days. Zane also used this to avoid talking to his uncle. His team, minus Simone since she was still in school, worked on packing up much of the house.

The move only took part of a day since before the truck had pulled up everything had been packed. There hadn't been a large number of boxes but each and every one had been labeled as to where they had come from. When they had started unpacking Tessa and Melony had told them they would deal with Olivia's room. They growled and grumbled until the boys had left to keep bringing boxes in.

Now unpacking had taken some time but they had gotten most of it done by the end of the day. Zane and Mike had been informed Olivia would be sent home the following week. Her cast had been replaced with a long walking boot. Once it had happened, Olivia had been encouraged to move around the room with the help of the twins. Zane had been so very pleased since it made both him and his wolf happy.

*****

By Friday the DA had finally reviewed the documentation and had finally returned their decision. They were going to start with a settlement hearing, to see if this could be cleared up without major legal involvement. Depending on what the settlement hearing turned up, if needed they might need to go from there.

Once it had been decided, the DA had sent out a letter informing everyone of the date of the hearing. It was, as mandated by law, ten days from when the letters were received and accepted. For this, the documents would be delivered via a certified mail. Once received, they could move forward.

CHAPTER 16

Mindy's Wishes

The rest of the week had been rough since Zane and the other two had been continuing the rotation through the pack work. After working in the laundry Zane had ended up working at the farm before moving to the house again and helping with cleaning and cooking. Melody and Rico had done much the same and thankfully Saturday afternoon, they had been released. For the other two, it had been nice but for Zane, he had the continuing education about what it meant to be a wolf.

The Enforcer training had been interesting but also exhausting. At the end of the last few days, Zane had barely been able to crawl into bed before collapsing and falling asleep. It didn't help each morning he had awoken with the scent of Tessa on his body. Zane now knew she had been massaging the oil on his back and neck, but it still bothered him. She was cute, and he was starting to sense she had a crush on him. It wasn't something he'd mentioned or talked about with anyone.

Later Saturday, Zane had made his way to Olivia's room and settled down in a chair. He leaned back and did his best to try and relax. In the end he was forced to groan, "Mike hates me, I think. I have been forced to crawl into bed the last few nights. Even when I wake up, I'm so sore it isn't funny. Darn it to heck, but I thought being a wolf meant I shouldn't be so sore and tired." Zane was so pleased Olivia had been released and was back home.

What had been rather annoying to Zane as well, was the packing had been done in-between everything else which had been going on. Thankfully, a good portion of it had been done by Tessa, Oscar, and their parents. Zane still had to do his share of the work such as pulling furniture apart like the beds. He also was helping to carry the boxes down and stacking them in the living room. It was one of the reasons why, when Zane collapsed in bed, he passed out almost immediately. Thankfully, there wasn't a great deal since Mike had indicated he'd just recently moved into the first house.

Olivia gave Zane a sympathetic look, "I have seen just how worn you have been. Tessa has been telling me how hard you have been sleeping." She had a feeling if she teased Zane about Tessa, he wouldn't react well, so she left it there, "At least you have today off. Maybe you can go and relax today and give your body time to recover."

Zane blushed faintly when she mentioned Tessa and he was glad Olivia didn't say anything else, "Thank goodness I do have today off. I was wondering if you wanted to come and relax outside, and we can have a small picnic." Since he really hadn't seen much of her, with all the work he had been doing Zane wanted some time with her. Time to talk and feel that she was doing better. He knew she was, but it would help, "It is supposed to be reasonably warm today, so you shouldn't worry about getting cold."

She gave him a really warm smile for the suggestion, "That sounds lovely though I'm going to need a chair and footrest." Although Olivia's leg wasn't hurting as bad as it had been, she still had a lot more healing to do. Olivia could only hope it indicated when she was fully healed, she would be almost normal, "Give me a hand getting up, since I want to go to the living room."

Zane stood and after helping her stand, gave her a good hug, though he was careful not to squeeze too hard. He knew for a fact he was getting stronger, and he didn't want to hurt her, "Sounds like a deal to me, sis." He held her arm while she picked up her crutches. Zane knew she would mutter if he did anything to help. Once she was up, he opened the door to her room and watched her work her way out.

Both Zane and his wolf could tell she really was doing better. She was taking pain meds, but Olivia simply didn't smell like she was hurting as much. There were still scents of pain and suffering, but not as strong. He was so pleased it wasn't funny. What was funnier, Olivia had a small pouch for the kitten. The silly thing was attached to Olivia at the hip. It was okay with Tessa and Oscar, less so with Zane and wouldn't have anything to do with the others. Zane hadn't asked about it, but he figured it was due to their dominance. The more dominant you were the stronger your scent.

Mike looked up as Zane and Olivia came into the living room. He could see the pleasure on his nephew's face, and it was so nice to see. For the moment, Zane was more open than he had been since waking up in the hospital. Mike watched Oscar stand and hurry over to Olivia, though he didn't offer her a hand until she went to sit down. Tessa had hurried over to Zane and given him a good hug at which Mike let a slight smile across his face. Even if Zane was dodging the conversation the Luna had suggested, it was obvious Tessa liked him. At some point, he was going to have to talk to Zane. For now, he had a feeling it was another subtle way to keep Zane distracted.

"It is nice to see how well you are recovering. It looks like, even with the leg brace, you are moving easier." He closed the folder he had been reading and set it off to the side. He wasn't going to mention Tessa or Zane, "So what are you going to do today? I know you can't leave the property but maybe a movie day?" He knew Zane and the others were pretty worn out thanks to everything they had been forced to do.

Zane furrowed his brows at his uncle, "Uncle Mike, fess up, you are deliberately keeping us worn out, aren't you? By the time I go to bed, I almost have to crawl up the stairs." He didn't make it a challenge but a question. He had a feeling he knew why, but even though the nocturnal trip hadn't been mentioned, he had a suspicion they knew, and Zane wasn't going to go there.

Mike smirked at him, “You are such a smart young wolf, Zane. It is true since if you are worn out, I know you won’t have the energy to remain too angry with David and Leon.” His expression became far more serious, “The last thing any of you need is further contact with those two. The worst thing you could do would be to confront them and kill or seriously hurt them. It wouldn’t be good for you or for the pack. You did what you needed to, you saved Tessa from further injury. You did exactly what was needed and then came to the pack and reported it. Now it is our turn to deal with this. You need to focus on your team and the twins. Don’t try and get revenge. Your job is to keep protecting your team. You are doing it b learning how the pack runs and with the training you are getting.”

Even while Zane was holding Tessa his expression became somewhat tense, “Beta Mike, how can I not want to do something to those two? They attacked the two junior wolves in my care. Their parents gave them over to me to protect and take care of. I accepted this. I know I’m having trouble reconciling my new wolf thoughts and human half, but I chose to take care of them.” His arms were wrapped around Tessa and holding her close. It was obvious Zane was asking an older more senior wolf for help.

Mike stood and walked to the kitchen and pulled some flavored water out before walking back. As he was doing that, he was thinking hard about how to answer. Once he settled back down and returned the serious expression on Zane’s face. Thankfully, the others were remaining silent, “Zane, wanting to do something to them is one thing. It’s understandable both from the human and wolf aspect.” He took a sip from bottle before leaning forward and catching Zane’s eyes, “Zane, I repeat; you did what was needed. You stopped the attack on Tessa. You have allowed them to curl up in your bed and comforted them. Your team has also taken care of them. I have seen Rico and Melody sit down and comfort them both in human and wolf form. Since you are an older pup, this falls into the category of letting the more senior *adult* wolves take care of the problem.” He stood and moved over and wrapped his arms around both Zane and Tessa, "When you took charge of them, when you protected them, and even more so, asked Damien to protect them since you couldn't... Damn it but I was so proud of you. It showed you were taking your responsibilities seriously."

Zane had rested his head against Tessa's as he was talking and before Mike had come over. When Mike came over and wrapped his arms around the two Zane and Tessa both leaned into the adult wolf. Both felt his dominance and protection wrap around them, "Thanks, Beta Mike." Both Zane and his wolf were pleased at the compliment from the Beta, "I will try to keep my homicidal urges under control. I will tell you if I even get an inkling those dog turds are even considering doing something, I will react. Last time Melody could reason with my wolf and me. Next time, it won't work. I will deal with the issue." There was no way he could do otherwise.

Mike gave the two one last hug before he went and sat down, "Which is exactly why we are keeping you at home and away from those two. It is also why we are keeping you too tired to think up some way to get back at them." He gave Zane a rather grim look, "I'm going to repeat what the Alpha said, do not leave the property without permission. If you do, believe me you will not like the punishment." After watching Zane lower his eyes he leaned back and relaxed, "Now that we have the important stuff out of the way, go and relax. Do the picnic you are thinking of, maybe a couple of movies, and just take the rest of the day off. I'm going to go and relax at the pack house. If you need anything, contact Abby." Mike had plans with a she-wolf he knew and liked.

Zane met his uncle's eyes for a moment longer than normal. **It does not please me, but I understand, and I will ensure my entire team obeys.** Once he had sent it, he lowered his eyes, "Sounds like a very good idea. I think a movie day sounds good as well. If anyone mentions the Underworld series, I will bite them." He glared around even as Melody started snickering.

"Nah, those movies are boring. I'm sure we can find something else to watch." Melody stood and headed towards the kitchen, "Zane, you want to help me get lunch?"

Even as she was talking Rico came over and collected Tessa from Zane, "Let's go and relax, Tessa, while they work on food." He gave her an amused grin at Zane's expression as Melody pointed him towards the kitchen.

Olivia had been watching during the entire conversation. It was rather shocking to hear her brother talking that way. When he said he would take care of the issue, Olivia knew Zane meant he would kill the two. It wasn't just 'I'll kill them' you heard from kids sometimes. It was *I will kill them* with grim determination. He definitely wasn't the brother she had known. Was this a side effect of having a wolf? If so, it was not a side she had seen before. It was another thing she was going to have to think about.

Oscar could hear Olivia's heartbeat speeding up during the conversation and he moved a bit closer to her. He wrapped an arm around her and let her relax against his side. Later he would talk to her since he was sure it was a very upsetting conversation to hear. It could wait until after lunch and the movies.

*****

Once Tessa had helped Olivia get ready for bed, Oscar slipped into her room, "Do you have a few minutes to talk, Olivia?" He settled at the foot of her bed, so he would be looking at her. With Olivia, he didn't feel the need to look away after meeting her eyes. Oscar knew it was because she was a human and it was rather nice, occasionally.

Olivia yawned at the question, "Only a few minutes. My medications are starting to kick in." She was already curled up. Thankfully with the light brace they had her in Olivia could move some. She could even bend her knee to an extent. Being able to move around even some was rather nice after being almost immobile for the two or so weeks.

He smiled at her as she yawned at him, "I wish you hadn't had to hear the talk this morning. Most wolves don't have to deal with kind of nastiness. With Zane, it is because he was forced into it. It doesn't mean he is a horrible person. It's just his wolf has to protect those more junior. He warned them, but they still went after us." He leaned forward and grasped one of her hands, "Please, he is still your brother. Sleep on it and I'll talk to you tomorrow."

She wanted to reply but the meds were really starting to kick in. Olivia mumbled something before she fell asleep, but it wasn't clear.

Oscar slipped into the bathroom and changed to his wolf form. Just in case Olivia had any nightmares, he was going to spend the night. Oscar hadn't had to yet but after the conversation she might just have one. Even with the pain medications, one could happen if she was worked up enough. Once he had settled down, he, much like Zane did, rested his head on her abdomen and closed his eyes. As he was starting to drift off, the kitten crawled up on his back. She found a good spot near his head, on his side, before laying down and falling asleep, purring gently. Oscar's wolf had to snort at the silly thing for using a wolf as a nap spot, even if the purring was soothing.

*****

The next morning when the mail was delivered, Kadrian frowned at the certified letter sitting on his desk. He glared at it for a while, and if he glared any harder the damn thing would burn. With a displeased growl, he very carefully tore it open and removed the contents. After reading it he had to struggle not to react. Thankfully, he was having enough of a problem trying to decide how to react, he finally ended up scratching his head. **Esther, can you come here? We finally have a letter from the DA's office. I'm going to have the lawyer come in as well.**

Esther had felt her mate's reaction to reading the letter, though she hadn't picked up what it said. When he finally settled down to utter disbelief, she hoped it wasn't bad news. **Just a moment and I will be over, love.** She neatly tucked the work she was doing away before leaving her office. When Esther walked in, she almost laughed at his expression, "Do I want to know what it says?"

Kadrian grunted at her, "No, no you don't, since it raises all kinds of really bad possibilities. Believe me, I really don't want to even think about the horrible consequences. Just wait for the lawyer to read this and explain what it means." He tossed the folded-up letter on his desk before holding his arms out to Esther. Kadrian knew the lawyer wouldn't even blink twice about his having Esther in his lap.

She showed up a short time later and before she did anything gathered a cup of coffee. Once she had she moved over to the desk and picked up the letter he waved at. Once she had read it, she rolled her eyes and shook her head, "I'm almost tempted to call the DA and ask if he is serious. I can understand trying to work something out in most cases but for this?" She was looking rather stumped at the idea of trying an out of court settlement, "Maybe we should just send a couple of coffins to the court? It would be a hell of a lot neater than anything else."

Esther frowned at the lawyer's reaction, "Okay, enough of the comments. What does the letter say and why are both of you seeing horrible things in the future?" It obviously wasn't good, and she wanted to know what was going on. It was especially true with them talking about it getting bloody and needing coffins.

The lawyer set the letting back on the desk, "The DA has reviewed the charges and evidence and forwarded this to a pretrial hearing. This is to see if the issue can be resolved without involving the legal system any more than it has been. If the issue can be adjudicated at that level, it leaves no court records. It is a way to try and keep the children from having a record, sealed or not." She glanced at the letter, "To be honest, in this case I'm somewhat surprised they went this route. The charges against David and Leon are serious enough I would have expected it to go to Juvenile court. Chances are since none of them have any sort of legal record they are starting with this route."

Esther had listened to what the lawyer was saying but she, much like her mate, could only stare at the letter now. When she finally reacted, it was about the only thing she could do, and it was to try to die laughing. She collapsed against her mate and bellowed out her laughter. She honestly wasn't very amused, but it was the only reaction she could come up with. Esther laughed to the point where she was almost blue in the face. At that point she finally had to gasp for breath, "Oh god, we might have to drag Zane there in shackles and chains." It honestly wasn't amusing but it was the truth.

Kadrian had a slightly amused expression on his face, while his mate was trying to control her laughter. When he glanced at the lawyer her expression was bemused at his mate's reaction, "Well it is better than her going wolf, I guess." Kad shook his head since it helped him step back from his surge of anger.

Michelle simply waited until the Luna was more under control, "I'm not really sure what to say about this. I can't see any way to get around it, since it was decided by the DA. I will obviously represent the children and their families, but I obviously can't control the children." Goddess, this was a frikken mess, and much like Kadrian, she didn't see it ending well, "The date of the session is ten days from today. I'm going to submit a request for all evidence involved. I don't know what they will give out, but I will ask. As far as the pups, I will let you deal with them."

Esther lightly punched him for his teasing her, "This is going to be rather interesting. Kad and I will deal with the pups. Between my presence, and Kad's orders, we will keep them under control. It is going to be rough on all of them. I will tell you now, I will not allow this to go unpunished as far as those two. I want you to see what you can do about getting hold of the school records for those two. While you are at it, get all the records for our pups as well. Hire a private investigator if needed to dig up all skeletons dealing with those two. If we can't get justice by law, we will blackmail them." Her voice was firm as she was speaking.

One of Kadrian's hands picked up his pen and started tapping it on the desk, "Do it but keep it as low key as possible. I will talk to a friend about doing some computer-based work. I will talk to the parents as well. This most definitely wasn't what I was hoping for, but we will run with it and do what is needed." He was starting to consider having the two families vanishing but now wouldn't be a good time. If they did, it was very possible the police would look at the pups and parents. That wouldn't be good at all, "Go do what is needed and send me an e-mail daily. If you need a meeting, contact me."

Michelle stood and with a polite nod she picked up the letter, "I'm going to take this with me for my records and I will get started. If you will excuse me, now that I know what the next step is, I can start formulating my defense." She left the office and hurried to hers. This was going to be interesting, as in the curse *interesting*. Michelle remembered hearing the old curse, 'May you live in interesting times.' It was looking like someone had cursed her with it.

Now that Kadrian and Esther knew what was going to happen, they discussed it. Tomorrow they were going to have a pack meeting to explain what was going on. They needed to update the entire pack on what was going on. He knew he was going to have to give several orders to keep the pack calm. As of now some of what had happened had gone through the pack and they were upset. It was the angriest he had felt the pack for a long time.

*****

When David and Leon's parents received the letters, they settled down at David's house. All of them had something to drink as they were discussing what to do and how to respond. Tomorrow they were going to talk to their lawyers but right now they were discussing options. David's father spoke first, "At least the DA has some sort of head on his shoulders. The charges should have been dropped but I guess they had to at least look like they did something. I'm sure we can force those others to drop the charges." He knew money wouldn't solve this, unlike other times.

Leon's mother snorted, "If he had a real head, he would have dropped the charges. It is completely unreasonable they kept the charges against our children. Those others I'm sure are just punks and jerks. I simply can't believe what they had to say about our children. Everyone knows those from that place are weird and freaks." She was still considering a lawsuit against Simone's parents for what they said at the meeting at school.

Leon's father was pacing back and forth as he was sipping on a tall glass of vodka, "I'm sure we can get these vile charges dropped and then we can sue them for slander and liable. I already have my lawyer working on it as we speak. Come hell or high water, I will have them paying for what they said about our children. In ten days, we will prove these are all lies."

Upstairs David and Leon were flopped on David's bed staring at the ceiling. Both had a beer they were working on, "God this is so frigging annoying. We can't go anywhere, do anything, and I'm about gamed out. Hell, I have gotten tired of watching porn on my computer as well. The homework sucks, since we can't get any help from our friends." By friends he meant those who hung with them to keep from being picked on. They also helped intimidate those who were harder to bully.

Leon took another sip before replying, "Tell me about it. I did find out Gene has a scanner. I told him to start scanning in copies of their homework to help us. He is going to start doing it today. As far as boredom, at least they are letting us spend time with each other, "If we had to be alone then this would really suck." They could skype, IM, and even use the phone. It didn't mean it would be fun though.

David let out a breath in relief, since his grades would have taken a hit, "Good. I know we are getting copies of their notes but that would really help." He also took another sip of the beer, "Fuck yeh, it does make it easier to deal with the boredom. At least while you are here it is easier to play the fun games." They had found a source for black market games. They had violence, sex, shoot whoever you wanted, and you could even specify the race of targets. They had a great deal of fun with those games. Tonight, chances were good their parents were going to leave later, and they could break some of them out. It would be a fun night for both. He rolled over and gave Leon a good kiss.

*****

When Zane and the others were done with their chores and training for the day, as usual they found Mindy at the house. Zane had finally decided he was going to talk to her. **Melody, get the others to work on their homework. I'm going to have a talk with Mindy. She has been helpful, and she stepped forward when she didn't need to.** He walked over to Mindy and murmured something to her before heading out back.

Once outside he walked across the yard and leaned against a tree. He was pleased Mindy had followed him. **Mindy what do you want? Just say it, since I don't have the energy to play twenty questions.** Zane was doing his best to be as calm as possible and not abrupt or abrasive.

Mindy leaned against the tree next to him and looked at the house. She had a feeling being blunt really wasn't the right way. Instead, she was going to try and hold a conversation with him. **Zane, you know my parents are Gamma's, right? You know one problem with being the pup of a more dominant wolfs?** For this she wanted him to think about what she wanted to say.

Zane almost growled but she had caught his interest. **How could I know Mindy? I wasn't born a wolf. I didn't become a wolf until some monster decided to destroy my world. He took my humanity from me, he took my family, and almost took my little sister. All I know is I suddenly have five people looking at me as their senior pup.** Thankfully she had caught his attention enough he didn't growl at her.

She leaned against him briefly before continuing. **That's why I asked, Zane. Many of the more senior wolves expect their pups to follow in their pawprints. For many, it isn't a problem, but for some of us, it is. It can be hard to get out of the wolf hierarchy, if your interests are different.** She turned and pressed a hand on his arm. **I knew some of what happened, you do have my sympathy, Zane.**

He had to frown slightly since he was still learning about the pack. Even though they had talked ranks this wasn't something he had experienced. All the parents had been very pleased Zane had taken their children as part of his team. **What is the problem? I have known other kids who have their parents breathing down their necks. What does this have to** *do with me?** When she lightly touched his arm he smiled slightly since he was slowly getting used to such contact.

Mindy sighed. **Because I don't want to be forced into one of their jobs. I want to go into graphic arts, computers, and that sort of thing. It might sound selfish, but if I can get connected with a group who can use technology, it's what I want to do. I don't have the urge to run the house, or even manage the property. It isn't what I have any skills at. I want to do something for the pack that helps it. Doing what they do won't help since I'd at best do a mediocre job.** It was obvious she meant what she was saying.

Zane frowned as she was speaking to him. It didn't sound right since everyone had the right to do what they wanted, even if it wasn't what their parents wanted. In this case it was his human side which was feeling rather offended and irritated. Some parents were that way, but it was a crock. **So that's the only reason you want to be around me?** If it was the case he was going to be feeling rather pissed.

She stiffened up. **No Zane it isn't the only reason, or not even the main reason. You are a human, well were.** She had to make a face. **You grew up a human and not a wolf. It is easier to talk to you about this. I have been watching and you are a good wolf even with the losses you've had. I think I could be of use to you, with what training. I can already design websites, I'm starting to learn graphics, and other things. All I'm asking is that you let me hang with you and do what I want.** Mindy really wanted a chance to do what she was good at, but her parents weren't going to listen until she found a team she could work with.

Zane contemplated what she had to say. **I'm going to have to think about this Mindy. I will talk to you in a day or two. I also need to talk to my team. I'm not sure this is the right way to deal with your problem. Thanks for being honest with me though.** He was going to seriously need to think about this, "I'm going back in since I have homework to do. Thank you for your help." He headed back inside.

Mindy followed, and they settled down at the table to do the homework. She helped as much as she could though it was hard since not all were her best subjects.

*****

The home schooling had finally been approved both by the school and the pack Elders. It was going to take a few days to get it set up for all the pups who were not going to school. The Elders in charge of the training had decided a few more days would be okay before the school started. The pups would be doing to school in the morning and their training or jobs in the afternoon. It was going to depend on how they actually did with the homework. That was the important part. They could excel at everything pack related but if they bombed high school, the best they could do in this pack would be senior to the junior wolves. Very rarely would they go beyond that, unless they upgraded later, which was much harder. For the most part, they expected all of their pack to graduate high school, and not to be ones which dropped out as soon as they could.

It was due to this pack valuing at least basic education a great deal, but some packs didn't and so were mired in thoughts and feelings of many years ago. In those packs, women, mates, and she-pups, were expected to run the house, bear pups, and take care of the he-wolves. It wasn't to say they weren't valued but they were limited in what they were allowed to do. With packs being able to determine how they were ranked, and how duties were assigned without interference, there was much greater differences between packs. What it did dictate was how well the pack fit into the modern world, as in many places that made them stand out. Many of the older thinking ones tended to remain isolated and only very slowly let modern ideas into the pack, as they didn't care for changes and had grown up when even being literate wasn't something most people had. Those packs were usually ranked either by the strongest through fights for advancing, or by who their parent's ranks were, and their parents before without regard of if they themselves had the mental abilities to perform the work. Those packs often had many leave, when they found out about more progressive packs and how some could advance and all could learn more skills, and if the pack didn't change, often died out.

In this pack, the diversification helped advance the pack and improve income and happiness of the entire pack. It was something the Alphas had been working on and it had taken him decades to get to this point of having the entire pack with high school diplomas and being literate. The Alpha didn't demand unthinking followers, only that they were willing to allow others to advance. It wasn't always successful, as some parents just wanted their pup to follow in their pawprints to whatever duties they had done, not what they wanted to do, which was totally different than it, and was resistant to their pup's desires. Mindy was an example of this, with her parents being more traditional than many of the others. They had decided to accept her wishes, if she could get find a team who would need her skills, otherwise they wanted her to continue with helping them out. It was a slow process to modernize the pack, and to have some give up their cherished traditional beliefs.

*****

The next evening, the pack was called to the meeting. Zane was informed about it in the morning when the three of them reported to the service office. He was annoyed, since it was Sunday, but they had to do what they were told. The three of them were tasked with helping to get the food ready for the meeting. As with all pack meetings, it was a buffet style, and the meat items came from the house. All other food came from the various families and was loosely rotated. Everyone enjoyed having a wide variety of entrées and sides.

For the three of them, it took lots of work but thankfully not as hard as the training in the afternoon. It was still hot and hard work as they helped to bring food from the freezer, pull out tables and chairs, and coolers for drinks. By the time they were done with setting up, Zane wanted to growl. It had been boring and tedious but import. Zane was definitely starting to get a feel for what went into taking care of the pack. It wasn't just the protection stuff but also making the pack comfortable, keeping them secure and taken care of.

When Zane finally was released, he hurried over to their new house, "Gah, so boring, but I think I learned a bit." He gave Tessa a hug before giving Oscar and Olivia one, "Liv, are you going to need a hand getting to the pack house?" It was a fair walk and he figured it would be too much for her.

Olivia didn't even bother considering trying to walk over. , "Uncle Mike is going to drive me over. Oscar is going to help me." She knew Zane would accept that.

He gave her one more hug in sympathy, "I figured it, but I had to ask just in case. I will make sure you have a good chair and foot stool as well. No reason for you to be uncomfortable." The brace alone almost precluded sitting in anything other than a well-padded seat. He'd seen how the brace rested just below her bottom and figured it wasn't comfortable. The brace went from the top of her leg to her foot. It had a joint at her knee and a footrest. It could be removed for short times such as taking a shower as well as when she was sitting down. If she was walking, it had to be on.

She made a face, "Thanks Zane, hopefully I will have this done with this soon." She gave him one more hug before lightly elbowing him to get him to move, since Mike had called that he was ready to leave, "Let's go Oscar." Since she was already standing, she started towards the front door. Oscar was carrying a small bag of things she might need. She wanted to blush, since he had an arm around her to help also.

Just for good measure when she elbowed him, he oomphed., "That's sibling abuse Liv. I might have to complain to Uncle Mike about it." He danced away when she tried to get him with a crutch. **Let's go too.** He watched Oscar help her out and she was looking so much better. It helped he and his wolf.

As they were walking out, Simone joined them and traded looks with Melody since Zane had his arm around Tessa. It didn't look quite like when he was just trying to comfort her. It was more, not possessive, but friendly for lack of a better word. It was just as obvious Tessa was enjoying being held by him. junior wolves didn't feel the need to try and hide certain things, because they knew there was no way to hide it from everyone so didn't bother trying. In this case Tessa was enjoying Zane's attention. **I think someone is feeling a bit more than protective. What do you think?**

Melody's eyes were dancing with interest since she had noticed his arm. She had more chances to watch them than Simone, since she wasn't at school. It had been obvious Zane didn't realize how he was acting around Tessa. She figured it was a case of he was just seeing it as his wolf being protective and nothing else. **Just a bit. I have been watching them when we aren't working or training. Tessa seems to be liking his attention too. I could almost feel jealous, but this is good for both o them.**

Rico was walking next to Zane, and they were just chatting. It was obvious they were rather oblivious to the others mentally chatting. They were talking about the training they were doing. It didn't take very long for them to reach the house and they were directed to the pack dining room. It was a room only used when the entire pack ate together. They traded looks and went to started carrying food to the buffet.

Eventually the pack started to line up. It was as usual very good, and people were enjoying it a great deal. The room was quiet since most everyone knew what the meeting was about. They didn't know the details, but they knew of the confrontation at the mall. It was not something easily kept quiet since there had been other wolves at the mall. The police visiting the pack was not something that happened very often. Many of the pups had known about the two bullies and knew there were some pups l not at school. The rumors were starting to get wild, and the meeting would hopefully stop some of them.

Uncle Mike, Zane and the others settled down at one table and as Zane had said there was a padded chair for Olivia, with her name on it. Olivia and Oscar were quietly talking. The rest of them were mostly quiet since they were feeling tense. They knew this was going to bring back memories for all of them. Zane could already feel his wolf coming forward and quietly growling. He was working hard to keep his eyes from changing but he knew they were lighter than normal.

Tessa was looking down at the food and mostly picking at it. Rico and Zane were on either side of her and she could feel their wolves reacting. She was trying hard keep from thinking about what was going to be said. It felt good having them almost hovering over her. Her wolf was doing her best to help Tessa stay calm.

Once dinner was over the Alpha and Luna stood. Kadrian cleared his throat and looked around the room, "I'm sure most everyone has heard about the incident last weekend at the mall. We have finally been contacted by the DA and I'm going to tell you some of what is going on. Normally I wouldn't but in this case the entire pack is pretty worked up which isn't normal. First and foremost, I'm giving everyone an Alpha order. Do not do anything in an attempt to get back at the Walpert's or the Baker's. This is going to be handed legally as much as possible. Now what happened was..."

Zane could feel Tessa start shivering as the Alpha was talking. He pulled her onto his lap and wrapped his arms around her and held her close. He rested his head on hers and closed his eyes and tried to take slow deep breaths. Abby and Brandon came over and settled down on either side, which also helped . He had a feeling Tessa was going to have more nightmares tonight. He might talk to Mike about having a sleepover in the living room. It might help having the entire group there for her.

CHAPTER 17

Discussion About Mindy

Eventually the meeting was over, and Zane was glad. He could tell Tessa was upset and not pleased. Almost across the board the senior wolves, young or old, were angry. Some had known but others knew only what rumor had said. He could tell that both Alpha and Luna were forced to apply their powers to calm the pack. At the table next to him, Zane saw Damien and one of his friends comforting Damien's junior wolves.

When Damien met Zane's eyes, there was an approving look in his eyes. Zane gave him a good nod before turning his eyes back to Tessa, **You will be fine, Tessa, feel the pack demanding satisfaction? This is for you and Oscar. He was hurt too, and they know this. We will protect you and we value you.**

Tessa had to shiver at the reaction from the pack since it was so angry. She also almost glowed as well, since she knew it was for her and her twin. Tessa and Oscar knew the pack cared but being so junior sometimes it was almost a generic caring. From Zane and his group, she knew they did care but it was still new to her and Oscar even as it was to Zane, **Thank you everyone.** Tessa's mental voice was grateful for the pack's reaction.

Oscar moved over and leaned against Zane and was very pleased when Zane wrapped an arm around him. He could feel the anger from the pack and especially from Zane. Oscar knew Zane would protect them. When he had asked Damien take care of them at school felt good. Much like Tessa he was feeling the caring from the pack and their almost unilateral support for the two of them. Oscar didn't say anything and simply settled for enjoying the feelings from the pack.

Zane lifted his head and looked around the pack. Most of the adults didn't move but several of the kids did. He still had trouble thinking of pups instead of kids. They had almost silently settled near Zane and the two junior wolves. He could feel their anger and desire to help take care of the junior wolves. Zane had to close his eyes. Damn it, this was beating his walls again and it scared him. When he finally opened his eyes, he sent to everyone, **Thank you for your support for what happened. Please do as our Alpha and Luna have asked and let our families deal with this. Protect those junior to you from bullies and nothing else. Protect Pack and don't go for revenge.** If something happened to any of David's lackeys, Zane would feel bad.

He lowered his eyes back to Tessa's head. **Uncle Mike can we please go home? I can't deal with this right now. I'm starting to get scared again and need some space.** Zane could tell the pack also wanted to protect him and Olivia as well. Thankfully Olivia more than him, or he would have wanted to claw his way out of the room.

Mike glanced at the Alpha, **We are going to leave.** He was going to protect Zane since it wasn't what the boy needed, **Tessa and Oscar are starting to get overwhelmed by all the emotions.** He knew the Alpha and especially the Luna would understand.

Esther gave the pack a very proud smile, "Thank you for wanting to protect pack members. As Zane asked, resist the urge to get revenge. I know we are wolves and to our other half protection means removing the problem, but don't. Kadrian and I are dealing with this and if we need, we will call on some of you for help. I'm sending Beta Mike and the others back to his house. The protective urges are appreciated but for the junior wolves, somewhat overwhelming. For those who wish, please remain and relax, since there is plenty of food and drinks left."

Zane stood up after helping Tessa to stand, **We will see you, Oscar, and Olivia, back at the house, uncle.** He had already received permission for the sleep over and all the parents had approved. Somehow Mindy had been included though Zane wasn't sure how that happened. Tonight he didn't care, since he did need to talk to her and his group.

Mike gave Zane an approving look, even as Oscar was turning to help Olivia up. She had been sitting long enough she was going to need help standing. He winced as Olivia grunted in pain and Zane tensed even though he didn't offer to help her. Mike led the group out of the room, "Let's get you back to the house and tucked into a comfortable couch. If you want to join the others in the sleep over, I'm sure they will let you have the couch." It was a comfortable couch and Mike had picked it just for Olivia.

Olivia had to take her time standing, though thankfully with Oscar's help, it wasn't too much of a struggle. She followed Mike to the car and with Oscar's help climbed into the front seat, "Thanks Oscar, it really helps." Moments after she was seated, she grimaced when he handed her a bottle of water and her medications, "Yay!!! Pills!!!" Olivia didn't bother trying to say no, since her leg was hurting again. The specialist doctor had been very firm when she had discussed taking the meds as prescribed.

Once everyone was back at the house Mike poked his head into the room Zane's team had taken over, "Zane, I need to talk to you for a few minutes. I have a meeting along with the other parents tomorrow about the hearing. I want to discuss this with you and see what your thoughts are." Mike knew Zane's first reaction was going to be kill the bastard and kick grass and dirt on the corpse. It wasn't going to happen, but he did understand.

Zane stood after giving Tessa a good hug and Oscar's shoulder a good squeeze. Melody was sitting next to Oscar even as he was sitting next to Olivia, **Go, we will take care of them.** She didn't have an arm around Oscar since he was relaxing against Olivia, but she was close enough to comfort them.

Rico moved over and settled down next to Tessa and gave Zane a good nod, **Taken care of Zane, I will comfort her for you. Go and deal with what is needed. It is why we are here.** He turned and looked at the game Mindy and Simone were playing, and he let out a groan, "Shoot me now, some girly game? I might have to cry!" He knew it would get him yelled at.

The girls turned and very briefly glared at Rico before going back to what they were playing. Melody wanted to snicker but didn't. She was tired enough after all the work today she was simply going to relax with the rest of their group.

*****

Zane followed his uncle out of the house and a fair distance away. Since his hearing was so much better than it had been he could understand. For the moment as they were walking both were relatively quiet and weren't talking. Eventually they were far enough away, and Mike flopped down before leaning back against a tree. When his uncle settled down Zane did as well against another tree, so he could look at his uncle, "What do you want Uncle?"

Mike leaned back against the tree behind him and enjoyed the scent of the forest, "Zane other than burying the body in some really deep grave, what do you want done with the two boys?" When Mike spoke, his voice was showing this was a serious discussion.

The boy had to sigh and tried to figure out how to reply. Frankly, his wolf did want blood and bodies, so the two wouldn't be an issue anymore. They had spent several hours talking to each other though. Eventually they worked out a few items, which they would both approve of. Zane's tone was clipped as he replied, "Anything that keeps them away from those I have extended my protection over. Out of school, restraining order, years in jail, I don't care as long as they are away from Tessa and Oscar. The others can protect themselves but those two can't." He knew if pushed too hard, the two would, but it would be erratic way. It was very possible for them to kill a human simply trying to get away.

Mike looked out in the darkness that was gathering. It was going to start getting cold soon since it was midfall and on the dry side of the mountains, even if they didn't get snow, it tended to get cold. He could read between the lines of what Zane was saying. It was essentially, 'keep them away, or I will remove the problem', "I understand Zane and it's pretty much what I figured. I will talk to the twin's parents tomorrow before the meeting. I have a feeling their reaction is going to be similar to or stronger than yours." He looked up at the half moon and enjoyed the feel of the light on his face.

Zane settled for looking into the not-darkness, since his eyes were so much better than they had been, "Damn it, Uncle, this is so frustrating for me." He wasn't sure if he wanted to huff, sigh, groan, or even scream, "I just want to be left alone but I keep getting dragged into crap that forces me to respond and do stuff." Zane knew he was whining but damn it he still, to an extent, wanted to be left alone. He wasn't being allowed to hide by both Melody and Tessa, "All I wanted was to get out of school without being bothered. Take care of my sister and cry over my parents. I find I'm some sort of more dominant wolf, drawing others to me and..." He didn't know what else to say and it was obvious he was feeling rather emotional.

Mike didn't smile though he wanted to, "Zane, welcome to your life. I know it has been a horrible introduction, but this is your life now. I do understand how you feel about losing your parents, because I cared a great deal for him and your mother. I don't think anyone has mentioned it, but your dad and I had the same mother but different fathers. My father was a wolf, and my mother had wolf DNA in her but hadn't been turned and when he died protecting the pack, she decided to not live with the werewolves and remarried. Your father's dad was human and that's why I'm a wolf, and he wasn't. You seemed to get a good portion of my mother's DNA which is why you are so dominant." There was more to it than that but for now Zane didn't need to know about how some werewolves had human pups who couldn't shift, and then their offspring would carry Werewolf DNA, even if they were human.

Eventually, he would share more of their family history with Zane, so he knew how their family often had more senior wolves.

It wasn't something Zane had known, since he didn't know his grandparents. They had died when he was young, and his parents hadn't said much about them. For whatever reason Zane hadn't had the urge to ask about them though he did know a number of stories. Looking back nobody had really talked about how his uncle and dad were related. They didn't look much like each other since Mike was tall and well-muscled and Zane's dad had been only average in height and shape, "Oh... I didn't know that."

Since the two of them were out there alone, Mike decided it was time to talk to Zane about Tessa. He knew his nephew had been dodging the issue, but they did need to talk about it, "Zane we need to talk about something else. You have been avoiding this, but we do need to talk. We need to talk about mates and when wolves are single." He was going to toss it out and see if Zane went for the bait.

Zane just knew this talk would be about his interest in Tessa, even without Mike coming out and stating it, he froze and looked away. Somehow, he knew his uncle wasn't going to let him get away with some mumbled comment. It was almost surly when he replied, "Fine, the Luna hinted that I needed to talk to you. What do you want to talk about?" He could feel his ears starting to get warm; he was glad for the semi-darkness.

Mike had noticed Zane's reaction and could tell he wanted to avoid the subject, but he needed to know. When Mike spoke again his voice softened and he was almost looking back in time, "Zane, most wolves find their mates at some point when they are what we could consider reasonably young. When I say young, I'm not talking as in teens unlike so many of the stupid wolf stories out there. Since we do live a very long time young can be in your forties or even older. Some even take centuries. Until we find a mate, female wolves don't get pregnant, except in rare cases. The last case I know of in this pack was a good fifty years ago.

Until we find our mates, older wolves tend to be active. I'm not saying I expect you to suddenly become active, but you do need to know this."

Since he could tell he had Zane's attention even if his nephew was embarrassed by the subject Mike kept talking, "Did you know at one point I dated Abby? We both knew it was simply because we cared for each other. Both of us knew eventually we would find our mates but we both cared for each other and enjoyed our time together. When she met her mate, I welcomed Brandon into my team with open arms. They have been and are very well-loved members of my team." Mike wanted to meet his mate but wasn't going to stress over it unlike some. Nor would he ignore it, like Lazy Jack.

It made Zane want to go and hide but he had a feeling Mike wouldn't let him. As his uncle was talking, Zane was slowly drawn into the conversation since he did need to know. The subject of maybe dating made him blush. His father wasn't there to talk to him, and Uncle Mike was the next best person to talk to. Zane wanted to know, but being the age he was, he was scared to ask or talk about it. Thinking about his father was starting to make him sad but he did his best to focus on what Mike was saying.

When Mike mentioned he had dated Abby he had to frown. Something didn't fit since his uncle wasn't that old. Even if he had dated her in high school or even a bit older, it would mean Abby was at least 34 years old or older. Neither Mike, Abby, nor Brandon looked that old. There was still so much he had to learn, and Zane's mind focused on the ages. Anything else was going to make him want to scream, "Uh, how old are you?" Zane couldn't remember the age of his uncle being mentioned.

Mike accepted the question at face value, "I'm about twenty years older than your father. Mom had me young and your father much later in life. I'm just about fifty-five years old. Abby is about fifty-three and Brandon a bit older than Abby is." He couldn't wait to see Zane's reaction, "Oh, and Kadrian and Esther are well over a hundred years old. Just remember it isn't nice to ask a woman's age." The Alphas were well over a hundred; they were almost two hundred and were considered young as Alphas went. If nothing happened to them, they would retire on their fourth centennial and become elders.

Zane turned and stared at his uncle and his jaw was on the ground as he stared at him. He had to really stop and think since Zane knew his father was thirty-five or would have been. Zane turned and stared at Mike, and it was all he could do. Kadrian and Esther looked somewhat older but over a hundred? It was almost incomprehensible. They looked maybe mid thirty's or at most forty. Zane shook his head and rubbed his hands against his eyes. He wasn't going to even go there and instead went back to the subject of the conversation. When he spoke, Zane was obviously trying to change the subject, "Uncle Mike, I think Tessa does like me, but I've never had a girlfriend. What am I supposed to do? This whole wolf thing... I think I like her, and she is pretty, and is really nice." His eyes were back looking at the ground.

Mike moved over to the tree Zane was against and settled down next to him. He had to smile as he contemplated his time with Abby and one or two other of the pack females he had been rather close to, "Zane, relax and enjoy the attention. Return the attention and be yourself. You do need to understand when you or Tessa do find your mates any former relationships you had will fade into a fond memory. Do what you would have done as a human such as movies, maybe a few nice meals. You might also find at some point you will end up spending time with others in the pack as well but that's normal. Enjoy the time you spend. I have some great memories of times when my team and I were young. Going for runs, playing, hunting, and even piling up in wolf form and snoozing. Be a kid, swear at homework, and even grumble at the stupid adults who are giving you too darn much homework. It isn't much different from being a human boy."

When Mike settled down next to Zane, he leaned against his uncle, "Uncle Mike, I'm still so scared of letting anyone too close to me. Tessa and Oscar, I can deal with, in a protective way. Melody and the others on my team are somewhat harder, but I'm slowly letting them in. Anyone else? It scares me more than I can admit. I know I keep getting told Pack is family, but my family was almost destroyed. How can I let the pack in knowing I might lose them, or some of them?" Now it was on a different subject.

Mike wrapped his arm around Zane, instinctively wanting to comfort him. He didn't bother trying to come up with some deep and insightful explanation, "Zane I wish I had something positive to say but this is life. There are no certainties. People die, and people live and the best we can do is to keep going. Losing my little brother hurt me deeply. I wanted to scream and though you might not have heard it, I have howled my pain out to the Goddess more than once. I had to keep going, since I had you and Olivia to deal with. It hurt losing my brother and your mom. I loved a great deal, even if they hadn't been told I was a werewolf." Kadrian had asked to wait till Zane and Olivia were adults before the entire family was told at once. It would need to be done before Mike had to either fade out of their life or the questions started about his not aging how a human would start. "If you keep isolating yourself, it will lead to a sad lonely life. Even if you only allow Olivia and myself in, it will be a lonely life and most wolves don't do lonely well." He knew of warning-stories from the elders of those who had ended up going rogue from it; they always ended in death of the one who went insane, but in some it was only after many others died too.

Zane was going to have to think about this for a while before he could really say anything. He finally stood up and looked up at the moon, "Thank you for the talk, Uncle Mike. I need to get back to my friends." As of now they were his friends and Zane could carefully admit it. He couldn't do anymore of the deep emotional stuff.

His Uncle stood as well and looked up as well. When he spoke his voice was warm, "Zane, let your team help and support you and your sister. My team, not to mention Abby and Brandon, have been so very helpful to me as well. I will talk to you later, Zane. Remember just how proud of you your parents would be. I am as well." Mike walked further into the woods since he needed some time alone much as Zane did.

Zane eventually made it back to the house and when he walked into the room, he settled down. There was a movie on now, but he didn't bother wondering what it was. Once he settled down in a chair, it was obvious he was heavily in thought. Melody glanced at Tessa and gave her a slight shake of her head. She settled down next to Zane and leaned against him. She hadn't chased Tessa off for any reason other than she had a feeling Zane needed to think, **Relax Zane and if you want or need to talk I—no, we—are here for you.**

Olivia looked at her brother and could see the strain in his face as Zane settled down and closed his eyes. She looked at Oscar before she leaned against him and wanted to cry. Zane was doing better but sometimes he was so different from the brother she had known. Other times he was as Olivia remembered. She really wished he would finally settle down and let his friends really help him. Instead of saying anything she leaned against Oscar and wrapped her arms around him and held on. If she cried or did anything similar, she assumed Zane would notice and react. Instead, she let her pills slowly drag her into drowsing.

*****

The next morning all the parents, or guardian in Mike's case, settled down in the Alpha's office. Michelle was there as well as Kadrian and Esther. She was at the other end of the table from the Alpha and Luna.

Kadrian called the meeting to order after clearing his throat, "Before anything else, keep your wolves under control. We are going to talk about this as reasonably as possible. We have to come up with a combined expression of what we want."

Before anyone else spoke Abby did, "Alpha, I will not accept anything less than they are no longer at the school, register as sex offenders, probation of some real sort, and some anger management classes. I do not wish to challenge anyone but it's the minimum I will accept." There wasn't any way in hell she was going to allow her children to go to school with those bastards.

Mike cleared his throat, "Alpha, Zane expressed much the same. He does want blood but will accept those two being kept away from those he considers under his protection. I know he is struggling to deal with his loss and becoming something like the monster who turned him. I'm not saying the monster disparagingly but that's how he sees it. He was turned, his family was destroyed, and now he is having to deal with emotions and feelings he never had to before. I will not accept anything less than what Abby indicated either." He glanced at Abby and Brandon before looking back at the Alpha.

Melody's parents looked at the Alpha as well before her father spoke, "We agree, though it is more to protect the pack than anything. If those two boys return to school, at some point Zane or one of the other pups will kill them. When it happens, it will endanger the pack. This pretrial thing is a load of crap. As far as we are concerned, it's the DA trying to pander to some well positioned humans. We understand we have to keep some aspects under control but not this time. Fuck the bastards and screw them to hell and back."

The rest of the meeting was much the same and by the time the Alpha excused everyone he had a headache. He didn't blame the others for what they had to say, since it went against being a wolf to accept some pansy ass excuse of punishment. When a wolf was punished, it was quick, to the point, and done with. If the wolf transgressed again with the same issue all knew what might happen, or at minimum it was a much harsher punishment. In a case like this, since they had been warned from harassing them, it would have likely been a permanent response, and it would have been considered justified. With a snarl he jerked upright, "Damn it, Esther, I don't see any easy way out of this." He was at the window again glowering out at the sky as Kadrian was trying to calm down.

Esther came over and leaned against him. She felt much the same way as he did not to mention the other parents. If something like this had happened to her son's junior wolves, she would have wanted blood as well. She forced herself into taking a number of breaths, they were in her nose, hold it, and then out her mouth. Eventually she felt better, "We will deal with this, my lovely mate. It isn't going to be easy, but we have dealt with stressful issues before."

*****

During the week following the meeting, even as Zane was doing what was required of him, he was thinking of two different issues. The first was Mindy and what she had asked of him. He had finally talked with Mike about it since Zane was most comfortable going to Mike for the hard Pack questions. The other was what to say or do with Tessa. Even now, Zane tended to crawl into bed and pass out and wake up with Tessa curled next to him. He wasn't sure if someone had mentioned it, but she had started changing to her wolf before curling up next to him.

In the case of Mindy, what she had said was something he could understand to an extent. Zane wasn't quite sure, or hadn't been, sure about what he had wanted to go to college for. Now he was a wolf, he was enjoying the training as an Enforcer. It was hard and demanded a great deal, but it clicked for him. From what he had seen, the Enforcers did a wide variety of security related issues. It wasn't just the thump your chest, 'me man, me tell you' crap, nor was it all males, there were some tough females too. They ran the security systems for the pack as well as did training for the pack members. They also provided computer security though there was another pack which managed the feeds and servers.

Zane had learned another pack was a major provider of computer and IT security for several packs in the state. They had a heavy security presence in Oregon and were considered some of the best in the region. When he had talked to Mike about what Mindy had asked, Mike had considered the idea for a while before coming back. He indicated it was something to think about. If she worked out it would be a good thing for the pack. Zane was going to think about it since he would have to consider accepting her into his team.

He finally decided to talk to his group, saying team still bothered him some, about Mindy. For this, it was just the four most senior of the group. Zane was going to have to make the choice, but he wanted input from the others. He finally settled down with Melody, Rico, and Simone, "We need to talk and just listen before saying anything." Zane looked at the others and when they met his eyes before lowering theirs his wolf was pleased.

"I talked to Mindy last week about why she was hanging around. What she had to say was fairly reasonable and made sense. Her parents are Gammas, but she wants to get into graphic design, computers, and tech things. I haven't talked to her any further, but it might be handy to have a tech on the team. What do you think?" He figured if they could get her into computer security as well, it would boost her usefulness.

Melody almost growled out an answer before she stopped and frowned. She started to lightly nibble on a fingernail as she tried to separate her gut reaction from what Zane had to say. It was reasonable, but it did bother her, and she really was going to need to think about it, "She is okay, but I just don't like the way she tries to hang around other groups. I'm going to have to think about it."

Rico was more mellow about it and shrugged. He rather liked Mindy though her occasional habit of being a hanger-on was annoying. All of them had grown up with her and she had been nice before they had started to really grow up, "I would need to think about it but as long as she is approved by you, I don't see a problem."

Simone liked Mindy and could understand where she was coming from. Working in her parents' shop was fun, but it wasn't what she wanted to do for the rest of her life. She didn't necessarily want to be an enforcer, but you didn't have to be one to work with them. Simone would have to do the training and be good at it. , but she could work the admin side of it rather than being an active enforcer, especially since few wanted that role. When she had talked to one of those who did it, they had shown respect as they described what she had to do to even be considered. "I like her, and we are friends. I didn't have to make the decision of going and asking for acceptance. You almost automatically did it when you extended your protection to the twins. I didn't have to ask or see if I would be allowed in, you just did it. I would say accept her."

Zane took a sip of his water and thought about what each had said before coming to a decision, "Think about this and I will talk to all of you in two days. At that point I will make the decision." He stretched and almost glowered at Simone, since she was obviously enjoying a soda, "I hate you being able to enjoy sodas, and I can't stand them now."

Simone simply smirked at him as she finished the soda, "I have to get home. See you in the morning." She stood and tossed the can into the recycling bucket and sauntered out of the house much to Zane's annoyance. The others stood and left the house as well.

Now that he had dealt with talking to his team about Mindy, he could think about Tessa. To be honest, he would prefer to worry about Mindy and what she wanted. That wasn't emotional or having to consider letting someone in even closer than most. If he did eventually ask her to become his girlfriend, it was an even deeper emotional connection. When she had been attacked at the mall, his first reaction had been anger and rage. Later when he had a chance to calm down, he had realized how much both Tessa and Oscar had come to mean to him.

It was different from Olivia or Mike since they were relatives. With Oscar, it was the junior wolf calling to Zane's wolf for protection. He liked him, and he was nice . What was even more important was Oscar focusing on helping to take care of Olivia. Since she tended to grump anytime Zane did more than a bit, having Oscar helping her meant so very much. Tessa was different though.

There was still the urge to protect her and take care of her, but she was really cute and nice. Even ignoring what his uncle had said about Abby, Zane was starting to really like her. She might be quiet and somewhat shy but around the team she did have an active sense of humor. Even her wolf was a pretty cute. Unlike his wolf, hers had a darker coloration. It wasn't an in-your-face coloration but had a darker stripe down her spine and a mixture of lighter and darker grays down her sides. Her body was slender and well proportioned, even if she was much smaller than his wolf.

As he was thinking he couldn't help but smile slightly even though he didn't realize it. Tessa or even Oscar didn't realize it, but their smaller wolf forms gave them an advantage. No, they weren't larger and more muscular, but they could get through places the larger wolves couldn't. They could turn sharper than the larger wolves as well. There were a few times she had caught him in play with an unexpected nip or dodge.

Zane mentally became more serious since he did want to think about this. It was so hard since his mind kept skittering off to other subjects. Much of it was trying to avoid what might happen if he did maybe date her and then something happened. If something did happen to her even now, it would hurt horribly. It was how he had felt after getting her away from David. It had scared him, and that was some of the reason he had been so angry and confrontational. Looking back Zane could see that though it was so very hard to admit.

Oscar quietly walked into the room and settled down next to Zane. He was quiet from habit, but he knew Zane felt him. Once he had settled down, Oscar leaned against Zane and smiled, **If it helps, Tessa likes you as well. I don't mind if you see her. I don't know if it's something you were worried about, but I think it would be good for you and her.**

Zane didn't move when Oscar came over. He had since learned if he twitched or moved away, other wolves took it as a sort of rejection. It was something he had been forced to talk about as well. It had been hard to explain it was a reaction from his human side and not his wolf. When Oscar contacted him, he sighed slightly, **No, that isn't the issue, Oscar. Tessa is a really nice girl, and she is pretty cute as well. It goes back to being scared because of losing my family.**

Oscar heard Zane's concerns over the pack bond, **We know, which is why we have been trying to give you as much comfort as we can. I haven't lost anyone like the two of you did but even the idea scares me. I have talked with Olivia a great deal and she is scared as well. She is also worried about you Zane. She wants her brother back. The brother you were before all this happened. She does understand this isn't quite possible, since you have a wolf now, but she wants her Zane back.** Oscar knew it was going to bother Zane to hear that but coming from him it shouldn't be a threat or criticism.

Zane had to wince before admitting he did know. She had tried to say it, but Zane simply hadn't been ready to accept it. Zane's wolf came forward and forced Zane to calm down and listen to their junior wolf. He finally replied, **I'm trying Oscar, I really am but it is so hard. I don't want to get hurt like that again. Just do me a favor and take care of my sister. Help her as much as you can since she yells at me when I try to help.** Zane needed to change the subject, **So are there any girls you like Oscar?**

Oh man, Zane asked a question Oscar didn't want to admit to, **There are one or two Zane. I must admit Margarethe is an attractive wolf.** Hopefully it would work.

Zane lightly elbowed Oscar, **The joys of noticing girls, right?** Zane had only seen Margarethe once or twice, so he couldn't really say much, **Good for you and yes, I'm attracted to your sister. I just don't know what I will do. I like her, she is fun to be around and talk to and now I'm going to bed.** Damn it, but he had pulled a muscle earlier, "I'm going to pass out and talk to you tomorrow." Damn it why was his room still upstairs?

Oscar watched Zane head to his room before he went to the bathroom and shifted. When Oscar jumped on Olivia's bed, that kitten found the spot it seemed to love by his shoulder and curled up. By now his wolf simply grunted in the back of Oscar's mind. For some reason Olivia thought it was rather cute and funny which made Oscar's wolf grumble but there was no way to dislodge the cat without hurting it, and it had four paws full of sharp claws it would use to hang on if they tried to shake it off, as they had learned. The others all came in and curled up with Zane later.

*****

By the time the prelim hearing arrived, Zane could tell he was growing into his wolf. With all the training, he had gotten much stronger and was far faster than he had been. He still had a way to go but he no longer felt like a brownie troop of she-wolves could take him down. Maybe a group of girl scout she-wolves but no longer brownies. Thankfully, the clothes he had still fit, though the shirts were starting to get tight around the shoulders and biceps.

When they headed towards the hearing, Kadrian had looked at all involved and especially the pups, "This is an Alpha order, do not let your wolves out. Do not growl, do not try to get to the others. You can be angry, glare, all the normal stuff. I can and will accept those. Anything else and you will be dealt with." Everyone climbed into several vehicles and headed to the courthouse.

Once they parked Zane, Mike, Oscar, and Tessa climbed out. Zane didn't even think twice before he wrapped an arm around Tessa, **I'm here for you and I won't let anything happen. I know better than to think anything they say is true. You are a really nice girl.** He blushed slightly when he almost blurted out his next comment, **Would you be my girlfriend?** The moment it came out he almost turned red.

Tessa leaned into his arm when he wrapped it around her. She already knew he would protect her; Zane had proven that several times. When he asked if she would be his girlfriend she blushed and looked down, **Thank you Zane and I would like that.** Her mother had talked to her shortly after Zane had offered his protection. It had been both embarrassing and informative. Tessa hadn't known that her mom and Beta Mike had dated.

Mike traded looks with Abby and Brandon though they didn't say anything as they headed into the courthouse. Going through security and the metal detectors almost made them laugh. If any one of them had decided to go on a rampage there, they weren't going to need a weapon. They also could get to any weapon the officers had before they could really react.

Eventually they made it to the room used for mediation. Thankfully both large tables were facing where the judge sat. It would mostly keep the parties from glaring at each other. The Pack Lawyer settled down at the end closest to the other table. She knew the others would think twice before going through her to get to the others.

Eventually the other parties were in the room and the judge walked in. Once they had done the entire 'stand for the judge' stuff everyone sat down. Before anything else was said Mrs. Walpert could be heard to say, "They should have just dropped the charges, this is such crap since David didn't do anything. Those others should have been charged and arrested!"

Abby didn't even think twice before she stood and snarled, "Your brat is a bully and coward. He assaulted my daughter! He has bullied both of my children and yours should be arrested and tossed in jail!"

CHAPTER 18

Mike and the Sensors

When they had been seated, Zane ensured he was sitting next to Tessa while Oscar was seated between their parents. Mike was sitting next to Zane and the others were spaced out. Since neither Kadrian nor Esther were directly involved, they were seated in a small viewer's section. When the Bitch, no, he wouldn't insult to both female wolves and dogs, the... Zane wanted to growl since he couldn't come up with a nasty enough term he was willing to use, and it was annoying. He finally settled for dehumanizing her and settled for 'it'. When *It* spoke, he didn't even blink since he just knew she was going act like that.

Now, when Abby had stood up and snarled out a reply, Zane was surprised. His Uncle had never really spoke about Abby standing up and snarling in the meeting at the school, so it wasn't expected. He was rather impressed with her mama-wolf reaction and mentally made a note not to upset her while dating her daughter. That thought alone made him almost pale slightly since now he was going to need to talk to Tessa's parents. It distracted him enough he jumped when the Judge reacted.

The judge was a rather frumpy looking older woman. She had thick glasses, short white hair in an old style, and the black robes which made her look almost like a ghost. When the two women snarled at each other, no, one was a whine while the other was a snarl, she banged her gavel,

"Order in the court. If there is another outburst like this, I will not be pleased. Control yourselves."

Abby looked up at the judge, "I apologize, Your Honor. I will control my reactions." She glanced at her mate before trying to relax. When he grasped her hand under the table, Abby started to calm down as she leaned into the mating bond helped.

Even though Mrs. Walpert settled for a grunt the judge accepted it, "This session is to see if we can work out a resolution without court, juvenile or adult, being involved. The charges are serious, and I would prefer to try and resolve them if possible." Based on the two women, not to mention the expressions on the others, the judge wasn't going to hold her breath, "Both lawyers approach the podiums. Mr. Lawless is going to go first simply because the charges from the Walpert's and Baker's were made first." She looked at the lawyer for the two boys and she had dealt with him before. He was a good lawyer; from the point of view of he was fairly successful. He also represented a number of clients she would classify as thugs, punks, and lowlifes.

Mr. Lawless waited until he and his counterpart were at the podium before speaking, "I have discussed the charges with my clients and would like to have the charges dropped. Neither boy has ever been in trouble with the law before and these charges are unfounded. Based on their statements to the police as well as to myself, they were attacked for no reason." He wasn't going to mention any encounters at school since he knew there had been some issues there. All charges of bullying had been dropped but better not to bring them up, "As per their statements they came out of the bathroom and the girl in question was in the hallway. They informed me she simply screamed for no reason other than to maybe get the others in the hallway. That was when the assault happened." He finished his statement.

When the Judge nodded at Ms. Carlson, she started speaking. Unlike Mr. Lawless she didn't bother with any sort of dramatic statements or flashy gestures, "Your Honor, the charges for both parties are serious, and we need to treat them this way. We do agree, if possible, we need to settle this outside of court to the satisfaction of all parties." God it was beyond total bullshit, since she knew that the best solution would be to bury the bodies so deep they would never be found. The least they would accept would be as had been mentioned, "Having said that, I have reviewed the police statements of my clients as well as having spoken to them as well. Before this incident ever happened, David Walpert and Leon Baker had interactions with Tessa and Oscar Fletcher previously. They also came into contact with Zane Donovan and not in a good way."

Ms. Carlson took a sip of a glass of water at her podium, "Based on talking to the twins, David Walpert and Leon Baker have bullied both Tessa and Oscar Fletcher before. In talking to Zane Donovan who stated that after he was forced to mention the loss of his parents, the boys in question were making derogatory comments that he could hear. While in school..." She wasn't able to continue since Mr. Lawless interrupted.

He lashed out, "These statements haven't been verified or brought to our attention. Unless and until these statements are reviewed, I demand an objection!" Mr. Lawless knew his clients were going to react to the statements. To be honest he didn't know what they honestly felt or thought about their boys, and it wasn't his job to care.

Mr. Baker jerked up right from glaring at the other table, "This is crap, my son wouldn't do this, and neither would his friend..." It was about as far as he got before the judge started banging her gavel.

She pounded her gavel before speaking again, "One more outburst like that from anyone and they will be held in contempt of court. Mr. Lawless, control your clients and their parents. If you don't, I will deal with them." She banged the gavel again before turning back to Ms. Carlson, "Please continue."

Mr. Lawless turned and spoke quietly to the parents, "Quiet or you will end up with a fine, in jail, or both. With every outburst, you are only making their case for them. It doesn't matter what the charges are, the more you interrupt, the guiltier your children look." He wanted to glare at the boys since they were not doing a very good job of looking innocent.

Even though he was speaking quietly, everyone at the other table heard him. It was all Zane could do to avoid saying something which would set them off again. He had been focusing on Tessa and to a lesser extent, Oscar to try and keep his wolf from being a pain in the ass. When the others started to spout off, it caught his attention, and something made him want to sneeze. Zane had to rub his nose to try not to though it didn't help. He let out a good sneeze and had to blow his nose before the urge to sneeze was gone again. When Zane finally inhaled again, he wanted to frown.

There was something about the scents which bothered him. Thankfully, his attention on the damn scent was distracting him from what was going on in the room. He had been trying to keep his eyes from reflecting the flat unemotional look he had used on David before. This was enough, for the moment, to keep his eyes from looking bleak. Even his wolf was starting to come forward to help identify the scent.

As he was thinking, Tessa slipped her hand over and lightly grasped his. Zane turned and gave her a smile before he went back to what had caught his attention. Even though he wasn't sure what the scent was, Zane had a feeling it was going to be important. He hoped Tessa would understand why he was being so distracted.

Even as Zane was focusing on smelling the judge looked back at Ms. Carlson, "Please continue Ms. Carlson and don't take too much longer." One more interruption and someone would regret it.

Ms. Carlson continued almost as if she had never been interrupted, "As I was saying during school both David Walpert and Leon Baker were whispering negative comments about Zane and his family. At lunch, Tessa and Oscar were walking past and the two in question started making nasty comments about them. Zane stood up for them and brought them to his table. This is what lead up to the assault on Tessa Fletcher at the mall. I have pictures and the statements to the police concerning it. because of the assault, the Fletchers have chosen to take their children out of school and home school them. I have talked to all parties and as mentioned, at the very least we request removal from the current school of the two children in question. They at the least also require supervised parole and anger management courses. Depending on what the court, as well as a psychological review indicates, registration as teen sex offenders would be required."

Even as she was speaking Mr. Lawless was speaking in a low and urgent voice to his clients. Personally, he didn't care what his clients had to say, since if they got stupid, he would get more money. It was one reason he tended to represent the dregs of society; he made more money. Since several of his clients were well heeled dregs, he stood to make some pretty good money in most cases. He was finally able to convince his clients to keep their mouths shut.

Once Ms. Carlson had finished speaking, Mr. Lawless indicated he wished to speak again. Once the judge indicated he could, Mr. Lawless started speaking again, "Your Honor this is hearsay since all we have is what they have said. What proof do we have of the veracity of these statements? Just because it is in a police report doesn't mean it is true. All it means is the police documented what they were told. There is no evidence there was an encounter in the lunchroom, or the two twins were spoken down to." Mentioning the term bullied wasn't a good idea in juvenile court, "What happened at the mall is much the same. We have bruising on my client's children indicating they were attacked. We have reports of some of the others nearby seeing the others charging down the hallway. It was a setup to bully my client's children." Now it was safe to mention bullying since it was against his clients.

When it was Ms. Carlson's time to speak again, she gave the other lawyer a disgusted look, "We also have evidence of hands having been laid on Ms. Tessa Fletcher. The pictures were taken by both our medical and the police detectives who came to the house based on the false claims of the two boys." She pulled some documentation out and held it ready to provide to the judge if needed.

Zane felt Tessa start to tense up and he kept her hand in his. He knew she didn't want the pictures shown, since it showed a good portion of her chest. Even though she was a wolf she had been raised well and there was a huge difference between generic nudity and this. Zane just knew if those little bastards got a chance to see the images they would get their rocks off, **Tessa I'm here for you and when we get home, we will curl up with you and protect you. I asked you to be my girlfriend, and nothing is going to change that.** Even as he was trying to deal with the emotions, he felt Esther sending comfort to them which helped.

Tessa couldn't help it but look down at the table and tears very slowly trickled out. She knew she hadn't been at fault but what they said had hurt, since she wasn't that type of girl. Their parents had taught them to be good wolves and she had done her best. When Zane contacted her, she couldn't help but lean against him and she didn't care what anyone made of it. Tessa needed the comfort of feeling her lead wolf and her boyfriend against her. Even as she was crying, Tessa wasn't sniffling or sobbing, simply the tears were trickling down her cheeks.

Zane spent the rest of the morning doing his damnedest to comfort her. Oddly enough, his urge to kill those two had been subverted with the need to comfort and take care of Tessa. When he had asked her to be his girlfriend his wolf had agreed. Now there was a new aspect to taking care of her. For now, the adult wolves could take care of this crap. The two weren't worth his time to deal with.

Even as he had been trying to comfort Tessa and Oscar, Zane could feel the others in his team helping. interestingly, he could tell it included both Simone and Mindy, though not nearly as strongly, since they weren't in the room. When the judge called for the end of the session, Zane was caught flat footed. If his uncle hadn't caught his attention brief moments before the Bailiff had called for them to stand, he wouldn't have.

Zane did stand and didn't even think when he kept Tessa's hand in his. Once they were done and released, he wrapped an arm around her again. Even though he didn't realize it, there was something more than simple protection to his actions.

Mike traded a mental smile with Abby and Brandon, he would speak to Zane again when the time was right. Mike also noticed Zane had grown and needed some new clothes. That was something he was going to have to talk to Kadrian about. To get properly fitting clothing, they were going to have to go to the mall. Even as he was considering it, Mike was glad the other people had gone first when leaving. If they hadn't, they would have noticed Zane looking very protective of Tessa. Behind him, Melody was comforting Oscar even as their parents were surrounding the two. Frankly, it almost looked like they were expecting a fight the way they were arranged.

The Judge had informed all of them she was going to consider all the briefs and the documentation provided. She would be ruling on what was going to happen within a week. It meant it was going to be the following Monday before they knew what was going to happen.

*****

Shortly before they arrived at the pack property, Kadrian contacted all the others, **Tell them to take the afternoon off, other than schoolwork. I know all of them are going to be stressed from this morning. Tomorrow, they will start up with what they were doing again. Mike, I need to talk to you once we get home.** Because of what was going on, Kadrian wanted to review the security systems with Mike to ensure they wouldn't have any problems. Even if the two families didn't do anything, it wouldn't be unexpected for a rogue group to try and take advantage to break in.

Mike had figured it was coming, since he had come to the same conclusion. He had been working with the Alpha and the Enforcer side long enough to expect this to be a good time for an attack. Most rogues nowadays were focused on different ways of getting money and illicit gains but not all, **Not a problem Alpha, once I drop them off at the house I will come to your office. I need to talk to you as well.**

Once Mike had parked at the new house, he ensured everyone was inside, "If you decide to go for a run, remain within the limits the Alpha gave you. I'm headed to his office for pack business I will be back as soon as possible." He gave both Zane and Olivia a hug. In Zane's case, he gave Tessa a hug as well before leaving at a trot for the pack house.

When he walked in, he headed directly to Kadrian's office and knocked before walking in, "What can I do for you, Alpha?" For the moment he needed the formality, or he was going to start snarling. Mike knew Kadrian would sense his reaction.

Kadrian was behind his desk and waved for Mike to come in when he knocked on the door, "Contact the pack who does support for our security network. I want a complete diagnostic. I don't expect any problems, but the Walperts have money and better safe than sorry. I know the network is secure and encrypted but the last thing I want is for them to manage to hire someone who gets lucky short term. Take care of it as soon as possible."

Mike listened to what the Alpha was saying and agreed that it needed done. The network was, from what he understood, one of the most secure in the world. It wasn't just the technology that secured it, but also had everyone's DNA profile. There were some very minor differences a normal human didn't have, which allowed them to secure the system. With the new biosensors on the market, a bit of code modification, and if you didn't have certain markers, you couldn't gain access. The markers were hard coded into hardware chips, and a hacker couldn't change those no matter what, since it required direct physical access to reprogram the chips on the control board. No, it didn't exclude a wolf from going rogue for a massive pile of money, but it did make it far harder, with other security measures which would prevent a rogue wolf from reaching the hardware.

"Will do Alpha and I will take care of it today. I will let you know what the status of the checks are as they are progressing." Mike stood and headed towards his office.

*****

Back at home, Zane led his team into the house and to their living room. He ended up standing there holding Tessa. As much as he hated to admit it, she felt really good in his arms. Zane settled for simply holding her and projecting what she had grown to mean to him. His face was more relaxed than it had been in some time and the others noticed it.

When they walked in, Olivia noticed what he had done and started to smile before Oscar squatted down in front of her. He shook his head at her, silently asking her to say nothing, since this was what his sister and Zane needed. Tessa needed to know what those two had said was wrong. Zane needed the attention, and yes, affection from his sister. Just to make sure he held a finger to his lips as he looked at Olivia. He leaned over and whispered very quietly in her ear, "Later, please." Before the other two could notice he stood and headed to the small kitchenette and started getting something for everyone to drink.

Mindy noticed the two but ignored them and followed Oscar into the small nook, "I will get some sodas while you make some tea or coffee." She already knew Zane didn't like soda anymore, so she simply grabbed a few sodas and waters and carried them over to the others and handed out what anyone wanted. She glanced at Melody, **Was it bad?**

Melody took a soda before glancing at Mindy, **It was annoying. Much of the morning, Zane spent comforting both Tessa and Oscar. We helped as much as we could, ,thank the Goddess, managing not to do something stupid.** She turned the TV on to see what there was to watch.

Rico left the room for the kitchen and started putting some sandwiches together. For today, he dug out as much almost-raw meat as possible along with piles of cheese. He found a large tub of Italian noodle salad and went to work. With how upset as everyone was, they needed the protein, and he found he had munched down a number of slices as he was working. By the time he was close to done Oscar was in the room helping, thankfully.

Zane had finally moved over to a chair and had Tessa in his lap. his eyes were closed and looked oddly enough, more relaxed than he'd been recently. Tessa was as well. She wasn't necessarily content but more relaxed than she had been.

Oscar came over and cleared his throat, "We have food and drinks." He pulled out two plates, one for Zane and one for his sister, "I hope you like them." He finally took his and Olivia's plate and settled down next to Olivia and started eating.

Zane opened his eyes and looked at Oscar and then the rest of the room. When he spoke, he couldn't help but look both pleased and shy, "I asked Tessa to be my girlfriend this morning." He kept holding Tessa close as he was talking. One thing he had learned was avoiding secrets from his team without good reason. There was no good reason to not tell, or even delay telling them he was dating Tessa. He had noticed it was very hard to keep secrets within the pack.

Olivia beamed at her brother, since it was a step forward for him. Even as she was beaming, she picked the kitten up and frowned at him, "You have kitty food, that's my sandwich and I'm hungry." After she gave the kitten a good hug, she set him on the floor and picked the plate up and took a bite. Olivia was both annoyed yet glad her sandwich was smaller than the others were.

Eventually they were done eating and Zane was tired, yet he wasn't. Today had been mentally tiring but physically he was used to so much more. when he tried to consider a nap, Zane knew he was going to end up waking up irritated and grumpy. Thankfully, Tessa had fallen asleep while the others were congratulating them on dating. All of them knew it wasn't permanent, unless the two became mates. Inside a team, it was incredibly rare for matings to happen. It could, and usually would, upset the team bonds negatively for a time. Zane didn't know this but eventually he would discover it.

Once Tessa was asleep, he glanced around the room before looking at Rico, **Take care of Tessa please, I need to go and spend some time to dealing with everything that has happened today.** It was the truth with a slight lie. He needed to go and talk to her parents, as well as time to relax. It was hard letting Tessa in more than he had; it scared him even as it was also needed.

Rico looked over at Zane and smiled as he held his arms out, **I will take care of her Zane, we will take care of them for you. Go and do what you need to do.** When Zane settled Tessa down in his lap, he gave his team leader a pleased smile for the trust he had given him, **Go and if you need us, we will come to you.**

Once Zane had silently left the house, Olivia leaned against Oscar, since he had settled next to her on the couch. She was so pleased for her brother, because he had looked more like what she had known. Olivia could tell when he said Tessa was his girlfriend, he had meant it and there was a slight change in how he sat.

Zane left the house. He leaned on his wolf as he opened the pack bonds up some to sense where Brandon and Abby were. Once he had it figured out, he headed towards their house. Zane wanted to talk to them. Partly it was to make sure they felt he was doing a good job of taking care of their pups and he also wanted to let them know he and Tessa were together now. As he reached the house, Brandon opened the door before he could knock.

"Come in Zane." Brandon opened the door and waved the young man into their house. It was a nicer house than many of the junior wolves had. Beta Mike took very good care of them which was why they were so pleased with Zane choosing to protect their pups.

Zane gave Brandon a tense smile and almost scooted into the living area. Even if he was going to be a fairly dominate wolf one of these days, he was still a pup. Knowing he was going to talk to them about dating Tessa only made it worse. Before he realized it, Abby had her arms around him, and he closed his eyes.

Abby had held Mike several times since his brother and sister-in-law had been killed. She knew it would help though not quite like the Luna, "Hello Zane and thank you for choosing our pups to be part of your team." She glanced at Brandon.

Brandon came over and settled for wrapping his arm around his mate, "We do mean it Zane, you have been so good for them. As wonderful as Beta Mike has been for us, we know you will be good for them too." Neither was going to push to know why Zane was there. He would talk about it when he was ready.

Their ready acceptance and approval helped him relax even though he could still sense their anger with what was going on. Zane gave Abby a good hug before looking at Brandon, "I asked Tessa to be my girlfriend earlier, I wanted to talk to you first, but I really wanted to ask her. It wasn't because it would help her but because I like her and..." What the hell was he supposed to say? He liked her, she was cute, they got along, and as she had helped him, he had helped her. It also felt good having her accept him as well.

Brandon didn't make any jokes, "Thank you for telling us, Zane, we appreciate your talking to us about your asking her. Good for both of you." He did mean it and glanced at Abby with a slight smile on his face.

Abby knew what Brandon was thinking and mentally growled at him over the mating bond, "All we ask is you be as good to her as Mike was to me and we will be happy. When they, our twins, find their mates, do as Mike did and accept them and what decisions are made."

Zane had to whine slightly, "So didn't need to know that, Abby. So, didn't need to know." He was going to need to train until he could nip his uncle's tail or something, "Thank you though and I need to get back." There was homework to do, and he need to go and hide as well.

The two of them traded mental smiles even as Abby let him go and watched him leave the house, "I feel so bad for Mike and the two pups, but I can't help but thank the Goddess for drawing them here." Their babies were going to be well taken care of. She had also heard Jason and Margarethe had been chosen by Damien. It was a good sign.

*****

Mike was in his office and was looking at what the computer systems were showing him. He wasn't the best at using them, but he had been working as hard as he could with the systems. Mike knew what the systems were showing as far as the status, but he didn't know why they were showing it. There were one or two younger wolves who had taken classes, but this was ultimately his job. The reports came to him which he could deal with but even as long as he had been using computers, they were just not his thing.

With a sigh he hit the autodial on his phone and thank goodness, he knew how to do that. He waited for the phone to dial. When it was picked up, he had to grin.

"Fossil Valley Help Desk, Julieanne speaking, how may I help you?" The woman on the other end sounded very professional.

"Good afternoon, this is Mike Donovan, and I need to talk to Joshua Develos, please? This is concerning a potential breach of security." He knew it would get the Beta's attention.

It was only a few minutes later before the woman came back, "I talked with Mr. Develos, he asked if this could wait a short time, or is it considered of a high, no, Alpha emergency?"

Mike didn't even blink an eye, "Alpha emergency please and hopefully this will only take a short time to deal with." It was probably a lie, but he didn't know the woman at the other end, but he did know Josh.

It was only a moment later when the call was answered, "What do you need Mike? I was going to contact you shortly about a potential rogue issue." Josh was sounding somewhat irritated since depending on what was going on this might be an emergency.

Mike tensed, "That we will talk about that momentarily, I don't want to ask if it's the issue, but we need a complete security check of the systems and sensors. We have an issue with some fucknut humans who attacked some of our pups. It is a teen pup slash human issue, but we need to ensure our system and sensors are working perfectly. This is to keep the humans from doing something stupid."

Josh sighed even as he glanced at Molly and Adam who were in the room with him, and with werewolf hearing, would have heard Mike perfectly, "Wonderful and crap, I will send you what I have on the possible rogues and are you going to need my attention on this? Can I delegate it to one of my specialists?" He dreaded the answer even as he was sending the information to Mike.

It made Mike give the phone a half-hearted smile, "Sorry Josh but I need you or Adam's attention, this is coming from my Alpha. Maybe if you or Adam supervise the specialist, I can run with it, but you know what I mean right?" Once in a blue moon dealing with this stuff was a pain. Normally this wasn't a problem since a specialist would do for the most part.

"Well fuck, I'm going to have to clear this with Andrew since we had a rogue attack earlier. I will call you back as soon as I can. I have to go Mike, and I was sorry to hear about the loss of your brother and his wife." They chatted for a few minutes longer before both disconnected.

Before Mike could snarl, Brandon walked into his office and placed a tray of food in front of him, "Zane came and talked to us. He wanted to let us know he asked Tessa to be his girlfriend. You have a damn good nephew." Once the tray was on the desk Brandon moved behind Mike and started working on his shoulders.

Mike didn't have the energy to deal with what Brandon said other than to be pleased. He leaned forward as Brandon rubbed his shoulder and neck, "Tell Zane I'm going to be home late and not to wait up please. I need some time to work on a few things." Once Brandon had finished with the massage Mike pulled the tray close and started scarfing down the food, as he realized how hungry he was.

*****

Zane had been informed Mike was going to be working late He was both glad and wished he hadn't been. Zane wanted the older—and more senior—wolf to be there, so he could lean on him and relax but since he couldn't; he had to be the most senior wolf. It had been a long evening since both Mindy and Simone had brought homework back with them. Until the home schooling started, they'd be continuing with what the school sent home. Several of them had to struggle through the homework but eventually they were done.

Once everyone had eaten and finished their homework, he had again asked for some time to himself. In this case it was because he wanted to talk to his sister. It had been several days since Oscar had talked to him about what Olivia had been feeling. Zane hadn't had a chance to talk to her alone for almost a week. So much of it was because by the time he made it home, he was bushed. Since he hadn't done much today, he thankfully wasn't tired. Once everyone was gone, he gave his sister a good hug as Tessa helped her up, "I want to talk to you, if you are feeling up to it." He really hoped she was willing.

Olivia returned the hug and was glad her brother was wanting to talk, "Let Tessa help me get ready for bed. Once ready we can talk for a few minutes." She had to make a face though the mandatory meds were getting less strong thankfully, "Unless the pills kick in immediately, I will have some time to talk to you." He let her go and watched her leave the room. She was moving much better than she had been. Zane was so very pleased.

Oscar came over and gave Zane a good hug, before watching Tessa and Oliva leave the room. Liv was moving so much better than she had been before the surgery and Oscar was pleased. He liked Liv and she was such a happy person even with her injury. It was like she was the polar opposite of her brother, but Oscar didn't have a problem with it. Zane exuded protection and Liv life. He was glad Zane had accepted him and his sister as his junior wolves.

Zane returned the hug and watched the two girls leave the room. He knew Tessa was maybe a year younger than him, but she was just a bit taller than Oliva. For some reason he'd never gotten around to asking their ages and didn't really care. She was so darn cute though and waking up next to Tessa had been both enjoyable and embarrassing. He was very glad she had accepted his asking her to be his girlfriend, "Oscar thank you for telling me it was okay to date your sister. It means a great deal."

Oscar couldn't help but smile at Zane and his comment. It was nice knowing Zane liked his sister enough to consider dating her, "You are welcome, Zane. If you don't mind, even though you are feeling better, I'm going to get the oils ready for your massage. You still need it to keep your muscles relaxed." He left the room since he didn't want any other questions or comments made. It was going to take some time, but Olivia was really nice, and she was rather cute as well.

Zane let him go. Since he was focused on the trial and what he was feeling for Tessa, he didn't think when Oscar left the room. To him, Olivia was still just a kid, even though she was in seventh grade. Hell, he still thought of himself as barely a teen even though he was fourteen now. How long he stood there he wasn't sure, but eventually Tessa let him know Olivia was in bed, **Thank you Tessa. Oscar is making sure whatever you use on my back is ready.**

When he finally walked into Olivia's room Tessa was already gone and he settled on the bed next to her, "Hey Liv, I wanted to talk to you. How are you doing?" This wasn't something Zane really wanted to talk about, but she was family.

Olivia stretched her leg out and even flexed it as allowed, "Better Zane and I do have an appointment in two days to see if they can remove the brace. I can't wait, and I so want it gone. It does hurt but not like it used to."

He sat down and wrapped an arm around her and tried to relax, "I know, since Uncle Mike keeps me up to date. I can smell you aren't hurting as much. Thank you for letting Oscar and Tessa help you." Zane looked away before he spoke again, "Oscar did talk to me and I'm trying Liv. With the help of the twins and my team I'm slowly dealing with my fears. I want to let everyone in, but it still scares me. I do care for you sis, so does my team."

Olivia returned his hug and then poked him in the ribs, "You had better let them and the pack in or else Zane. I do have a crutch hidden and will use it if needed." She gave him another hug, "Love you Zane and don't be stupid or I will brain you with my crutch." Olivia settled down in bed and yawned even as she was pulling the covers up.

Zane growled at her just for good measure even as he stood up, "See if I try and open up with my horrible sister in the future." He made sure she had the covers up before stomping out of the room and heading to his. When he passed the living room, he glanced at Oscar even as he kept going.

When he walked into his room, Tessa was there waiting for him. She had on some sleeping shorts and a jammie shirt which made him blush. Instead of saying anything he settled on the bed and groaned, "Do your worst, I'm still sore and tense, darn it. I thought being a wolf made us heal like yesterday!"

Tessa snickered at him even as she blushed slightly as well. Before Zane settled on the bed, he had pulled his shirt off and flopped down. He was a good-looking wolf and when Tessa did find her mate, she hoped he was as nice as Zane , "I will do my best Zane." Even though he couldn't see it, she wrinkled her face at him.

CHAPTER 19

Decision About Mindy

The tech from the Fossil Valley Pack had shown up late the night before. As soon as he had arrived, he had been shown to Mike's office, "Come in and have a seat, please. Due to the lateness, unless there is something urgent being reported, start the work in the morning. Mostly we are worried about a couple of human pups getting stupid and getting killed. Did Josh inform you of what is going on and why?"

Tech Jason met Beta Mike's eyes before lowering his, "He briefed us. I have been on the road since I was dispatched to come and do a security check on all your systems and sensors. I'm sure I will have an update waiting when I log in, but if it wouldn't be a problem, tell me what you can." Having Josh tell him was different than what the client did. Sometimes Josh had a better idea and other times the client did.

Mike leaned forward and rested his arms on his desk, "Long story short, two human brats decided it was a good idea to push around a junior she-wolf pup. My nephew took exception to this, since she and her twin recently became members of his team. When they found an opportunity to push the young wolf around, the only thing that saved the two was the quick thinking of one of his team members. My nephew has already stated if they get close to the she-wolf again, he will kill them. We would rather like to keep it from getting that far."

Jason's expression didn't change since it was a very valid reason for a security check. If the humans got too close, they would die and all kinds of awkward questions would be asked, "Thank you for the information, Beta Mike, and I'm sure Beta Josh has already saved a diagnostic report to the system. I will check on the stats and presuming nothing major is at fault, I will touch base with you in the morning." He started to stand when Mike waved him to sit back down.

"One last thing, once you report to me, if there is anything that is going to require inspection or even replacement, make sure I know. Unless it is a major security issue, I think it would be a good idea for my nephew to help with the heavy work. Maybe his future second as well. Check with Josh to see if this would be acceptable. If he would prefer not, tell me. I'm simply trying to keep the pups busy and worn out."

The other wolf did smile at Mike, "I understand, and I will talk to Josh, since it could impact on the treaty for services. I will talk to you in the morning Beta." Jason stood and left the office.

Once Jason was shown into his room, he connected his laptop to the systems and logged into the local security server. While it was calling up the logs and diagnostic data, he pulled out his cell and placed a call to Josh. He needed to check in and pass on the request from Beta Mike.

*****

The next morning, Zane discovered their training had been altered. Now they were going to school in the morning, since it was set up, and enforcer training in the afternoon. Depending on how things went, they were still going to be doing chores but not like they had been since the fight at the mall. He was glad but for some reason, it almost felt like the pack work they had been doing was just waiting to catch them when they were the most tired.

When Zane walked down to breakfast, he found Tessa and gave her a good hug and a quick kiss before sitting down. Once he settled down in his usual chair and yawned as a cup of coffee was put in front of him, "Thanks Tessa, breakfast smells good." It smelled like there was some ham instead of sausage and most definitely pancakes and bacon, "I can't help but wonder how much bacon the pack goes through on a weekly basis. There is some very rich farmer out there somewhere." Zane smiled as Oscar made sure Olivia was comfortable.

When Zane gave her a hug and kiss Tessa couldn't help being pleased. She could feel her wolf responding as well to the affection, "Here is your coffee and breakfast will be done shortly." Keeping up the routine of helping all of them helped her to deal with what was happening. It wasn't much longer before she helped carry the food out.

After giving Zane his plate, Tessa gave him a light hug before sitting down next to him with her plate. For the moment, since she was his girlfriend, she could sit next to him, and nobody would say anything. If she hadn't been his girlfriend, if he had asked, she would have sat next to him, but normally she and Oscar were furthest away. It felt rather nice being here surrounded with his scent even though she knew eventually she would end up back next to Oscar but for now she was going to enjoy it. Occasionally, she would lean against Zane as they ate.

Zane noticed Melody had a pleased smile on her face and after thinking about it, he returned it. He had debated frowning at her but to be honest Zane was rather pleased. She was his first girlfriend, and she was a really nice girl. He leaned back when Tessa leaned against him and both he and his wolf enjoyed the attention too.

Soon breakfast was over, and it was time for everyone to head to the school room in the pack house. When Olivia stood up, she crutched over to Zane and wrapped her arms around him, "Love you Zane and congrats on seeing Tessa." She remained leaning against him as he wrapped his arms around her as well, "Don't forget my appointment this afternoon and if you go wolf, I will use a crutch on you."

She got a muffled snort from the others though nobody said anything. Zane gave her a light squeeze, "My wolf is pouting now just so you know Liv. He might chew up a crutch just because." He let her go and watched Mindy and Simone walk Olivia towards the bus stop. She was moving better than before the surgery which great. His face showed just how much it meant to him seeing her moving easier.

Tessa could feel his thoughts and wrapped her arms around him, **It is so very good to see Olivia moving so much better. I'm really happy for her. Now it is time for school.** Just to distract him she leaned up and gave him a soft kiss.

Zane returned the hug though he kept his eyes on his sister, **It is, it still hurts knowing what we lost but this does help.** The kiss he really wasn't expecting and before he realized it, he had returned it before furrowing his brow at her, "That was sneaky Tessa. My wolf might have to nip at you later." He kissed her again before he frowned at the others there who were grinning.

"It goes for the rest of you as well. I might just have to take each one of you on a run and growl and nip at you as well." He couldn't help but start laughing even as he grabbed his backpack and holding Tessa's hand, headed to the pack house. When they eventually arrived there, they headed straight to the room being used for school.

*****

Jason had received approval to have several of the older pups' help, based on Josh's relationship with Mike. They both knew each other well. Mike was much older than Josh, but both had a great deal of respect for each other. How the relationship had developed, Jason didn't know, and it wasn't his concern. All that mattered was they knew and respected each other.

Between last night and this morning, Jason had dug through the diagnostics and reports. The servers were fine and were reporting no issues. There had been a complete virus and malware scan. Several different types of intrusion scans, and a complete hardware test of the servers and the connected remote-ware. For the remote-ware, it included but wasn't limited to hardwired and wireless. To bypass any of the sensors required a registered DNA scan. It had to be fresh blood as well. If someone tried to take a sample and preserve it, the sensors were designed to check and verify certain chemicals.

There were a few issues, nothing that could be considered major, that he was going to look at more closely. Most of the glitches appeared to be related to connectivity issues, which normally wouldn't be a problem. They were connected and would register intrusions, but the signal was slightly degraded. It was mostly likely a case of the connections needed to be reseated and it would resolve the issue. Normally this would be taken care of during the bi-yearly visit but due to what was going on, it needed to be resolved.

After reviewing and making a list of problems to examine, Jason headed to the security office. After checking in and having his access verified, he was allowed into the server room. Jason ignored all the racks except the single sealed enclosure. He inspected the tamper seals on both the front and the back, which were still intact and had the ID code they should have, before he broke the front, so he could access the controls to unlock it. After swiping his card, using his biometrics scan, and a code, the enclosure opened. For this server, it was not connected to anything but a very highly encrypted tunnel from here to the pack Jason belonged to. There was a total of three computers in this house it was connected to and again it was a dedicated link with separate wired network ports, to the switch near the top of the rack, and didn't have any other wireless or internet connection. To access it, you had to be in Josh's office, the security room at Jason's pack, via the console at this server, and the security office for this pack. Even changing the computer out had to be registered, as it would detect and authenticate the specific computer.

Yes, it was possible to gain access, but it would require someone to use a direct connection to the server or one of the computers connected to it. It would require someone very high up in the pack to become a rogue and give out some sort of access. While it was possible, it was very unlikely. When anything new was connected to any of the systems, it had to be approved before it would function. There were only a few authorized who could approve new hardware. Even with reseating a connector it would be detected and had to be in a diagnostics mode or an alert would flag it, and the sensor would be considered suspect until approved.

Jason had to shake his head as he chased his thoughts about the design of the systems out of his mind. The last one that crossed his mind was living a very long time had some use. Somehow Josh had found a wolf who had helped build the ENIAC and had been programming ever since. The amount of computer information in his brain was both fascinating and depressing.

After logging into the computer, he started entering commands and while they were running, he inspected the physical structure of the system. Nothing had broken any of the security seals or measures for the enclosure. Eventually lunch time rolled around and he was done with the checks on the server and connected hardware. Now came the enjoyable part – locating the actual sensors and resolving any issues. He was glad the freezing weather and snow hadn't come yet, otherwise it would be much more work to locate them.

He left the security section after re-securing the enclosure, including placing a new tamper-seal and recording the unique ID number, and headed to Mike's office. After knocking, he walked in and settled down in the chair indicated, "Beta Mike, there are an even dozen sensors I'm going to check. They aren't having any problems as of now, but they are indicating potential failures. Chances are very good it is simply connectivity issues, but as you mentioned, better safe than sorry. I have also received permission from Beta Josh to have some of your trainees assist with carrying equipment."

After listening to what Jason had said Mike leaned forward and looked at a few papers the printer had kicked out, "That sounds good and looking at the information I have, I think I know which sensors you are talking about. I will have Zane, Melody, and Rico report to the security office after lunch and assist you. Feel free to have them carry anything and everything. Hell, feel free to 'accidently forget' something and make them run back for it. As I mentioned I'm trying to keep them busy and tired."

Jason couldn't help but return Mike's slightly mischievous look with a knowing grin, "I can take care of it, Beta, and I do understand. I think

I should have everything resolved this afternoon. Before I leave, I will have Beta Josh run another diagnostic and discuss it with him." When Mike dismissed him, he headed towards the dining room since he was definitely hungry. He was looking forward to the differences that were inherent in each pack's food, even if each were equally delicious.

*****

The afternoon, once Zane was released from running stuff for the computer tech and watching him play with the hidden sensors, learning lots about how they worked and what sort they had, he headed directly to medical. Mike had already informed him Olivia was there, and they were waiting for him to arrive. He dashed into the room and paused before slowly walking over to his sister, "Hey Liv, ready to see how you are doing?" He didn't even bother trying to hide both his concern and his hope. Olivia had pretty much asked him not to try and hide his feelings from her, so he was trying. Zane wanted her to be as healthy and pain free as possible, and it showed.

Olivia grasped his hand and gave it a squeeze. She had talked with Oscar, or she should say he talked to her. It was more a conversation about not trying to force Zane to stop helping her. It was also a conversation about Zane asking Tessa to be his girlfriend. Even now after being here, in the pack, for several months, there was just so little she understood. Oscar and Tessa were helping her understand more about how the pack worked. They had been very careful to explain why Zane was acting the way he was. Not the hurt and tense Zane, but the over-protective wolf-Zane and why it hurt him when she yelled. Olivia still did at times, just to keep him back to an extent. This was something she had to work thru as much as she could. Trying to explain it to Zane didn't seem to be working very well.

To be honest, if it hadn't been for the twins, Olivia's and Zane's relationship would have been far rockier than it was. She simply didn't understand, and he didn't have the ability to explain why he was acting the way he was. To have someone simply say 'it was his wolf' just didn't help. Mrs. Esther had tried to explain it, but she was an adult and just didn't have the right words for her. The twins were her age, or close enough they spoke much the same language.

Olivia looked at Mike and then Zane, "Just remember if you go wolf, I will do something, maybe exchange your underwear for something tie-dyed..." She gave him an insouciant grin when she threatened him.

Zane lifted a corner of his mouth and showed a few teeth even as he growled at her, "I am still going to find out how you managed to swap my shirts and get you back." He finally gave her hand another squeeze as the surgeon came in and greeted them.

"Good afternoon, I have been keeping track of the reports on Olivia and she does appear to be healing well. She has been responding even better than I had hoped, which is a good thing. I have a feeling it is a combination of the traces of her wolf DNA and the blood provided. Now let me do my thing and I will give you further information." Olivia was already in a gown, so she shifted it enough to get to Olivia's leg and did as she had before.

It didn't take long, though longer than before, since she wasn't just checking on the injuries. She was checking on the injury and the healing and how much was left. Once she was done, she flipped the gown and sheet back over Olivia's leg and sat down on a stool, "Well, you are healing quite well, young lady. As of now the calcification of the fixed bone is advanced enough you don't need the brace at home. I still want you to keep using the brace at school for two more weeks but at home you don't need it. It is significantly better than it was, and I'm going to talk to a Physical Therapist colleague of mine. We will come up with exercises you need to do to strengthen your muscles and help you finish healing. As of now it looks like you will be back to about ninety percent of full function. Eventually, unless you are in extreme situations, you shouldn't have more than minor issues with it." She had told Mike that Turning her likely would restore full function, leaving it to her guardian to tell her when or if he decided to do so. Each pack was different in how they dealt with Turning, especially for pups. She knew some packs who refused all Turns except for Mates, and refused to even teach that it was possible and taught that it would kill those who weren't mates if a turn was attempted. Other packs would turn anyone who could show they had the knowledge and mind to understand it, and consent to the Turn, even if they didn't feel it was good fit, and they then later had to put them down when they failed to adapt. Both extremes were rare, and most fell into the middle.

Zane listened intently to what the doctor was saying and was forced to lower his head. Both him and his wolf were beyond pleased with what the doctor had to say, and it showed. Even though they were happy with what the doctor said, they were still upset by what had forced this. Zane had to lower his head to the exam table and the tears started coming.

Mike stood up and indicated for the doctor to leave the room. He also asked for Tessa and Oscar to stay and help. Mike and the doctor walked out of the room and closed the door behind them, "Doc, I know this is covered by the pack, but I want to do something for you. It could be a donation to your pack, a charity of your choice or anything else. Let me know and I will take care of it."

She knew the question was coming, it was a common request, and knew he wouldn't take no for an answer, so had her ready answer for him. "Then donate to St. Jude's for the human children. That would be what I want, Mike. Nothing more and nothing less." She watched him move down the hall and lean against the wall as he was dealing with his emotions. She left the medical section since she wasn't needed any longer.

He turned and moved down the hallway. It was obvious he needed some time.

Inside the room Oscar settled down next to Olivia and lightly grasped her hand. He was rather pleased as well by what the doctor had to say for all of them. This would help Zane continue his healing and it would help Olivia return to what she had been before the accident. Without really thinking about it, Oscar reached over and stroked her cheek, "I'm very pleased for both of you, Olivia."

Tessa had wrapped her arms around Zane and was doing her best to help him relax as he processed his feelings. For now, she was going to let him cry, since her mother had recommended it. When Zane had started to cry, Tessa had linked with her mom and asked for suggestions, and it was what she had recommended.

*****

Zane and the others were finally done with their homework for the evening. The elder who had taken charge of the home schooling was both very good and very abrupt. She had informed them she knew they didn't need the entire day to learn what she was teaching. She had muttered something about 'since there were only a few of them and they had almost one to one instruction they had better do good or else'. She had taken the time to threaten Zane with the cows, Rico with the rabbits, and even Melody with more dusting and cleaning. For some reason she didn't bother threatening the twins with anything, which Zane felt was just wrong.

Now that he had collapsed in his chair, he flopped his head back against the back of the chair and let out a slow sigh. It was mostly a way to try and let the tension drain out of his body. It didn't really help but it was worth an attempt, "Oscar, Tessa, I need to talk to Melody, Rico, and Simone. Will you please give us some time? I will let you know when we are done talking." One thing he had been taught was to try and avoid involving the most junior wolves in team issues unless it directly affected them, as they would just follow what he decided.

Once they left Zane looked at the others, "At the hearing on Monday, I felt Mindy trying to help support both Tessa and the team. I'm going to talk to her tomorrow and accept her into the team. If she is willing to do that for Tessa and Oscar, I can't say no. She hasn't asked or talked about joining since I talked to her and then you. She has brought over the homework and helped us with it. I haven't sensed any ulterior motives from her. What do you have to say?"

Melody had been paying close attention to Mindy and she hadn't felt anything negative from her. She had felt Mindy was more comfortable than she had been for a long while, "I don't want to say yes or no, but she has been helpful and does seem to really want to join the team. It is your decision Zane but if you do say yes, I will accept it."

Rico had to shrug since he had already stated his position, and it hadn't changed. Zane was the leader of the team, and he would go with what he decided. If it was something Rico had really strong feelings about, he would make a stand, politely, as needed. Now wasn't one of those times.

Simone gave Zane a very pleased smile, "I do think she will be a good addition to the team Zane. I think at this point, we need to hold off on admitting others. Mindy might have come across as a suck up or hanger on, but she really isn't." She felt Mindy was just trying to find a team to accept her but didn't have a senior pup she was close with to have just been folded into the team as it formed, so would try to get close to a team before being told to back off, and then having to try with another. "Others might see our accepting her as saying we will accept anyone. Right now, those we have in the team including the twins are what we need. Eventually you might add more but it can wait."

Zane listened to what each person had to say and after thinking about it decided, "I will talk to her tomorrow. Each of you have made your opinions known and thanks." He had to make a face, "I know I'm supposed to be in charge, but I want opinions and thoughts and not yes or no people. I want the best team we can build. Now if you don't mind, I'm going to go and collapse in bed." He stood and stretched even as he yawned, "See you tomorrow."

The rest of the week passed reasonably quickly for the pups. When Friday evening rolled around Zane was looking at the mirror in his bathroom and couldn't help but grin. Before all this he had been in good shape, but he had been a runner. His body had been lean and well-muscled, for someone his age from his running. Between gaining a wolf and the almost constant exercise for the last few weeks, he was definitely bulking up. No, he wasn't ever going to be one of the over muscled body builder types, not that he wanted to, but he definitely had larger muscles. It was obvious to him even without looking in the mirror. The clothing he had either had before, or picked up upon arrival, no longer fit very well.

They were tight across his chest and around his upper arms. Even his pants were starting to get tight in the thighs and he was starting to worry about ripping something at the wrong time. If it was a sleeve, it was one thing but, on his legs, or groin that would be so damn wrong. With a slight smile he trotted downstairs and found his uncle, “Hey Unc, I really need some new clothes. Sorry but I gr some and most of my clothes no longer fit quite right.” He had deliberately made ‘grew some’ sound like ‘gruesome’ just for good measure.

Both Tessa and Olivia stared and then started groaning at the horrible joke, “I agree you are gruesome since you are a horrible brother.” Olivia even went so far as to pick up a crutch and wave it in his direction.

Mike simply looked up at him and cocked his head, “Really? I hadn’t noticed. I guess we will have to go shopping tomorrow. I know just the place, since you do those shirts Olivia asked me to pick up so very well.” He had figured by now Zane should have figured out he had done it at Olivia’s request. If he had been a wolf for longer, he would have known immediately, as he didn’t try to hide his scent, just minimized how much he touched them.

Zane stomped his foot at his uncle before laughing, “I had rather figured it out, since Oscar and Tessa told me they wouldn’t do it to me. I know Melody and the others wouldn’t have either, so it didn’t leave many others who could. I want you to know, I’m training so hard just to give me a chance to bite your tail, ears, or paw. I will get you for this.” He grinned at Olivia, “My wolf already decided what we are going to do to get you back so be worried, very, very worried.”

With a shake of his head Mike smirked back, “Good luck Zane and when you do… Well, I will figure out some way to reward you. I have already talked to Kad and tomorrow we are going to go shopping. Rico and Melody’s parents have mentioned the need for some new clothing as well, so we decided to make it a group shopping trip. It will keep you out of trouble and keep trouble from getting to you."

The twins and Zane almost shuddered, "Oh heaven yes, I don't want any more trouble, damn it. I want things to calm down, so I can go back to school and do the teen thing again." He rolled his eyes even as Tessa came over and wrapped her arms around him. Zane returned the hug before letting her go and moving to his chair and held his arms out for her to sit down in his lap, "Seriously Unc, even as much as I still want to leave certain individuals as eunuchs, I want to keep getting to know my friends." Even now saying healing was something he couldn't admit to.

Olivia had to think about the word before she made a face and stuck her tongue out in reaction, "Ewww, that's nasty!" She was starting to understand, and she cared for Oscar and Tessa as well. Tessa had been so hurt by what had been said by those two, but Olivia still had issues with how Zane appeared to be blood thirsty now.

Zane glanced at his sister and shook his head, "Believe me Liv, I feel so much the same at times. My wolf tends to have a rather direct outlook. Kill them, then they won't be a problem. From what I have learned it is sort of senior wolfy thing." He looked at Mike, "Unc, I'm going to go for a run since I can feel the moon calling. I will talk to you later." He gave Tessa a good hug before standing up.

Mike stood as well and stretched, "I think I'm going to go for a run as well though in a different direction. Since I'm not under pack property arrest, I want to go for a good long run. It has been a good week, but I need to stretch my legs and let my paws feel the earth." He walked out of the front of the house.

Zane stretched after he urged Tessa off his lap, "Later sis and Oscar will probably join you once we are back. Not sure why they have a room anymore since they simply refuse to sleep in their room." He grinned when he said it, only to have Tessa growl at him. He headed outside and knew the rest of his team would show up including Mindy. He had talked to her and accepted her as part of the team.

Olivia snorted even as she turned back to the TV and changed the station to what she wanted to watch. As the others left, she settled further into the couch and relaxed as one of her shows came on.

*****

Annaliza had arrived at the pack with a document from her pack. It wasn't urgent, but it was an official document and since she was one of the couriers from her pack to others, it was her job. After arriving, she had briefly talked with Alpha Kadrian and turned it over. He had cracked the seal and after reviewing it told her to relax for the evening and he would deal with it in the morning. As expected, she had been told she had the run of the property though hunting wasn't included, which was more often than not what freedom she was given at other packs. In the rare case she had a need for doing a hunt, usually it could be arranged, sometimes it was just needing to pay for it. She had been in time to have dinner, so it didn't matter.

She cheerfully took the offer up and once she had settled into the guest room and shifted to her wolf, headed out back. This pack she did enjoy, since they were fairly relaxed and accepted, with permission, others running around on their property. She settled for a good run on one of the paths she had gotten used to running, as she had been here several times. She was still young, for a werewolf, as Annaliza had just turned forty, but she had been doing this job for years and knew the place.

As she was running, she enjoyed the feel of her muscles flowing and moving as the kinks of the drive were worked out. Eventually she found the one clearing she really enjoyed and stopped by a small creek to lap up some water. Once she was done, she lifted her head and let out a contented howl. It wasn't anything but to let the Moon Goddess know she was very pleased to have been able to run and enjoy it.

Before Mike had left the house, he had been informed a courier was here with some official document. It wasn't a problem and was reasonably common, but since he was the Beta Enforcer, he needed to be informed. Couriers were relatively sacrosanct, even when their packs were at war. It allowed the packs to maintain communications even at the worst of times. The only time a courier could be challenged was when one was accused of a council transgression. Even then they were to be delivered to the council for investigation and discipline as needed. It was rare, but they could be stripped of their courier status and turned back over to the pack for discipline after being proven that they had made a serious transgression. Like Elders, even though they couldn't be challenged, they could make a challenge for cause and have a fight in a ring. Otherwise, they were only allowed to fight in self-defense, and even then, they were expected to run instead of standing to fight.

He didn't even bother wondering what the courier had been carrying, since Kadrian would tell him if he needed to know. Sometimes they were private communications between the Elders or anyone else who wished to use the services. As long as Mike knew there was a courier as their guest on the property, he was satisfied he had been kept in the loop. He settled into his run even as she, the courier was and settled for stretching out his legs and body into a mile eating run. As wolves, they could run all day and night as needed. It was a mixture of running and a slow ground eating lope which could cover vast miles in a fleeting time. Tonight, he simply wanted to exercise his body and had headed to one of the densest parts of the property.

Mike wove between trees, going over or under obstacles such as berry bushes, fallen trees, and terrain issues. It helped keep their wolves familiar with the property. It would also teach their wolves how to slow down and possibly even shake off a rogue chasing them just by knowing the way the land was. Eventually he had worked his body enough he needed a drink and headed to a nearby stream.

When he approached the stream, he noticed a strange wolf and slowed down. Mike checked the link and discovered this was the courier, so he kept moving forward instead of calling an alert. When he stopped on the other side of the stream, he gave her a brief yip of greeting before leaning down for a lap of water.

When the other wolf came into the small clearing, Annie, as she preferred to be called, tensed, and then relaxed. Since she was downwind of the other wolf his scent hit her hard. Almost before she realized it, she had easily leapt over the stream and slowly approached. As she was approaching, she was whining slightly in desire. The wolf was obviously powerful though she had long dealt with strong wolves. The color of his coat was lovely in the moon light as well but again she had seen so very many lovely wolves. She had spent time with many as well, but this wolf had an added scent which drew her. It smelled of an earthiness as well as piney resinous mixed in. There were traces of sadness as well which made her want to whine even more.

Mike could tell the direction of the wind was going to take his scent to her even as it kept hers away from him. It was somewhat annoying, since he liked to know the scents of all who were on the property. As he was watching her the other wolf startled him when she leapt over the small creek. It wasn't huge in any way, so the leap didn't require hard work, but it still startled him. When she whined at him, he cocked his head before standing and moving towards her. When he was close enough, her scent hit him hard as well. She was lithe and sweet looking. She had a very proud carriage as she moved, which drew him. The she-wolf was obviously comfortable with who she was and knew her job and position. When he scented her, his ears shot up. To him her scent was of the upper meadows when the wildflowers were blooming and the warmth of the sun in spring.

Mike kept pacing forward towards her until they met, and he took two steps even closer and rested his head on her shoulders. When he did it, he felt the tingles and there was a delicious shiver of attraction as well, **Mine. My mate, how I have waited patiently for you.** He pressed even closer to her as he sent to her.

Annie froze when he moved even closer and pressed against her. Her eyes dilated, and the tingles started as well. Oh goddess, this was not something she had expected even though she had been wanting to find her mate . Annie had been here several times and after the first few times she figured her mate wasn't here. She didn't realize Mike was normally gone a fair amount of the time as he fulfilled his job role. It was why she hadn't seen him or really gotten a good scenting of him, **Mine as well and I have been waiting for the Goddess to bless me too.** They stood there for some time as they enjoyed the feeling of having found their mate.

*****

Zane and his team had been running when he felt a surge over the link with his uncle and stumbled. When he stumbled, he ended up almost braining himself on a rock he had been working on going around and ended up landing on his bottom. When he did, it was with a definite thump, and his eyes were somewhat glassy in reaction to the impact of what he was feeling over the bond. Even as he was trying to shake his head, the others were coming back to check on him.

Melody approached him and nuzzled one cheek, **Zane? What is wrong? Did you step wrong?** It wasn't unheard of for something to slip under a pup's paw and an accident to happen. She even knew of a few adult wolves who had it happen to them.

Zane shook his head again and blinked his eyes several times before he started to get his focus back, **Um, something from Beta Mike...** He dropped his head as he tried to keep clearing his mind and make sense of what he was feeling. It didn't make any sense though other than it had something to do with a she-wolf, **Ah, something about Mike and a she-wolf, um, they smell good to each other maybe?** About then the link closed off which helped.

When Zane looked up, he twitched since all the others were giving him a very amused look. All he could do was stare back and wonder why.

CHAPTER 20

New Mates

How long Mike and the she-wolf stood there as the sensations flowed through them, they weren't sure, but it felt like an eternity . He finally lifted his muzzle to the moon and howled to let any wolf nearby know she was his. Even though there was joy in his howl there was sadness as well even as so much of Zane's howling had the same, **Alpha I have found my mate and she is the courier, I do believe.** He had to let Kadrian know.

Annie had lifted her muzzle and let out her own howl in thanks to the Goddess. As she listened to his howl, she heard the underlying sadness and wanted to know why. Something had hurt her mate, and Annie was not pleased at all. Once she was done howling, she nuzzled him and used to her body to express her concern.

Kadrian was relaxing in his suite with Esther when Mike contacted him, and he immediately started laughing, **Take her to your suite here and I will have Esther let Zane know you will talk to him in the morning. Go relax and get to know your mate. I will ensure the pups are taken care of.** He had included Esther in the sending and he turned and gave her a good kiss, "I'm so pleased for him and I can only hope this will be good for Mike and his family."

Esther returned the kiss and gave her mate a very pleased smile, "I'm so pleased for him and I'm sure this will be good for all of them. It might be rough for a time, since Zane is going to continue having problems.

I think in the long run it will be good." She kissed her mate again and gave him a good hug, "I'm ready for bed, how about you?" She batted her eyes at him when she said it.

*****

Zane returned the stares and twitched his ears at his team, **Why are you staring at me?** He was most definitely feeling confused. When Esther contacted him, he was even more confused.

Zane, Mike is going to be busy this evening. Something came up and he is needed at the pack house. It isn't anything related to the two idiots, in case you were wondering. Go back to the house and as I said, he will talk to you later. She let Zane go and hoped he wasn't going to ask too many questions.

Zane let out an annoyed growl, since he had been having fun with the run, **Okay guys I was told to head back home, and Uncle Mike is going to be busy this evening.** He stood and gave his head a good shake since he was still feeling slightly out of it.

Melody walked over and pressed her body against his, **Zane, I think what Mrs. Esther didn't say was Beta Mike probably met his mate. He is going to be busy the rest of the night as he gets to know her. I'm so pleased if that's what happened.** She had to work to hide her amusement on how bewildered he was; that your mate would be the best smell ever was something 'all werewolves knew' but seems that Zane hadn't known it.

Zane had leaned against her when she came over to comfort him. When she mentioned mate, he tensed and almost felt like he had been punched in the gut. What was this going to do to what was left of their family? Was Mike going to pay more attention to her than him and Olivia? He could feel his heart starting to beat faster and his chest tightening up with fear. Zane wasn't worried Mike would send them elsewhere; he just was scared Mike might focus on his mate more than on Olivia.

Rico felt Zane's reaction to what he had been told and settled down on Zane's other side and leaned against him. He felt Melody lean even more against Zane and the two pretty much sandwiched him. Both of their wolves were giving him as much support as possible. Simone, Mindy, and the twins came over and pressed as close as possible to help provide comfort.

Melody rubbed her head against his, **Zane what has you so scared? Having a mate is a good thing.** She could smell the tension as well as hear his change in heart rate.

Zane felt them leaning against him and it really did help. He could feel the comfort from their wolves, and he leaned into it and took several slow breaths, **Just a stupid concern. I will be fine.** He returned the head rub and then gave Rico a nudge, **With the support of our team I will be fine.** Zane had finally decided he was most comfortable using the inclusive 'we' as far as the team was concerned. He might be the leader of the team, but as far as he was concerned, it was *their* team not *his,* and he was going to treat it that way.

Mindy was standing in front of him and gave his muzzle a lick, **Are you sure Zane? I can still hear your heart racing and your breathing strained. Will you tell us what is wrong?** She hoped it wasn't related to Beta Mike's finding his mate.

He took a slow breath and stood up, **I will be fine. It is something I will have to deal with. Your support is all I need, and I will be fine. It is time for us to get back home. I will see all of you tomorrow.** Zane stood and stretched after nudging Melody and Rico away from him, **Night all.** He headed back towards the house since he didn't want to discuss it.

Melody moved away before giving Oscar and Tessa a concerned look, **Keep an eye on him. See if he will talk to you Tessa.** She deliberately bumped Zane before trotting off towards her house. If needed, she was going to talk to the Luna in the morning. It was going to depend on how Zane reacted, if Mike had found his mate.

For the moment Zane was going to try and ignore his fears and talk to his uncle in the morning. For now, he was going to go back, curl up on his bed and do his best to sleep. As he trotted away from the group Tessa and Oscar followed. It didn't take them long to reach the house and head inside. As Zane headed towards his room Oscar headed towards Olivia's.

Oscar made a stop in his room and shifted and pulled on some shorts before quietly walking into Olivia's room. She was still awake, and he settled on the edge of her bed, "Hey, unless you need me curled up next to you, I think Zane might need Tessa's and my presence. It looks like Beta Mike has found his mate and Zane is upset."

Olivia had been reading a book when Oscar had knocked before coming in. When he mentioned Zane needing the two of them, she looked concerned. She had discussed mates with Tessa since it had piqued her curiosity. At the mention of their uncle possibly have found his mate it was obvious Olivia was struggling to not squeal like the girl she was, "Go be with him tonight. If I need anything, I will give you a call. I'm moving much better than I have been."

*****

Mike finally stepped back from his mate and gave his fur a good shake. He ran his tongue across her cheek before he turned away and looked over his shoulder. Once Mike was sure she was following him, he leapt over the stream and took a direct path to the pack house. When she joined him and trotted next to him, he was pleased. Normally he would have taken the time to play with her but even as overjoyed as he was, he was worried about Zane.

Zane was doing so much better than when he had woken up but there was still a great deal of scared pup inside. Letting even Tessa and Oscar close had been hard for Zane and much of it was related to his wolf almost forcing it. Since he had talked to Esther and even Kadrian, he was doing better but he was still very resistant to letting very many close. He was going to have a serious talk with his mate about Zane and to a lesser extent Olivia.

As they were heading back to the pack house, Annie was feeling the tension from her mate. It was somewhat upsetting since she simply didn't know why he was tense and sad. She wished they had the mating bond already, so she could ask. It was going to be the first thing Annie was going to ask him. The rest of what they were going to have to talk about she was going to ignore for the moment. Normally when you found your mate, the female would leave her pack, but Annie had a very important job. She didn't have any idea what her mate did though she could tell he was dominant. She could also smell pups on him though they didn't smell like *his* pups. Related maybe? Was that why he was sad?

The two of them were deep thought as they trotted into the house. Mike headed up the stairs to his suite and through the doggie door. Once inside, he shifted to his human form and pulled on some shorts, "Don't know if you want a shirt or something but if you do here is something you can wear." He pulled out a long shirt and some smaller shorts from his dresser. Tomorrow he was going to have to clean out the miscellaneous female clothing. He wouldn't have any more use for it.

Annie changed as well and pulled the shorts and shirt on as well. She would have preferred to settle down with lots of skin contact, but they needed to talk first, "I'm courier Annaliza from High Valley Pack and I'm very pleased to have found you, my mate." Even though they needed to talk she was being drawn to Mike and she wrapped her arms around him and leaned against his body. Goddess, he felt good in her arms. He was just enough taller she could rest her head on his shoulder and press her nose against his neck.

Mike couldn't help but appreciate her body. She was tall, slender, and in very good shape. He was glad she had decided to pull the shirt on, or he wouldn't have been able to control his wolf's urges, "I'm Beta Mike, the senior enforcer for the pack. I'm glad I have found you as well." He wrapped his arms around her and rested his head on hers. Mike could feel his body responding to the tingles and her scent, it was like his entire body relaxed. As they were standing there, tears slowly started to trickle out in reaction to holding her.

Annie couldn't help but preen slightly knowing her mate was so senior. Mike would probably be one of the top five or six wolves in the pack, not including the Alpha and Luna, "Why are you so sad, my mate?

I could hear it in your howl, and I can sense it now. What has you so hurt?" She didn't lean back or look up; she kept the hug going and felt his body relaxing even more.

He swallowed before responding, "My nephew was attacked by a rogue just after the end of the school year, last spring. He was in a coma for most of the summer and while he was in it, his parents were killed in a car wreck. Olivia, his younger sister, was badly hurt in that wreck and ended up partially disabled. None of them had known about werewolves at all; my brother was waiting for them to come of age before they were told. He woke to find this out and it has been extremely hard for him to deal with. Toss in suddenly being a monster, his words, like what attacked him, being fairly dominant, and forming his team... It has been a very hard few months. There are some other issues as well but those are the biggest ones." He paused and spoke quietly, the agony heard, "I miss my brother and sister-in-law so much."

Annie had to lean back in shock as Mike was speaking, her eyes saddened as well, "I'm so sorry to hear it Mike, so very sorry." She leaned back against him and settled for holding him and sent as much love as she could. It was horrible to have happen, and especially the attack by the rogue, "How are the two pups doing? How is this going to impact on them? What can I do to help and keep from upsetting him?" Changed humans could be odd when it came to matings and how they happened. Pups were very important, and even at times more important than the adults.

Mike finally lowered his head down and pressed against hers. He had cried previously, and Abby had helped but this was his mate holding him. The tears started flowing even more before he quietly started sobbing. It hurt knowing he could never introduce his mate to them. It hurt so badly knowing he would never see his brother and sister-in-law again. It hurt knowing how badly it had hurt Zane and Olivia. He cried for a while before he finally moved away from her, so he could blow his nose.

Once he had splashed water on his face and patted it dry before walking back into the bedroom. Mike noticed Annie had crawled into bed and he smiled. It was a strained smile but a smile nonetheless. He moved over to the bed and slipped between the covers and smiled somewhat more when he only felt skin. She had panties on, but Annie had taken her shirt off and the tingles were so comforting. Mike sighed and wrapped his arms around her, "As far as Zane, I'm not sure. It is going to be one day at a time. He was so hurt he wouldn't even allow the Luna to comfort him for weeks. Tomorrow we are going to the mall to get him some new clothes. Why don't you come with us, and we will simply spend time with each other?"

Annie had moved towards him when he crawled in and wrapped an arm around his waist, "If needed, I can stay in your suite here while he comes to terms with our becoming mates." Neither she nor her wolf liked the idea, but this was a hurt pup they were talking about. Pups were more important than them being together. Even her wolf knew the pups came first. Just jumping in with both feet probably wouldn't be the right way to deal with it, from the sounds of it.

Mike frowned at the idea since he wanted his mate next to her, "We will see but I don't like the idea. I want you in my arms and in my bed. I need you in my bed and my life. It has been so hard trying to deal with my feelings, Olivia's injuries, and Zane forcing people away. Even with the help of my junior wolves, it has been very hard to stay upbeat for them." He tucked his nose in Annie's neck and settled for inhaling her sweet scent.

Annie tilted her neck, so he had better access and slowly started stroking Mike's back and damn it, she wanted him. She turned her head and pressed her lips against his, "Make me your mate Mike. We will deal with what has happened to your family in the morning. For tonight please just love me and make me yours before I make you mine."

Mike felt her lips find his and he leaned into the kiss and let his wolf come forward slightly. Since he had his arms around her, he rolled on his back and settled her on his chest, "We can do that; we will become one and deal with everything together." He pulled her into a far from chaste kiss even as his hands slid down her back and cupped her firm, shapely bottom.

*****

The next morning, Zane was relaxing in his chair with Tessa curled up on his lap. He had slept fairly well last night, and he had a feeling it was a combination of his wolf and Tessa being there. Oscar had left partway through the night. When Mike hadn't shown up for breakfast, Zane had decided to remain at home since he was sure Mike would eventually show up. The team had told him they were going to meet up when they went to the mall. This was so his family could have time to talk. While they were waiting, Zane was talking with Tessa about her childhood and what it had been like growing up in a pack and as a wolf. For the moment, this was their time, and he was going to enjoy. There was the occasional kiss mixed in, and he was holding her hand as well as she was leaning against him.

Tessa was enjoying their quiet time. Oscar and Olivia were relaxing on a couch quietly talking. He was keeping an eye on Zane, but Oscar was mostly relaxing next to Olivia as they were talking. She was really nice, and she had a lively sense of humor. The shirts she had foisted off on Zane were an example. Olivia hadn't let anyone know she was going to do it, other than as a threat. Beta Mike might have done it, but it had been her idea.

When Mike walked in with a strange female, Zane sat up and urged Tessa to stand. He turned and faced Mike and the woman, "I guess you found your mate, Uncle Mike? Congratulations to both of you." Zane turned to the woman, "I'm Zane, this is Tessa, one of my junior wolves and my girlfriend. The wolf next to my sister Olivia is Oscar and Tessa's twin. I will introduce you to the rest of my team later." He sounded almost painfully polite.

Annie slowly moved over and held her hand out, "I'm very pleased to meet you Zane, and thank you for the introductions. It is nice to meet the rest of you as well. Mike mentioned going shopping because some of you are growing. If you don't mind, I would like to go with you and start getting to know all of you and your team."

Zane took her hand and gave it a good shake, "I have been worried about ripping the seat out of some of my pants. I really don't want to do it, since I know my sister would snicker at me and she does it enough. I will warn you; she likes to threaten to use her crutches on me. I felt you needed to know."

Olivia glared at him and lifted one of her crutches and waved it in his general direction, "I will deal with you later." She lowered it back to the ground and carefully stood up and crutched over to the woman and wrapped an arm around her, "Congratulations and we didn't get your name. I'm pleased for the two of you. I don't quite understand, but I have been learning about what it means to find your mate." Oscar had talked to her when she had woken up.

Annie gave Olivia a good hug and glanced up at Mike. It was obvious she appreciated the willingness of Olivia to hug her, "Thank you Olivia. Mike and I talked this morning. I know this is going to toss everyone for a spin, but I will do my best not to upset the balance all of you have gained. My name is Annaliza, but I go by Annie." She looked at Zane and gave him a warm smile, "Mike told me about what happened, and I'm so sorry. If you need room or some space let me know, please."

Zane looked down when she gave him her sympathy and leaned into Tessa's hug, "Thank you Annaliza for your sympathy." He was not going to cry now, "If you would like to come with us, please do, you are Uncle Mike's mate, and it would be wrong for me to ask you not to." Damn it the walls were starting to come up slightly. Nothing like what they had but they were there again.

Mike settled for that, "If you are ready, we can go, Olivia if you want to come with us also, please do but remember the brace and I have a wheelchair for you to use. I know you don't want to use it, but I don't want you straining yourself. If I let you hurt yourself, the doctor might brain me, and I have a feeling Annie might object to it."

Olivia made a face, but their uncle was right about the wheelchair. She needed to start getting her endurance back. Lying in bed for two weeks as well as the surgery had taken their toll, "I understand, and I might even let my brother push me around. Might give his wolf some satisfaction about protecting me."

*****

David and Leon were relaxing in David's bedroom again and both were flopped on the bed. They were glaring at the ceiling before David finally rolled off the bed and pulled on a shirt, "I'm going to talk to mom about going to the mall. I'm about ready to scream in boredom and frustration. If that dick hadn't caused problems, we wouldn't be restricted to our houses. The mall shouldn't be a problem." He left the room and stomped downstairs.

When he found his parents, David walked over to his mother, "Mom, can we go to the mall? We are so bloody bored, and I'm sure the mall would be fine." They hadn't been placed under house arrest or anything like it as far as he knew. They just couldn't go to school or come near those fucking brats. Chances were they wouldn't be at the mall, though some of the others might be. It would be hard, but David would restrain his urge to push anyone around. They had been warned the others could use it against them.

His mother glanced at him before going back to working on her nails, "That's fine, and I will have one of the workers drive you there. If you see those people, just go the other way, and call for a ride. I don't want them hurting my little baby boy again." Even as she was talking, she carefully applied a fake nail before looking up at him, "I will put some money on your card. Get yourself something nice, maybe a new game or a couple of videos."

David walked over and gave her a generic hug before he ran back upstairs, "We have permission to go to the mall. She even gave me money to spend so let's have fun." He knew his mother would transfer more money to his card than he needed, and Leon's family would as well. Today might just be a good day.

*****

When Zane and the others finally arrived at the mall, he slipped out of the SUV and helped Olivia out before letting Oscar take over. For the moment, the wheelchair would remain in the SUV until Olivia needed it. When she did, someone would come and get it for her. For now, she had insisted on walking. When Oscar stood close to her, Olivia gave him a smile.

Zane wrapped an arm around Tessa, and they started walking into the mall, "No damn sunrise tie-dyed shirts and I want my others back to see if they fit." He glared at Olivia before turning away and ignoring her snickers.

Annie smiled but didn't snort or laugh. She was too new to the relationship to really comment. Thankfully, Zane had been polite, though Annie could feel the slight distance he had place between himself and her. He had taken the time to introduce the rest of his team before they had left, which had been nice. Annie could tell they were dedicated to Zane as their team leader, and it was a good thing for him.

The rest of the adults were there as well, and she had been introduced to them as well. She could immediately tell who the twin's parents were, without even using her nose. They were staying close to their pups, and it was obvious they were upset. Mike had told her what was going on with the pups and why they were being home schooled for the moment. She wasn't happy with what happened to the twins either. There was still so much Annie was going to need to learn about but just the basics of what Mike had said had her upset. To combat her urge to growl, Annie settled for relaxing in Mike's arms and let the flow from the mating bond help her relax.

Zane was looking around and had to make a face, "I feel like I have been allowed out of prison for a couple of hours. It's a rather disturbing feeling." He shuddered before trading a wry grin with Rico.

Olivia giggled at his comment and reaction, "At least you haven't been confined to a hospital room or the house for a month." She was so happy she would get to go back to school soon. She wanted out of the house and off the property. Her friends among the pack made a point of visiting frequently but there were other friends she wanted to see.

Melody gave Zane a sly grin, "Well I'm sure the House Manager could find something for you to do. It would get you out of the house and keep you occupied." Zane and the others started laughing when Olivia's expression changed, and she whacked Zane with a crutch, "You are the leader, so you deserved it."

The rest of the adults were smiling at the pups as they were chatting. It was nice to see them laughing and relaxing. All of the adults knew the anger was just below the surface and would be for quite a while. Even once the boys were dealt with, it was going to take time for everyone to calm down. Since the pack was angry, it would filter through the bonds and slowly go away as individuals in the pack calmed down.

When they walked into the mall Zane felt Tessa almost shrink into herself and he pulled her a bit closer, "Relax Tessa, you will be fine. It's how I felt going to see Liv in the hospital. It was like there was a sign only I could see which read 'Enter at your own Risk!'. It was one of the hardest things I have had to do recently. I'm here, Oscar is here, Uncle Mike is here and all the other parents. We will take care of you." He tried to project security to her the way he had been taught to do.

Olivia glanced at Zane and Tessa and felt bad for both. Since Zane had told her about his reaction to seeing her in the bed, she could see just how much medical scared him. For Tessa, it was going to be much the same, only here for a while. She leaned over and gave Tessa's arm a gentle squeeze before they continued walking in.

Mike could feel the muscles in his jaw clench for a short time before he forced them to relax. Thankfully, he was holding onto Annie and leaned against her for some comfort. He felt her wolf supporting him as he tried to calm down, **Thank you Annie, you are bringing a stability to me that I need.** Even having dallied with several she-wolves hadn't helped a great deal. Last night they had sealed the mating bond.

She simply turned and kissed him and made it a rather sensual kiss before releasing him. When Annie did, she gave Mike a knowing look since he was still leaned towards her, **You should feel better now.** When he growled at her, she simply smiled and kept walking with him.

Once inside the mall, they didn't hurry but they didn't dawdle either. They needed to make sure they had what Zane needed, since he was growing into his wolf. Once they had some new clothing for him and several of the others, everyone decided to get some food. Zane glanced at Melody and Rico with a grin, "I feel some more greasy pizza coming on with some cheesy bread." It was enough just thinking about it to start drooling again.

Even Tessa perked up and gave the others an appreciative grin, "With lots of cheese and sausage. Oh, and mushrooms and onions." It definitely sounded like a good idea to her. It would help clear the memories out as well.

When they walked into the food area Mike slowed down and sent a thought out to everyone. He carefully inhaled several times and gave a slight nod, **There is a family of wolves here. I don't recognize their scents and it smells like several pups and a mated pair.** He sent several other commands before he started moving forward again.

Zane caught the scents shortly after his uncle mentioned them. He glanced around as well and almost automatically focused on a family at a table in the corner, **Simone, take Tessa, Oscar, and Olivia over to a table. Rico, stay with them and protect them if needed. Melody, stay close to me in case we are needed.** As the group started to separate, to him it was obvious what was happening. Abby and Brandon followed their pups over to a table. The rest wandered towards some of the food venders though it was to surround the strange wolves.

Zane stayed somewhat back since he knew Mike wouldn't want him involved if something happened, he did get a feeling from his uncle, that he was to be in charge of the retreat of the other pups and his juniors and to keep them safe. Instead, he contemplated the food options and was casually talking to Melody, or hoped it was casual. Zane knew he wasn't a good actor, but he was doing his best.

Mike walked over to the family as soon as they were mostly surrounded, "Morning, mind if I have a seat and have a talk?" He settled down and glanced at the family, "I'm the Beta Enforcer for the pack Mac Tire' Dona. What brings you into town and why haven't you checked in with my boss yet?" As soon as he had noticed them, he had sent a request to Malcom to see if they had any new lone wolves, and there hadn't been any he knew of.

The man sat up straight and met Mike's eyes before looking slightly away, "We just made it to town and decided to get something to eat. We are simply traveling through and weren't planning on stopping for more than a few hours. We mean no harm Beta and are registered with the council as lone wolves."

He gave the man and his mate a good look before glancing at the pups. The two pups, the boy was maybe Zane's age, and the girl was maybe ten or so and they looked scared. Mike gave them a relaxed smile, "Relax please, I'm simply doing my job. I have a nephew about your age", he nodded at the boy, "And a niece somewhat older than you." He nodded at the girl before turning back to the adults. If they were just traveling through and didn't have plans on stopping for more than a few hours, it wasn't a problem. Technically they should have at least called but just traveling through was an acceptable reason not to have.

Mike sighed, "My Alpha would like to speak with you. This is simply because it was brought to his attention. If everything checks out, if you want, we will provide you a room for the night, a couple meals, and you can continue in the morning." As he was speaking, he could feel the pups starting to get scared. Their parents weren't nearly as concerned but the pups were shaking a bit.

Zane, bring Tessa and Oscar over. This is just a lone wolf family group traveling through. Their pups are scared and having your junior wolves come over should help. He smiled at them again, "I asked my nephew and two of his team to come over. They are just going to say hello and if you would like to relax with us, I'd appreciate it. No strings, no threats, just relax with fellow wolves for a while. Once we finish eating, we can run to the property and go from there."

Zane waited for Tessa and Oscar to join him, and he told Melody to go and relax with the others. When Tessa came over, he wrapped an arm around her and strolled over to where his uncle was, "Hey, nice to meet you. This is my girlfriend Tessa and her twin Oscar. How are you doing?"

The two adults glanced at each other and shrugged since they didn't have a choice. They had simply wanted to travel through and not get hassled. So far, the Beta seemed nice, and he wasn't demanding they follow him now which was nice, "Yes Beta we do understand." The mother moved towards her pups and wrapped an arm around her daughter. It had been a while since they had encountered other wolves, so their pups weren't as comfortable. A few packs they had encountered recently had treated them almost as if they were rogues. As if being loners made them somehow deficient.

When Zane wandered over with the twins the adults glanced up and the mother had to smile. The she-wolf was blushing at the introduction. It was obvious she was a very junior wolf and she belonged to the he-wolf. Her brother did as well, and they looked well treated though the boy's eyes were tense and there were strain lines around them. She lightly sniffed and finally decided it wasn't anything to do with them, "It is nice to meet you Zane and hello to you as well Tessa and Oscar. Our daughter is Pauline, and our son is Peter. Beta Mike asked us to join all of you for lunch. We are mostly done but it would be nice to sit with some others like us for a while."

Mike let Zane take over as far as the pups were concerned. He stood and glanced at Zane, "Introduce them to your team before you get some food." Mike knew the two adults would follow them over. By now the rest of the group was settled down at several tables though they were surrounding the pups. Due to the potential threat from those two families they wanted to be able to keep anyone away if needed.

Zane mentally grumbled at Mike at the mention of his team. The grumble was just to tease his uncle even as he moved back, "Come on over and if nothing else my sister will tell you horror stories about her mean older brother." He gave Peter a knowing grin and received a tentative one back. He nodded to Oscar to walk next to them, so they would know there wasn't a threat, or they should know it. Since Zane had never dealt with lone wolves before he wasn't sure what the pups might have been taught.

Once at the table he flopped down next to Olivia, "This is my sister Olivia, and I will warn you she is fast with her crutches." Zane winced when she thumped him in the calf with one, "I rest my case. You should be safe, since she reserves any and all crutch thumps for me. She says it is my fault for some reason." He got thumped again and he frowned at Olivia and ignored her angelic smile.

The mention of crutches definitely got the two's attention, and both gave Zane an odd look. He leaned forward, "She is human, I was turned, don't ask." He wanted to say please but he wasn't going to answer any questions.

Both blinked before lowering their eyes and nodding, "What are you doing here?" They had noticed the clothes bags and felt it was a safe topic.

Olivia decided not to poke Zane again since she could sense his wolf hovering. It was annoying, but it also helped her feel safe. She glanced at the bags and elbowed Zane, "Someone is growing and needed more clothes. For some reason he decided he needed to replace his tie-dyed shirts." When he quietly growled at her she poked him again.

Peter gave Zane an odd look before glancing at Olivia and he had to cover his mouth, "Oh, that's a horrible thing to do." It broke the ice though the new wolves were being very polite and careful as they were talking. Once everyone was done eating, they cleaned the mess up and started to leave the mall.

As they were walking out of the mall the adults again surrounded the pups, including the two new ones. For the adults, it was mostly an instinctive need to protect the pups. Just before they walked out of the mall, those two walked in. Zane instantly turned and faced towards them, and his expression became blank and emotionless. His eyes met David's and again begged David to do something stupid.

David started to sneer, until he noticed Zane's expression and the number of people giving him and Leon much the same look. He forced the sneer as they walked past and did his best to ignore the implicit threats from the others. As long as they didn't do anything overt, the others couldn't do anything without a report being made. Just for good measure David let his eyes briefly travel over Tessa and the sneer changed to a smirk.

Zane didn't do anything more than take a deep breath and make his face expressionless. When he inhaled, he stopped and his head turned towards the two even more and Zane inhaled again. He started frowning since there was something in the scent which was bothering him. It was right at the edge of his senses which made him take another deeper breath. He finally figured out what the scent was, and his jaw dropped before he started laughing, **Melody, take a deep scent of David and Leon...**

Melody had already turned and faced the two when Zane told her to scent them again, she did. When she did her expression mirrored Zane's before she started laughing, **Oh goddess so wrong, yet so right. Oh goddess, blackmail material for the next few years. Oh man...** She turned back and kept walking. As they were walking others in their team caught the scent and started laughing as they walked out of the mall.

Mike glanced at the team and frowned slightly since he wasn't quite sure why they were laughing. It was quite possible they were doing it just to annoy the two, but it didn't quite make sense. He would ask later, when he was done talking to the Alpha.

CHAPTER 21

The Laugh

The evening before, Jason had run a second diagnostic scan after all the work he and the young wolves had done. He knew Josh would do much the same from his end as well. As the diagnostics were running Jason trotted down to the dining area. He grabbed a couple of snacks and a drink from the snack area and headed back to the computer area. Food and drinks didn't go in, so he settled down at the outer security office where he could see the monitor and waited for the diagnostics to finish.

It took some time since he had to run the initialization and calibration of the repaired and replaced sensors. Once he was done, after reviewing them he would contact Josh and see what he said. Chances were good, in the morning he would be leaving. Eventually the testing finished, and he walked into the secured computer section. He entered the room that held his equipment and reviewed the report. He was satisfied with the results and using the secured VOIP phone in the room called Josh.

Josh figured Jason was going to be calling later in the evening, so he had remained up. Adam, Molly, and Josh were relaxing in his office discussing some of the information they had received about the rogues. When the call came in Josh accepted the connection, "I just finished reading the report on this end. Return in the morning. If Mike is still up report to him otherwise catch him tomorrow. Good job Jason and thanks for being willing to go on such short notice."

*****

When Zane and the others started laughing at David and Leon, both flushed deeply. What made it even worse, was even the stupid girl was giggling slightly as they walked past and out. As usual Zane's expression sent chills down his spine. It had been very hard to keep the sneer going, though leering at the girl had been satisfying. Zane's expression seemed to say, 'try me and I'll kill you.' It had been satisfying, until they started laughing at them, which was humiliating. Even as he was trying to keep the smirk going, he felt chills going down his spine. He knew Zane was being serious, so he turned and did his best to ignore them.

Leon had flushed as well, though unlike David, he wasn't as scared of Zane. Mostly it was because Zane had focused on David and ignored Leon. He hadn't had the focus of a dominant wolf threatening him. What he noticed that David hadn't, was how Zane was holding the little cunt. It was obvious they were more than just friends or Zane trying to look good comforting her. His smirk was far more natural. Once they had passed the other group, Leon elbowed David, "Did you notice how Zane was holding her? The little slut is putting out for him. He was definitely looking satisfied with showing she belonged to him."

David returned the elbow though a bit harder to remind Leon he was in charge. It took a short time for what Leon had said to penetrate. When it did David turned and gave Leon a questioning look, "Huh? I didn't notice, I was enjoying see her shrink when I stared at her." He was trying to shake the feeling of a descending doom off.

Leon gave David a questioning looks as well. He didn't sound quite like his normal self, even if what he said did. Had Zane's threats bothered David more than he had been letting on? "What I'm saying is Zane and Tessa look like they are dating. I'm sure she is doing it to suck up and keep him protecting her. Wonder if she is any fun." He slyly glanced at David when he said it.

David had to glance over his shoulder in the direction the others had been going but they were gone. Thinking about it, Zane had been pretty protective of the little pansy. His mind roamed back, and he was going to have to look at the next hearing date, "Huh, what do you know. Might be something we can use against them. We will have to mention it to the lawyer as something he set up to make himself look good?" He still wanted to bust Zane's face for all the humiliation David and Leon had faced. They kept talking as they continued down the mall.

*****

Once Mike climbed into the SUV he glanced over his shoulder at the pups in the vehicle, "So why the laughter? Did you do it just to irritate the two? If so, it's better than glaring and cursing at them." He was missing something which bothered him. Normally, even the thought of David or Leon was enough to set him and his wolf off. They had started that way and even Zane's wolf was feeling somewhat amused.

Zane had to close his eyes and breathe slowly before he could answer, "Ah, David and Leon smelled like they had been, um..." God, he wasn't sure if he could continue with what he felt he had scented from the two. He was starting to turn pink even though it was beyond funny even thinking about it.

Mike sighed even as he read Zane's body language and sampled his scent. It didn't help much, "Zane, I don't want to make it an order, so just spit it out." Great use of an unplanned pun which didn't help Zane.

When he heard what Mike had to say he lost it again and had to cover his mouth to try and keep his laughter in. It was too much since spiting it out might just be the right term for the two. He tried to control the laughter, but it was just too much, and the laughter was helping him relax.

Tessa spoke for Zane with a great deal of malicious intent, "Beta Mike, what Zane is trying to avoid saying, is it smelled like David and Leon had been intimate recently. I'm not sure how intimate but there were traces of certain scents around them and somewhat blended." It was more than obvious she had greatly enjoyed saying it.

Olivia almost choked when Tessa spoke, and she covered her ears, "Oh ick! I don't want to hear about it. Talk to them at home, Uncle Mike. Ick!!!" She shuddered and looked utterly revolted at the topic.

Mike's face went blank for a moment before he looked like he had been gob smacked, "Oh... Ah, we will talk about this later. I would hate to have Olivia try and brain you with her crutches in the car." It wasn't something he had expected. Mike had been expecting Zane to say they'd done it simply to irritate the two.

Annie was somewhat startled as well but since she didn't know the people involved, it didn't mean much to her. When Olivia reacted Annie shook her head, "I will share some ice cream with you, and we can have some girl time." Her voice sounded sympathetic as she talked.

Olivia shuddered one last time, "I like that idea and maybe some caramel sauce on top. I don't do many sweets, but it sounds really good." She did lean against Zane, since it seemed to keep his wolf somewhat content. It was one nice change, that he liked to be touched now.

The rest of the drive home was relatively silent even though Zane did occasionally have to fight down a laugh. **Everyone, come to my house. Uncle Mike asked why we laughed, and Tessa ended up telling him. He wants to talk further about it at the house. Olivia was sounding somewhat traumatized by what Tessa said.** Olivia's reaction was pretty good, though he wasn't going to tease her about it.

When they walked in, Zane headed towards the back after asking Oscar to remain with Olivia. Zane was starting to conclude Oscar sort of liked his little sister. It sounded rather strange to Zane but if it helped Olivia let Oscar help her, he was all for it. When he walked into the lounge in the back of the house, he flopped down and smiled when Tessa settled in his lap. He gave her a quick peck before he looked at his uncle.

Mike smiled at the two since they looked as cute together as he and Abby had back when they were dating, "So just to make sure of what you said", he glanced at Tessa, "David and Leon smelled like they had been in some way intimate?" Since he had time to think about it if the two were, it wouldn't really surprise him.

Melody snorted and had to cough to clear her throat, "That's what it smelled like, Beta Mike. We didn't get a really good sniff due to where we were but there were traces of their smells intermingled. It wasn't just them spending time together but traces of arousal and other scents."

Rico was openly grinning as was Simone. Mindy was trying to remain neutral since the incident hadn't involved her other than simply being on the edges. The rest of them confirmed what Zane had scented. They pretty much decided the reason Zane had picked up the smell first was because he was still getting used to his new senses. They still tended to cycle through one after the other unconsciously and sometimes it could make a person more sensitive.

Mike wanted to laugh and groan, since this was prime blackmail material for the pups. It was also a very good way to start a fight with the other two. Just the mention both might be either gay or in the closet with everyone else would start a fight, "Do nothing with this information when you next see them. I can see how it is both amusing yet also tempting to use to make them start a fight. I will not have any of you using this that way. Do not mention it to anyone else either." About then he received a message from Kadrian asking him to come to his office, "Work calls, pups, and thanks for the information. Relax for the rest of the day. Depending on what the Alpha and lone wolves have to say, I might invite them over for dinner. It would be good for their pups to mingle with some Pack wolves."

Zane shrugged, "I really hadn't planned on doing anything with it," he hadn't even considered it. He was grinning, "To be honest Uncle Mike it was just so unexpected, and I just reacted by laughing. My first thought was overcompensation, also known as earthworm syndrome." He grunted when Tessa elbowed him in the ribs even though she giggled, "We won't use it Uncle Mike and I will talk to my team about it later as well. If you want to invite them over or even if they would like to be shown around while their parents talk to the Alpha, we can keep them occupied."

He thought about it and Mike nodded at Zane, "I will send to you." He stood and left the room and headed towards the main house.

*****

Annie was sitting in the kitchen with Olivia as they contemplated the bowls of ice cream. There had been two flavors, Pralines and Cream as well as French Vanilla. Olivia had the caramel she had asked for on hers while Annie had given hers a light dusting of some chocolate powder, “Olivia, if it isn’t too painful, can you tell me what happened to you and your brother? Mike mentioned , but I wanted to talk to you about it as well.” Mike was very concerned about how Zane might react to their mating, “If you have any questions for me, please ask.”

Olivia took a sip of milk since she had just eaten a bite of ice cream and caramel, she tensed slightly before speaking, “We were called and informed he had been hit by a vehicle and then later found he had been bitten by some animal. He has some ugly scars on one shoulder and his back.” She had to bite her lip as it was bringing memories back. They were still almost raw and ugly, and nobody was talking about them. She wanted to know but from what she’d decided they felt she was too young to understand.

Annie moved her chair over and wrapped an arm around Olivia even as Oscar leaned against her other side as he placed his own bowl of ice cream on the table but stayed silent. “If it is too hard to talk about Olivia, it’s fine. I’m just trying to get to know you and what happened. I know I’m going to cause a shift in your family. Mike is my mate, but I also know he has a responsibility for the two of you.”

Oscar leaned against Olivia but kept eating the ice cream. If she needed something, Olivia would tell him, and he would take care of her. He knew Zane had entrusted him with his sister, which meant the world to him.

She leaned against Oscar as he leaned against her. Annie’s arm was warm around her, but she still didn’t know the woman, “Annie, it is hard. We have finally started to settle down into what we have now. Zane has finally started to recover. I don’t know what to say, what I can say, or what I should say. It hurt waking up knowing my parents were gone and I had been in the wreck, and unlikely to walk normally again. Zane woke to find out about mom and dad as well as finding out I was hurt." She didn't want to talk about it anymore.

Annie gave her shoulders a light hug before moving back slightly since she didn't want to force her presence on Olivia. Instead, she changed the subject, "When do you go back to school? Mike mentioned you should be going back soon. Looking forward to it?"

Olivia relaxed slightly into the hug and once Annie moved away started eating the rest of her ice cream, "It has been almost a month since my last surgery, and I go back on Monday. I can't wait to see some of my human friends. Anne and several of my wolf friends have visited me a lot. I want to get back to school and a routine." She sat up and finished eating the ice cream.

"Good for them, I'm glad you have had your friends around. It usually makes it easier to deal with problems." She took a bite of the ice cream and let a pleased smile cross her face, "I do love Pralines and Cream. I would say 'go school', but it has been a while for me. So, Oscar, how did you meet Zane, if you don't mind my asking?" Annie had so little knowledge of what had been going on, she just didn't know what to ask or how.

Oscar wasn't bothered by the question and honestly looking back he had decided he was pleased with what had happened. It hadn't been a good meeting, but it had helped him, and Tessa find their leader. Zane had fought the idea but even then, he had cared, "Zane protected Tessa and I from some teasing and invited us to his table. He didn't realize what he was doing by inviting us over and especially with what he did after that, but he stood by it and accepted us. I'm really pleased we found him, and he accepted us." It was obvious he was happy.

She wanted to groan since it seemed like every question had some negative connotation to it. With such junior wolves though she could understand, "Good for him and I think he has made a good choice. Would you mind me asking, what today was about? Mike gave me some information, but I still feel like I don't know what al is going on." Right now, she was just talking to try and get to know the two pups.

He gave her a pleased smile, "It wasn't the best way to meet Zane, but Tessa and I are very pleased. Zane has taken his responsibility to us very seriously." Oscar glanced at Olivia and blushed very slightly, "He even entrusted us with the care of his sister and that..." He couldn't even explain how it meant to the two of them. It let them know Zane trusted them a lot, as they knew his sister was the most precious thing to him.

When he finally spoke about earlier, he looked down at his ice cream, "Several weeks ago, those two assaulted Tessa at the mall and said some really nasty things. Zane almost killed David and would have if Melody hadn't stopped him, as they had ignored Zane's warning to stay away from us. They are no more than poodle turds and Zane protected us." He couldn't think of anything lower than a poodle turd since he didn't like poodles at all. They were whiney nasty dogs for the most part.

Annie reached across Olivia and lightly patted Oscar's arm, "Good for him and it sounds like you have a really good team leader. Now before the ice cream melts... If you have any questions for me, please ask." They talked for a while longer before Zane poked his head in.

Zane looked into the kitchen, "I'm running over to the Pack house and see if the family is going to be spending the night and invite the kids over. Oscar, if you want to talk to the others about something for dinner, it would be nice. I'm thinking some sort of barbeque since I don't know when Mike is going to be back."

Tessa poked her head in as well and gave Annie a nice smile even as she was leaning against Zane, "Maybe the brined and sugared chicken as well? It sounds really good." It was something their parents taught them not too long ago.

Zane pretended to groan, "Chicken? I want an almost mooing cow, darn it!" He laughed when Olivia waved a crutch at him, "Sorry sis, you are too far away, and I'm not scared." When Tessa poked his side, he twitched and grumbled at her to everyone's laughter.

*****

When Zane and Tessa reached the pack house, they did find the two pups in one of the lounges with Damien. They were relaxing as much as they could though Zane could smell the tension in the room, "Hey Damien, I was going to see if they wanted to come over to our house." He assumed their parents were with the Alpha and Mike.

Damien gave Zane a good look and he looked better than he had for a while. He had seen how Olivia's hospitalization had devastated him. It wasn't including the impact those two ass wipes had on Zane and the twins. For the moment Margarethe was relaxing next to him though he hadn't asked her to be his girlfriend, "That's fine since they would be at your house. If you want to go for a run, it would be fine. Just respect the limits you have been ordered to." It would probably be good for the two to shake their fur out.

Zane paused for a moment even as he wrapped his arm around Tessa and a smile crossed his face, "Now that would be nice. Oscar is working on getting dinner ready, but it will be a while. It would be nice since I could stand to shake my fur out." He paused before reporting of the issue at the mall to one more senior to him, **Just so you know at the mall we ran into those two, they smelled of each other.** The mental bonds could share much more than just mere words... he shared the memory of the scent itself, and what he thought it meant as well. Later he would realize that he had been able to get around his uncle's order to not share it, by thinking of it as just reporting it to a more senior.

Damien gave Zane a toothy grin, "I might come over with Anne and join you for some food, it would be rather nice. Go and have fun. I will let dad know you have taken charge of them for the moment." When Zane contacted him, he gave Zane an evil smile, **Oh my... There have been hints before but... Oh my, if they end up at school again, they are so screwed. We don't need to do anything, just a few whispers and they are screwed.** The wolves wouldn't need to do anything.

He glanced at Damien with an angelic expression, **We were ordered not to take advantage of this information. I would have to say for my team to pass this information around would break the order. I simply can't suggest this information be passed around.** He couldn't but others could.

That generated a slight disapproving look from Damien, **Of course, I would expect you to obey such orders from your uncle. I will ensure none of your team has a chance to pass this information on.** There was an understanding which passed between them.

Even as they were trading the information Tessa moved away from Zane and over to her friend. She gave Margarethe a good hug, "Good for you, I'm so very happy you found your team." Their parents were friends and Tessa was very pleased for her friend.

Margarethe returned the hug and gave Tessa a small smile, "Good for you as well and congrats on being asked to be Zane's girlfriend. It's really nice to have been asked to be part of Damien's team. He is a very attentive wolf." They started to quietly talk as the other two talked.

Zane met Damien's eyes for a short time before lowering them in submission, "Peter and Pauline, I have permission to invite you over to my house. We are going to do a barbeque this evening, and if you would like we can shift and go for a run." He did his best to go with a relaxed feel.

Peter sent to his father to check and see if it'd be okay, "Thank you Zane and it would be nice to be able to go for a run. It has been a while for us." He stood so he was somewhat between Zane and his sister. Even if he was less dominant than the other, it was instinctive.

Zane noticed what Peter had done and glanced at Tessa, and she moved over, "Peter, I will ensure your sister is taken care of. As I'm sure you can tell I'm one of Zane's junior wolves and he told me to take care of her. I can't go against his orders, and she will be fine." With a slight grin she decided to tease Zane, "If I didn't, Olivia might take a crutch to Zane and then me."

Peter gave her a tentative look and a sort of smile, "Thank you Tessa, we appreciate it. Mom and Dad said we can go over. They are talking to the Alpha and the Beta Enforcer." He stood and waited for his sister to stand.

He gave Damien another glance and there was a knowing smile on his face. One of the reasons he had come over had been dealt with. Once

Damien had given him a returned smile, Zane turned to the two lone pups, "Uncle Mike will probably show up right as the food is done. Let's go and we can do a run and play for a while." He collected Tessa and waved the other two to follow them.

*****

Once they reached the house Zane led the two inside and gave them a quick intro to his team and Annie and Olivia, "This is my sister Olivia and my uncle's mate Annie." He looked at his pack and considered what had been done towards dinner, **Oscar do you want to come with us for a run? I told these two we could go for a run and want to know if you want to go.**

Oscar came over and leaned against Zane for a moment before going back to what he had been doing, **Don't worry about it, Zane, I can go for a run later. Take them and go have fun. I want to make a good meal for everyone.** He would like to go with them, but this was his job.

Zane gave Oscar a light nudge and left the room. He led everyone outside, and they quickly changed. after, he gave a really good stretch since it had been a while since he had last changed. After the stretch, he gave Tessa a good nuzzle and swipe of his tongue across her muzzle, **This way and keep an eye on the two. If any pack have questions, answer them, and then forward them to me.** Chances were good they would have been informed but he didn't want to take a chance.

For the moment he headed towards one of the large clearings, so they had room to play. When they arrived, he found Damien and his team there. After a brief submission, Zane dove at Damien and the play was on. As they were playing, Zane and his team ensured the two lone pups were watched. Zane wanted to make sure they weren't hurt by the rough housing. When Tessa and Damien's junior wolves took charge of the girl he was pleased. After playing for a while, Zane was feeling far more relaxed than he had been. For the moment, his bad mood was temporarily broken.

The rest of the evening had been fun for Zane. Having the two strange pups over had helped him to relax and step back. He had a feeling it also had something to do with discovering what he had about David and Leon. Even if he couldn't say anything about it, Zane could gloat and smirk at them with a knowing smile. It would drive them nuts as they would have no idea what he had learned and that alone was almost worth it. Eventually everyone left for their houses for dinner. Zane tried to not think of the next day, as it was going to be hard for him since Olivia was going to be going back to school.

He knew she would be fine, but it was going to drive his wolf nuts. At home he had Oscar and Tessa to watch over her. At school, it was going to be wolves he didn't know as well or trust nearly as much. He was going to be a very irritable wolf for the next few days.

*****

As Zane had expected, the next morning when he got up his wolf was not happy. They both knew she had to do this, but they were starting to stress again. Both knew she was going to be fine but those two were out there. They didn't know if they knew anyone at the school who might decide to harass Olivia. Zane knew Anne and the other wolves in her school would be keeping an eye out, but it didn't help much.

When he finally made it down to breakfast, Zane was doing his best to remain civil. He knew part of what was going on was he was starting to think about when he woke from the coma. It was also a reaction to when he had seen Olivia after her surgery. Both had hurt him deeply and was still simmering under the surface. He gave Tessa a kiss and hug before he settled down and picked up his coffee and took a sip, "Morning all."

Mike had briefly talked with Zane and Annie had moved in. She was sitting next to Mike and obviously enjoying the food Oscar had served her, "Mike, I have to say Zane's junior wolves are darn good cooks. Both you and Zane are very lucky with those who are part of your teams." She neatly ate a slice of bacon; she took small, neat bites and took her time eating as she savored the taste.

Mike settled for making a satisfied sound as he was eating. He had to admit she was right since Abby, Brandon, and their twins were very good at what they did. When he paused for a sip of coffee, "Oh my yes, the four of them have to be some of the best in the pack. I knew I was lucky but now with the four of them? Both my team and Zane's team are making others jealous." He took another sip and looked at Zane, "Annie and I are going to be gone for several days. We need to go to her pack and let her Alpha know about us being mates. He has been informed but it is good manners. I will be back before the next meeting with the judge."

Zane didn't bother getting upset or even doing more than a brief pause from eating, "I had rather expected it, Uncle Mike. Abby and Brandon have indicated they will be keeping an eye on us. Something about ensuring we behave or something. Makes me feel like we are being babysat." He started eating again and did his best to keep from looking at Olivia, though it was hard.

Olivia glanced at Zane and then their uncle, "Annie talked to me about it this weekend and I understand. As long as someone doesn't get too uber protective, it should be fine. If he does, I will leave the bent crutches in your office." She understood how Zane was going to react, but she wasn't going to let him push her around.

After a very brief conversation with his wolf, Zane turned to Olivia and let out a low sad whine. Just for good measure, he gave her puppy dog eyes and looked really sad at what she had said. Normally he would mutter at her but they both decided she deserved this.

When he gave her rather a sad and pathetic look Olivia wilted, "Fine, some uber protective is okay but back off when I tell you to." She was feeling bad for making Zane feel bad and didn't realize he was playing her.

He sniffed slightly and went back to eating though not quite as fast as he had been. His entire body posture showed he felt bad for wanting to protect his sister. Even Tessa and Oscar bought it for the time being.

Annie watched the entire thing and glanced at Mike before narrowing her eyes at him, **Don't even think about trying that on me. I know the whole puppy dog eye thing!** She passed Zane her card, "So we are going to leave after breakfast and if you need anything, call Mike. On some off chance you can't get him here is a card with my numbers and the main pack number. I'm sure Alpha Kadrian can get hold of us as well."

Mike stood and handed his plate to Oscar, "We will talk to you later and as Annie said, call if you need anything. you can always go to Esther or Kadrian, and they will take care of you until we get back." He helped Annie up and they left the room.

Zane finished eating and waved Oscar off when they stood, "Let me walk you to the bus stop Olivia. I'm glad you are going back to school, but I won't lie, it does have my wolf worked up." He helped her stand and gave her a hug. He was careful not to squeeze too hard, but he held her for several minutes, "Love you Liv, I know I haven't said it much, but I do. I'm glad you are feeling better."

Olivia almost yelled, but at least he was admitting he was trying not to be too over-protective. When he gave her a hug, she could feel his tension and she leaned into him and returned the hug. Zane telling her he loved her made her feel so warm. It had been a long time since she had heard it from anyone. She leaned even more into the hug before finally pushing him away, "I gotta go, darn it. You are going to make me late and I will have to poke you!" Olivia let Zane grab her backpack and walked out of the house with him. She did have her crutches and knew if needed, they had a wheelchair at the school for her. Olivia wasn't going to be stupid but damn it she wanted this over and done with. When they arrived at the bus stop, she watched Zane hand the pack to Anne before giving her another hug and leaving.

He walked away from the bus and since he had his backpack with him, he wrapped an arm around Tessa. She had come with him, and Oscar had caught up to them as well, they headed towards class at the pack house. Once they reached their destination, he made for the kitchen and filled a travel mug with coffee before settling down for school.

*****

Early evening, Mike and Annie made it to the pack she was from. It had been a while since he had last been to the High Valley pack. When they arrived, he was directed where to park, and they were shown directly to her Alpha's office. This was going to be interesting, since he and Annie were in senior positions and most packs hated losing powerful wolves. He was a Beta, and she was a courier. Both were very respected positions, and it was going to affect both packs. On the other hand, it would help build the bonds between the two pack. To have two wolves linked at this level gave both packs a bond having lower ranked wolves mate wouldn't.

When they were shown into the office as expected, both the Luna and Alpha were present. He let Annie show him in and do the introductions. He had already introduced her to his Alpha and Luna, so it was her turn.

Annie led him in, "Alpha Benson, Luna Leigh, I would like to introduce you to my mate, Beta Enforcer Mike Donovan of Pack Mac Tire' Dona. Beta Mike these are my pack leaders Alpha Benson and Luna Leigh Hanrahan."

Mike met the Alpha's eyes and then the Luna's before lowering them, "I'm pleased to meet the pack leaders of my mate." He kept his eyes on the Alpha's ear as he spoke again, "Alpha, Luna, before anything else is said, I can't leave my pack, though I would for Annie if I had too. I have guardianship of my niece and nephew. Their parents were killed in a car accident, Zane was turned by a rogue, and to leave what they know..." He couldn't say anything else.

Both the Alpha and Luna started to tense when Mike almost became confrontational. When he explained what was going on the Luna came over and gave him a light hug, "Have a seat and will you tell us about what else is going on? I can smell your tension and concern." Needing to stay at his pack for the needs of pups was a valid reason for needing to have Annie released.

Annie hadn't joined Mike's pack yet, so she could still send to her current pack leaders, **I have checked and what Mike has said is true. His nephew, Zane, was turned by a rogue before he was hit by a car. His sister Olivia was involved in a wreck and was critically injured. Zane is just starting to deal with what happened, but I can tell he is still a badly hurt pup. There are some other issues as well which Mike needs to talk to you about. Please allow me to join Mike's pack, since to try and force them to come here would seriously hurt the pups.**

Mike lowered his eyes, "Sorry Alpha, sorry Luna." He settled down next to Annie, "As I said, Zane and Olivia lost their parents in a terrible wreck. Olivia was badly hurt and not long ago underwent surgery to help repair her leg and hip. On top of this, Zane is dealing with being a wolf and forming his team. He is a rogue-turned wolf and his life, even more than Olivia's, has been tossed over and turned into a mess. Several human pups at his school decided to try and pick on him. It almost ended in the death of one and now there is a legal issue dealing with that. The two-humans attacked one of his junior wolves and we have a follow up hearing at the end of this week."

Both tensed and then relaxed, "I see, I'm sorry to hear about everything. I have to admit losing Annie is not going to be something I wish to do. I can understand and respect your need to take care of the pups, and you have an obligation to your pack. I will release Annie from all pack obligations, though I'm going to talk to Kadrian about this, and possibly see if someone is interested in moving here. I'm planning to talk to him about strengthening the bonds between the two packs. Go relax for the evening and go back to your pups with our blessing."

Some pack leaders might try and use this to their advantage, but it tended to be with older alphas. Many of the packs in the pacific northwest were more forward thinking and it showed. It was one way packs moved members, by trading those that had an interest in moving to another pack. For some it was a change of scene, others the lack of advancement opportunities in their chosen field, and a few because of unreconcilable differences with another packmate. Most Alphas didn't have a problem with moving between packs, as long as they were leaving in good standing, or could convince the new alpha the reasons were legitimate.

Mike stood and met both of the leaders' eyes, "Thank you Alpha and Luna. We will head back soon." Even now it was obvious he was feeling somewhat stressed, and he knew it. Annie's friends were helping to pack her stuff up and was glad there wasn't too much.

*****

Friday, those involved with the David and Leon case met at the courthouse. They walked in and all of them had taken the time to look their best. They were all clean, had tidy hair, and nice clothing. They weren't going out of their way to impress the judge but to look clean and nice, and it showed they respected the proceedings. Today when Zane walked in, he had his arm around Tessa. He was making a point and Zane was going to rub it into David's nose, **Remember everyone, don't let them get to you. It doesn't matter what they say, simply relax and give David and Leon a knowing smile as needed. I do not want any confrontation, if anyone acts up, I want it to be those two and their parents.** It wasn't what he wanted to do, but he made it an order. When the others submitted his wolf was pleased and Zane felt bad.

Everyone had ensured their pack jewelry was polished and showing. The humans might not understand but others would. Zane still felt odd wearing a fortune of gold and jewels, but it was expected. Being a pup, his necklace wasn't anything like his uncle's, but it was still worth quite a bit.

Once they were all seated at the tables again, Zane kept his eyes on their lawyer. When the bailiff came in and called the room to order everyone stood. It was obvious the other party thought this was a waste of time. It wasn't what they said but how they stood and acted. Their scents also told a story and again David and Leon's scents were intermingled, letting the wolves know it wasn't a single time.

Once the judge sat down and the bailiff told everyone to sit down, they did. The judge glanced around and then at her papers, "I have reviewed all the notes, briefings, forensics, and statements. As of now from what I can see, Mr. and Mrs. Walpert and Mr. and Mrs. Baker feel the charges are unfounded. As far as the other party they feel the two named defendants are at fault and demand at the least some counseling, structured parole, registration, and removal from the school. Based on what I have reviewed, neither party is willing to change their stance on this issue. Because of this, I'm going to pass this to a penal court. As of now, all charges are valid until they are judged to be innocent or guilty. If anyone pushes, all children involved will be sent to Juvenile Detention until the court date is reached." She banged her gavel once she was done speaking.

The Walpert's and Baker's jerked upright and started yelling and screaming even though the others remained calm. Zane and his team gave David and Leon slightly knowing smiles though Tessa had a rather malicious smirk on her face.

CHAPTER 22

The Contempt

When the Walpert's and Baker's stood and started screaming at the judge, Zane had to stare at them. How stupid could they be? Even at his age he knew it was a really bad idea to do that. Based on what he was getting via the pack bonds from the adults, they were finding it rather funny. He had to pause for a short time before he realized why. All they were doing was making everything look even worse for them.

Before he had a chance to think more about it, the judge tapped her gavel several times, "Order in the court. If you do not settle down this instant, you will be held in contempt of court." She banged her gavel several more times as their lawyer tried to calm them down.

Mrs. Walpert glared at Mr. Lawless, "The charges are crap! My son is a good boy and would never do what they are accused of. It's that boy and his group of friends who are out to get my son. I want the damn charges dropped and those put in jail!" Her voice had raised until it was nothing but a screech.

Mr. Baker was doing much the same much to the amusement of the wolves, "I agree, Leon is a good boy and is doing well in school. Why would he attack *that* girl? He has a girlfriend and wouldn't have any reason to do what is being said about him. This is causing him problems with school and his reputation has been damaged!"

When Zane heard Leon's father mention his having a girlfriend, he barely managed not to die laughing, **And a boyfriend as well, right*

*Tessa?** He aimed the thought at her since he had felt her start to draw back. It was his way of helping her stay present.

Tessa had started to withdraw when Zane contacted her. His comment made her giggle very slightly before she managed to control it, **Very true Zane and thanks.** She was holding his hand under the table and gave it a good squeeze.

Mike was quietly murmuring to Abby to keep her from doing or saying anything. She was still pretty worked up by the assault. If anyone was going to react to what Mr. Baker had to say she would be the one. Brandon was doing much the same from the other side as well. The rest of the table was trying to look serious, but it was hard. Small smirks and grins kept breaking out only to be wiped off their faces then reappear.

When the Walperts and Bakers refused to listen to the judge, she banged the gavel again. "Bailiffs, detain the parents for contempt of court. Detain their children as well until I have this sorted out." Several deputies came out and it almost turned into a brawl as they detained the six.

The parents were not obeying orders and more officers ended up in the courtroom. When all was said and done, all six were in handcuffs. Zane mentally grumbled because the two boys hadn't resisted unlike their parents. He had to look at Mike and was at a loss on what to say. Watching adults act that way shocked him. His parents had taught him well how to behave and respect authority. As a wolf it only reinforced what he'd been taught to the point it was nearly instinctive.

Mike raised an eyebrow at Zane and shook his head, **Later Zane, we will talk about it. It was rather amusing watching the wicked witch taken down though.** Mrs. Walpert wasn't looking nearly as faux elegant as she had been. Her hair was a mess, her blouse had partially come untucked, her makeup was smeared.

The judge banged her gavel one last time, "Additional charges may be added to the contempt of court after review by the District Attorney. As of now you are going to be placed in a cell. David Walpert and Leon Baker will be sent to Juvenile Detention until family services can find a location for them. Depending on what charges are made, they might be remanded to Juvenile Detention, pending trial. Court is adjourned."

Zane's side stood and filed out of the courtroom and towards the vehicles. All the kids were feeling rather shocked at the blatant display of disrespect. From Tessa and Oscar, he could feel a sense of satisfaction for what had happened. They were the most affected, so he could understand why. Once they were in the SUV Zane, Tessa, and Oscar could only stare at each other.

The drive to the pack territory was silent until they reached the house. Once they walked in, Tessa started giggling before it turned into a belly laugh. She finally collapsed against Zane since she was laughing so hard. By the time she was done laughing Tessa was gasping for air. She shouldn't have laughed but it had been too much, "Oh Goddess that was funny!" Tessa gasped.

Zane held her, as she was working hard on proving you could die from too much laughter. He had found it funny to watch, but Tessa's reaction seemed excessive. Then again, she had been assaulted by the two boys, so he decided it was okay for her to react that way, "It was but I have a feeling you had more enjoyment watching David and Leon getting arrested than anything else."

Abby and Brandon had walked in as Tessa gasped her last laugh. They gave Zane a quizzical look, **What had her so amused?** Abby was pretty sure she knew but had to ask.

He almost started laughing when Abby asked him about Tessa, **It seems she found the arrest of the other families hilarious for some reason. We walked in before she collapsed in my arms from laughing so hard. She couldn't even stand without help as she howled.** He couldn't help grinning as he replied. His arms were around Tessa as her arms were around his neck with her face pressed against his neck. She was warm and enjoyable to hold though as the thought crossed his mind, he blushed slightly.

Brandon couldn't help being pleased by Zane's reaction to holding Tessa. He wasn't going to tease him since he remembered being that age. It was both pleasing and amusing to watch the two with each other.

It was obvious they liked each other and enjoyed the company of each other. Zane was a good boy, and Brandon knew Zane would take care of his little girl. He had noticed Oscar spending more time than needed with Olivia as well. When she was old enough, if Oscar still liked her, she would be a good first girlfriend for their son, "I have to admit I wanted to gloat as they were arrested and taken away." Helping keep Abby from doing anything rash helped him not make things worse.

Mike rolled his eyes at the two, "I have work to do. You are off until lunch and then your normal day starts. I would say have fun with the Enforcer training but..." He grinned at Zane when the boy made a face.

Zane resisted sticking his tongue at his uncle, since it would only make Mike laugh. Instead, he went with a nice and proper reply just to tease him, "We will be at training, and we will enjoy it. I know the enjoyment is mandated, and we will obey such mandates."

Tessa poked him for that and got up, "Time to start working on lunch. Anything in particular anyone want?" They had had to wait until later in the morning to see the judge and so lunch was delayed.

Mike shrugged, "Sandwiches will be fine and maybe some soup to go with them. . Nothing special needed. I'm sure we will appreciate whatever you make. Zane, have your team come over this evening for a group meeting. Nothing major but it is about this morning." Zane had been as shocked as the other kids at the actions of the other adults. It was one of those things that one knew happened but when you saw it you were shocked.

Zane finally had to ask, "Uncle Mike, how can adults actually think they can get away with what they tried to? Don't they know the meaning of common sense? Keeping your mouth shut at times? I don't understand." He had seen adults acting like children before, but that display was seriously shocking.

Mike had to pause and think before he could really come up with a reply. Partly because he was a wolf, he didn't really understand that sort of behavior. Yes, they had those who were disrespectful and flouted authority but hardly ever like the way that other family had done, they just didn't last as wolves, as acting like that to orders from the alpha would get them kicked out of the pack, at best. If a loner was disrespectful within a pack territory, they were then usually treated as rogues and dealt with permanently, although some packs might just revoke their permission and kick them out of the territory; it usual depended on how bad the disrespect was. "Zane, I wish I had a good answer for you. Part of it is how they were raised and what they were taught growing up. Some is their personality. They just have a sense of entitlement, and think don't have to listen to anyone else." He shrugged since there just wasn't much more he could really say. He never had to deal with someone with that sort of blatant refusal to show respect to authority.

Annie made a face and spoke as well, "I have had to deal with people like them before, Zane. It is just part of life. Maybe this will smack some sense into them. I'm not going to hold my breath, since I rather like living but we can hope... As Mike said there are a number of reasons for people to act that way. I have a feeling in this case, it is that the adults simply don't believe anyone else can be right and they can't be. If they don't get their way, the other person is at fault. They will toss a hissy fit and pout and make everyone know they are being put upon. With their kids, I'm guessing they are passing it down to them. It makes them think that since they are wrong, they don't have any authority over them." She moved over to Mike and wrapped her arms around him and gave him a kiss.

Zane ran his fingers through his hair and tugged on it, "My brain hurts after watching their actions. I think I'm going to find a tree and beat my head against it." When Annie kissed Mike, Zane deliberately caught her eyes before scrunching up his face, "Ick! Not in front of an innocent young wolf!" Now just for added effect he stuck a bit of his tongue out as if he had tasted something horrible.

Annie looked at him when he caught her eyes and started to frown. When he pulled the whole icky thing, she could only stare at him. It caught her flat footed and she wasn't sure how to react.

Mike had to stare also before frowning. Just for good measure he pulled Annie into another much deeper kiss, "Deal with it and don't even try pulling the 'innocent wolf' thing. I know better." Just for good measure he winked at the boy.

Zane started laughing at both, "Since Olivia isn't here, I had to pull the 'ick' thing to support her." He was grinning as he turned and wandered towards the kitchen. He started helping Tessa getting lunch ready.

*****

Kadrian was again in his office talking with Ms. Colburn, "So what is going to happen from here? I need to know and understand, since I'm going to have a meeting with the parents this afternoon." His wolf wanted to understand as well.

She pulled out notes she had already prepared. She took a few moments to do a quick review before speaking, "I will need to check on a few items before I can give you concrete answers. When I originally talked to you, I told you the first option was out of court mediation. After that, it would be passed to a Jurisdiction hearing. That's where they decide how the case should be handled. Depending on the results of the review of the charges, the parties could be forwarded to a Disposition hearing. If the charges are declared without merit, then the charges are dropped. If the charges are found valid, it will go to a Disposition hearing. In that, the judge will decide on the sentence."

Kadrian started tapping his pen on his desk as he considered what she had said. After thinking about it, he gave her a sharp nod, "I don't currently have any further questions right now. Based on what we witnessed this morning, what are your thoughts on what might happen?" He held a hand up before she started speaking, "Based on your experience and I understand this is simply a guess."

Ms. Colburn gave him a brief grin, "First, I can tell you the other party definitely made a negative impression on the judge. I'm sure she will do her best to ignore how they acted, but it will affect how she perceives them, as their action within the court room can be used. Best case, she will reflect on the actions of the boy's parents. She will take it into consideration when she reviews the evidence and charges. Best case, she will uphold those charges. Other than Abby speaking out the first morning, our children have acted well behaved, the parents have respected the bench, and we have remained civil. Best case she will drop the charges for the pups. I'm leaning towards her dismissing all charges against the pups. That's my personal opinion, based on experience." Even though she had expected some of what had happened, she, along the others, had been appalled at how over the top the disrespect had gone.

He didn't bother making a face at the mention of the actions of the parents. Kadrian had been expecting it and he hadn't been shocked. He had dealt with both parents before and none of them understood the concept of restraint. They were loud, obnoxious, convinced their shit didn't stink, "That's what I am thinking toas well. Go and take care of business; Once you get any information let me know. I'm especially wanting to know when we might end up going back to court."

After tucking her notes into her folio, she stood, "Will do Kadrian. I will head to the courthouse right now and see what they might have." Since he had dismissed her, she left the office.

Kadrian leaned back in his chair now he was alone, letting a slow malicious smile cross his face. It had been way too fun watching those people get their comeuppance. Before their brats had assaulted Tessa, he had to mostly ignore them as they hadn't done anything worthy of his attention. Now? Both he and his wolf were pissed off and they became something to be noticed and possibly dealt with. They would wait for the court case to see if it dealt with them enough. Depending on if they had court monitoring, they would have to stay paws-off, as to not bring more attention to the pack, as retribution was something the human courts didn't allow. When Esther came in, he could feel her satisfaction as well, "This morning was so very enjoyable. I wish I could have had a camera and taped it."

She had a pleased and contented expression on her face. Anyone looking at her would assume she was having a nice day. Behind the façade it was totally different. She was gloating as much as her mate was. When she settled down in his lap instead of saying anything, she leaned against him. Esther started sucking on his neck and nibbling as well. She knew what it was going to do to him. When she received a growl from him, she knew it was working.

Kadrian stood up with her in his arms as he went over and locked the office door, **Evil woman, trying to distract me when I should be working.** Once the door was locked, he carried her over to a couch and dumped her on it.

*****

The Judge was sitting in her office and staring at the stack of motions already filed by Mr. Lawless. By the time she had returned from lunch, she already had half a dozen of the documents. From what one of the bailiffs had said, the adults had been very vocal all the way down to the cells. They would be transferred to the city jail later, after she decided what was going to be done with them. As far as the boys were concerned, they had already been sent to Juvie.

The two had been so shocked at what had happened, they had been silent and didn't fight it. Maybe this would teach them a lesson and they would straighten up. She wasn't going to hold her breath on how their parents accepted what happened. It was rather obvious the parents hadn't taught their children well. She was tempted to drop the charges against the other children.

She read through all the various documents available. Based on everything she read, it did look like the three kids had been protecting the girl. She had seen the pictures of the bruises left on her chest. Sexual assault was one of the crimes she took a very dim view of. It wasn't going to take long to make her decision., but she had to do come thinking about the two boys. If she just tossed out a decision it could look bad.

As a member of the community, she had heard of rumors pay-offs to cover up other incidents with their kids, since neither side had brought up anything, as well as being inadmissible unless they brought the other party in to give a statement, she put the thought out of her mind, as she dealt with only the evidence that had been presented and their contempt of court charge. She wished she could do an independent investigation, but that would open her up to being asked to recuse herself. She was supposed to be independent and neutral, and dealing with only what she was told in court that was admissible.

*****

When Judet came in the next morning, there was even more motions from Mr. Lawless. She flicked through them and rolled her eyes. It was rather obvious he was trying to bury her under so many motions she would give up. Considering the two of them, had dealt with each other before he should have known better. He would still do it just for annoyance's sake. The only thing this really resulted in was his clients would end up in jail for longer as she dealt with the motions.

While her assistant was working on those, Judet logged into the computer. She pulled up one of the programs she used for legal documents. With a great deal of judicial displeasure, she started creating the contempt of court sanction. Once she was done, she had fined each of them $500.00 for the initial charge the day before. She also indicated the defendants would remain in jail until such time as they formally apologized to the court. For each day they were in jail under the contempt of court, each would be fined an additional $500.00. She thought it would be the days in jail would be more impact than the fines.

Once the document was done and being printed, she typed up another document. To keep everything equal, a copy would be sent to both lawyers, even if it was mostly directed to Mr. Lawless and his clients. In it she informed them she was referring any possible charges from the day before to the D.A. Once they received the information, the D.A. would decide if any charges should be brought. She sent it to the printer and the moment they were out, she signed them and handed them over to her assistant, "Take care of these first, as you are done organizing the motions and put them on my desk. I have a court session I need to go and take care of." She left the office after pulling her robes on.

*****

Mr. Lawless was relaxing in his office and contemplating the day before. His clients were far less than happy at the moment. When he had checked on them last night and then this morning, they were still screaming. Well by now, it was more general frothing, since their throats were sore from the screaming and yelling. When he tried to talk to them, they had just demanded he get them out of there immediately.

He did find it rather interesting it was Mrs. Walpert and Mr. Baker who were the most vocal. The other two were relatively quiet for the moment. He had finally managed to get them to shut up by threatening to leave. Once they quieted down, he carefully explained what contempt of court meant. After making sure they understood, he explained the sanctions which could be taken against them. He hadn't received the letter about the sanctions, or charges being forwarded to the D.A. for review, but was expecting something.

Mr. Lawless had knocked out several motions, both the day before and before going to see his clients. His next stop was to see their sons and see how they were doing. He had a feeling going to Juvie was not going to be a pleasant experience. They were bullies and by nature bullies were cowards. They might think they were tough, but they weren't. He had watched the boy who the other kids seemed to follow. Now he would probably have taken over Juvie. He was muscled, had bleak eyes, and just came across as uncaring. It wasn't that he just didn't care so much as he didn't care what happened to him personally. It was reinforced by how he'd comforted and taken care of the girl.

He had one of his various P.I.'s look into the kids' background to see if there was anything he could use. It ended up being a bust. Zane had been a good kid where he had lived before. Being in a coma and losing most of his family wasn't something he was going near. He could try the 'coma changed his personality' but if the mention of what happened to his sister and parents came out, it would become sympathetic. For the other children involved, they were much the same. Good kids with few issues at school and decent to good grades. There just wasn't anything there he could use.

The problem was that his original clients weren't good kids, and everyone knew it. Their parents were respected only because of their position in the city which was because they had money. They had several companies and employed a large number of people from the community that paid a modest wage and had few turnovers of employees . He was going to do what he always did and fight to get them off or as light a sentence as possible.

As he was thinking he couldn't help but grin, he had traded parries with Judet a number of times. They both disliked each other but they also respected each other. He was a good lawyer, and she knew it. She was an honorable judge and stood by the law. Just for good measure, he knocked out one more motion. Once he had it done, he turned to one of his other cases. The Walperts and Bakers still wanted to sue for slander and libel. He needed to wait to file. If he filed it now, and then the children were convicted, or the others let off, it would be tossed and it would open themselves up to the other side being able to counter sue, and also sue for trying to silence them and they would likely win and tack on all their court costs.

*****

Since nobody knew when the judge might rule one way or another, Zane had decided he was simply going to go with the flow and try and be a kid again. One thing he knew was he needed to go and have a talk with Annie. He had been trying to be open with her, but it had been so very hard. She hadn't pushed in any way and neither had Mike.

Olivia seemed to get along with her quite well and so did Tessa and Oscar, and even the rest of the team; he was going to trust their judgement. He figured it was because they were junior wolves and didn't have anything tied up in it. Zane finally walked over to Mike's office right after Enforcer training. When he knocked and was answered, he walked in and closed the door. He flopped in a chair across from Mike's desk.

"How can I help you, Zane? Is there a problem with the training or school?" Mike couldn't think of what might be bothering Zane enough to come see him in his office.

Zane met his eyes and looked down. This was going to be horribly hard, "Uncle Mike, I would like to talk to your mate. I know I have been distant with her. I want to talk to her and try to get to know her. Olivia gets along with her, along with the rest of my team. I know you and Annie have worried about me but..." He didn't know what else to say.

Mike met Zane's eyes before he had lowered them. As Zane was talking, he listened and wanted to cheer to the sky. His nephew was taking steps to keep healing, even if he didn't see it, "You didn't need to come and talk to me. I appreciate you taking the time. Would you like me to ask her to come here rather than the house?" She was working on getting her Courier credentials moved to this pack, but that involved waiting on the regional council.

Zane visibly relaxed as his uncle started talking, "I had to talk to you first Uncle Mike. You are her mate, and it felt wrong to talk to her first. I'm trying Uncle, but it is still hard. I know you as well as Olivia and the Luna are worried about me. I am still scared. My team and Tessa, are helping me a great deal." He swallowed before he started speaking again, "If you don't mind Uncle Mike, I really like to talk to Annie."

Mike passed on Zane's request, **Annie, Zane would like to talk to you. Would you mind coming to my office?** He knew she would feel his pleasure at what he was telling her. He felt her agreement and she was on her way. He stood and walked around the desk and leaned over and gave Zane a good hug, "I'm proud of you Zane. She will be here shortly."

It was only a few minutes later when she walked in. While he waited, he was relaxing in his uncle's arms. It really did help him and his wolf, since they could feel his love. They did know it, but Zane had been very hesitant when it came to some hugs. Tessa was one thing, but Mike, the Luna, and the Alpha were totally different. He was starting to get used to how much more touchy-feely werewolves were compared with the way he was raised as a human. He did like how the bonds allowed him to know without reservation how much he meant to his uncle, and how proud he was. It also let him know he wasn't alone in grieving for his parents, and the elders had said "Pain shared is pain halved" and while he hadn't known it then, he was starting to see how it helped to share the feelings, and it seemed to reduce the pain he felt.

Annie stopped at the door to the office after opening it and smiled. It was good seeing Zane accepting affection from his uncle, "Hello Zane, why don't we go elsewhere and talk. I'm sure Mike has all sorts of horribly important Enforcer stuff to take care of. No reason to occupy his office." She wasn't going to force Zane to give her a hug. This was more than she had been hoping for.

Zane let his uncle go and stood, "I would hate to distract my uncle from all those horrible Enforcer duties he has. If I did, he might talk to the trainers, and I would start crawling up the stairs at home again." When Mike laughed, Zane did too as he followed Annie out of the office.

She was grinning at the two, it was obvious they did love each other. Zane was still processing what happened while he was in a coma. Annie had talked with Mike about Zane and Olivia. She had respected his decision to respect their privacy. They were mates, but this was a very complex family situation. Once they left the office, she glanced at him, "Feel like getting something to eat? I know of a good place in town. Since I'm with you, you can leave pack territory." She knew feeding him would be a good way to get to know any young wolf.

Zane's wolf lifted his head and looked interested at the idea of food. He had to snort, "Well as long as it is rare and not something off the wall, it sounds good. I have to admit I would love to have a Gyro, an authentic one. Not one of those pseudo-American ones." He hadn't had one since arriving. There had been a place back home he could walk to, and they were killer. He much preferred the vertical rotisserie the difference in spices, over the oven-baked loaf, as the American one was too heavy on the spices.

Annie gave him a toothy grin, "Oh goody, I do know of a place, a lone wolf runs it, and Mike took me to it recently. Shall we?" They walked outside and to her car.

Zane lifted an eyebrow at the car since it seemed almost un-werewolf. The darn thing was a Subaru Impreza wagon. It was a good car, but he had long since decided wolves like cars that were big, bigger, and frigging massive. This had to be one of the smallest cars he had ever seen a wolf drive, "Ah, I was expecting something larger."

Annie laughed at his comment, "If you did as much driving as I do you would have something very fuel efficient. I get about 33MPG and believe me, it saves a goodly amount. Besides, I don't have to have some monster SUV or muscle car to prove I'm a wolf."

He almost giggled at the sharpness in her voice., "I see, that does make sense. It just seems wolves just want a big vehicle." Zane settled in the car and remained quiet while she drove to wherever they were going.

Once they arrived, he stepped out and inhaled, "That smells good! Thanks!" They walked into the place, and he had to smile. There was the vertical skewer with the mutton or beef stuff. He took several slow deep breaths and almost blushed when his stomach spoke. It was a loud and demanding rumble.

From behind the counter a woman, who Annie knew was a lone wolf, started laughing, "I think someone is hungry and what can I get for you?" She had inhaled and knew both were wolves. She had met Annie before and gave her a grin.

Zane had to swallow several times since his mouth really started to water, "Um food, lots of it, and soon. I would hate to try and eat the counter to get to the meat." All he could do was stare at the skewers as they were slowly rotating, even as his wolf was forward and watching the meat the same way he did a choice bunny who was taunting them by being at the opening of a burrow.

The woman started laughing, "One large meal for a hungry teen coming up, what would you like Annie?" She turned and started slicing a fair amount of meat off and made several larger Gyros for him. For good measure she tossed in several sides and slid his food across the counter before working on Annie's food. It didn't take very long before she had what both wanted, "Enjoy, there is plenty more where it came from, if you want it."

Annie snickered at Zane's reaction as he was staring at his tray. It was obvious he was debating how much he could eat and how quickly, "Go, there is a table in the corner where we can talk." She grabbed her tray following him over, **We can talk this way, so we aren't overheard.** Since they both had bonds through Mike, they could talk, even if there hadn't been a full moon for her to join the pack. It also meant they could eat and talk at the same time.

He did his best to be polite and wait but it didn't happen. The first bite of the Gyro almost melted in his mouth. The sauce and cucumbers were fresh and crisp. He finished his Gyro e before he could reply, **Sorry Annie, I didn't realize how hungry I was. Enforcer training makes me very hungry!** Once he finished, he took a good sip from his drink, a flavored sparkling water and started munching on a side.

Zane was glad when Annie didn't press him to talk. If she had he would have replied but it would have been irritable, **Annie, don't take my reserve or lack of reaction to you wrong.** He stopped eating for a moment and looked at her before looking back at the table, **I'm sure Uncle Mike has told you what happened. When I woke to find my parents dead and Liv so badly hurt... It scared the crap out of me. Everything I knew had been destroyed. To make it even worse, I woke hearing voices, and I'm now something like what caused all of this, and not like I was...** He working to come to terms with what had happened. He did like his wolf and was starting to understand him.

Annie kept eating though not as fast as he was. She had dealings with other turned wolves and he was still figuring who he was going to be. Annie watched him eat, even if he hadn't noticed. He was eating more than the other wolves, because he was growing and training, **I don't blame you for being so scared and upset. I'm not going to bother pretending to imagine what it might be like because I have never lost my family or** *world.** She'd have to think on how she could help him, but would want to know what her mate and the pack had tried first.

She reached over and rested a hand on one of his arms and lightly stroked before she went back to eating, **I know Mike and I becoming mates has thrown you for a loop. I will not come between you, your uncle, or Olivia. All I wish is to be able to settle into living with my mate. I want to become part of this family. I will try not to push or ask too much from you. Please talk to me if you have a problem with anything I do. I will do my best to work with you to help us become family. Family is so very important to me.**

Zane moved a hand over and pressed it against hers before he went back to eating, **You becoming mates scared me , Annie. I was afraid Uncle Mike would ignore us. I think I could have dealt him ignoring us since I have my team. Olivia doesn't have a team to help her. Oscar really cares for her, but it isn't enough She almost needs Uncle Mike more than I do, since he is her only other family. We both need a parent in our lives and the thought of losing him was terrifying.* * He dropped his hands to the table.

What he had said punched him and he had to blink. What he said was his team was now part of his family. Tessa was his girlfriend and he had meant it when he had asked. He did like and care for her. His choice had little to do with her and Oscar taking care of Olivia. He and his wolf just plain liked her. Olivia couldn't know what the pack bond was like since she was human.

Zane had to take a slow breath as he tried to understand what his team meant to him. He put his food down and drew in a ragged breath. After several he finally lifted the food back and started eating, **I have my team as well as Olivia and Uncle Mike. Olivia only has Uncle Mike or me. I think having you is going to be good for her.** He couldn't say anything else.

Annie had watched him and what he had been thinking about had really hit him hard. She hadn't quite joined the pack, since by custom, it had to be done on the full moon. Because she was mated with Mike, she could sense some of his feelings. When he finally spoke, she again reached over and rested her hand on his arm, **Zane you have family as well. Mike and Olivia love you. I will do what I can to help you. I'm hoping someday we will all become family. Are you still hungry?**

His stomach grumbled, "Yah, food!!!" He grumbled as he finished the second Gyro. Even now he was eating more than the others in his team, "Heaven help the bacon bill." He scarfed up all the food on his plate.

Annie giggled at him. They talked a while longer before getting some ice cream from a different shop and heading home.

*****

Judet was looking at the document she had just finished writing. She decided to drop the charges against Zane and his friends. She had taken several days to really contemplate repercussions of her decisions and for the legal basis for it. Each time she had reviewed documentation she had; it came up the same. The two boys were at fault because they attacked the girl. She was most definitely an innocent in this issue. So far there had been no proof provided to support how their statement of being 'good boys' was true, while the other side had facts with documented proof to support their side.

With each time Judet had seen her, Tessa had been quiet and almost painfully shy. She simply couldn't imagine the girl working with the others to do a setup, so Zane could have a fight with David. Judet had also reviewed the doctor's notes about Tessa. They showed the young woman was trying to accept that the assault happened. The first day when she had started crying her entire body showed her trauma.

Seeing Zane's reaction also proved to her . He wasn't possessive or overbearing. His actions showed he truly cared for Tessa. Judet had to wonder about his reserved and painfully hurt expression. She did know about his parent's dying but what else had happened? He looked like a badly hurt and scared teen.

After much rumination, she chose to drop the charges against Zane and his friends. The other parents hadn't been willing to submit a formal apology to the court. That also colored her considerations on the case. One group had come across as willing to accept her authority and respect her position. The others didn't. If the parents didn't respect her authority, then the children wouldn't.

With her decision made, she created a document indicating the next court date. Both parties had to appear for her judgement and punishment. It was going to be ten days from the date of her decision. It would give both parties time to prepare any motions and rebuttals. With a slight smile she had the documents sent out.

CHAPTER 23

The Pictures

Once Zane left with Annie, Mike shut down his computer and put his files away after finishing what he was working on. He had a surprise, and he hoped they would appreciate it. With Olivia now going back to school and Zane away in the afternoon, he had made some plans. HE had all of their things from their old house shipped to the pack property and put in storage where they could access it whenever they wanted to.

What neither child knew was Mike had gone to their house after the wreck while Olivia was recovering from her initial surgeries. He had selected a number of pictures of their family and packed them separately himself as he arranged getting the rest of their belongings packed. At first, he hadn't hang them, because the doctors suggested it would do more harm. Now that Zane healing, there had been too much going on. With Zane starting to heal, it was time.

Mike had talked with Abby and Brandon and showed them where he wanted the various pictures and paintings placed. His sister-in-law had been a good artist, even if unknown. He chose to not have the paintings she had done for him hung in the first house. Again, it was to keep from hurting Zane and Olivia. Now they, as well as others, were going to be hung for all to see.

Abby and Brandon had subtly browbeat the rest of the team into helping get everything ready. Everything was ready for when they got home. Just for good measure he had ensured Tessa and Oscar—Mike knew about Oscar's slight crush on Olivia—were there. Olivia was going to get home first, so they could comfort her.

When Zane came home, Tessa would be there for him. Mike was expecting tears and all kinds of emotions. One picture he had hung in the main room was of him in his wolf form. His sister-in-law didn't know it was him. His brother had given her a high-quality picture and asked her to do a painting for him. When he gave it to Mike, he had almost broke down. It showed his wolf standing in part of the forest. There was snow on the ground and a dusting of snow on his back, head, and muzzle.

As Mike was thinking about this, he walked to the house and met Olivia on the porch. Oscar had her pack over one shoulder, and she looked tired. She had been back to school for only a few days and was worn out by the end of the day, "Hey Olivia, I have something I want to show you. I hope you like it." He gave her a good hug as Oscar opened the door.

Olivia gave him a curious look even as she leaned into the hug, "As long as I can sit down for it that's fine. I'm tired and sore. Nothing like before the surgery, but I need my meds and a chance to rest."

Mike lightly tweaked her nose just because he could, "Maybe a bit of walking but not outside of the house." He helped her into the house. When she froze, he carefully sniffed to see what she was feeling.

She almost grumbled at the tweak, but she was too tired. When they walked in, she immediately noticed the family pictures on the wall of the entranceway. Her eyes widened, and her lower lip started to quiver. She didn't expect to see those pictures ever again and as the tears came, she turned and wrapped her arms around Mike. They were what she needed to make this place home, and she loved seeing the pictures even as they brought memories back. It also was one more thing which meant they couldn't go back to the way it had been.

He wrapped his arms around her and held her as she cried. Based on her scent she was both pleased yet sad. It was what he had hoping would happen for her.. All of them needed the slice of home it provided.

*****

Annie hadn't known what Mike was planning, though she had felt the emotions from him. When they walked into the house after talking Zane's reaction caught her off guard. They walked in and he froze before bursting into tears and turning to her and holding on for dear life. She glanced at the hall and noticed the pictures hanging where there hadn't been any before. Annie had to look at one or two before she finally understood. They were pictures of his family before all the crap happened.

Tessa had seen the pictures and knew Zane was going to be overwhelmed by them. When he turned to Annie and started crying, she hurried over and wrapped her arms around him and leaned against his back, **It is nice to see your family, Zane.** She held on and pressed a kiss against his neck.

Mike and Olivia stepped out of the main living room. Mike settled for leaning against the door jamb as Olivia slowly moved over and leaned against the three, "Uncle Mike did this for us, Zane. He had the pictures and paintings put out, so we could have memories of our parents here." She started sobbing as well.

Abby and Brandon were there, and they wrapped their arms around Mike as well. He was as upset as the others, even though he wasn't crying. He needed them, and they would be there for him.

Eventually Zane stopped crying and gently worked his way out of their arms. He moved over to his uncle and leaned against him and gave him a good hug, **Thank you Uncle Mike, thank you so much. I have wanted our pictures of mom and dad and us.** He couldn't keep up the hug for very long before he needed to escape.

He needed some room before he broke down again. Zane almost ran out of the house and stripped down as he was running leaving a trail of clothes. Mid run he shifted to his wolf and kept running. He needed space. Eventually he reached *that* clearing again, with its gentle comfort and peace, and lifted his head and started howling again. His howl ranged from loss, sadness, happiness at having the pictures, to wanting his family back and knowing it could never go back to the way it had been. After exhausting himself, he didn't know everything he'd howled about but he felt better.

Zane flopped down on the flowers and grass and panted from all the howling and crying. As tired l as he was, he quickly fell asleep. As he slept, he dreamed. In it he saw his parents, and both gathered him close and held him, even though he was in his wolf form. When he eventually woke, he didn't know what they had said other than the feeling that they were proud of him. It was a feeling that would stay with him for a long time.

While Zane left, Tessa followed though she hadn't been able to keep up. Even if she was smaller and faster in some ways, Zane was a dominant wolf, and it showed. By the time she found him, he was asleep in a lovely clearing. She slowly padded into the clearing and settled down next to him. She had listened to his howls and right before they ended, she knew he was going to fall sleep. Tessa curled up next to him and rested her head on his flank. She closed her eyes and went to sleep too.

Waking was a slow process . He hurt but was feeling better after the howl. It had been some time since he had let out a howl like that. On the moon nights, he did howl, but he had been keeping them as neutral as possible. He found Tessa there curled up next to him. He leaned over and nuzzled her before he stood and moved to the side. Right now, he needed a good stretch. He lowered his chest to the ground and slowly moved forward until his nether region rested on the ground and his back legs were stretched out. Just for good measure he gave his tail a good stretch.

Tessa started waking up as Zane was stretching. Once she was awake , she joined him in a good stretch. When she finished, she moved over and leaned against him and ran her tongue across an ear. She had to yawn again, **The pictures really were lovely, as were the paintings. I'm so glad Beta Mike was able to get them for you.**

Zane returned her affection as he listened, **Mom painted many of the pictures I saw. It was her hobby and gave her time from the business of our lives. I have been wanting our things from our family home and they* *help.** He yawned as well, **Time to get back to the house I suppose.** He was feeling better now. It was going to be hard seeing the pictures again. He hoped the pictures would change from hurting to see too good memories. It was going to take time.

She yawned again and gave her head and ears a good shake, **True, since it is late, and we do have school and training tomorrow.** She lightly bumped him and started out of the clearing. Her tail had a contented curl to it as she moved away from him. For a werewolf, spending the night as a wolf outside and sleeping wasn't unusual. It was one reason why they had Enforcers patrolling and the sensors.

Zane returned the bump and followed her back towards the house. It did take some time to get home. When they changed and walked in the lights were out and it sounded like most were asleep. He didn't bother wondering what time it was and settled for pulling some shorts on and collapsing in bed. When Tessa joined him, he curled around her and was quickly asleep. He never thought about the fact someone had to clean up his clothes he left on the floor.

*****

Kadrian and Mike were in Kadrian's office when the mail was delivered. Kadrian flipped through it until he reached an envelope from the courts. He held it up and away from him just in case it was booby trapped. With a sigh he pulled out a small knife and slit the envelope open. He steeled himself before pulling the letter out and reading it.

Mike watched the entire thing and frowned. Based on Kad's reaction, he had a feeling it was from the courts. He wanted to know what it was about, but he had to wait until Kadrian read it. It was an agonizing long wait as the Alpha read it, blinked, and read it again. Finally, it was too much, "Damn it, Kad, what does the flipping thing say?"

Kad had to blink before he remembered Mike was in the room. Just to be a butthead he gave the letter a sorrowful look before folding it up. He handed it over to Mike across the desk and heaved a tired sigh. He didn't say anything as he held the letter out to Mike.

Mike tensed, and a low growl started even as he slowly reached over and snatched the letter. Based on Kadrian's reaction, it wasn't good news. It took a force of will before he was able to open the letter and start reading it. When he finished a very grumpy grunt was forced out, "Damn it, you are an ass of an Alpha." He tossed the letter back across the desk and stormed out of the office. As he was leaving, he could feel the laughter from Kad over the link as well as hearing it.

He growled and snarled as he stalked angerly out of the house and into the forest. While he was dealing with the teasing, he still felt his Alpha's laughter over the bonds, "Damn uppity irritating know-it-all Alphas." He swore for several more minutes before he felt a hand pressed against his back. He could smell Annie's scent wrapping around him and could feel her in the bond.

Annie had finally finished what everything needed to be accepted as a Courier for this pack. Now she had to wait for the approval of the elders, Alpha, and Council. When Mike's irritation hit, she sat upright and frowned. He had been doing okay not too long ago but now he was definitely unhappy. She followed the mating bond and eventually found him. When she paused before approaching, he was making some rather horrible comments about the Alpha. She moved over to him and pressed her hand against his back, **What is wrong Mike? I can feel your... displeasure.**

He growled out a few more insults before he started laughing, **Our so lovely Alpha pulled a fast one on me. While I was in a meeting with him, he received a letter from the court. When he read it, he acted like it was bad news. When he finally handed the damn thing over, I found Zane and company were cleared of all charges. The others not so much. He was jerking my tail and he deserves to be sworn at.** He finally ended up coughing from laughing so hard.

Annie started laughing as well. It was good to know the Alpha could joke and was trusting enough of his Beta to allow teasing. Now the swearing had been somewhat insulting, **You do know you shouldn't* *swear at your Alpha like you did, right? Even if he is poking fun at you, it is rather disrespectful.** Her tone was teasing.

Mike growled at her for the teasing and whipped around and pulled her close, "I'm going to get you for that, woman." He leaned over and started nibbling on the side of her neck on the mating mark.

*****

Esther walked into Kadrian's office and settled for smacking him before walking back out. What he had done was both funny and mean. She had felt Mike's reaction and he had been badly worried about what the document had to say. When she finally walked back into her office, she sent a thought to the kitchen supervisor to have Kadrian's meat cooked well done for the next week. Granted she'd started laughing but it had been wrong of her mate to do that with something so important.

*****

That night, Mike had asked Zane to call his team to the house. Normally they were there but this was official, and it needed to be official. When Zane had given him an odd look, Mike told him to do it. He didn't want to come across as an ass, but it wasn't up for discussion.

Zane met his eyes before submitting. He sent the call out for everyone to be there at 7pm. He told them his uncle had something to talk about, but he didn't know what. Once he had taken care of that, he left the room and went to work on some homework. They had been given a report to write that was going to take some time. It was researching a past historical figure who might have been were-creatures of some sort and how they had changed their country and history. He chose to write about Richard the Lionheart.

When 7pm rolled around Zane was in the main living room with Tessa. As the others came in, he gave each a tense smile. He had a feeling it had something to do with the court case. Once they were all seated, Mike and Annie walked into the room and settled down.

Mike looked at the teens and all of them were focused on him yet respectful of his rank, "The Alpha received a letter from the Judge looking into this issue. As of now, the three of you are cleared of all charges.

They have been dropped and no longer valid. The charges against David and Leon are being upheld and there is going to be a punishment phase in ten days." He was looking very pleased when he told them.

Zane had tensed as Mike was talking, since he figured it was going to be bad news. When his uncle finished talking, he could only gape at him before finally closing his mouth. He pulled Tessa close and rested his head on her shoulder as he took several shuddering breaths, **Thank you for telling us Uncle Mike. I can't even begin to explain just how freeing it is. I feel like the weight of the world has been removed from my shoulders.** His shoulders were twitching in response to the news.

Olivia was there too, since it was her brother, they were talking about. After Mike spoke, she almost screamed in happiness. The only reason she didn't, was because she knew the wolves would flinch, "Oh god, I'm so happy for all of you." She shifted and settled on Oscar's lap and leaned against him and tried not to jiggle with excitement. This was what Zane and the others needed. They knew they had been in the right, but this proved they were.

Oscar blushed slightly when she moved to his lap and leaned against him. Yes, she was too young to ask if she might be interested in being his girlfriend. It didn't mean he didn't wish he could. It was going to take time, but if she still felt the way he hoped in a couple years, he was going to talk to her after he talked to Zane. He wrapped his arms around her and gave her a good hug, "Good, now they can get what they deserve." It had been a while, but he and Tessa were still having the occasional nightmare.

Melody flopped back against the couch she was sitting on and let out a whoof of air, "Thank goddess, I'm so sick of being restricted to the property. I have enjoyed the short school days and the Enforcer training, but I want to get back to school. I miss my human friends." Even she had gained muscles from the intense training, she was still less muscled than the other two. She had also had a growth spurt as well. Since everything had gone down, she had gained a bit over an inch in height.

The rest of Zane's team had reacted similarly, and the sense of relief was obvious. All of them, even the ones going to school, had been affected. Because Zane was their team leader, his stress had fed down to them and they felt his sudden relaxation.

Mike looked around the room and it was obvious all of them felt the sudden release, "Go and relax. I'm going to excuse you from class and training tomorrow. Take the time to recover, go for a run, play, and do teen stuff. Mind you, the day after you are going to be hating school, adults, and training again but for the moment enjoy the time off." He stood and gathered Annie to him and walked out of the room and headed towards their room.

*****

Judet was in her office with Mr. Lawless and Ms. Colburn, "What do you wish to talk about Mr. Lawless? The motions have been filed, reviewed, and recorded in accordance with the laws. If you want leniency for the parents of the two boys, it isn't going to happen. They refuse to apologize, from what I understand." Her voice was calm and relaxed as she was talking to him.

Mr. Lawless knew that and unless someone beat some sense into the parents, they would be there until the extent of the law was exhausted for the contempt, "Your honor, I simply wish to discuss some possible pleas with you. I might be able to talk my clients into a plea deal, if the sexual assault is dropped." He had a feeling taking it off the table wasn't going to happen, but he was going to do what he could.

Ms. Colburn didn't bother with any reaction other than to speak, "Your Honor, it isn't going to be possible. I have talked with the parents of Tessa. I have reviewed the evidence, the reports, and the medical records for the young lady. She was assaulted, had sexually explicit words used against her, and even threatened with rape. My clients will not accept having those charges dropped. Other charges might be dropped or lessened but the sexual assault, it won't happen."

Mr. Lawless had decided he needed to be reasonable. This wasn't the time for histrionics, "Your Honor they don't have any prior record and a record of sexual assault will have an impact on them. They are still young and made a huge mistake. Don't punish them because an issue between the two boys and Zane. Add some anger management counseling to the punishment but not sexual assault."

Judet was listening to the two of them as they traded offers and counteroffers. If she could get this resolved before the actual sentencing, she would be happy, as would also mean they wouldn't have an endless set of appeals tying up court time. For now, she was going to listen to them and hoped they could work it out, "Ms. Colburn?"

She shook her head, "Tessa's mother might accept it, as long as there was the sexual assault mention, until both boys are cleared by a Mental Health professional. Before Mr. Lawless suggests a counselor, it will have to be a neutral party with no connections to either party. If they can be shown what they did was wrong, then they might accept it. I would have to say they would want the children removed from the environment they were living in. Their parents' actions show just how little they care about authority or respect for others. They ignored the courts demand for respect while in session. They fought against the charge of contempt of court and then fought being arrested. The parents are not good role models, and they need to be removed from such a poisonous environment."

Mr. Lawless knew it wouldn't happen, their parents would fight removal of their children with everything, "I might be able to talk them into counseling for both the boys and as a family. I doubt I can get them to allow the boys to leave their homes, without a court order. As far as a Counselor I agree a neutral party, assigned by the court, is a promising idea. Might we consider a weekly visit by CPS? Have them come in, talk to the parents, children, and even the Counselor and go from there?"

The three of them, well the two lawyers with assistance from Judet, tried to hammer out a possible plan. As far as Ms. Colburn was concerned, right now almost anything that would resolve this issue and keep the wolves' content. Eventually, they had a possible deal. She was going to need to talk to Kadrian and the parents. It wouldn't be good to involve the children.

*****

Ms. Colburn requested an appointment with the Alpha. For this she had come to the pack house and settled in his waiting room and would remain until he was free. When she was shown in, she wasn't surprised when it was shortly after she had arrived. Before he even waived at the chair she settled down and pulled the draft agreement out and handed the folder over to him.

Kadrian had called for Esther to join him in his office, and she was sitting next to him in her chair. When they took the document they slowly and carefully reviewed it. Once they were done, they read it two more times just to ensure they thought they understood what was being said.

Esther chose to speak, "Just to make sure I understand what is being said. Tentatively, counseling for the pups, the parents, and as a family is on the table. Until the counseling is completed, they would have a tag of sexual assault. Once cleared they would lose it, and their records would be sealed? As far as jail time, it would be minimal, though they would have supervised parole. Is that correct?"

Ms. Colburn nodded, "Correct Luna. Mind you, this is going to require acceptance from all the parents. I'm not going to hold my breath they will agree. It is a decent deal and will punish the other parties. Oh, and they would be removed from this school. They would have to be accepted by another or go to a school which deals with juvenile offenders."

What do you think Kad? It is reasonable, even if my wolf is still wanting blood. It punishes them and their parents. I think the only person who might need some convincing is Abby. Not even the Alphas would force anyone to accept the punishment, that was offered as the solution. In this case, it was the parents who had to accept on their behalf. She did feel it was the best solution for everyone.

Kadrian laced his fingers behind his head and looked up at the ceiling as he thought, **What I think doesn't matter much. What matters is if their parents will accept it. You are right, Abby is going to be the hardest* *to convince. Call them over and let's deal with this now.** For this he was going to need the Luna of the pack to make the call.

He looked at Ms. Colburn and shrugged, "I'm having the parents and guardian called over now. We will get this resolved today, if possible. What the other parents have to say, we can't control. We can deal with this from our side though." He called for drinks and food. It was going to be a long afternoon and possible evening.

It didn't take before all the adults involved showed up. Kadrian had already had the conference table readied. He and Esther were sitting at the head of it and let the others settle down in the chairs based on their dominance. Once everyone was seated, he looked around the table, "Ms. Colburn has a possible plea deal for your review. I'm going to ask, not order but ask, for you listen and do your best to think about the suggestions. Ms. Colburn tell them what you discussed with Mr. Lawless and the Judge."

She handed out the potential deal before speaking, "Page one of the plea concerns the sexual assault charge..." She laid out the various charges and possible plea deal offers.

They ended up spending several hours working on what had been suggested. There had been a few changes offered. As expected, Abby and Brandon had been the hardest to convince. It took Mike talking to them to change their minds. He simply asked them how much more trauma they wanted their twins to deal with. He was sympathetic to what they were feeling but he also was looking at it as a dominant wolf. By accepting the plea deal, they were protecting both the pack and their children's team. That was what was most important.

When Mike had asked them, Abby looked stricken and had leaned against her mate. It was obvious they were discussing everything. They were being serious while were talking, and it showed. They talked for some time before Brandon spoke, "We aren't completely satisfied, but it will do what you said. This will take care of our pups and the rest of the team. If what we have worked out is approved, we'll accept it."

Mike and Annie moved over and gave them both a good hug . They quietly talked to them for several minutes before sitting back down. Mike looked at the Alpha, "I'm taking my junior wolves home to let them relax. If you will excuse us..." He stood and sandwiched them between him and Annie as they walked out of the room.

Kadrian watched them walked out and looked at the other wolves. From them he could feel their acceptance of the decisions made. For their pups it wasn't as traumatizing. They would and could fight. It was the junior wolves who were the most affected.

*****

Once the details had been hashed out by Zane's guardian and the other parents, the document was forwarded to Mr. Lawless and the court. He had reviewed the document and dropped it on his desk as he leaned back and contemplated it. To be honest, the deal was better than he had expected. If it had gone to court, it would have been much harsher. Now came the fun part, he had to convince the parents it was the best they were going to get. For this, he was going to talk to each set separately.

Since they had sat in jail since that disastrous day, they had started to wear down. It was a case of having to wear a jumpsuit, not having their personal sanitary products, go by their schedule, and jail food. Even though they were still ranting, it was almost like they simply didn't know how else act. It was going to be his job to talk to them and convince them this was the best they were going to get. If needed, he would tell them they could challenge the decision and go from there.

If he could get them to accept the deal and convince them apologizing to the court was in their best interest, they would fold. With a desire to get this issue resolved, he packed his briefcase with all the files he had. It wasn't a huge amount, but it should be enough to overwhelm them . Once he was ready, he checked his suit and walked out of his office.

As Mr. Lawless had expected the visit to the jail had been a pain in his ass. It had taken several hours of talking as well as laying out the case multiple times. He made sure to hit on the pictures of the bruises not to mention the statements of other kids, along with how all the other witnesses and video had shown the girl in the hall, while their statements had said she had left before. While talking, he kept a conciliatory attitude which even if not true, the evidence showed it happened. The deal he was handing them was the best they could expect. If it went to court, they could expect far worse for their children, at minimum it would have a record of a conviction. He also hinted at how it would hurt on their businesses and social standing, because it would become public record. Sections would remain sealed, since it dealt with minors, but it still would follow them.

Just for good measure he hit on how it was already impacting their businesses. They had lost customers, mostly from the other families involved and those connected to them, and how it was impacting their income. If they kept fighting this, it would cost them even more, as knowledge of it would spread father.

Eventually, they bowed down and even promised to do their best to apologize and make it sound real. Once he was satisfied, he had them sign the plea and left the jail. This was going to be a nice payday for him. It made him smile as he walked out of the building with a jaunty step and a whistle on his lips.

The next day, the signed document was delivered to the judge and the other parties. Judet was impressed with what Mr. Lawless managed to accomplish. It showed he was as good as his reputation said he was.

With the court date already set, she passed the agreement to her assistant to file. She would deal with it on the date assigned. Until then she was going to focus on other cases.

*****

Once they had received the agreement, Kadrian took time to work through the implications. He needed to see if it solved all the problems. It would solve some, but it was just a patch. The conflict between human and wolf culture had to be considered. A good enemy was a dead enemy to most wolves. Their human side knew it wasn't always that simple . The world was so much more connected that you couldn't just kill them and hide the body.

After thinking about it for some time he finally decided it was an acceptable deal. It would keep the two from the pack pups. It would keep the two boys safe unless they chose to get stupid. If it happened, then so be it and he would deal with it. Kadrian signed the document and sent it back to Ms. Colburn. Once that was dealt with, he sent a message to the parents of his decision to accept the plea deal, which they had hashed out.

*****

Mike settled down with Annie that evening and curled up with her. He was somewhat ambivalent about the decision, but the Alpha was right. It was a sensible option, short of killing the two families. Killing them would draw too much attention their way. Mike decided he would talk to the kids in the morning.

Annie was feeling his thoughts as she was relaxing against him. She gave him some time to think before she straddled his lap and faced him. Annie leaned forward and gave him a very passionate kiss before returning the favor of sucking on mate mark, **Remember this from the other day? Well, you had better, since you are going to be a father. I just entered heat when you nibbled on my bite. I was going to tell you, but you decided to distract me. Now it is my turn...** Her heat wasn't lining up with the others here, but it didn't really matter to her, next year it probably would. She smiled, in her pack, it was known that sometimes when two werewolves mated, it triggered the heat immediately. She would be surprised if Mike's pack didn't know that.

Mike couldn't help but tense when she flipped over and settled on his lap. When she started kissing and sucking on her bite on his shoulder, he leaned back and felt his erection grow. She was so damn sexy and goddess she had rocked his world the other day. He had been trying to tease her, but they had some damn fine love making. What she said went unnoticed by him as he enjoyed her attention. He let out a low sexy growl and rolled her over and returned the favor and attacked his bite on her neck.

Eventually they finished the love making and he drifted off to sleep. He finally woke and looked at her, “Huh? What? Did you say pregnant?” It was the middle of the night and Annie simply let out a comfortable sound and didn’t bother waking up. She was too content to bother waking unless he forced her to. If he did, he would probably be bit hard somewhere tender. He finally decided sleep would be good and that he could ask her in the morning. He spent the night dreaming of their pups.

*****

The next morning Mike collected the four pups and settled down at the table, “I have some news for all of you. Annie told me last night that she is pregnant. I’m so thrilled and wanted to let you know!” His expression was jubilant.

Both Zane and Olivia felt their jaws drop at the news. The two had only been mated for a short time and they had never even thought about them having babies. As Olivia stood and carefully walked over to Annie she was squealing in excitement, “Oh goody, a baby to help with!!!” She was almost bouncing as she was hugging Annie before turning to give Mike a good hug.

Zane could feel one of his eyes twitching and decided to tease Mike. He crossed his arms over his chest and glowered, “I don’t do diapers! Tessa will I’m sure, but I don’t!” When she growled at him, he started snickering before grumbling again, “I don’t want to move again. Add onto the house but no moving, Uncle.”

Mike almost snapped at Zane before what he said hit and he started laughing, “I will have a talk with Abby and I’m sure she will be more than happy to teach you, Zane. You will be his or her cousin and there are certain obligations involved. I might even have the baby’s room constructed next to yours.”

Annie kicked Zane’s closest leg and frowned, “Just for that, I will ensure you babysit on all the good nights. You know the ones where your friends are going to movies and on dates. If Tessa doesn't bite you, I might on the next run."

Olivia even joined the 'tease Zane' group, "I will loan you one of my extra crutches Annie. It already has a few dents on it so don't worry about damaging it."

Mike became more serious, "Kadrian has accepted the plea deal I talked to you about. The parents of the other pups are letting them know as well. Once the punishment part is over, you can go back to school. You will still have enforcer training after school though. Consider this done and you are not to even consider doing anything to any flower beds. You are wolves and not squirrels."

Even as Olivia gave Mike an odd look, Zane submitted, "I won't do anything to them unless they start a fight. I will protect the pack and my team as needed." He had come to accept they were his to protect, support, and lean on.

Mike nodded at the submission and statement. It was more or less what he had expected, "Good. Now go and relax." It was Saturday, so they were being given the day off.

Once the pups left, Annie gave Mike an odd look, "Not squirrels? What do you mean by that?" She hadn't heard the story and wanted to know.

He snickered, "Um, before Tessa was attacked, several wolves visited David's house and chewed up anything not nailed down. Just for fun, they left piles of wolf crap around. Rumor has it, David's mother stepped in a pile on the porch before she realized what had happened." He was doing his best to keep his voice and laughter down.

Annie stared at him for several minutes before she felt her lips twitching, "Um, oh..." It was all she could come up with.

*****

The court date finally arrived, and Zane woke with his alarm. Tessa was resting partially on his chest and was still snoring quietly. He yawned and prayed this would take care of everything . He finally nudged Tessa awake. He gave her a peck before urging her to move and rolled off the bed. For this occasion, he had been thinking a great deal about what to wear. He settled for his boots, black pants, a white shirt, and his leather jacket. Those dicks didn't deserve anything else. Besides if he had a chance, he was going to give David and Leon a blank look.

Tessa gave him a hug and returned the kiss before she slipped out of bed and headed to her room to get ready. Even with Zane there with her, today was going to be hard. . She settled for a nice skirt and a pretty blouse. There was no reason for her or Oscar to have any sort of tough guy image. After taking a few minutes for a light touch of makeup and braiding her hair she was ready.

Oscar was similarly dressed, though he had on a nice button up shirt and slacks instead. He gave his sister a firm hug after they were both ready, "I'm glad this is going to be over. It really hurt knowing what they said and did to you. Zane is a good wolf and thank the Goddess for his picking us." Zane had been good for Tessa as well. Since he had asked her to be his girlfriend, she had really started recovering from the assault.

Everyone met up at Mike's house and they left as a group. Kad and Esther were going to meet them at the courthouse. The drive was quiet, since all the kids just wanted this done with. They weren't in the mood to talk or joke around. Even when they walked into the courthouse and then to the courtroom, they were quiet.

They settled down at the table and waited quietly. It wasn't much longer before the Walpert's and Baker's were escorted into the room. Seeing them in orange jumpsuits and cuffs was rather satisfying for all the wolves; in many cases, they considered being locked up one of the worst punishments, since werewolves were not able to handle that sort of confinement without going insane. Tessa and Zane completely ignored them and simply sat there waiting.

The Judge came in not much later and the court was called into session. After she sat down, she looked at Mr. Lawless to see what he might have to say.

He stood and urged the parents to stand as well. He had run through this enough times, it should go smoothly. Mr. Baker started, "Your honor, we apologize for any and all words said to you in this room. It will not happen again." It sounded like he was chewing on something vile as he was speaking.

Judet considered his statement and chose to ignore how it was delivered. She looked at his wife and received much the same statement.

Mr. Walpert spoke as well, "I do apologize, your honor. The way we spoke and acted was wrong." He didn't quite spit the words out, but it was close. Mrs. Walpert repeated the same thing verbatim.

Judet nodded to the two, "The court appreciates your apology and accepts it. Remember this when or if you are in court again. I will have my assistant take care of the paperwork to have you released." She turned to the two boys, "In accordance with the plea deal agreed on, you are going to be incarcerated for an additional sixty days. Once you are released you will report to your assigned parole officer. You and your families will undergo court monitored counseling. Upon completion of the counseling, depending on the opinion of the court and counselor, the sex offender tag will be removed. As of now this case is closed." She struck her gavel in finality to close the session.

*****

Zane and his team were sitting at the house and staring at each other. With the case closed they simply didn't know what to do next. They had been so angry and frustrated for long enough suddenly being told 'it's over' simply didn't work. Melody summed it up for them, "What do we do now?"

The decision and how it just ended shocked them. They had the next week still being schooled at the pack before they were going back to regular schooling. The other two were not returning to the school, as with the plea deal, they would be going elsewhere, and were not allowed to be on the school's property without an escort, nor were they allowed to approach the pack's compound.

It was going to take a few days for them to get their minds around the fact it is all over, and as far as they were concerned, the two bullies were out of their lives.

Teaser for Why Us 2

This is the start of the next book... Zane and Olivia's mother had a sister... but nobody had known where she was to tell her what had happened...

Jolene walked into her apartment and dropped her bags next to the door. It had been the beginning of June when she had last been home, and now it was almost Thanksgiving. Before anything else she wanted a hot shower, a long hot bath, and some real food. She loved being a wildlife photographer and being out in nature, but she did miss a few things. Somethings like hot water, real food, and other amenities of civilization.

She had just gotten back from an extended trip into the jungles of Borneo and couldn't wait to call her sister. Even though they led totally different lives they had always been close. She might even go and visit with her and see her niece and nephew. It had been almost a year since she had visited them, and she knew the kids had to be getting taller. As she was walking into her bedroom the more she thought about it the more she liked the idea.

After changing into some clean lounging clothes and her silk robe, she strolled into the bathroom. When she walked past her home phone, she noticed the flashing message light but ignored it. There wasn't anything much more important than a shower and then a long soak in a bath. Her skin felt dry and a good soak with some oils in the water would be perfect. Tomorrow she would probably go to a salon and get a good skin treatment.

Jolene settled in the tub after her shower and let her body relax. She had her head leaned back and turned the jets on. The bubbles felt so good against her skin. She was going to sleep like a log for most of the day and tomorrow would be soon enough time to look at the messages and stack of mail she was sure to have. Thankfully one of her friends had been collecting anything important and she had noticed a large stack on her table. Any junk mail had been shredded or tossed.

Eventually, she slipped out of the bath and toweled off before working some lotion into her skin. One drawback to her job was a lack of a boyfriend. She wished she had someone there to work the lotion into her back. Something else would be nice as well but she would deal with the urge later. For now, some food and her bed were calling her name.

After she flipped through her stack of takeout menus, she settled on Thai since, even though it wasn't quite dawn, knew this place was open 24-hours. Jolene called and placed her order before grabbing some bottled water from her fridge. There was a bottle of wine, but she rarely drank and only for special occasions. Coming back from a successful trip wasn't her idea of a special occasion. When she settled down at her table, she looked at the stack of mail and decided to at least look.

It could wait but she wasn't in the mood for watching something or even listening to music. She just wasn't in the mood for noise, so this would do until the food arrived. As Jolene was sorting through the mail, she came across an official looking letter from her lawyer. With a frown she opened it and started reading through it. Before she had finished the letter fell from her fingers and she started crying.

The letter was informing her that her sister and brother-in-law had died in a car wreck. It requested she contact him as soon as possible to deal with the estate. It also informed her Zane and Olivia had been sent to live with their uncle since she wasn't able to be contacted. There was more but for the moment all she could do was cry.

Eventually she fumbled for her cell and looked up Mike's number and called him. She had to go out and see the two as soon as possible. When the phone was answered, she was surprised to hear a female's voice, "I need to talk to Mike please. Tell him Jolene is calling."

*****

Annie glanced at the clock when a forwarded call from Mike's cell showed and wondered what it was about. It was very early in the morning and Mike was gone for the moment. He had been sent to talk to another pack about a rogue issue, "Morning, how can I help you?" She listened to the woman on the other end and wondered who it was, "Mike isn't available right now. Can I help you? I'm Annie, his girlfriend." They hadn't gotten around to filing a marriage certificate yet.

Jolene had to take a deep breath, "I'm his sister-in-law. I just returned from a trip and... I need to talk to him." She almost dropped the phone as she started sobbing again, "I need to talk to him about what happened to my sister and her husband, and I have to see Zane and Olivia."

Annie had been told there was a sister out there, but they hadn't been able to contact her. If she was out of the country, it would explain why she hadn't been heard from, "I'll contact Mike once I let you go. Right now, his phone is being forwarded to mine due to the job he is doing right now. Would you like to talk to Zane and Olivia? I'm watching them for Mike." *And living in his house as well as having his pup,* she thought to herself, with some amusement.

"Could I? Please? I need to come out and... Oh god, why did I have to take the job? I should have been here for them." She managed not to start sobbing even harder.

Tessa, contact Oscar and have him bring Olivia to my room. Bring Zane as well. I have their aunt on the phone, and she just found out about their parents. She decided it was easier to have his junior wolf wake him, "Give me a few minutes to get them and then you can talk to them. I'm going to talk to Mike's boss to see about having him call you." This was definitely a good reason to wake an Alpha up, even if she mentally cringed, since her old alpha hated being woken up and he usually did something in revenge like a very nasty shift if he felt it wasn't a good enough reason, **Alpha I just received a call from Zane and Olivia's aunt. She just found out about Marlene and Steve's deaths. She wants to come and visit.**

When Tessa woke Zane, he glanced at the clock before looking at her, "It isn't time to get up, is something wrong?" Not only was it early based on the clock, but it was also still dark out.

She leaned against him, **Your aunt is calling and wants to talk to you and Olivia. She just found out about your parents.** She gave him a gentle kiss before slipping off the bed.

Zane rolled out of bed and almost tripped. If Tessa hadn't caught him, he would have face planted against the wall in his haste. Once he was mostly stable, he dashed out of the room and ran to Annie's. When he walked in, she handed the phone over and he held it to his ear, "Auntie Joli? It's Zane..." He didn't know what to say. He felt Tessa wrap her arms around him and lean into his back which helped so much since he could feel tears starting. With their hearing, even though it wasn't on speaker, any in the room would hear the other side just fine.

Jolene felt horrible for not being there for them. She should have been and taken them in. Marlene was her sister, and she should have known, "Hey Zane, I didn't know, I was on a photo shoot in Borneo and just got back. I'm so sorry I wasn't there for you. Are you and Liv doing okay?"

Zane was used to his aunt being gone for extended lengths of time. He hadn't even considered her not knowing. His mom had usually been the only one that kept tabs on where she was at any time. Waking the way he had, had driven everything else from his mind. It hadn't helped having those two pricks causing problems either, "We're doing okay. Uncle Mike and Annie have been helping us recover from everything. Liv is healed from her most recent surgery to fix her injured leg."

Jolene felt like she had been slapped, "What? Why did she need surgery? What happened?" All that she had read in the first portion of the letter had indicated was her sister and brother-in-law had been killed in an accident. It hadn't mentioned anything happening to Olivia or Zane in the part she had read. Since she hadn't read the entire thing, it was possible it had been mentioned, but it was an unwelcome addition.

Her response caught him flat footed, "Ah, she was in the car when it was hit. She had a badly broken leg and damaged hip. Liv had to undergo several surgeries to repair it. They were coming to see me in the hospital when mom and dad were killed." He was starting to babble.

Anne took the phone back from him, as she could see he was starting to lose control, "Jolene, it is a long story, but I think it would be best for Mike to talk to you. Olivia is going to be here in a moment to talk to you. I know you want to find out what happened, but this is just bringing up bad memories for Zane and Olivia. I'll have Mike contact you as soon as possible."

As she was talking Zane was holding onto Tessa and he was still crying. Olivia walked in and she moved over to the bed and settled down next to Annie even as Oscar settled down next to her. She took the phone from her, "Hi Aunt Joli, are you going to come out? We would really like to see you." Olivia loved the stories her aunt told about her trips and wanted to see her again.

Jolene choked back a sob as Annie talked to her before Olivia answered, "I'm going to talk to Mike and see how soon I can get a flight out. I'm going to come and see you as soon as I can Liv. I'm going to let you go. I need to take care of a few things here since I just got back." She hung up and started sobbing again. The food had been forgotten and she ignored the buzzer from the building entrance.

Olivia leaned against Annie as Oscar settled down next to her. She started crying again as well. It had been nice to talk to her aunt, but it had brought back sad memories.

*****

Kadrian was awakened by Annie contacting him. He rolled over and grabbed his cell and made a call to Andrew, the Alpha of the Fossil Valley Pack, as Mike was there, and he wouldn't have his cell on him while he was helping deal with a rogue issue. It was early, but this was important and couldn't wait. When Andrew answered with a grumble Kadrian grumbled back, "Hey, I was awakened early so why not you too? I need to get a message to Mike. His sister-in-law, Jolene, called because she just found out her sister's death. He needs to come back home as soon as possible. I'm sending Malcom up to replace him."

Andrew gave Kad a 'Wah' sound before becoming serious himself, "I will pass the message onto him and Malcom, another senior enforcer will be fine to replace him. I'm going to let you go and get Mike on the road." He had to find him first since Josh, Mike, and several other wolves had gone to see if they could find any trace of the rogues that were being a nuisance to his and some other packs. They tended to come and go so they were harder to track down to deal with.

He gave Mina a kiss before he slipped out of bed and shifted. He trotted out of the room and once he hit the back door he contacted his son, **Josh, where are you? I have an urgent message for Mike. It is from his Alpha.** He had a rough idea where they were and headed in their direction. This was not something he could pass to someone else, and he couldn't reach Mike at this range to let him know directly.

After finding their location he settled into a ground eating lope. He was pushing but not going all out. He would be at their location within two hours. If he pushed, he would be there somewhat sooner but though urgent, this wasn't a time sensitive issue to push harder and chance an injury. When Andrew finally arrived, he shifted back to his human form.

"Mike, Kadrian contacted me. Someone named Jolene just found out about her sister's death. Kadrian is sending another senior enforcer to replace you. Go back to the pack house and pack up. Go and take care of this issue." He didn't understand all of it, but it was family and involved pups, and this was something any senior enforcer could help deal with.

Mike listened and nodded before he left at a run. Mike was pushing it since he had to be there before Jolene arrived. She didn't know they were werewolves or Zane was one now as well. Better he was there before she arrived. It wasn't even mentioning she didn't know where they lived. As soon as he reached the room he had been provided, he picked up his phone. After checking it, he placed a call to Jolene.

When she picked up, he could hear the tears in her voice, "Jolene, it's Mike. I'm sorry you had to find out this way, get a ticket to Medford Oregon. Send me the itinerary. I will be there, or I will have someone there to pick you up. I'm going to let you go since I'm not at home and have a fair drive ahead of me. If you need anything let me know and I will do what I can." They talked a few minutes longer.

When he hung up Mike leaned against the wall. This wasn't something they needed at all. He had met Jolene and for some reason they just hadn't hit it off well. They were civil, and it wasn't a dislike, just they were too different from each other. He had to hide what he was, and she could somehow sense he was hiding something. She kept trying to get him to tell her what he was keeping from her. Likely, she was going to need to be told now, but that decision was up to the Alpha not him. He pushed away from the wall and started tossing his stuff into his bags and prepared to leave.

About the Author

Brian had been writing for many years before working to get his stories published on Smashwords (Which unfortunately has taken them down) and Amazon as an eBook (Which still has several available, at the time of the publishing of this book).

He was born February 27, 1966. He served 20 years in the US Navy (1984-2004) first as a Hospital Corpsman, later he went to school and became a medical tech repairman and repaired machines in several duty stations. He had been stationed in San Diego, CA, Yokosuka, Japan, Hawaii, Denver, and several other duty stations. He had also been stationed abord the USS Knox (FF-1052) in the 1980s and the USS Tarawa (LHA-1) in the 1990s. After retirement he moved back to his hometown where he continued to keep medical equipment running correctly. He was a "veteran enjoying his semi-retirement" while he did something he loved, writing stories.

He has three children, who have also served in the US Armed Forces.

He loved telling the stories from his life in the military. The ones he loved best were about his days as a corpsman and the many different people he met. He enjoyed meeting people and hearing their stories. He loved zooming around on his motorcycle when he lived in Hawaii and San Diego.

He passed away in June 2019. His actions touched on a great many other authors, and helped them get started, or encouraged them to make their stories available for others.

Books he had Published:

The Folican Chronicles:

1: Dog Got Your Tongue

2: Homecoming

3: The Temple
4: We Have to Keep Moving Forward
5-12: Located on Wattpad only

Magic Girl Satire Series
I'm a Magic Girl?!
Prequel of *Magic Girl Cherry Blossom* and Sequel *I'm a Magic Boy* are on Wattpad

Wolf of the Emperor
Love Rejected - Love Found: A Peace Bringer Story (Stand-alone werewolf story)

He had many other stories which in addition to these which are available on Wattpad to read for free.

The Folican Chronicles are planned to be released in print, posthumously, eventually.

Goodbye to Max, by Adam Webster

I took the time to get the copyright from Brian's estate, as they had no plans to do anything with his stories. I have felt that his stories needed to be shared with more people, as he is a very good author, and in the case of *Why Us*, and the sequel *Why Us 2*, they tie into my Wolf Tech series and are almost a prequel to *Wolf Tech 3: The Alphas*, and extend the ideas for my own stories, which Brian did help co-author parts of *Wolf Tech 3*, and then the subsequent books. The following letter I wrote shortly after he had passed, while I was fighting back tears, and I had a couple hours cry after finishing it, knowing there isn't anything I could do beyond that.

It was posted to Wattpad to share my feelings, and to allow others to share in it, partly as an announcement to the readers at large of his passing. It was also read at his military funeral, which unfortunately I could not attend. Mostly I thought of him as "Max" as his account name on Wattpad is MaxD01. Some changes have been done from that version, and some parts have been expanded.

My Goodbye to Max:

I met Max, as I thought of him, when I was reading some werewolf stories and came across his on Wattpad. I can't remember which one I found first, but soon became addicted to reading all of his stories. I think it might even have been this story, which was incomplete at that time. One of my first interactions was to a comment of having to stop reading *Folican Chronicles 4*, where one of the main characters dies. His reply to my comment was "Yes!!!! Nailed another reader. (does happy dance)" Needless to say, something about that made me want to get to know him.

I started just chatting in the comments of his stories, especially the unfinished ones and especially adding to the howls of outrage over the cliff hangers which he put into his chapters and speculations on the resolutions. When he put out a request for an editor for the third *Folican Chronicles* book, I offered, and started collaborating with him on that, and eventually also did editing for the then titled *Mate Rejection Thang* but was published as *Love Rejected - Love Found*.

When I sent him a link with a chapter or two of my own story, he read it and was very enthusiastic on me posting it to Wattpad. Before I knew it, he had done a shout out for it, then before I could think further, I had quite a few people who read what I had wrote and were clamouring for more! That was the single thing that got me writing my story. The continued encouragement kept me writing my stories.

The request to co-author a section of *A Pregnancy Story* (Wattpad name for the story, which even he didn't really like, but never worked out a better name for) when I was starting my third book was a request that really touched me, nor one which I could turn down. The fact that an author who had become one of my favourites and a person I liked and respected had wanted my input to their story? It stunned me hard for a while and made me feel exceptionally good. That co-authoring, I think, wasn't planned to go beyond a couple of scenes, tied into my third book (*Wolf Tech 3: The Alphas*) and was used there as well.

The end of *The Pregnancy Story* tied into this story, which I related to personally and had been one that he had stopped writing about halfway, and may have been my urging, along with many others, to finish, that I then started asking about borrowing characters from. After a few weeks of work to get permission to use them in my story, they appeared as guests of the pack, late in *Wolf Tech 3*, which overlapped and fit into part of his *Why Us 2*, with Brian writing their side of the story. Then with an offer late in that book, the characters (Zane and his Team) became major characters in *Wolf Tech 4*. Towards the end of that book, he surprised me with a request to have them permanently become part of my story (instead of just the one book), with him co-authoring the parts of the story they dealt with. That lasted through another four novels, and three short stories!

I had also enticed a local friend to write a story of Were-Tigers and he had it tied into our shared world. For one story, *Thawing of the Ice*, all three of us worked on it.

I even had a chance to co-author parts of Book 11 of *Folican Chronicles, We Come in Peace* (Which he always has to add "Shoot to kill, Shoot to Kill" as a parody to a Star Trek skit song) and of Book 12 (We're Back), the last book written in the series. He had planned to write at least one more book in the series.

I had started two new stories, one where I had some wolves, which were distantly related to those in my Wolf Tech series, decide to emigrate to Folica, which almost would be Folican Chronicles book 13, and one which was follow-up to an offer which was made in *Folican Chronicles 12*, which had a bunch of packs emigrating to another planet, one where they would be in control of it instead of the humans. He threw me a curve, by adding in a part of a request from some characters from the *Folican Chronicles* wanting to move to the planet with the Weres.

I had about five chapters into each of the books, before I got hit with a bad case of Writers Block, and had a few other interests start up, along with being very busy at work, and fewer of the readers hounding me for updates, I let it slide one day, then two, then a week, then a month… and had been three months since I last posted anything when he passed. It is extremely hard to go back to the stories and try to be true to the characters that he was writing, while getting more content out. In the case of both, as of 2025, neither have been finished, even if I have started and finished two novels and a short story. Another two have been started.

I am going to very much miss our nearly daily chatter about weather, our lives, his dogs licking his toes or jumping on him, and most especially the banter and working together. My stories would never have gotten the exposure without him, and beyond my first three books, I don't think I would have had much content, as it was his push to do better and write better. He never said it in so many words, but the fact he kept wanting to co-write more, showed how much he respected me as an author, and wanted to help me write my stories, and wanted to be involved in the stories.

I have had times that I found something funny or interesting that I wanted to share, and keep starting to send it, before remembering he was gone. It is going to take a while to get over it, from doing it the last three or four years. I am very much going to miss my friend.

The only fitting legacy I can think I can give Brian is to work to have my books published and out for more people to read and enjoy his work that is linked to mine. Maybe we can give him everlasting life through his stories, that he gave so much to accomplish.

Now, since then, I have had *Wolf Tech 1: New Beginning*, *Wolf Tech 2: Finding Their Place*, and *Wolf Tech 3: The Alphas* published, and even though this book was planned to be published before Wolf Tech 3, due to delays with formal transfer of the copyright, it is after. Next, I plan on publishing *Why Us 2* next, then *Wolf Tech 4*. I am also considering the Folican Chronicles series to be published, but it means a lot of work.

A portion of the profits from his stories will be given to Veteran charities, to help those who need it, after leaving the military.

If anyone wishes to contact me direct, I can be reached at books-interact@adamwebster.ca even if it is just to chat!

www.ingramcontent.com/pod-product-compliance
Lightning Source LLC
Chambersburg PA
CBHW070643310726
48982CB00001B/400
* 9 7 8 1 7 3 8 0 4 7 3 9 0 *